WHICH WAS THE MOST DANGEROUS?

The nymphomania of a ravishing Balkan countess on her nightmare estate?

The ruthless determination of an embattled Turkish general fighting his way out of a deadly trap?

The blood-hunger of a rebellious Arab chieftain in his desert kingdom?

The depraved desires of an all-powerful Indian rajah in his fabulous pleasure palace?

The cunning of a conscienceless Chinese warlord in his fortress-like stronghold?

Or the explosive chemistry of two handsome, gallant men and a beautiful young woman in a world of rising passion and rousing excitement?

Nothing was safe on—

HIGH ROAD TO CHINA

JON CLEARY

High Road
to China

WARNER BOOKS

A Warner Communications Company

WARNER BOOKS EDITION

Copyright © 1977 by Clearview, N.V.
All rights reserved.

Published by CBS Inc. by arrangement with
William Morrow & Company, Inc.,
105 Madison Avenue,
New York, N.Y. 10016
Distributed by Warner Books.

Warner Books, Inc.,
666 Fifth Avenue,
New York, N.Y. 10103

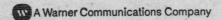 A Warner Communications Company

Printed in the United States of America

First Warner Books Printing: April, 1983

10 9 8 7 6 5 4 3 2 1

To Marina and Aubrey Baring

AUTHOR'S PREFACE

William Bede O'Malley died in Fort Lauderdale, Florida, on 22 July 1974, aged 80. He left behind him an autobiography called, plainly, AN ADVENTURE; it ran to over 1500 pages of manuscript. He left no instructions as to whether he wished it to be submitted for publication. After much discussion his family offered it to me, a distant cousin, to use as I thought fit.

I decided to tell the story of what I think was one of the best of Bede O'Malley's adventures and it was agreed that I could use excerpts from his manuscript. I wished to include them because I thought that, with some minor editing, they would give a sense of perspective to a story that took place when I was only three years old, a time of which my memory is, to say the least, hazy. The year 1920 is almost as remote as 1492 or 1066 to a lot of people today.

I found that certain incidents did not accord with historical fact in respect of time, but Bede O'Malley was writing without benefit of diary or notes and an old man's memory does not always recognize the calendar. But it does not alter the truth of what he experienced.

He was an adventurer, a dying breed: but who of us does not still dream of being one?

CHAPTER 1

1

"So far I've shot only one man." Eve Tozer patted the gun-case beside her as if it were a vanity bag containing all she needed to face the men of the world. "Elephants are easier."

"Of course." Arthur Henty kept his eyebrows in place. "Did you kill the, er, man?"

"One couldn't miss at ten yards. He was a perfectly ugly Mexican who was trying to rape me."

"Ten yards? That was rather distant for rape, wasn't it?"

"He was trouserless. His intention was distinctly obvious, if you know what I mean."

Henty hung on to his eyebrows from the inside, wondering if one could dislocate one's forehead. He was a tall balding man in whom the bone was very evident, as if the skeleton had already decided to shrug off the flesh; but his eyes were bright blue, shrewd and amused, and he had no intention of stepping into an early grave. Not while women as attractive as Eve Tozer presented themselves to his gaze. Even if that was as far as the presentation of themselves went.

He had never met Bradley Tozer's daughter until he had gone down to Tilbury this morning to escort her from the ship that had brought her from China. Several people in the Shanghai head office of Tozer Cathay Limited had written him that she was every inch her father's daughter and now, with a glance at the gun-case on the seat of the car, he was prepared to believe they were right. He studied her, wondering what the perfectly ugly Mexican had thought of her as, trouserless and lance pointed, he had rushed towards her and the fate worse than he had anticipated.

Eve was staring out at London as it slid by outside the car and Henty looked at her closely, yet managed not to stare. It was a trick he had learned in ten years up-country in China, where the stranger's gaze could never afford to be too frank. He saw a girl above average height with a figure that would attract men less violent and point-blank than the unfortunate Mexican. She was dressed in a beige silk travelling suit with tan stockings and shoes that, even to his inexpert eye, looked expensive and hand-made. The skirt, he noticed, was of the fashionable length, just below the knee; his wife Marjorie was always trying to educate him in such trivialities. But he also noticed that she was wearing her dark hair cut unfashionably short and there was a touch of rouge on her cheeks, something that Marjorie would have labelled as "fast."

"It is six years since I was last in London." Eve looked out the window of the Rolls-Royce as they drove along the Embankment. Grey skies and a thin muslin drizzle of rain had not kept the August Bank Holiday crowd at home; the English, she guessed, were as dogged about their pleasures as they had been about winning the war. England was still settling uneasily into the new peace; during last year's summer holidays, she had read in *The Times,* there had still been a disbelief that the long agony was really over. This long holiday weekend, however, the citizens were determined to enjoy themselves, come what may. Buses, bright in their new postwar paint, rolled by; on their open top deck passengers sat beneath their umbrellas, teeth bared in resolute smiles. Excursion boats went up and down the Thames, their passengers bellowing "Knees Up, Mother Brown" as they went past the Mother of Parliaments. A newspaper poster said, *Woolley: Duck,* and Eve wondered at the strangeness of the English language as spoken in England.

"What's a woolly duck?"

Henty frowned in puzzlement, looked back, then

laughed. "That's Frank Woolley, one of our more famous cricketers. He scored a duck. Nil runs."

"Oh. Some time, not this trip, I must go to see a cricket game. When we were last here, Mother wanted to see one, but Father wouldn't hear of it. Said it was too slow for him. Instead we went to Wimbledon. We saw Norman Brookes beat Tony Wilding in the men's singles. I remember I fell in love with Tony Wilding."

"He was killed in the war. At Neuve Chapelle. My two brothers were killed there, too."

"Was that where you got your, er, wound?"

"No, on the Somme." Henty tapped his stiff right leg with his walking-stick. "The bally thing plays up occasionally. When it rains, mostly."

"You shouldn't have come all the way down to the ship." But she turned away from him, looked out the car window again. She could shoot animals without a qualm and had shot the rape-minded Mexican and left no mental scar on herself; but she felt helpless in the face of other people's suffering. "That was a beautiful summer, 1914, I mean. I read that they are calling it the long golden summer, as if there'll never be another like it."

Perhaps there never will be, thought Henty, but not in terms of weather. It had been a summer, he mused, which even some people not yet born would look back to with nostalgia. But he had looked up the weather records and they had shown that it had not been a "long golden summer:" that had occurred four years before, in 1910, the late season of the Edwardian reign, of a king meant for pleasure and not for war. But memory, Henty knew, had its own climate and regret for a time gone forever created its own golden haze. So people now believed the sun had been shining through all the months and years up till August 1914. Suddenly his leg began to ache. But he knew it had nothing to do with the rain or the shrapnel still lodged beneath his kneecap.

The Rolls-Royce turned up towards the Strand and a few moments later pulled into the forecourt of the Savoy Hotel. It was followed by the smaller Austin in which rode Anna, Eve's maid, and the luggage. Henty, who did not own a car and usually rode in buses and taxis, knew he had done the right thing in hiring the Rolls-Royce in which to bring his boss's daughter up from the ship. He had been warned that Bradley Tozer expected nothing but the best for his only child; and, Henty had remarked to himself, evidently Miss Tozer took for granted that only the best was good enough for her. At least she had made no comment when he had escorted her off the ship and down to the car. The Rolls-Royce was good enough for the Savoy, too: a covey of porters and pages appeared as if royalty had just driven up to hand out grace and favour pensions to the common herd.

The head porter showed no surprise as Eve handed out her gun-case: it could have been that American ladies arrived every day at the Savoy with their guns, Annie Oakleys every one of them. He passed the gun-case on to a junior porter, then took the small lacquered wooden box which Eve pushed at him.

"Tell them to be careful with that. My father would have my scalp and yours if what's inside that box should be broken."

"Yes, miss," said the head porter, wondering if the father of this dark-haired beauty could be a Red Indian; but miffed at the suggestion that anything, other than perhaps the guests' virginity, should ever be broken at the Savoy.

Going up in the lift Arthur Henty said, "I'm sorry your father couldn't come with you. I was looking forward to seeing him after so long. It is almost seven years since I said goodbye to him in Shanghai."

"He hasn't changed."

"So I've heard," Henty ventured and was relieved to see Eve smile.

"He still believes China belongs to him."

Inside the suite Eve moved to the windows, opened one of them and looked out on the river, dull as unwashed quartz under the grey skies. It had stopped raining, but it was still a miserable day. A day for going to bed with a good book or a good man. She smiled to herself: her Boston grandmother would have commended her for the first thought and banished her for the second.

Henty studied her again, the heiress to the Tozer fortune, legatee of that part of China which her father thought belonged to him. Tozer Cathay had been started in Shanghai in 1870 by Eve's grandfather, a windjammer captain from Boston turned merchant. Rufus Tozer had died in 1903 from a surfeit of bandit's bullets while estimating a price for a repair job on the Great Wall of China: or so the company legend went. His son had run the firm ever since, had built it into the major competitor for trade in China of Jardine Matheson, the British firm that, until Tozer Cathay began to develop, had thought that *it* owned China.

"How do you feel about China?" Henty himself had loved it and its people, but he knew his leg would never allow him to go back there and take up his old job as a traveller. He had been grateful when Bradley Tozer had made him general manager of the London office.

Eve shrugged, turned from the window. The reflected light from the river struck sideways across her face, accentuating the slight slant of her eyes and the high cheekbones. Years before, Rufus Tozer had taken home a half-caste Chinese bride and Boston, already feeling itself invaded by the Irish, had resented this introduction of a possible further invasion, this time by the Yellow Peril. Since then, however, Pearl Tozer, having conveniently died at the birth of her son, had been forgiven and forgotten for her intrusion into decent Boston society: after all, her son had grown up to play quarterback for Harvard, gaining both All-American selection and a bride who was a distant cousin of the Cabots. Pearl's granddaughter, grown to extraordinary beauty, was admired and, though given to such eccentricities as big-game hunting, piloting an aeroplane and smoking cigarettes in public, was still considered more acceptable than the Irish.

"It's not my cup of tea, if that's the appropriate meta-

phor. I get upset by poverty, Mr. Henty, and there is so
much of it in China. I like to see happiness everywhere."

He hadn't thought she would be so shallow-minded and
his voice was a little sharper than he intended it to be.
"The Chinese are happy. Things could be better for them,
but they are not *un*-happy."

"You think I'm shallow-minded for making such a remark, don't you?"

Henty hung on to his eyebrows again. He should have
recognized that she had probably inherited her father's almost uncanny perception. But he was not a cowardly
man: "Your remark did suggest that to me. I apologize.
Perhaps we had better talk about something else. What
are your plans while you are in London this week?"

Eve smiled, forgiving him. He was right, of course: she
was shallow-minded. At least if that meant preferring
happiness to misery. "I want to do some shopping at Har-
rods and a few other places. And Father wants me to order him some shirts at Turnbull and Asser's. They have
his measurements. How long will they take to make
them?"

"Two, three days, no more. I have tickets for the
theatre every night—you can take your choice. *Chu Chin
Chow*—" Then he, too, smiled. "But not if you don't like
China."

She shook her head. "I'd like to see some of the new
matinée idols. I'm mad about good-looking men, Mr.
Henty. Does that shock you?"

"Not really," said Henty, wondering if she took her gun
when she went in pursuit of good-looking men. "I understand it's a perfectly normal thing with young girls."

"I adore you, Mr. Henty. You try to sound like a
stuffed shirt, but you're not, are you? I read about a new
leading man, Basil Rathbone. I'd like to see him, no matter what show he's in."

He held up a fan of tickets. "He's in a new play opening next week, one by Somerset Maugham. I've included
it amongst these."

"You're perfectly slick, Mr. Henty."

He took it that that was a compliment: he was not up on the latest American slang.

Then the luggage arrived, supervised by Anna. She was a tiny Chinese who had been born in New York and had hated every moment of the three months she and her mistress had just spent in China. She had a New York accent but a Mandarin attitude towards servants less than herself. And in her book hotel porters were much less than the personal maid to a millionaire's daughter. She clapped her tiny hands in tiny explosions and fired off orders with machine-gun rapidity. The two porters, silent and expressionless, Leyton Orientals, but boiling with thoughts about Yanks and Chinks who were mixed together in this midget witch, carried the trunks and suitcases into the main bedroom of the suite.

Eve took the small lacquered box from the page-boy who had brought it up and put it on a table. "When I left Father he was heading for Hunan to look for the companion piece to this. It's a jade statue of Lao-Tze, the Taoist god. I believe there is one something like it in a museum in Paris, but Father says if he can get the pair of these, he'll make all the museums and collectors sick with envy. You know what he's like about his collection."

Indeed Henty knew. On their trips into the Chinese hinterland all Tozer Cathay representatives were expected to keep an eye out for any items that might prove worthy additions to the famous Tozer collection.

"Isn't it risky, carrying it with you? Wouldn't it have been safer to have shipped it straight home to America?"

"That was Father's original idea, but then he became afraid it might be stolen on the way. I persuaded him to let me bring it with me. I—" For the first time she looked embarrassed. "I wanted to prove I could be useful. I owe my father a lot, Mr. Henty."

Henty felt at ease enough to be frank: "I understand he thinks the world of you. So perhaps the debt is mutual."

"You're perfectly sweet, Mr. Henty." She smiled, then shook her head, nodding at the gun-case lying on a sofa.

"He took me tiger hunting in Kwelchow this summer. He didn't want to go, he was frightfully busy, but I wanted to go and he took me. He's been doing that ever since my mother died, spoiling me terribly. He's a kind man, Mr. Henty, too kind. At least to me."

Henty was glad of the qualification, though he couldn't detect whether she had said it defensively. Bradley Tozer had no reputation in China for kindliness; he hunted business with all the rapacity of an old China Sea pirate. Henty guessed there would be few people in China who felt they owed Bradley Tozer anything.

He was saved from an awkward reply by the ringing of the phone. Eve, a lady who, despite the admonitions of her maternal grandmother, could never resist the temptation to answer her own telephone, picked it up. It was the reception desk.

"A gentleman to see you, Miss Tozer."

"A gentleman? English?" Basil Rathbone, perhaps? Eve was not so spoiled that she didn't have girlish dreams occasionally. "Did he give his name?"

A hand was obviously held over the mouthpiece downstairs. Then: "Mr. Sun Nan. A Chinese gentleman."

Eve looked at Henty. "Do you know a Mr. Sun Nan?"

"No. Is he downstairs? I'll go down and see what he wants."

Eve spoke into the phone again. "Mr. Henty will be down to see him."

She put down the phone, but almost at once it rang again. "I am sorry, Miss Tozer, but the gentleman insists that he sees *you*." The tone of voice suggested that the Savoy reception desk did not approve of the cheek of a Chinese, gentlemen or otherwise, insisting on disturbing one of the hotel's guests. The hand was held over the mouthpiece again and then the voice came back, this time in a state of shock: "He insists he see you *at once*."

"Send him up." Eve put down the phone once more and stopped Henty who, leaning on his stick, was already limping towards the door. "You had better stay. This Mr.

Sun evidently has something important he wants to tell me."

"If he's selling anything or wanting to buy, he should have come to the office. Let me handle him."

"No, leave him to me," Eve said, and Henty suddenly and ridiculously wondered if Mr. Sun, whoever he was, might meet the same fate as the unfortunate Mexican.

Mr. Sun Nan was brought up to the suite by one of the reception clerks, as if the hotel did not trust pushy, demanding Orientals to be wandering around alone on its upper floors. He was ushered into the suite, a smiling *li-chi* of a man who seemed amused at the attention he was being given.

"A thousand apologies, Miss Tozer, for this intrusion. If time had allowed, I should have written you a letter and awaited your reply." He spoke English with a slight hiss that could have meant a badly-fitting dental plate or been a comment on the barbarians who had invented the language. "But time, as they say, is of the essence."

"Not a Chinese saying, I'm sure," said Eve.

Sun smiled. "No. I only use it because you will be the one to profit by our saving time."

Henty introduced himself. "If you have anything to sell or wish to buy, you should be talking to me."

Sun smiled at him as he might have at a passer-by, then looked back at Eve. "It would be better if we spoke alone, Miss Tozer."

Henty bridled at being dismissed and Eve stiffened in annoyance at the smiling, yet cool arrogance of the Chinese. "Mr. Henty stays. If time *is* of the essence, don't waste it, Mr. Sun."

"I was warned you might resemble your father in your attitude." Sun gave a little complimentary bow of his head, then the smile disappeared from his face as if it had been an optical illusion instead of a friendly expression. "The matter concerns your father. He has been kidnapped."

Through the open window there floated up from the Embankment the cheerful mutter of London on holiday:

the ordinary, reassuring sounds that made Eve think she had not heard Mr. Sun correctly. "Did you say *kidnapped*?"

"I'm afraid so." The smile flickered on his face again, but it was no longer apologetic or friendly; Sun smiled as a relieving movement to relax what was indeed a badly-fitting dental plate. "My master has him in custody and will kill him on 21 August by your calendar, eighteen days from today. Unless—"

Eve went to the window and closed it, shutting out the ordinary, locking in the macabre. The clouds were lifting a little, but there was no break in them. She caught a glimpse of a plane high in the sky to the west: it had just written a giant O in dark smoke, an empty circle barely discernible against the grey sky. The pilot's effort at sky-writing on such a day seemed as ridiculous as what she had just heard Mr. Sun say. She turned back into the room in a state of shock.

She heard Henty say, "Is this some frightful joke by Jardine Matheson? If so, I think it's in deucedly bad taste."

"It is no joke, Mr. Henty." But Sun smiled at the thought of Jardine Matheson's being involved; he thought *that* was a joke. "My master is a very serious man at times. If he says he will kill Miss Tozer's father, then he certainly will."

"You said *unless*." Eve had to clear her throat to get the words out. "Unless what?"

"You have a small statue, I believe. Of the god Lao-Tze riding on a green ox—"

Surprised, puzzled, Eve gestured at the box on the table. "It's in there. But it belongs to my father—"

Sun shook his head, face stiff now with impatience and denial. He was a Confucian, but he had a more immediate master, the *tuchun,* the war lord, in Hunan who laid down timetables which had no place for etiquette and ritual. "It belongs to my master."

"Where did your father get it?" Henty asked Eve.

"He bought it from some provincial governor. General Chang something-or-other."

"Chang Ching-yao," said Sun. "My master's enemy. My master has the twin to the statue. He owned both of them, but Chang stole one of them from him. Open the box. At once, please!"

Henty grasped his stick as if he were going to use it for something other than support for his leg. "This has gone far enough! I think we had better call the police—"

"It would be foolish to call the police." The hiss in Sun's voice was even more pronounced now. "My master does not recognize any other authority but his own. Even in China."

"Miss Tozer, you can't let him get away with this! How do we know this isn't some bluff to swindle you out of that statue? The cleverest swindlers in the world are the Chinese—"

Sun bowed his head again, as if he and his countrymen had been paid a compliment. Then he took a gold watch and chain from his pocket. He was dressed in a dark suit that was too tight for him and he carried a black bowler hat; he looked like a civil servant, a non-white from Whitehall. He looked at the watch, then held it out on the palm of his plump hand.

"Do you recognize this, Miss Tozer?"

Eve took the watch: it ticked like a tiny gold bomb in her hand. "It's my father's. I gave it to him last Christmas."

"Your father was captured the day he arrived in Hunan province, two days after you left Shanghai on your ship. I travelled overland to Hong Kong and the intention was to speak to you there. Your ship was supposed to spend four days in that port."

"We were there only two days. The schedule was altered for some reason or other. None of us minded," she said irrelevantly; then added very relevantly, "At the time."

"I caught another ship and followed you, but at each port I just missed you."

"You could have sent a wireless message to the ship."
Eve, assaulted by reason, now believed everything she
was hearing: no swindler could be so cool about his facts.

"How to word it, Miss Tozer?" Sun smiled again, as if
admitting even the cleverness of the Chinese would have
found such a code beyond them; he marvelled sometimes
at the stupidity of white foreigners, whose minds never
seemed to work as quickly as their tongues. "My master
wants secrecy. If I had sent a wireless message, even if
you had believed it and not thought it a hoax, you would
have contacted the authorities in Shanghai, am I not correct?"

Eve nodded, and Henty said, "You said something
about—how long? eighteen days?—in which to return the
statue. Return it to where—Hunan? That's absolutely impossible, you know that."

"I regret the limited time allowed, but I am afraid there
is no way of changing my master's mind. If I do not have
the statue back with him on the day appointed, I too shall
be killed." Sun was abruptly grave, as if the thought of
his own possible death was suddenly a surprise to him.
Then he shrugged away the possibility: he was that acrobatic philosopher, an optimistic fatalist.

"Why is there such an absolute deadline?" Henty
asked. "Can't you ask your master for an extension?"

Sun shook his head. "The only wireless in Hunan is
controlled by Chang Ching-yao. I should have told my
master before this that I had missed you, had it been possible. I have been in a veritable state of frustration ever
since I took ship at Hong Kong. What to do? I kept
asking myself."

"How did you manage to arrive here today then, if you
were always so far behind Miss Tozer?"

"My ship went to Constantinople—I caught the Orient
Express from there. A very funny name for a train, one
that stops over 4000 miles from the real Orient. But very
comfortable and full of very strange people. It saved me
several days getting here."

"It hasn't saved us enough to get us to Hunan in eighteen days."

Eve looked at the watch in her hand. Somehow she knew, with a sickening feeling of certainty, that it was all the evidence she needed to know that her father had indeed been kidnapped. But with despairing hope she said, "What if I don't believe your story, Mr. Sun? You could have stolen this watch—"

Sun Nan produced a piece of folded notepaper from the inside of his jacket and handed it to her. As soon as she unfolded it she recognized the handwriting, bold, assertive even while it asked for her help: *Eve darling, These fellows, I'm afraid, mean business. Give them what they want. And don't worry. Dad.*

"I don't understand why the Shanghai office hasn't cabled us your father is missing," said Henty.

"Mr. Henty, China hasn't changed since you left. Upcountry, two days out of Shanghai, and you could be on the other side of the moon as far as keeping in contact." She turned back to Sun Nan. "Will your master, whoever he is, really kill my father if he doesn't get back that statue?"

"I'm afraid so, Miss Tozer. He does not value lives highly, especially those of foreigners. He often jokes he would have made a very good imperialist." He smiled, but Eve and Henty did not share the joke.

"What about you? Do you value foreigners' lives?"

Sun spread his hands. "I value my own. I am a humble messenger. Does the telegraph boy carry the burden of every telegram he delivers?"

"Good Christ, now he's spouting bloody aphorisms!" Then Henty hastily looked at Eve, wobbled on his stick. "I'm frightfully sorry. I usually don't swear in front of ladies—"

"It's all right, Mr. Henty. Everything is bloody at the moment."

Eve felt choked: with helplessness, fear, premature grief for her father who was about to die. She had felt grief before but that had been bearable; her mother, gone

suddenly with cancer, had been spared what the doctors
had said would otherwise have been a long lingering
death. But Bradley Tozer, for all his adventurousness, had
always seemed to her invulnerable. Though they had often been separated in the years during and since the war,
she living in America with her grandmother and he coming home from China on his annual visits, she had never
thought of life without him. The bond between them had
never been severed or even frayed by distance.
Distance . . .

"How far is it from London to Hunan by air?"

"By air?" Henty's eyebrows went up this time as if he
had had a sudden spasm; then they came down again in a
puzzled frown. "By aeroplane, you mean? But there's no
aeroplane service *that* far. The furthest it goes is to
Paris."

"I can fly. Father and I have our own machine back
home. We usually fly from Boston down to our winter
place in Florida. We were planning to do so next month."
She heard herself already speaking in the past tense; and
tried to sound more resolute. "We can buy a machine
here and fly to China. How far is it?"

"I don't know. Seven, perhaps eight thousand miles as
the crow flies. But you wouldn't be flying as the crow
flies. It's out of the question, Miss Tozer—"

"Nothing is out of the question, Mr. Henty, if it will
save my father's life. Unless you can think of an alternative?"

Henty thumped his stick on the carpet in frustration.
"No, I can't. But such a flight—" He trailed off help-
lessly.

"Some men—what was their name? Smith?—flew out
to Australia only last year."

"Ross and Keith Smith. But there were four of them,
they had an engineer and a mechanic and they flew a
Vickers Vimy bomber. Even so they took longer than
eighteen days. A month at least, I think. And another half
a dozen chaps have tried to follow them and got less than
half-way."

"China is not as far as Australia and the Smiths were not as hard pressed for time as I am."

"I wish there were some other way—"

"There isn't," said Eve. "Where can I buy an aeroplane?"

2

Extract from the William Bede O'Malley manuscript:
George Weyman always said he could read my sky-writing better than he could the handwritten notes I used to leave for him in our office. Perhaps that was because he suffered from what we now call dyslexia; or perhaps it was because the only skywriting contract we ever had was for Oxo, the meat extract. Or more correctly, nearly had. Because at the time I am writing of, we were no more than on trial. The first sky-writing had been attempted by an American way back in 1913, but nobody had yet come up with a formula for keeping the smoke coming consistently out of the exhaust pipes of our machines. Letters kept breaking off in mid-stroke; if the world at large had been able to read Mr. Pitman's shorthand we might have been successful. There were plenty of advertisers waiting to use our services once we proved, as it were, that we were not illiterate. That summer we had been approached by a sweets manufacturer who wanted his name, plus a gumdrop in green, sketched above half a dozen seaside resorts. The producers of the motion picture *Why Change Your Wife?* had also been in touch with us; they wanted the name of their film in purple smoke and that of the delectable actress, Miss Gloria Swanson, in red, hung, as one of their publicity men described it, on God's marquee. The thought of Miss Swanson in cirrocumulus across London's sky had excited me, but reason had forced us to say no to them. There was no point in taking on a 35-letter contract when I still hadn't succeeded in spelling out Oxo.

This weekend was our last chance and our luck was running its usual course. George and I had stood in our shed all morning watching the rain; as soon as it stopped I took off. The clouds were still too low for good sky-writing, but that couldn't be helped. The writing, if I managed to get it out of the exhaust, was going to be just that much lower to the ground. The short-sighted citizens, if not the executives of Oxo, would be pleased.

I finished the first O, shut off the smoke and took the Sopwith Camel up to begin the first stroke of the X. But half-way down the stroke I knew our luck had finally run out; there was nothing but a dribble coming from the exhaust. I did a half-look and climbed back up again, rolled over into another dive. But it was no use: Oxo was no more than a giant cypher in the sky, drifting west towards Berkshire, a county not noted for Oxo drinkers. I cursed the smoke mixture, the weather and God Himself and headed back towards earth and bankruptcy.

I took the Camel down over the Thames towards Waddon aerodrome near Croydon. I passed over the Oval. Surrey was playing Notts that day and play had started; spectators sat around the ground in their raincoats and watched the flannelled fools on the mud-heap out in the middle. I hoped Surrey was batting and I waggled the Camel's wings as an encouragement to Hobbs and Sandham. Cricket is, or was then, a peaceful game; but none of the cricketers down there knew the peace I sometimes felt up here in the sky. Excitement, too; but mostly peace these days, as if the air was my one true element, the one to be trusted. Debts were never airborne with me, nor any other worries. That gave the sky a certain purity, if nothing else did.

Waddon aerodrome came up on my starboard wing and I banked to go in, making sure there were no other machines with the same idea at that particular moment. I could see four or five machines at various heights around the aerodrome; they would be the joy-riders, ten minutes for ten bob. There was a control tower at Waddon, but they had little control over you if you chose not to look in their direction. It was the days before the bureaucrats began cutting up the sky into little cubes with aeroplanes' markings on them. Too many damned people flying these days. Egalitarianism should never have been allowed to get off the ground.

I came in over the long sheds of the Aircraft Disposal Company. I always wanted to weep when I thought of what stood there beneath those long roofs. Hundreds of aircraft, like birds that had died at the moment they had spread their wings for flight. Pups. Camels. SE5a's, Bristols, DH4's and 9's, Handley Pages, even some Spads and Nieuports: the no-longer-wanted chariots of a war everyone was trying to forget. The Aircraft Disposal Company had brought them all here when the war had ended. It had been expected there would be a rush to buy them, everyone wanting to be airborne on the euphoria of peace and a cheap aeroplane. But it had turned out that the wartime pilots had other, more pressing things to do with their money. Such as getting married (what use was a Sopwith Pup to a couple intent on adding to the postwar baby boom?), buying a house if you could find one (the housing shortage wasn't a recent invention), emigrating to Canada or Australia: money went no further in 1919–20 than it does now. There's just more of it now, that's all, like promiscuity. The satisfaction with what you get hasn't been increased.

There were a few of us who felt no immediate need of a wife, a house or a new country. I had no nostalgia for the war, none at all. But two years of tossing an aeroplane about the sky, uninhibited but for a natural desire to avoid German bullets, had worn threadbare any yearning for what the editorial writers were then calling the fruits of victory. Already they, the fruits not the editorialists, looked speckled. Though come to think of it, what those editorialists wrote had the sound of second-hand words in which they didn't truly believe, the harangue of men caught at a corner where they weren't sure from which direction came the echoes they could hear. In that year the Roaring Twenties was still just a distant whisper.

In the meantime some of us flew aeroplanes, ignored our debts and called Waddon home.

There were two landing fields at Waddon in those days, separated from each other by a public road, Plough Lane. I put the Camel down on the grass of the field called Wallington, holding it against the cross-wind. Landing was usually no problem, if you watched the wind; but taking off, a cross-wind could sometimes flip you over on your back. You don't get that sort of thrill these days in those damned great cattle trucks they call jumbos. I swung the machine round at the end of the field and taxied back towards the level crossing over Plough Lane, feeling as I always felt when I came back to earth, deflated. I've heard it likened to post-coital blues, though personally I never felt any such blues till I was too old to be coital.

I crossed the road, waving a royal hand to the envious and resentful motorists and cyclists waiting beyond the gates, and taxied towards our shed near the ADC's hangars. George Weyman was waiting for me, ready to put the Camel away as he always did. George still flew, but he was the mechanic of the two of us and he looked after our single machine as if he, and not the Sopwith Company, had given birth to it. He loved it as an aeroplane, but he also loved it as our only asset.

"Someone has just been on the telephone," he said when the Camel was safely stored away in the shed that was its hangar, our office and our home. We could not afford a telephone and I knew he must have been called over to the ADC's office. "Chap named Henty. He said you would remember him, Arthur Henty."

"We were in the same battalion together, before I transferred to the RFC. What did he want? Not some bloody regimental reunion, I hope."

"He said something about wanting to buy an aeroplane. Or maybe two."

"We're not going to sell him the Camel," I protested in anticipation. "We'll pay off our debts some other way."

"What other way? I saw what just happened to Oxo." He nodded up towards the sky. The O I'd written was now just a flat dim vowel in the greyness. "You're not thinking of taking up joy-riders, are you? They'll expect a seat, not be standing out on the wing."

George Weyman was a big man with a high voice and a low boiling point. He never went looking for a fight or an argument, but somehow he seemed to spend half his time swinging his fists to defend a point or holding someone down to force an argument down his throat. He was prickly with prejudices and one had to be careful one didn't rub against them; which was not always easy to do, since they seemed to cover the whole spectrum of human bias. So why did I choose him as my friend and partner? Because he was loyal, honest, good company when he wasn't arguing and the best damn aeroplane mechanic I'd ever come across.

"Did Henty say why he wanted to see me? If he wants a machine, why doesn't he just go over to the ADC?"

"He said he'd like your advice as an old army mate."

"Henty would never use the word *mate*."

"Righto. *Friend*. He said he'd be down within the hour. What are you thinking about? You've got your swindler's look again."

I was staring across at the ADC's sheds. "How many cheques do we have left in our cheque-book?"

"Four. There's just one snag. We don't have any money in our account. They closed our overdraft on Friday."

"Today's a bank holiday. If I write four cheques, who's going to be able to call the bank to see if there's any money in our account to meet them?"

"What are you going to write four cheques for?"

"Deposits on four machines. We'll give Henty a choice—you said he wanted a machine, perhaps two. You said he also wanted my advice. My advice will be to buy from us, not the ADC. We'll be more expensive than the ADC, but he won't know that."

"I don't know how you got your commission as an officer and a gentleman. I was only a bloody sergeant and I'm twice the gentleman you are."

"You're wrong, chum. Honesty has nothing to do with being a gentleman—that's a myth put out by gentlemen. Simmer down, George. I'm not about to do something they can send me to Wormwood Scrubs for. All I'm going to do is put our name—"

"Your name. Not mine."

"Righto, my name. I'll sign the cheques and leave them with the ADC. If Henty buys a machine, or two, I'll cancel the deposits on those he doesn't want. I'll get him to give us his cheque today and we'll be down at the bank in the morning when it opens to deposit it to meet the cheques we've paid out. Now what's dishonest about that?"

"It's not what I'd expect of a gentleman, that's all."

"That's because you're not a gentleman. You socialists always expect more of us than we claim for ourselves. You secretly wish you had our honest hypocrisy."

Half an hour later we saw the Rolls-Royce pull up outside our shed. It came down the perimeter of the field as if the chauffeur wasn't quite sure that he wasn't going to be attacked by the aeroplanes coming in and taking off. Arthur Henty got out, steadying himself with a walking-stick. He turned and helped out a girl. Even through the dirty windows of our office one could see she was a stunner, an absolute beauty. I know I'm looking back through a rose-coloured telescope and the girls of an old man's youth always have an aura about them. But Eve Tozer was not only beautiful, she had what was later known as It or, still later, sex appeal; and she also had what is now known as class. Even through the grime of that office window and the rheum of an old man's eyes, I can still see her that afternoon fifty years ago and still remember the feeling that, up till then, I had only experienced when looping the loop. And not in bed.

"Holy Moses, did you ever see such a girl!"

"They've got a bloody Chink with them," was all George said. He was only slightly prejudiced against women, but he had a consuming aversion to all the world's populace who weren't white, especially those outside the Empire. "We're not going to sell any machine to him! Those buggers want to conquer the world."

"Let me do the talking, George. Just don't declare war on China till we hear what Henty has to say."

We went out to meet them. A Chinese had come round from the passenger's side of the front seat and stood by the rear door behind Henty and the girl. As we walked towards them I whispered to George, "The Chinaman looks like a butler. Stop worrying about the Yellow Peril."

Henty introduced himself and Miss Tozer, ignoring the Chinese, and came straight to his point. "Miss Tozer needs an aeroplane for a long-distance flight, O'Malley."

The *O'Malley* was a measure of the sort of friends we had been. We had been fellow officers sharing a mess and several trenches together, but he had been wounded and demobbed before we had been through enough to get down to first-name terms. "How did you know where to find me?"

"I saw that piece in the *Illustrated London News* on your attempts at sky-writing. I cut it out and kept it. One likes to keep track of chaps one knew in the army, y'know."

It wasn't a liking of mine, but I was glad it was one of his, if it meant he brought Miss Tozer to meet chaps he'd known in the army. "How long is the flight you're planning, Miss Tozer?"

"To China." I felt George start beside me. "I'd like to leave tomorrow at the latest."

"Are you serious?" said George, starting to boil. "We don't like having our leg pulled."

"I've never been more serious in my life, Mr. Weyman. I am an experienced pilot, I know what I'm attempting should have more preparation than a day's notice allows. But I just don't have the time. I am flying to China because it is urgent, terribly urgent, that I get there by a certain date."

"How soon?"

She looked at Henty, then back at us. "21 August. I'll

need an aeroplane with maximum range and a good cruising speed. One that will carry myself as pilot and a passenger."

I glanced at Henty and he shook his head. "Not me. Mr. Sun Nan."

The Chinese behind them stared at George and me. I almost said *inscrutably*, but there was a certain nervousness about him, tiny cracks in his mask. "Does Mr. Sun Nan fly?"

"No," said Henty. I became aware that he and Miss Tozer did not want to take me and George into their confidence. This flight they were talking about was no eccentricity, no madcap adventure by a bored rich girl; they were far too serious for that, too strained-looking. But I was certain that Miss Tozer, for all her claims to being an experienced pilot, really had no idea of what lay ahead of her. Henty must have seen the sceptical look on my face, because he went on, "On our way down here I've been talking to Miss Tozer about taking a second machine and pilot with her."

"Mr. Henty vouched for you as a pilot and a gentleman," said Miss Tozer.

George coughed and ran his hand like a crab over his mouth. I wasn't sure that Henty knew anything about my value as either a pilot or a gentleman; but he was one of those, now almost all gone, who believed that if a man came from a certain class he was taken as a gentleman until proven otherwise. He had told me so one night in our mess at Salisbury, before we had gone to France and found the Germans made no class distinctions as they shot at us. He knew nothing about my cynicism: that had developed after we had parted company.

"What would the pay be?" I said, ungentlemanly.

"We could come to terms," said Miss Tozer. "There would be no quibbling on my part. My only concern is to get to China as soon as possible. And I think we are wasting time even now. May we look at the aeroplane you suggest I buy?"

"It's over there in the ADC sheds," I lied. "They let us store our machines there. We have four."

"Five," said George, determined to get a grain of truth in somewhere. "We have a Sopwith Camel, but that would be no good for your purpose."

Mr. Sun Nan stayed with the chauffeur and we led Miss Tozer and Henty across to the Comapny's sheds. Being a holiday there was only a skeleton staff on duty; no salesman followed us as we made our way down past the long lines of parked aircraft. The first machine I showed Miss Tozer was a Vickers Vimy. It could carry four people and extra fuel tanks could be fitted; it had been a good bomber in the last days of the war. George had not come across with me to look at it when I had paid one of our rubber cheques as a deposit on it; but ten minutes' inspection now told him it would need at least a week's work before being ready for any long-range flying. It was the same with the De Havilland 9 and 4 on which I had also paid deposits; I could see our quick profits disappearing even quicker than that O in Oxo. We were left with only the Bristol Fighter at the end of the line.

"There's another DH4 at the other end of the shed." George suddenly sounded as if he had been a used aeroplane dealer all his life. "But I'd take the Bristol over it. The range is about the same, but the Bristol is about five miles an hour faster and it can climb about five thousand feet higher. You'll be crossing a lot of mountains, I suppose."

"What's the range?" Miss Tozer asked.

"The Bristol will stay up for three hours," I said. "I flew one for a while during the war. Say about three hundred miles or a little over."

"We could stretch that by fitting extra tanks," said George. "Assuming you cruise around ninety to one hundred miles an hour, with the extra tanks you'd probably get another hundred, possibly more, to your range. Let's say four hundred and fifty miles maximum."

Miss Tozer stared at the Bristol Fighter. It had been a great warplane, a two-seater almost as manoeuvrable as any single-seater and twice as effective because it had carried two guns, one fired straight ahead by the pilot and the other able to be fired in a complete circle by the observer. George and I had flown as a team in one of them and in three months we had brought down nine Huns. Miss Tozer walked round the machine, then came back to us.

"Mr. O'Malley, could you get us some maps? I think we need to sit down and have a talk. Perhaps we could go back to your office?"

Two people in our office crowded it; a four-person conference would have split it at the seams. "We'll go back to our shed—we can find a spot there where we can have a talk. George will have to scout around for some maps— all we have are some of England and some old war maps of France and Belgium. But before he goes scrounging—"

"Yes?"

"This machine won't do for what you have in mind. For one thing, it can carry only you and Mr. Sun Nan. There won't be room for a second pilot. You mentioned the possibility of a second machine, but all we have is our Camel. It wouldn't have sufficient range."

She was quiet for a moment. She had a habit, that I was to come to recognize later, of holding her chin in one hand, almost as if she had a toothache; but it was her pensive attitude, as if she were holding her head steady while she deliberated. Then: "How many other Bristol Fighters are there here?"

"At least half a dozen," said George. "Two of them are in as good condition as this one."

"They happen to be two on which we have an option," I said.

"I thought you might have," said Miss Tozer, and suddenly I knew she had already begun to doubt Henty's recommendation of me as a gentleman. "How much would they cost?"

I almost quoted the ADC price; but then I thought, nothing risked, nothing profited. "Roughly £750 each. How many were you thinking of buying?"

Miss Tozer looking at George, the honest broker. "What would *you* say they would cost, Mr. Weyman?"

George swallowed, didn't look at me. "By the time the extra tanks and everything had been fitted, about £750." There went our profit: I had forgotten all the extras that would be needed. "It's a fair price, Miss Tozer."

"I'm sure it is, Mr. Weyman," she said, not looking at me. "Do you have a pilot's licence?"

"Yes."

"Then I'll buy three." She took her hand away from her chin; she had all her thoughts sorted out. "I'll fly this one and you and Mr. O'Malley can fly the other two. We'll fit extra tanks to each of them—we can put an extra tank on the top wing, can't we?—but your two machines will also have extra tanks in the rear cockpits. In other words we can carry our own emergency supply dump."

I was amazed at the calm, cold efficiency of this beautiful girl who, without benefit of maps, with no knowledge of the route she would have to fly, had already anticipated some of the basic problems such a trip would present. It was as if she had had a satellite's view of the world between England and China. Except, of course, that in those days anyone would have been locked up who had suggested such a view was possible. Only God's eye was the empyrean one then and I'm sure He occasionally shut it in disgust at what He saw.

"Could you find some maps, Mr. Weyman? In the meantime, Mr. O'Malley, I'd like some tea."

George, looking slighty dazed, went off. I said, "Pardon me for mentioning it, Miss Tozer, but I don't think George and I have yet agreed to accompany you. I'm not taking off at twenty four hours' notice to fly all the way to China and not know why I'm going."

"You'll be well paid. Isn't that good enough reason for going?"

"It's a good reason, but it's not enough."

We had now walked back to our shed. The Camel stood in the middle of it, the star lodger. Against one wall were the camp beds of the other two lodgers, George and me. Near the beds were a kitchen table, two chairs, a cupboard with a sagging door, a stove that looked like something that had fallen off George Stephenson's Rocket; pots and pans hung on nails on the wall, like the armour of the poor, and a length of old parachute silk was a curtain that hid the rack on which hung our skimpy wardrobe. In the far corner there was a chipped bath and a rough bench on which stood a basin and a large bedroom jug. The bench continued along the wall, holding all George's tools, till it came up against the cubby-hole that was our office. The only hint of affluence in the place was the Camel and it already showed the pockmarks of the surrounding poverty.

Miss Tozer looked around her. "Who lives here?"

"We do."

Even Henty looked stunned, as if he had bought a ticket for Ascot and found himself in the Potteries. He rushed to our defence: "It's only temporary, I'm sure."

"That's what we said when we moved in here over a year ago. Don't apologize for us, Henty. We're broke. Kaiser Bill could raise more credit at our bank than we could." Since George had already wiped out the profit I'd been anticipating, I could afford to be honest; it was about all that I could afford. I turned to Miss Tozer, took a nose-dive. "Never mind the reason why you want to fly to China. We'll go with you. As you said, the money is good enough reason."

"I admire your honesty, Mr. O'Malley." But she sounded as if she was surprised by it, too. She walked out again to the open doors of the shed, stood staring off into the distance—towards China? Perhaps: she was looking east. She took something from the pocket of her suit, fondled it without looking at it: it was a gold watch and chain. Then she came back to us. "I'll tell you why I have to fly to China."

Which she did, her voice faltering only once, when she mentioned that her father would be killed if we did not reach Hunan by the deadline date. My ear faltered, too, because I found it hard to believe what she was telling me. But the proof was there in her face and in that of Henty behind her.

"It may be dangerous, Mr. O'Malley. Perhaps now you won't want to come."

"She needs your help," said Henty before I could volunteer to be a hero; then looked at his crippled leg with hate. "I wish to God I could go!"

George came back, one big hand clutching a roll of maps, the other holding a school atlas. I told him why Miss Tozer wanted us to fly to China with her. He listened at first as if I were telling him about a proposed joy-ride to the Isle of Wight; then abruptly he exploded. He swung round, pointing a rifle-barrel of an arm at Mr. Sun Nan still standing beside the Rolls-Royce.

"Is he part of this? You mean you take that sort of threat from a—a damned Chinaman? I'd kill the swine!"

"If we kill him, Mr. Weyman, we'll probably also kill my father. If you dislike the Chinese so much, perhaps you'd better not come with us."

"He'll come," I said. "We need him. We'll go with you, but it will cost £500 for each of us and our return fares."

"Five hundred each!" Henty, I hadn't suspected, had a bookkeeper's mind. "That's preposterous! You're making money out of someone else's difficulty!"

"I'm not going to bargain—"

"Neither am I!" Miss Tozer was suddenly fierce. "You sound as if you're putting a price tag on my father's life!"

"On the contrary. I was putting a price on *our* lives. I don't think I've over-valued them. We're cheaper than the machines you're buying."

"I'm sorry." I had the idea that Miss Tozer was not accustomed to apologizing. I also had the idea I had hurt her and that hadn't been my intention. "I'll pay whatever you ask. Now may we please get down to planning the trip?"

I made tea, got out our four cracked and only cups, pulled the chairs and two boxes up to the kitchen table, spread out the maps and got down to planning an 8000-

mile trip to China, everything to be ready within 24 hours. Moses, Columbus and Captain Cook, three other voyagers, would have laughed at us. The roll of maps George had scrounged took us only as far as Vienna. The rest of the proposed route, over which we had some argument, was sketched out on a school atlas on which the inky fingermarks of its former owner, some unknown juvenile, were sprinkled like a warlock's mockery. I began to wonder what George and I had let ourselves in for. I felt like Columbus or Magellan, heading for the edge of the world, flying into an unknown sky.

"We can't take a direct route," George said. "We'll have to fly by way of places where we can refuel. And there's no guarantee we can do that all the way. There are bound to be stretches where they've never seen an aeroplane."

"We'll have to risk that," said Miss Tozer. "Can you have everything ready by tomorrow morning?"

George nodded. "I've already asked half a dozen chaps to stand by to help us. I promised them a pound each if they would work right through the night—all right?" Eve nodded, but Henty looked as if George had promised them life pensions. "I didn't tell them where we are going, just that the machines have to stand up to some hard, long flying. They'll have them ready in time."

"I'd like to take off at noon tomorrow. Is there anything I can get up in London, things we'll need?"

I had been making out a list. "We want to keep things down to a minimum because of weight, but there are still essentials. You'd better get flying suits for you and Mr. Sun—"

"Let the swine freeze," said George.

I ignored him. "We have our wartime suits. You'll need some good strong boots—just in case we have to walk. We want a spare compass for each machine—and you'd better get us a spare sextant. Four sleeping bags, a Primus stove and eight water-bottles, two each. Make sure the bottles are silver or nickel-plated inside, the water tastes better. You can buy them at Hill's in Haymarket. We'll need a medicine kit—John Bell and Croyden in Wigmore Street will make up one for you. And maps—the best place will be the War Office."

"I'll get those," said Henty.

"We'll supply the cooking things. A rifle will come in handy, just in case we have to shoot something for food. You can advise her on that, Henty."

"Miss Tozer has her own gun. I gather she is very competent with it."

"What do you shoot?"

"Elephant, tiger. And the occasional man."

George and I looked at her with cautious interest this time. Then George said, "We'll bring our service pistols. And I'll fit machine-guns—the ADC has some spares."

"Isn't that illegal?" said Henty. "I mean arming a civilian aeroplane?"

"Yes," said George. "But we'll be out of here before anyone knows. I'll put a couple of Vickers forward on Bede's and my machines and I'll mount a couple of Lewis guns on the Scarff rings in our rear cockpits."

"I hope we shan't need them," said Miss Tozer soberly.

We were all silent a moment. The machine-guns suddenly made the other equipment seem superfluous; George and Henty and I were all at once back to the values of war. For the first time it struck me that the actual *flying* to China might not be the worst part of the trip.

"We'll wait till they fire first," I said, denying a wartime principle. "Whoever they are."

Henty took out a cheque-book and I left him to George, who was our book-keeper, when we had books to keep. I got up and went outside. Miss Tozer followed me. She took a cigarette from a gold case, fitted it into an ivory holder, looked at me.

"I don't smoke. I haven't any matches, I'm afraid."

She searched in her handbag, took out a box of matches fitted into a small gold case, handed it to me. I don't think I was awkward with women, even in those days; but I was fumble-fingered just then. I had never lit a woman's cigarette before; I held the spluttering match towards her like an apprentice on Guy Fawkes's team. She smiled, puffed on the cigarette, then stood looking around the aerodrome as the last of the joy-riding machines came gliding in.

"Mr. Henty told me you were an ace. Thirty-two aeroplanes, is that right?" I nodded. Or 44 men, if you wanted to count it another way: some of the machines had been two-seaters, such as the Albatros C7. But I never counted it that way, couldn't. "Do you miss it all? The war, I mean?"

"No. Only lunatics and generals love war."

That's a glib statement these days, something you see on demonstrators' banners, but no less true for being glib. But the Battle of the Somme was only four years behind us then: 1 July 1916, when the British Army alone lost 60,000 men, the day that finally put an end to the glory of war. I was there that Saturday morning, in the third wave to leave the trenches. I saw the men ahead of us going up the hill, strung out like a frieze against the skyline, a frieze quickly ripped to pieces as the German machine-guns cut them down. The second wave went on, never hesitating, just walking smack into death. When I led my platoon over the top I already knew half of them would not live to reach the top of the hill. They died like flowers under the scythe and by the time I reached the top of the hill and could go no further, was trapped in a shell crater with three dead men and another one dying, I wasn't wanting to fight the Germans but to turn back and go hunting for the blind, stupid, living-in-the-past generals who had ordered this massacre. I survived that day and I didn't go hunting the generals. Instead, I joined the Royal Flying Corps, where you were above the carnage and the muck and, if you had to die, you died a clean, sensible death.

"I miss the thrill of flying, I mean the way we flew in the war. I'm grateful for this job, Miss Tozer. Not just for the money."

"It won't be fun, Mr. O'Malley. Not for me, anyway."

"I wasn't thinking of it as fun. I was thinking that once again I'll be flying an aeroplane somewhere for some purpose."

I looked east, toward Kent, the Channel, France and everything that lay between us and China. In the foreground stood Mr. Sun Nan, bowler-hatted, black-suited, patient-faced. I couldn't hate him, not even if I'd had George's prejudices. He was the one who had rescued me from Oxo and all the other graffiti I had planned to scrawl on the sky.

End of extract from O'Malley manuscript.

3

General Meng had started life with the burdening name of Swaying Flower: his mother, going against the grain, had wanted a daughter instead of a son. At the age of six, already ferocious, he had changed it to Tiger Claw; by the time he was eighteen and had already killed six men he had had half a dozen other names. Now, at fifty and with countless dead behind him, he called himself Lord of the Sword. He knew there were people who called him other names and if he chanced to hear them he terminated their opportunities to call anyone any name at all.

So far Bradley Tozer had called him nothing but General. "You are a respectful man, Mr. Tozer."

"Not really, General. Just circumspect. I call you other names, but only to myself."

General Meng nodded, unoffended; if he had to kill this American he would do so for other reasons. He pulled back the sleeve of his voluminous blue silk robe and waved a decorated fan in front of his face. He had come originally from the cooler steppes of Sinkiang and he had never really become accustomed to the more humid heat of Hunan. He was a tall man with a handsome Mongolian face and a head of thick dark hair that was his main vanity. Every morning one of his concubines brushed the black hair for fifteen minutes. It shone like the feathers of a mallard, reflecting any lights that shone on it; the walls of his *yamen,* his palace, were lined with mirrors to add to the light. Meng could admire himself from any angle at any time of day and his head, the object of his admiration, gleamed like an evil totem to the scores of people who served him in the palace.

He looked at himself in a convenient mirror, then back at the American who could have been his half-brother. "I'll kill you if the statue is not returned in time. I am a man of my word. At least, when it pleases me to be."

They both spoke in Mandarin, the words a little awkward in their mouths: each in his own way was a foreigner to Peking. Tozer could also speak Cantonese, but Meng had only contempt for the dialect of the shopkeepers from the south. They were not warriors like himself.

"My daughter will bring the statue. I told you, General—I prize the statue, but not above my own life."

"Are you afraid, Mr. Tozer?"

"No," said Tozer, hoping he sounded unafraid.

He was taller than Meng, with a hard-boned thrusting face and impatient eyes; he had inherited some of his mother's features but none of her placidity. Never having known his mother, he had decided to be an American: to have been chosen All-American had brought him a double satisfaction that no one else had known of. He had no time for fools or incompetents, but he was a fair-minded man and he paid better wages than his competitors, and those who survived his stringent standards and demands usually stayed with him for years. He was also a sensible man and he knew there was no sense in applying standards or demands in the present circumstances. Also, he knew enough of Meng's reputation to believe that the General would be a man of his word. When it pleased him to be.

"Why is this statue so important to you, General?"

Meng continued to fan himself. He looked at the two body-guards standing behind him. They were Mongols from the Tsaidam, muscular men in blue coarse wool robes, worn with a sash beneath which the skirt of the robe flared out. Their riding boots had upturned toes and each man had his long pipe stowed in the side of the boot. The robe was worn with one arm free and the shoulder exposed, a décolleté effect that was more threatening than provocative, since the hand of each bare arm always rested on a broadsword hung from a loop in the sash. The martial effect was only spoiled by the flat tweed caps they wore, suggesting a trade union frame of mind that had so far escaped their master. They hated the local Hunanese and were in turn hated, a state of affairs that kept them constantly alert for their own safety and, by projection, that of General Meng.

He waved the fan at them, dismissing them, and they went out of the small room, their heels clumping on the bare wooden floor. Meng waited till the door closed behind them, knowing they would take up their stance outside it, then turned back to Bradley Tozer.

"Neither of those men speaks Mandarin, but one can't be too careful. I can't have them thinking I'm less than perfect." He looked at himself again in a mirror, nodded in satisfaction as if the mirror had told him he was as close to perfection as it was possible to be. "I am superstitious, Mr. Tozer, my only failing. The twin statues of Lao-Tze have brought me good fortune ever since I acquired them some years ago."

"How did you acquire them?"

"I made their owner, a landlord in a neighbouring province, an offer he couldn't refuse. It's an old Chinese custom which I believe a certain secret society in Italy has now copied from us."

"What was the offer?"

"His head for the statues. Unfortunately, one of my bodyguards misunderstood an order I gave and the landlord lost his head anyway."

"I hope your bodyguards don't misunderstand any orders you may give about me."

Meng smiled. "I admire you, Mr. Tozer. I think you

are secretly very afraid, but you won't lose *face*, will you? It is so important, *face*. That is why I want my statue returned."

Tozer knew not to ask how Meng had lost the statue to Chang Ching-yao in the first place; the matter of *face* forbade such a question. He waited while Meng fanned himself again, then the General went on:

"The dog Chang came to see me, under a flag of truce, to suggest an armistice between us. We have been fighting for two years now, as you know. I welcomed him, being a man who prefers peace to war." He looked in the mirror again, but the sunlight coming in the window had shifted and the mirror was, by some trick of refraction, momentarily just a pane of light, like a milky-white blind eye. Annoyed, he turned back to Tozer, his voice taking on a ragged edge. "While he was here, enjoying my hospitality, he had one of his men steal the statue he eventually sold you. How much did you pay him for it?"

"Ten thousand American dollars."

The fan quickened its movement, like a metronome that had been angrily struck. "Aah! You know it is worth much more than that, don't you? Even so, it is enough to buy him two or three aeroplanes. You know that is what he wants, don't you? He is already recruiting foreign pilots down in Shanghai. I knew it was a dreadful day when he stole that statue. So many things have gone wrong since then. Our harvest has been poor, I've had four opium caravans ambushed, yesterday I learned two of my concubines have got syphilis—" The fan stopped abruptly, was snapped shut and pointed like a pistol at Tozer. "My good fortune will not return until that statue is returned, Mr. Tozer. And neither will yours."

CHAPTER 2

1

The three Bristol Fighters took off on time at noon on Tuesday. O'Malley and Weyman had worked till midnight the previous night, then left the servicing of the planes to the six mechanics Weyman had engaged. Extra tanks were fitted into the rear cockpit of two of the planes and an extra gravity-feeding tank was mounted on the upper wings of the three aircraft. Spare parts were split between O'Malley's and Weyman's machines to divide the weight: a spare propeller, six magnetos, vulcanizing kit for repairing burst tyres, an extra-strong lifting jack. When the mechanics fitted the Vickers and Lewis guns they asked questions, but George Weyman told them to mind their own business. Just before take-off he turned up with four boxes of ammunition.

"All we can afford to carry. We're right on our weight maximum."

"Have you filled the tanks?" O'Malley asked.

"Right to the brim. Three and eightpence a gallon— I'm glad our lady friend is paying and not us. It'll be a pleasure to get away from inflation. How did she handle the machine when you took her up this morning?"

O'Malley had taken Eve Tozer up on a test flight to see how she could handle the Bristol. He had warned her that it had its peculiarities: an inadequate rudder, ailerons that were inclined to be heavy, a tendency for the elevators to be spongy at low speeds; and when he had got into the passenger's cockpit behind her he had wondered if perhaps they might not get further than Purley, just over the ridge at the end of the aerodrome. He had fitted the Go-

sport tubes into the earpieces in his flying helmet, picked
up the speaking tube and wished Eve good luck, then sat
back rigidly in his seat and waited for possible disaster.
Like so many pilots he was a passenger. However . . .

"You'd have thought she'd been flying Brisfits all her
life. She's a natural, George."

"I don't think she liked me laying down the law about
how much baggage she could take with her. That Chink
maid who came down with her must have thought she
was going in a Zeppelin. She'd packed four suitcases for
her."

Henty, Sun Nan and Eve came across from the Rolls-
Royce, where Anna, the maid, stood with the three
suitcases that had been refused by Weyman. Eve and Sun
were dressed in brand-new flying suits and both wore helmets; Eve carried the lacquered wooden box, now
wrapped in hessian, under her arm and Sun carried his
bowler hat under his. Eve looked pale but determined and
Sun looked pale and scared.

"Mr. Sun tells me he has never flown before," Eve
said.

"Glad to hear it," said Weyman. "We could run into
rough weather all the way across France."

"Mr. Weyman, we had better get one thing straight before we leave. I need both you and Mr. O'Malley, but I
need Mr. Sun much more than either of you. He refuses
to tell me who his master is or where he is to be found,
for fear that as soon as we take off Mr. Henty will cable
the authorities in Shanghai and try to have a rescue mission mounted from that end. I shouldn't want to risk my
father's life by having such a mission look for him, but
Mr. Sun doesn't trust me. So I need him to guide us to
where my father is being held captive. Don't forget
that—and keep your anti-Chinese feelings to yourself. I'm
paying you for your skill as a mechanic and pilot, not for
your opinion on the Chinese."

Weyman flushed and for a moment it looked as if he
was going to explode in a fury of abuse and walk away.
Eve wondered if she had been too outspoken; if George

Weyman did walk away it might be too late to get someone to replace him. But she could not back down; he had
to understand there were other considerations that over-
rode his stupid prejudices. She stared at him, painfully
aware of the tightness of her jaw; her tear ducts were
ready to burst, but she kept them dammed. She was determined there would be only one boss on this journey
and it would be she. It was her father they were setting
out to rescue and nothing was going to stop her.

"Righto," Weyman at last said, ungraciously. "But
don't ask me to let him ride in the cockpit behind me. I'll
never trust the blighters."

Then he did turn and walk away, but Eve knew she
had established who was boss. Eager to be gone before
more complications arose, she went across and said goodbye to Anna, who wept, then sat down on the suitcases,
like a refugee stranded with nowhere to flee to. Eve left
her and went back to Henty.

"Goodbye, Mr. Henty. I'll cable you whenever possible
to let you know how we're progressing."

"I have your route," said Henty. "If there is any word
from your father in the meantime, I'll send a wireless
mesage to the British embassies. Good luck."

He ignored Sun Nan, passing him to shake hands with
O'Malley. Then he walked back to the Rolls-Royce and
stood beside it, now and again jabbing his stick into the
ground, still frustrated by his helplessness. He knew
China better than any of those who were about to take
off, with the exception of Sun Nan, but he knew his leg
would not have stood up to the journey that lay ahead.
Sick at heart, envious, he watched the three planes taxi
down to the end of the field.

In the lead Bristol, O'Malley checked his instruments,
looked to either side of him at the other two planes, then
raised his hand. He pushed the throttle forward, set the
rudder to neutral, let the plane pick up speed as it began
to roll. He had always flown by the seat of his pants,
knowing the exact moment when whatever had to be done
should be done; but this Bristol was carrying a bigger

weight load than he had ever taken into the air before and
he kept an eye on the airspeed indicator. He saw it go
past the 45 miles an hour when one could usually lift the
machine off the ground; he let it build, 50, 55, then he
gently pulled the stick back and felt, or rather sensed, the
ground slip away from beneath him. As soon as he was
airborne, knew he had enough power to keep climbing, he
looked back. But there was no need for him to be anxious. Eve Tozer and George Weyman were climbing behind him, coming up smoothly and banking to follow him
as he set the course down through the valley to Redhill,
then to follow the railway line to Ashford in Kent and on
to the coast. They were flying wartime V-formation with
O'Malley as leader. Three armed warplanes flying in war
formation, heading for some sort of showdown on the
other side of the world: I'm dreaming, thought O'Malley.
Then he looked up at the clouds closing down on him,
heard the sirens of the wind singing as they brushed by
him, felt their fingers against his face, knew the dream
was the heart of reality and rejoiced.

That day the world was having its usual convulsions.
Bolshevist troops were advancing on Warsaw and falling
back before Baron Wrangel's White Army in the Crimea;
Parer and McIntosh landed in their DH9 in Darwin, having taken exactly eight months to fly the 10,000 miles
from London; there was heavy selling on the New York
Stock Exchange; Landru, the French Bluebeard, was
swapping jokes with newspapermen while police sifted the
ashes in his villa for the bones of his victims. News was
being made that might become history or just another tick
in the continuing tremor of time passing.

But O'Malley, Eve and Weyman knew none of that and
would not have cared if they had known. Sun Nan, heart
in mouth, bowler hat pressed to his stomach like a poul-
tice, had never had any interest in the world outside
China anyway. He peered ahead through his goggles,
looking for the Middle Kingdom beyond the grey horizon.

They crossed the coast at Folkestone, O'Malley
watching the thunderheads building up in the Channel to

the south of them. Twenty-five minutes later they were over the mouth of the Somme, the thunderstorms behind them.

A few more minutes' flying, then familiar territory to O'Malley and Weyman lay below. O'Malley looked back and across, pointed down at the ground. Weyman nodded, then O'Malley saw him thump his gloved hand on the cockpit rim in an angry gesture. O'Malley understood, but gestures now were futile and too late. He looked down at the flat landscape, searched for the hill he had walked up that July morning four years ago; but at this height there were no hills. He saw the trenches zigzagging across the earth, the scar tissue of war; weeds and bushes and wild flowers were growing in them now, but in his mind they were only proud flesh on the wounds. He flew over the shattered towns and villages, saw the rebuilding going on; people stopped in the squares and looked up, but nobody waved. A cleared patch of ground stood in the loop of a winding road; crosses, like white asterisks, stood in ranks, the dead drawn up for inspection. They died in ranks like that, O'Malley thought. *Oh Christ!* he yelled aloud into the wind and behind his goggles his eyes streamed.

Eve saw the wings of the plane ahead of her wobble; she moved up closer, wondering what message O'Malley wanted to convey to her. But he didn't look towards her; instead she saw him push his goggles up and wipe his eyes with a handkerchief. Then she looked down at the ground, saw the trenches and the ruined farmhouses and the church with the shattered steeple like a broken tooth, and remembered Arthur Henty telling her that more men had died that first morning of the battle on the ground below her than on any other day in the entire history of war. And for what? Henty had said; but she had known he had not been asking the question of her. Then she saw O'Malley looking across at her and she lifted her hand and waved. It was meant to be a gesture of sympathy, but there was no way of knowing that he understood it.

They landed at Le Bourget to refuel. The French aero-drome official checked them in, looked at their planes, went away and came back with two gendarmes. He gestured at the rear cockpits of O'Malley's and Weyman's planes. The Lewis guns were locked in position and covered by canvas sleeves, but there was no mistaking what they were.

"It is not permitted, m'sieu, for private aeroplanes with machine-guns to fly across France."

"These are not private machines." O'Malley's French was adequate if not fluent. A six months' affair with a girl in Auxi had improved his schoolboy French in every possible way. "We are delivering them to the Greek government in Athens."

"Have you papers?"

"We were told the Greek embassy in Paris would arrange for our transit. Everything was done in a hurry. The machines were only ordered yesterday. Things are very bad in Thrace, as you know."

The official didn't know, didn't even know where Thrace was, but he wasn't going to admit it. He said doggedly, "You need papers."

"M'sieu, I admit we should have papers, but there wasn't time. It was a holiday in England yesterday—the French embassy was closed—and everything is so urgent. As you know, the Turks are attacking and winning."

The official once again didn't know, which was just as well, since the Turks were losing badly. But the sergeant of the two gendarmes opened his eyes wide, then nodded. "Damned Turks. I fought against them in Syria. We were supposed to have beaten them."

"The Greeks will beat them with these machines," said O'Malley. "Your government is also supplying them with some of your wonderful aeroplanes. With your Spads and Nieuports and these machines of ours, the Turks will be beaten in a matter of weeks."

It was the official's turn to nod, but he wasn't going to give up so easily. "Who is the lady?"

Eve, whose French, learned at Boston's Winsor School, was good enough to allow her to follow the conversation, was about to introduce herself when O'Malley, with a bow to her, said, "She is the daughter of the Greek Foreign Minister. She is hurrying back to be with him."

"Does she speak French?"

Before Eve could answer for herself O'Malley said, "Unfortunately, no."

"Does she have a passport?"

"As you know, the Greek government, since the war, has not got around to printing passports."

The official once more didn't know; as O'Malley hoped he wouldn't, since he didn't know himself what was the Greek situation on passports. "Who is the Chinese gentleman?"

"The Foreign Minister's butler. The Minister used to be the Greek ambassador in Peking."

"Let them go," said the sergeant. "We're holding up giving those damned Turks a hiding."

The official sighed, shrugged. "Just don't fire your machine-guns at anything before you cross out of France, m'sieu." He bowed to Eve, shook hands with George Weyman, then followed O'Malley across to his plane. As the latter climbed into his cockpit the Frenchman said, "I always admire a good liar, m'sieu, and the English are so good at it."

"And the French, too," said O'Malley, taking a risk. "Let's give credit where credit is due."

The Frenchman acknowledged the compliment. He was a thin man with sad, bagged eyes in a bony, mournful face. He was still weary from the war, too old to be hopeful about the peace. "Just where *are* you going, m'sieu?"

"China."

The Frenchman smiled. "A good lie, m'sieu. Keep it up. Bon voyage."

They took off again, heading almost due east. They ran into rain squalls south of Strasbourg and O'Malley gestured to the others to widen the gap between them; they flew blind for ten minutes, then came out into bright, almost horizontal sunlight. They flew on yellow rails, through brilliantly white clouds, and at last slid down towards the sun-shot blue of Lake Constance, the Bodensee. They landed at Friederichshafen, going in past the huge Zeppelin sheds. They parked their planes at the end of the field and at once saw the big Mercedes staff car speeding down towards them. It skidded to a halt on the grass and two men jumped out.

"Sprechen sie deutsch?" He was a plump, blond man, hair cut *en brosse*, a personification of the cartoon German.

"Unfortunately, no," said O'Malley. "Sprechen sie englisch?"

"Yes," said the plump man and twisted his little finger in his ear as if getting ready for the foreign language. "I was a prisoner of war for two years."

The other German, a younger man with dark hair and eyes that would never admit surrender or defeat, only half-hid his sneer. "Herr Bultmann is proud of his English and where he learned it."

"At least I survived," said Bultmann, as if that had been the purpose of war. He explained to the ex-enemy, "I flew in Zeppelins. Unfortunately we were brought down. Herr Pommer was ground crew. He learned his English from a book." He looked at O'Malley and Weyman, as if he knew they would understand that ground crew could never be shot down. Then for the first time he saw guns on two of the planes. "You are armed? Why?"

"We are on our way to Turkey," said O'Malley. "As you know, things are going badly for your ex-allies there. These machines have been bought by the Nationalists."

"*British* aeroplanes?"

O'Malley shrugged. "You know what governments are like, even our own. They will sell anything to anyone, if there is a profit in it. Herr Weyman and I are just paid civil servants."

"But the Treaty of—where was it? Sèvres?—I thought the Turks were not allowed to have any military equipment. Like us."

"Ah, what are treaties? They'll be turning a blind eye to you, too, in a year or two."

"If they do, the wrong people will get the equipment. Who is the lady?"

"Daughter of the ex-Foreign Minister of Turkey. She speaks neither English nor German, unfortunately. The Chinese is her father's butler."

"I am sorry," said Bultmann, still smiling and friendly, his prisoner-of-war English impeccable. "I do not believe a word of it. You will have to come with us, please."

Then another car came speeding down the field. This was another Mercedes, but this one had never been a wartime staff car; it was a private one, badly needing a coat of paint but still looking huge and powerful and opulent. The man who got out of it, though not huge and powerful, also had a suggestion of opulence about him. He wore a homburg, a winged collar with a grey silk cravat, black jacket, grey waistcoat, striped trousers and grey spats. He could have been a diplomat, a successful laywer or a gigolo. Only when he got closer did Eve, who had an eye for such things, see that everything he wore was like the car, pre-war and frayed at the edges.

"What is the trouble, Herr Bultmann?" He spoke in German in a soft voice that didn't quite disguise the harsh Prussian accent.

"No trouble, sir. The English party just have to explain why they are flying armed aeroplanes over German territory."

The newcomer turned to face O'Malley and the others. He was a very tall, lean man with a bony, handsome face that gave no close hint of his age: he could have been an old twenty or a young forty. He had cool, insolent eyes, a sensual mouth and an air of contempt for the world and everyone in it. Eve thought him one of the handsomest men she had seen in a long time.

He took off his hat, exposing sleek blond hair, clicked his heels and bowed to Eve. "I am Baron Conrad von Kern," he said in English. "I live just along the lake. I saw your aeroplanes come in and I was curious. The last time I saw a Bristol Fighter was two years ago. I shot it down in flames."

"Bully for you," said O'Malley.

"It was pointless," said Kern, not looking at O'Malley but at Eve. "We had lost the war by then. Where are you taking these machines now?"

"To China," said Eve, and introduced herself, O'Malley and Weyman. She did not include Sun Nan in the introductions, but Kern had already dismissed the Chinese as baggage that could be ignored. "It is imperative, Baron, that we are not delayed."

"There is something fishy here, sir," said Bultmann, showing off his colloquial Enlgish. "A moment ago the lady was supposed to be Turkish and unable to speak English."

"You said you didn't believe us," said O'Malley, as if that disposed of his lie.

"How soon do you wish to leave?" Kern was still giving all his attention to Eve.

"Tomorrow morning." Eve recognized the Baron for what he was, a lady-killer, and she accepted the opportunity to take advantage of it. After all, there was little risk of his attempting to emulate the unfortunate Mexican. "All we want is an hotel where we can spend the night, to refuel our machines in the morning and be off first thing."

"One has to be careful, sir," said Bultmann. "You have read what the Bolshevists have done in Saxony, they have taken over some of the towns, declared soviets."

"Do we look like Bolshevists?" said Eve indignantly.

"If I take them as my guests and leave their aeroplanes in your charge overnight, will that satisfy you, Herr Bultmann?" Kern put it as a request, but he made it sound like an order.

O'Malley looked at Bultmann and Pommer. He hated Prussian militarism, had fought against it, had rejoiced that it had been defeated. But it had not been, not entirely; and now he was glad of it. Bultmann stiffened to attention, clicked his heels.

"Yes, Herr Baron. First thing in the morning I shall telephone my superiors for instructions."

"Do that, Herr Bultmann. In the meantime, Fräulein Tozer—" He gestured towards his massive car.

"Thank you," said Eve. "What about Mr. O'Malley, Mr. Weyman and Mr. Sun Nan?"

Kern looked at the three men as if surprised he should be asked to play host to them. Then he looked at Bultmann. "Can't you accommodate them, Herr Bultmann?"

Bultmann was prepared to go just so far in interpreting a request as an order. He allowed himself a touch of Bolshevism: "It will be enough for me to look after the aeroplanes, Herr Baron. They are your responsibility, sir."

Kern lifted his chin and his mouth tightened. But he didn't threaten to have Bultmann court-martialled: he knew better than any of those present that the old days were over. He stalked to his car. "You will ride in front with me, Fräulein Tozer."

George Weyman spoke for the first time. "I'm not leaving these machines here with these Huns."

"It is some time, Herr Weyman, since Attila and his Huns were through here," said Kern. "Herr Bultmann and Herr Pommer are good Germans, nothing more, nothing less."

Weyman looked as if he was about to deny there were any good Germans, but O'Malley cut in: "George, we don't have any choice. These aren't our machines, they're Miss Tozer's."

"And I say we leave them with Herr Bultmann," said Eve. "Get into the car, Mr. Weyman."

Weyman flushed, looked at O'Malley as if accusing him of being a traitor. But the latter was already pushing Sun Nan ahead of him into the back seat of the car. He pushed Sun Nan across the seat, sat himself in the middle. "Come on, George. You're next to me."

Reluctantly, still awkward with rage, Weyman got into the car, left the door open and sat staring straight ahead. Kern drew himself up; then he closed the rear door with a slam. He went round and got in behind the wheel. He nodded to Bultmann and Pommer as they clicked their heels and stood to attention, then he swung the car round.

"Wait!" Eve suddenly cried. As Kern jerked the car to a halt she jumped out and ran across to her plane. She came back with the hessian-wrapped box and a small overnight bag. "Thank you, Baron. Flying is no good for a girl's complexion. I'll need my creams for repairs."

"I have never seen a complexion less in need of repairs."

In the back seat the two Englishmen and the Chinese glanced at each other, joined for a moment in their contempt for such flattery. The United Kingdom and the Middle Kingdom knew how much encouragement was proper for women.

They drove out of the airfield, past the vast hangars where two airships were moored, their noses sticking out of the sheds like those of giant porpoises. The Zeppelins looked harmless enough, but once on leave in London O'Malley had seen one caught in a web of searchlights over the city and he could never remember seeing anything so eerie and menacing. He looked at George Weyman, who had lost his parents in a Zeppelin raid.

"And they're worried about a couple of guns on our machines," said Weyman bitterly. "All of those should have been burnt."

"It's all over, George," O'Malley said, and tried not to sound too weary of Weyman's hatred; after all, his own parents were safe in Tanganyika, profiting from what the Germans had lost. "Try to forget it."

"Not bloody likely."

The road ran along the edge of the lake. Sail-boats were coming in, the sun behind them turning them into huge translucent moths. The water shone like a burnished shield and summer was a great green bloom of trees. If the war had been through here there was no evidence left of it.

"I was on my way to a tea dance over in Constance," said Kern, gesturing at his clothes. In the back seat the three men glanced at each other again: going dancing in the *afternoon*? "I was driving to catch the ferry when I saw your aeroplanes fly over. I turned round at once. I am still fascinated by war machines."

"What did you fly?" O'Malley could not resist the professional question.

"Albatros D's and Fokker Triplanes. I was with von Richthofen."

"How many kills did you have?" said Eve.

If Kern noticed the slightly sarcastic edge to her voice he gave no sign. "I shot down thirty-two machines. But I never looked upon them as kills."

"The same number as Mr. O'Malley. It's a pity we aren't staying longer. You would have a lot to compare and talk about."

"We might have had, at the time," said O'Malley. "You forget, Miss Tozer, I told you I was glad the war was over. That part of it, anyway."

Eve didn't look back, but at Kern. "And you, Baron?"

But Kern didn't answer. He turned the car off the main road and it began to climb a hill. On the crest, on the edge of a sheer drop that fell down towards the lake, stood a small castle. Spired and turreted, light as a pencil drawing, it looked unreal as it perched against the salmon sky.

"It's like something from a fairy tale!" Eve exclaimed. "Is it yours?"

"It is now," said Kern, taking the car across a drawbridge and under a portcullis into a small courtyard. "It belonged to my uncle, but he and my two cousins were killed in the war. Then my aunt died of a broken heart. Women do," he added, not defensively but challengingly, as if the others doubted him.

"So do men, occasionally," said Eve gently.

Servants came out, two men and a woman, all elderly: museum pieces, O'Malley thought, prewar waxworks figures wound up and put back into service. They bowed to the Baron and his guests, but not to Sun Nan; obviously they thought he was just an Oriental mirror of themselves. But their faces showed no surprise when Kern told them to show Sun Nan to a room of his own with the other guests.

"You have had a long flight," said Kern as he led them into the high-ceilinged entrance hall of the castle. The walls were darkly ornate with carved timber, but the floor was flagstones and their heels echoed hollowly. Skeletons walking, thought O'Malley; and shivered. And wondered how many ghosts Kern entertained here in his moments alone.

"Take a bath and rest for a while," said Kern, speaking all the time to Eve; the others could do what they liked. "We shall dine at eight."

An hour later Eve walked out of her bedroom on to a terrace. Refreshed, wearing a clean blouse and skirt that had been in her overnight bag, she felt pleased at the day's progress. She still had a long way to go to save her father, but the trip had started well. She took the gold watch from the pocket of her skirt, opened it and watched the moving second hand: again the bomb image sprang to her mind and her hand jerked of its own accord as if to throw the watch over the wall of the terrace. Instead she snapped the lid shut and shoved the watch back in her pocket.

She stood beside the stone wall and looked down at the lake turning blue-grey in the soft twilight. Pigeons murmured in the trees below her; out on the lake a last sailboat drew a silver line behind it towards home. It was all so peaceful, and on the other side of the world her father might already be dead. She put her hand to her throat, feeling the sudden thickening pain inside it.

"It all looks untouched," said O'Malley behind her. "It's hard to realize they lost the war."

"Those in the cities know they lost it." She took her hand away from her throat, recovering quickly. "That's what I read. Millions of unemployed, money not worth the paper it's printed on."

"You sound sorry for them."

"I might be, if I thought about them. I was a long way from the war, Mr. O'Malley, and I didn't lose anyone in it. No fathers or brothers or even a cousin. I might feel differently if I had. Did you lose anyone?"

"No relatives. Just friends." He turned back to looking out at the lake, closing a door on the war. "We may be in trouble tomorrow morning if Herr Bultmann gets officialdom on his side. German officialdom is the worst kind."

"We can't afford to lose even a day, not so soon. What do you suggest?"

"I don't know. I've run out of invention. And Bultmann thinks I'm a liar anyway.

"You are a liar, Mr. O'Malley, but I'm not sure how serious a one. You are also not averse to swindling a lady out of some money, making a quick profit if you can. Am I right?"

O'Malley smiled, unabashed. "Anyone who makes a profit out of you, Miss Tozer, deserves a medal. I talked to Arthur Henty yesterday before you went back to London. I wanted to know a bit more about you before I started following you to the ends of the earth. I gather your grandfather wasn't above a bit of swindling if he could make a profit."

"Did Mr. Henty say that?"

"No. But I put two and two together. I don't think any white man would make a fortune in China if he was entirely honest and stuck to his scruples. I must ask Mr. Sun about it some time."

"My father is honest."

"Arthur Henty didn't say he wasn't. And I'll take your word for it.

"Until you ask Mr. Sun, is that what you mean?"

Eve realized she was looking at O'Malley carefully for the first time. She had always had a lively interest in men and she had had two serious affairs, one of which had petered out and the other had been broken off sharply when she had discovered the man in question had been as interested in getting into her bank account as getting into her bed. But there had been no disillusionment; as she had told Arthur Henty in London (only yesterday?) she was mad about good-looking men. Quite apart from the worry and distraction of what had happened to her father, perhaps she had not been interested in O'Malley purely as a man because he was not good-looking. He was just above medium height, well-built, clear-skinned and healthy-looking; but he was not handsome. He had brown curly hair that was in need of a cut, a broad blunt face with a long upper lip only relieved by the well-shaped nose above it, and eyes that were too mocking ever to offer an invitation to a girl who believed in romance.

"I don't think Mr. Sun would be the man to ask. He'd be too influenced by his master, as he calls him."

"Just who are you, Mr. O'Malley, besides being an ex-ace?" She cupped one elbow in her hand, put the other hand under her chin.

"An ex-infantry officer. No kills that I can claim, if that's your next question."

"Who were you before the war?"

"Nobody." He grinned. "I'm an only child, like you. My father is in the Colonial Service. He and my mother are out in Tanganyika now, trying to educate the natives that the British Empire will be better for them than the German one was."

"Do you think it will be?"

"I don't know. If ever I meet a native, I'll ask him. My father won't. He believes the British Empire is the closest thing on earth to a well-run Heaven. It may well be. I'm just not interested in propagating the idea."

"You sound like a radical. Were you one before the war?"

"No. I was at Oxford playing cricket and rugger and drinking beer. One term I tried drinking sherry, but I discovered I'm no aesthete. Not as a drinker, anyway."

"Was that all you did—played cricket and rugger, whatever that is, and drank beer?"

"No. Occasionally I read History, but it was considered bad form to swot. I was very much against bad form in those days."

"But not now?"

He shook his head and grinned again. "I saw too much

of what was good form during the war. It killed more men than bad form ever did."

"You don't believe in duty?"

Kern had come along the terrace. He was still dressed as he had been earlier, still the lady-killer; and Eve wondered if he went to the tea dances over in Constance and actually was a gigolo. But despite his foppish image there was something about the Baron that said he would never sell himself to anyone. Least of all to fat matrons at Constance. Though Eve wondered who, in these days of incredible inflation, had money to buy a partner even for a dance. But perhaps, she thought, absorbing some of O'Malley's cynicism, not all Germans had lost the war.

"You sound like our government in Berlin," said Kern. "Schneidermann and Erzberger sneer at the sense of honour we had in our army."

"I don't sneer at a sense of honour," said O'Malley. "I just don't admire stupid generals who expect too much of it."

Kern bit his lip, then nodded stiffly and reluctantly. He was an honest man, too uncomplicated for dialectics; he was a past pupil of an old school that was now just ruins. He turned his attention to Eve. A sense of honour was not so necessary with women: he knew that most of them privately had too much common sense to expect it.

He offered his arm, a courtier from the old school. "Shall we go in to dinner, Fräulein Tozer?"

Over dinner Kern held the chair. "I am from Koenigsberg. The Poles have our city now. You English and Americans don't know what it is like to have your home city given away to another country."

"You asked for it," said George Weyman round a mouthful of potatoes. His dislike of Germans did not extend to their food. He had had two helpings of soup and the meat course and was on his third glass of wine. But he sounded only amiably argumentative. "You had to give up something. You can't lose a war and get off scot-free."

"Perhaps Mr. Sun has something to say about that,"

said Eve. "They have had wars in China for far longer than we've had them."

Sun Nan was seated beside Weyman at the table. O'Malley and Eve were opposite, with Kern at the head. He had said nothing since they had arrived at the castle, but his eyes and ears had been open, absorbing everything that surrounded him. He had been impressed by the castle; he wished his master were here to take an example from the circumstances. The *yamen* at Szeping had begun to look like nothing more than a grandiose tenement.

"Losers in our wars lose everything," he said. "We are not so foolish as to expect mercy."

"You sound as if you have never been on the losing side," said O'Malley.

Sun smiled, and seemed annoyingly smug to the others. "My master is a very able general. Not stupid."

"He is a swine." Weyman abruptly looked less amiable.

Kern, sitting very still, looked in turn at each of his guests. He still did not understand the presence of the Chinese, but it was against his code of manners to ask. The atmosphere had changed; but he was curious rather than annoyed. He had been bored ever since coming here to the Bodensee six months ago and he welcomed anything that would spark a little electricity in his dull existence. Any war was welcome, even one at the dinner table.

"For wanting to be master of his own province?" said Sun Nan, looking sidelong at Weyman as if doing him a favour by answering him at all. "You foreigners have no right to be in China."

"We have the rights of trade." Weyman was flushed; it went against his grain even to argue with a Chink. "There are treaties."

"They mean nothing. You Europeans invented them to cover up your lies and greed." Sun Nan waved a hand of dismissal; then turned to Kern. "I am sorry to be in an argument in your house, Baron. But the bad manners are not mine. Forgive me, I shall retire."

He bowed his head and stood up. But as he pushed

back his chair, Weyman grabbed his arm. Ordinarily, despite his low boiling point and his consuming prejudices, he might have contained his temper at a stranger's table: he was not without social graces. It was ironic that it was German wine that made him lose control of himself.

"I'm not taking that from any damned Chink!"

"Getyourhandsoffme!" The hiss in Sun's voice ran all the words together; his mouth ached with the awkwardness of his teeth. He said something in Chinese, glaring down at Weyman.

"Who the hell do you think you are!"

His hand still grabbing Sun's arm, Weyman pushed back his own chair and stood up. O'Malley, sitting on the other side of the table, saw Sun's left hand go to his pocket, guessed at once what was going to happen but was too slow to act. The knife came out of Sun's pocket and slashed at Weyman's hand; the latter cursed, let go Sun's arm and swung his other fist. But the knife flashed again and Weyman flopped back in his chair, holding the inside of his right elbow with his bloodied left hand. He drew his hand away and looked in amazement at the blood pumping out of the rip in the sleeve of his jacket. He tried to move his arm, failed, then suddenly fell off the chair in a dead faint.

Kern and O'Malley were already on their feet. Sun Nan, still holding the knife out in front of him, backed off. He was working his jaw and his mouth, still battling with his dental plate, but he looked neither afraid nor apologetic for what he had done.

O'Malley knelt down beside Weyman, wrenched off blood-stained jacket and wrapped a napkin round the punctured artery. "Get a doctor!"

"I shall get the police, too." Kern made for the door.

"No!" Eve stopped him. Her mind was a confusion of shock and anger, but at once she saw the danger of further delay if the police were called in. "Not the police—please! I'll explain later. Just get a doctor. *Please!*"

Kern looked at them all again, then he went out of the room.

Sun Nan moved round to the other side of the table, picked up a napkin and wiped his knife. He put it back in his pocket, did up the buttons of the jacket, bowed his head to Eve. "I am not used to being treated like that, Miss Tozer."

"Not even by your master?" She was rigid with anger at him.

"No white man is my master. Or mistress. You had better remember that, Miss Tozer."

He left the room, turning his back on them and moving unhurriedly as if he knew neither Eve nor O'Malley would dare to touch him.

"The bastard!" said O'Malley.

Weyman stirred, opened his eyes and tried to sit up. But O'Malley pushed him back, while Eve found a cushion and put it under his head. She wrapped another napkin round his wounded left hand. Weyman looked at his right arm, propped up on O'Malley's knee, and shook his head, as if he still couldn't believe what had happened to him.

"I could kill him."

"I'd stop you first," said O'Malley. "You heard what Miss Tozer said this morning. She needs him more than us. And he knows it."

Weyman looked at both of them, then at his arm. "How bad is it?"

"I don't know. It's not good, that's about all I can say."

Kern came back. "The doctor will be here in ten minutes. Where is Herr Sun?"

"Gone up to his room," said Eve. "He won't run away."

"Perhaps you would do me the favour of explaining all this?" Kern was coldly polite.

Eve hesitated, then told Kern everything. He listened without any expression on his face. When she had finished he looked down at Weyman. "Herr Weyman is not going to be able to fly tomorrow."

George Weyman was stubborn, but not stupid: at least not about practical matters. "I couldn't handle a machine, not the way my arm feels now."

"We'll have to fly on tomorrow," Eve said. "We can't be delayed. Can we leave Mr. Weyman and his machine here with you?"

"There is no alternative," said Kern. "But you still have to have your other aeroplanes released by Herr Bultmann."

"Can't you help us there?" Eve pleaded. "You can see how much even a day's delay may mean to us."

"I'll see what I can do. In the meantime we should get Herr Weyman up to his room."

"What do we tell the doctor?" O'Malley asked.

"That it was an accident," said Kern. "This man was my uncle's doctor for years. He won't ask awkward questions."

The doctor didn't. Old, thin, looking like his own most regular patient, he came, fixed up Weyman's arm, ordered him to rest. "You have damaged the tendon, too. It may be a long time before your arm is perfectly well again."

"What did he say?" asked Weyman, irritated by the doctor's inability to speak English. Kern told him and he shook his head in angry disappointment. "When you get to China, Miss Tozer, throw that swine out of your machine, will you? From a great height."

Eve smiled, though it was an effort. "Just get well, Mr. Weyman. Go back to England. You'll be paid in full." Then she turned away, put a hand to her forehead. She closed her eyes for a moment, then opened them as she felt herself sway. "I'm tired. I'll go to bed, if you'll excuse me, Baron."

Kern took her to the door of her room, kissed her hand. "We'll solve your problem, Fräulein Tozer, Just get a good night's sleep."

"My problem isn't here, Baron. It is in China."

She closed the bedroom door, undressed, got into the

big four-poster bed. She stared out through the open window, saw a star fall across the purple-black sky. She believed in omens, but, exhausted emotionally and mentally, couldn't remember what a falling star meant. But it reminded her of the flash on Sun Nan's knife as he had plunged it into George Weyman's arm. *That* had been some sort of omen, she knew; and cried for her father, the prisoner in a land of superstitions. She wondered if her father, staring out of his window wherever he was held, had seen the same star fall. Then remembered that it would be already dawn in China, the beginning of another precious day to be marked off by the man who held her father captive.

2

In the morning, at breakfast, Kern said, "Would you allow me to take Herr Weyman's place?"

Eve looked at O'Malley. There were only three of them at the table. Weyman was in his room, still asleep. Sun Nan, careful of his manners, had asked to be excused from eating with them; munching an apple, he was now out on the terrace, admiring the scenery like any unworried, conscience-free visitor. Breakfast made a mockery of the claim that people further north were on the verge of starvation; eggs, bacon, sausage, fruit, three sorts of bread loaded the table like some harvest offering. The fruits of defeat, thought O'Malley, who hadn't had a breakfast like this in longer than he cared to think about. And looked at Kern and wondered if he could put up with the arrogant ex-enemy.

"It's up to you, Miss Tozer." He sipped his coffee, tasted the mushy bitterness of it; at least the coffee in England wasn't made from acorns, as this was. "If it won't offend the Baron to fly a British machine."

"You are a flier like me, Herr O'Malley. You know real pilots draw no distinctions between aeroplanes. Your fliers had as much admiration for our Albatroses and Fokkers as we had for your SE's and Bristols. All one looks for is a machine that gives him pleasure to fly."

"At least we have that much in common." O'Malley tried not to sound too grudging. "If the Baron flew with von Richthofen, he'd be a good pilot. I *know*—I flew against the Circus."

"We may even have flown against each other," said Kern.

"The thought had occurred to me. Were you ever shot down?"

Kern hesitated, but his honesty was equal to his pride. "Once. I was flying an Albatros and we ran into an English formation above Rosières. I shot down two machines, two Camels, then a third one got above me, put me on fire. I got back to our own lines, but only just. My mechanics dragged me out, but not before I was burned. Here." He ran his right hand down his left side and left arm. "It was 22 July 1918."

O'Malley looked at his coffee cup, pushed it away. "I still fly that Camel back home in England."

Kern showed no surprise: the war in the air had always been a local affair. "Did you claim me as a kill?"

"I'm afraid so. I thought you were a dead duck."

Kern shook his head, smiled thinly. "Your count was wrong, Herr O'Malley. So I am one up on you, thirty-two to thirty-one."

"Are you finished, both of you?" Eve, worn out, had slept soundly; but she had woken depressed. The offer by Kern had given her a momentary lift, but now she was annoyed by these two men and their reminiscences that had nothing to do with what concerned her so much. "This is not a lark, Baron—"

"The war was no lark, Fräulein."

Eve ignored that: she knew it had been no lark, but these two talked as if it had been some sort of deadly game in the air. "Our arrangement would be a business one. The same terms as I'm paying Mr. O'Malley. Five

hundred pounds and your return fare. I don't know what
that is in marks."

Kern smiled. "Who does know? Yesterday it could
have been a billion marks, today a trillion. The money is
immaterial, Fräulein Tozer. But I'll take it."

He's as broke as I am, thought O'Malley. The castle,
the big Mercedes, the servants, the big meals: it all
floated on God knew what depth of credit. The Junkers
still survived, though O'Malley wouldn't bet on how long.
Not even a credit bet, if anyone would give *him* credit.

Eve stood up, suddenly eager to be on their way again.
"Could we leave in half an hour, Baron? We hope to
make Belgrade tonight."

"I shall have to telephone Herr Bultmann before he
talks to his superiors."

"Is he likely to hold us up?"

Kern shook his head. "Herr Bultmann is one of the old
school."

What the hell does that mean? O'Malley wondered;
but didn't ask, because he had already guessed. Certain
areas of Germany still echoed to the click of boot-heels;
the workers' soviets might be taking over towns in Saxony,
but not here around Freiderichshafen. He determined
there would be no heel-clicking between here and China.

Kern went away to make his phone call to Bultmann
and Eve and O'Malley went up to say goodbye to Weyman. He was more comfortable this morning but far from
cheerful. "This is a right do, isn't it? Stabbed by a blasted
Chinaman, replaced by a Boche. I did better than that in
four years of war."

"Stop laughing, chum."

O'Malley would miss Weyman on the flight. His mer-
curial temper was a handicap and they would be flying
over terrain where his prejudices would have flourished
like weeds; but he was an excellent mechanic and
O'Malley had little confidence in his own ability to keep
the machines going if any of them should break down.
But he was becoming more and more aware of Eve
Tozer's concern for her father, could see that the air of

cool control she affected was now no more than a veneer, and he did not want to add to her worries by mentioning what, with luck, might not happen.

"Good luck." George Weyman put out his bandaged left hand, made the gesture of a handshake. "You'll get there in time, Miss Tozer. You can put your money on Bede."

Eve, an affectionate girl, kissed Weyman on the forehead; he blushed as if she had pulled back the sheets to get into bed with him. "Good luck to you, too. See Arthur Henty when you get to London. Tell him so far we are keeping to schedule."

"Second day out," said O'Malley sardonically. "I should hope so."

"That's the only way I can bear to think," said Eve. "Day to day."

"Sorry," said O'Malley, and bit his tongue to remind it to be more careful in future.

An elderly servant drove Eve, O'Malley, Kern and Sun Nan in to the airfield. Sun Nan sat in the back with Eve and O'Malley, completely indifferent to the change of pilots in the third plane. He made no reference to Weyman, not enquiring about how his victim was this morning; and on the surface he looked equally uninterested in Weyman's replacement. But he was studying Kern, certain that the German aristocrat, in his own way, had as many prejudices as the English working man. They were all the same here in the West and he would be glad to get back to China, where all the prejudices were honourable ones.

Bultmann and Pommer were waiting for them at the airfield. One of the airships had been brought out of its hangar and floated against the morning sun as it nosed a mooring mast. The Mercedes drove through the shadow of it and went down to the end of the airfield and the parked Bristols. Kern looked up at the huge shape above them.

"Some day the sky will be full of those. There will be no room for fliers like us, Herr O'Malley."

"Let's take-off, do a circuit and come back and shoot them down."

For the first time Kern smiled directly at O'Malley. "Jolly good idea."

The car pulled up in front of the three Bristols. O'Malley, certain that Kern was going to get his way with the class-conscious Bultmann, went to his plane and began to dismantle the Lewis gun in the rear cockpit. Then he did the same with the gun in what was now Kern's plane. He stowed the guns in the cockpits, but left the Scarff rings still mounted. He jumped down from Kern's plane as the latter and Eve came across to him.

"We can put the guns back when we get into hostile territory," he said.

"What is the point of them with nobody in the rear cockpit to fire them?" said Kern.

"They were Weyman's idea. If we're going to have to fight anyone, it'll be on the ground, not in the air."

"A pity, don't you think?"

"Stop that sort of thinking, both of you!" Eve snapped, turned and strode across to her plane. She gestured curtly to Sun Nan to get aboard, then she clambered up and settled into her own cockpit.

Kern looked across at her. "She would be a fiery woman in bed."

The thought had crossed O'Malley's mind, but he wouldn't have voiced it. He was glad of an interruption from Bultmann. "I had all the tanks filled, Herr Baron. But there is one, er, small point. Who pays?"

Obviously the thought of payment had not occurred to Kern. He looked at Bultmann in surprise; but O'Malley came to his rescue. "Fräulein Tozer will pay you."

"A woman pays?" said Bultmann.

"A new custom," said O'Malley. "Equal rights."

Bultmann, shaking his head at the decadence of the English and the Americans, went across to Eve. There was some discussion, then she handed him some English money. Bultmann looked at it as if not sure of its value, then he stepped back and bowed to Eve.

"Do you want to take your machine up for a test flight before we start?" O'Malley asked Kern. "You haven't flown one of these before, have you?"

"Hardly. But you and I are fliers, Herr O'Malley. Would you wish to have a test flight?"

Yes, thought O'Malley; but said no. But told himself it was the last time he was going to swap bravado with the arrogant Baron. "Shall we start then? Vienna is our first stop, to refuel."

They took off into a cloudless sky, with O'Malley once more leading the way. He looked behind him and saw Kern lift his Bristol off the ground too soon: the Baron hadn't allowed for the extra weight. The plane flew flat for several hundred feet, the nose threatening to point down; but Kern, as he had claimed, was a flier, a pilot who was part of his machine. O'Malley saw the plane wobble and he waited for it to stall: then the nose lifted and he knew Kern had it under control. It climbed steadily, swung round in a steady bank and fell in behind O'Malley. They headed east and soon were skirting the northern flanks of the Bavarian Alps. The flying was easy and O'Malley lay back in his wicker seat, occasionally turning his face up to the sun, listening to the music of his engine, marvelling at his good fortune. He felt sorry for Bradley Tozer, was apprehensive for him, but the American millionaire, involuntarily and through his daughter, had bought him a few weeks of escape. He looked across to his left and wondered if Kern had the same thoughts.

They landed at Vienna after three-and-a-half hours' uneventful flying. Kern was first out of his plane and moved across at once to help Eve down from hers. Sun Nan, plump and awkward, was left to feel his own way down to earth. O'Malley, finding an English-speaking official, was left to superintend the refuelling of the planes and Kern, taking a small picnic box that his servant had packed, led Eve to the shade of some near-by trees.

Eve called to Sun Nan, gave him some food and asked him to take some across to O'Malley. The Chinese didn't rebel at being asked to act as servant; he knew he was as

much a partner in this foursome as the others, uneasy
though the partnership might be. He gave O'Malley his
lunch, then sat down under the wing of Eve's plane and
began munching his bread and sausage. The food was
awkward in his mouth, dislodging his dental plate, and he
longed for some nice smooth noodles.

"I was here in Vienna before the war." Kern lay back
on the grass. He had brought a wartime flying suit with
him, but was not wearing it; like the others on this hot
summer day he wore just street clothes. He was dressed in
grey flannel trousers, a wide-collared silk shirt open at the
neck and black-and-white shoes; again Eve had the mental picture of him as a gigolo. He looked at her apprais-
ingly and she waited for him to pat the grass beside him
and invite her to lie down. "My father was at the court of
the old Emperor for six months. He was there on loan as
a military adviser."

"Where is he now?"

"He was killed at Verdun. My two brothers also."

She changed the subject. "I came here when I was a
girl, with my mother and father. We did the Grand Tour."

They were both silent for a while, lost in the contem-
plation of something that now had the fragile structure of
a half-remembered dream. A bee buzzed above the picnic
box and Eve lazily brushed it away. In the distance the
end of the aerodrome shimmered in the heat like quivering green water. Eve lay back, somnolent, but wide awake
enough not to lie too close to Kern. China, and her father,
all at once were as remote as the lost empire of the
Hapsburgs.

She heard Kern say, "I fell in love with the women of
Vienna. They were beautiful, always flirting, in love with
love. But I was too young for them then, only eighteen. I
vowed to come back and enjoy them when I was old
enough. But it's too late now."

"Why?" she asked dreamily.

"Because romance blossoms best on a full stomach.
One does not flirt when one is hungry—I learned that in

Berlin last year. The women of Vienna, I'm sure, are thinner now than they used to be."

Eve sat up, no longer dreamy. "I fear you are a ladies' man, Baron. Don't expect any opportunities on this flight of ours."

Kern, still lying back on the grass, hands behind his head, smiled up at her. He *is* handsome, Eve thought; and chided herself for the admission. But it was a pity she had not met him in other circumstances, when she could have pitted her wits against him in the flirting game that seemed to be his favourite sport. Then was conscience stricken as she thought of her father. She stood up quickly, brushing the grass from her skirt. Pulling on her flying helmet, she walked across to O'Malley, who stood leaning against the wing of his plane, finishing his lunch.

"The Baron offend you?"

"What makes you think that?"

"Just the way you got up and left him. I've had girls walk away from me the same way."

God, she thought, are both of them going to give me trouble? "How do I pay for the gasoline?"

"What did you bring?"

"Pounds and dollars. It was all I could get at such short notice."

"They'll take either. Our money is more welcome than we are. They're a sour lot, these Austrians."

"That's not what the Baron has been telling me."

But she didn't elaborate, just turned her back on him and went across to pay the two men who had brought down the drums of petrol in their ramshackle ex-army truck. Then she moved to her plane, pulling up short as Sun Nan suddenly rose up in front of her from beneath the wing. Preoccupied, thoughts building up in her mind like a honeycomb, she hadn't noticed him seated in the shadow of the wing.

"Miss Tozer, if either O'Malley or the Baron makes trouble for you, let me know. I shall take care of you."

"Make trouble?" Then she understood what he meant, marvelled that he should have been so observant. She laughed at the irony that he should be her protector, the defender of her honour. "I'm sure I have nothing to fear from them, Mr. Sun. But thank you."

"We have to stick together. Your father is depending on us, not them."

"You don't have to remind me, Mr. Sun. But Mr. O'Malley and the Baron may still be necessary to us."

They took off five minutes later. They flew south-east this time, soon crossed into Hungary. The countries lay below them, one merged into another; treaties had broken up the Empire, but the boundaries were only on maps; at 5000 feet nothing appeared to have changed. Harvest-yellow, dotted with green lakes of forest, the lost empire was unmarked: not here the scars of trenches. Then they were over Lake Balaton, sparkling under the afternoon sun like a vast spill of Tokay wine; the sails of fishermen's boats drifted like tiny moths caught in the web of sunshine. Then Eve, looking up from the bright glare of the lake, saw the clouds ahead.

They hung in the sky like great baskets of evil purple blooms, a hot-house of storm stretching away to the south-west. Lightning flickered, blue-silver against the purple, and she imagined she could hear the crash of thunder above the roar of the engine. She looked back over her shoulder at Sun Nan, saw the fear on his face below the opaque mask of his goggles, wondered what her own face showed. She hated storms, was afraid of thunder and lightning even in the shelter of the safe, weather-impregnable houses she had called home. In America she had never dared fly in the face of a storm, had always looked for a place to land even when she ran into squalls of rain.

Then up ahead she saw O'Malley wiggle his wings, point to his left and then bank away to the east. He was going to try and take them round the storm.

3

Extract from the William Bede O'Malley manuscripts:
It was a bitch of a storm, the worst I had experienced up
till then. I have never been a religious man, at least not
down on the ground; and if one is going to be religious,
that's the place to be it, down among the selfish, the
cheats, the murderers who are there to test your Christi-
anity or whatever you profess to believe. No, the only
time I've been religious is when I've been up in the air:
marvelling at God's genius and charity in creating the sky
or cursing Him for the storms He could whip up out of
nowhere, showing off His wrath. This was one of His
most wrathful.

The turbulence hit us long before we were into the
clouds. I had turned east, hoping to fly round the edge of
the storm, but it was moving too fast for us. The edge of
the giant waves of air as they hit us. I had looked down
it caught us and in a matter of moments we were bucking
just before the clouds enveloped us, but there was
nowhere to head for as a landing site. We were over hills
that rolled up into mountains; and the thought of the
mountains frightened me. I had jerked my hand upwards,
hoping Miss Tozer and Kern were watching me, then
pulled back the stick and began to climb. If we were
lucky we might get above the storm, but in any case we'd
be above the top of the mountains. Mountain tops and
aeroplanes still have an upsetting magnetism for each
other and even today, at 30,000 feet, I can't fly over a
range of mountains without feeling them scraping my
bottom.

I lost sight of the other two machines as soon as the
cloud, a wild dark sea, rolled in on us. From a distance
the clouds had looked purple; now they were black and
green. The air had suddenly turned cold, made even
colder by the rain that hit me like a barrage of knives. I

continued climbing, fighting the stick that shook in my hands and threatened to break my arms at the wrists and elbows. The turbulence was like nothing I had ever known before; the yo-yo hadn't been invented then, but I should have got the inspiration and patented it. The noise was more than noise: it was a physical assault inside my head. I reeled in my seat with it, punch-drunk, deaf but still able to hear. Lightning had been exploding behind the clouds, throwing them into bright relief, making them look solid and impenetrable. Suddenly it burst all around me, a great flash of blue-white light that blinded me, yet in the moment before blinding me painted everything in frightening detail: I saw things, the dials on the instrument panel, the worn rim of the cockpit, the tear in the back of my right-hand glove: I saw them, yet I was *inside* them. It was an effect I had once experienced as a child during an attack of *petit-mal*, the splitting of oneself in a split-second dream: you are inside and outside the objects you are witnessing at the same moment. I felt sure now that I was about to pass out, that I was seeing the final, meaningless revelation before dying.

The lightning went and I looked up. And saw the plane only half a dozen feet above me. I didn't know whose it was, Miss Tozer's or Kern's: all I knew was that the pilot couldn't see me. We flew almost locked together, the wheels of the plane above only a foot or two from my top wing. Lightning flared again; half-blinded I saw the plane above tremble and dip. I plunged the stick forward, hit turbulence, shuddered, then fell away from beneath the other threatening machine. There was no time to look up to see if it was following me.

Then the Bristol flipped over, flung sideways by the greatest explosion of sound I've ever felt: not *heard*. My head reverberated with it, an echo chamber that threatened to drive me insane. Sanity, fortunately, has nothing to do with the urge to survive. Unbreathing, paralysed, mind and body dead, the unthinking me refused to let the aeroplane go. My hands and arms worked of their own accord; then feeling came back into my legs and feet. I fought with the only two weapons I had, the stick and the rudder bar; yet they were the machine's weapons, too, for it was fighting me. It was not in a spin; we seemed to be plunging in a series of tight bucking slides. I still couldn't see; lightning glared around me again, but it was only a lightening of the darkness in my blinded eyes. I worked by *feel*, fighting the plane by instinct, going with the slide at times, pulling against it at others, praying all the time with the mind that was slowly coming back to life that the wings would not tear off, that the machine would not disintegrate and leave me sitting there for the last moment at the top of the long drop to eternity. I believed in God then and hated Him for wanting me to join Him.

Then I found I was winning. The Bristol slid to starboard, kept sliding and I let it go, feeling I was getting it under control. I eased the rudder to port, pulled the stick back; the plane responded, straightened out. The wind and the rain were still pounding at me, but now the Bristol and I were part of each other again, ready to fight together. I held the stick steady and we drove on through the storm, the wings trembling as if ready to break off but always holding, the engine coughing once but then coming on again with a challenging note that gave me heart. I glaced at the altimeter: I had dropped 3000 feet since I had last looked at it. I had no idea of the height of the mountains I had glimpsed (were they still ahead of me? Below me?); but I dared not try to climb above the storm again. I had to ride it out at this level; the galleries of hell were topsy-turvy, one stood a better chance of survival in the lower depths. I wondered where Miss Tozer and Kern were, if they were still flying or had already crashed, but there was nothing I could do about going looking for them. I shivered when I thought how close I had been to that other Bristol in the clouds.

It took me twenty minutes, forever, to fly out of the storm. Then, as so often happens, I came out abruptly into bright mocking sunlight. I checked the compass; we

were miles off course. But there was no hope of correcting
just now; over to starboard the storm still stretched away
to the south, its darkness lit with explosions of lightning. I
looked back and around for the others. Then I saw them
come out of the clouds, too close to each other for comfort; Kern swung abruptly to port to widen the distance
between them. I throttled back, waited for them to come
up to me. Miss Tozer waved to say she was all right; but
Kern pointed to his top wing and I saw the tattered fabric
and the splintered strut. He was holding the machine
steady, but he would have to do that if he was to keep it
in the air; any sudden manoeuvre would rip the wing to
shreds. I waved to him, then looked down and about for a
possible landing site. But there was none: we were over
mountains that offered no comfort at all.

There was nothing to do but keep flying, hoping Kern's
wing would hold, till I saw some place where we could set
down without his having to put too much strain on his
machine. It was just as likely to fall to pieces as he eased
the stick back for the gentlest of landings, but that was
something we had to risk.

Then at last I saw the long narrow valley ahead, with
the straight white road running down the middle of it. I
waved to the others to circle over the valley while I went
down to inspect the road. I slid down, aware of the workers in the fields on either side stopping to look up at me,
at some of them running in terror for the shelter of neighbouring trees; but I kept my attention on the white dirt
road, looking for the thin shadows in the afternoon sun
that would tell of ruts or holes in the surface. There appeared to be none and I banked steeply and climbed
back. I made signs that I would go down first, Miss Tozer
would follow and Kern would be the last to land.

I went back to the end of the valley, passing over a
large mansion standing among trees, then slid in above
the road. There were no telegraph poles bordering it to
offer a hazard; and it ran without a bend in it for almost a
mile. I put the Bristol down, felt the smoothness of the
dirt and knew I was safe. I rolled down the road, eased to

a stop and swung off into a field. I jumped down and ran
back to the road.

Miss Tozer came in, steady as a bird, bounced a little
as she touched, corrected and ran down towards me. She
swung off into the field, got out and came running back.
She stood beside me and watched as Kern, coming round
in a wide flat bank so that he didn't strain the upper wing
too much, prepared to land. He came down steadily and I
knew how he would be: one eye on the nose, the other on
the wing above him. He was ten feet above the road,
holding the nose up, when the wing started to shred off. It
went back over his head in tatters at first, as if he had run
into a flock of starlings; then a big strip tore off and I saw
him duck as it flew straight at his head. Miraculously he
jerked neither his hand nor his feet; he kept the plane
steady while the upper wing disintegrated above him. I
felt Miss Tozer clutch my arm, but I didn't look at her,
just kept my eyes on Kern as he brought his plane down
to earth in as beautiful a landing as I've ever seen. He
came rolling down the road and swung in beside us.

He climbed down, looking much less the dandy who
had climbed into the cockpit this morning. I had recognized him for what he was, a womanizing loafer on whom
time and his testicles hung heavy; but, God Almighty, he
could fly a plane and that in my eyes forgave him a lot.
Only I wasn't going to tell him. With his bloody arrogance he'd have just nodded his head and agreed with me.

"I got a bolt of lightning." He unwound the long silk
scarf he wore, tied it round his middle like a belt; he was
a Fancy Dan all right, and I wanted to throw up. But he
was as cool as if he had just come in from ten minutes of
uneventful circuits, and even my prejudiced eye could see
that it was no act. He had probably got out of his burning
plane, the day I had shot him down, with the same cool
aplomb. "Fortunately, it was a small one."

"I'm just glad you're safe." Then Miss Tozer sniffed
the air, looked around. "What's that smell?"

"I thought it was your perfume." She had let go my
arm, but still stood close to me.

"Roses," said Kern. "What a beautiful sight."

I turned my head to look behind me, following the direction of his gaze. Intent on watching Kern bring his plane down, I had not noticed before that the whole valley was one vast rose garden, split up the middle by the road. There were workers scattered throughout the fields; the closest were four women on the other side of the road. As Kern and I looked at them they flung their skirts up over their heads, hiding their faces; but everything they owned below the waist was exposed. Pubic hair and bare bottoms are common sights nowadays, but in 1920 we didn't have the broadening education of television and only those with the fare to Paris or Port Said ever saw a blue movie. These women stood modesty on its head, but every woman to her own standards.

"A charming custom," said Kern. "Purely local, no doubt."

I looked at Miss Tozer, but she was staring up the road. In the distance there was a cloud of white dust, quickly coming closer. Then we saw that just ahead of it was a white horse galloping at full speed and a few moments later we recognized the rider of the horse as a woman sitting side-saddle. She came down on us like a Valkyrie, bringing the horse to a rearing halt only yards from us.

"Good God, we must be in Roumania!" said Kern. "It's Queen Marie!"

But it wasn't, though we didn't know that at once. She quietened the prancing horse, sat elegantly in the saddle and looked us up and down. She said something in a language I didn't recognize, then she spoke in heavily accented English. "You are English, yes? Those are English aeroplanes, are they not?"

"We are English, American, German," said Miss Tozer and introduced us individually.

"I am the Countess Ileana Malevitza." She had to be an aristocrat of some sort, or an eccentric; or both. She was wearing a bright red tunic, braided with silver and with silver epaulettes, over a royal-blue shirt and dark

blue trousers tucked into riding boots that came above her
knees. She had a black fur shako on her blonde head and
a short sword swung in an enameled sheath at her waist.
Despite her coating of fine dust, the effect of her was
striking. We've flown through that storm into Ruritania, I
thought, and waited for the Drury Lane chorus, somewhere out among the rose bushes, to burst into song. I
looked across the road again, ready to be bemused again
by the bare bottoms and bellies, something I had never
seen at Drury Lane, but the women had dropped their
skirts now and stood watching us. That somehow made
everything real.

"You are welcome to my valley," said the Countess.

"Thank you," I said, and found myself doing a Kern: I
clicked my heels and bowed. "Where are we?"

"In the Valley Malevitza. The border between Roumania and Bulgaria runs down the middle of this road,
right through my house. You are in Roumania at this
moment."

"And the young ladies are Bulgarian?" Kern gestured
towards the women standing among the rose bushes on
the other side of the road.

"Young? Your eyesight is not very good, Baron. Only
one of them is young." The Countess gave them only a
cursory glance, as if they were no more than thorns or
faded blooms on the bushes.

"I don't think the Baron looked too carefully at their
faces," said Miss Tozer.

The Countess laughed heartily: it came up out of her
belly, like a fat man's. "It is the custom among some of
the women. They dare not show their faces to a strange
man at first. What else they show is not an invitation.
Their menfolk would cut the stranger's throat if he
thought it was."

I saw the men standing further back in the rose fields.
They had risen up from among the bushes; more women
and children were also appearing. There must have been
a hundred of them spread out through the fields on either
side of the road, dark, silent figures among the blaze of

red, pink and white blooms. Each man's hand glittered: it was a moment before I realized each of them held a sharp pruning knife.

Sun Nan had got out of Miss Tozer's plane. He looked pale and sick, but he put on his bowler hat against the fierce sun and stood holding on to the lower wing of the machine, doing a good job of looking dignified. The Countess glanced at him, but made no comment: like Kern she dismissed him as a servant. Nobody, in her book, would have an Oriental with him or her unless he was a servant.

"Why did you land here in my valley?"

I explained the circumstances and pointed to the remains of Kern's top wing. "I'm afraid the Baron can't take off again until we repair that. Is there somewhere around here where we can stay, an inn or something?"

"You will be my guests. Follow me." She swung her horse round. I wondered if we were supposed to gallop after her on foot.

"Countess, I don't want to leave the machines parked here with no one to look after them."

I don't know what I really expected to happen to the planes, unless I thought the rose-gatherers would attack them with their pruning knives. It struck me that none of these peasants, wild-looking and isolated in this mountain valley, had seen an aeroplane before, at least not on the ground and quite possibly not even in the sky. I had vague memories of reading of Balkan superstitions and there was no guarantee that these particular Balkans trusted the strange contraptions that had fallen down out of the clear hot sky into their midst. I had only a hazy idea where we were, but Dracula country couldn't be too far away.

"Bring them with you." She dug her heels into her horse and went up the road at full gallop, trailing a long thin veil of dust.

I shrugged, turned to the others. "She's the hostess."

"I think she's mad," said Miss Tozer. "Do you think we should stay with her?"

"What choice do we have? Even if I can find some canvas and varnish right away, it's going to take me at least two days to rebuild that wing."

She hid her dismay, but I knew she had guessed it was not going to be a ten-minute repair job. Kern said, "You can go on without me and I'll try to catch you up."

I waited for Miss Tozer to give the decision, but she was looking at me. She was the boss, but with George Weyman's departure I had become what I suppose one would call the technical manager. "I think it's better we stick together, at least for the time being. We still have a few days in hand."

"We can work on the wing together," said Kern.

"Yes," I said, but I doubted if he could darn a hole in his sock let alone rebuild an aeroplane wing. He had the sort of hands for stroking flesh, not stretching canvas. If he had done a hard day's work in his life there was no evidence of it.

"Mr. Sun could help, too," said Miss Tozer.

Sun Nan had moved across to stand beside us. "I could be of help. My father was a fisherman on Lake Tung-Ting. I used to help him make his sails when I was a boy."

His hands looked as soft and unmarked as Kern's. But there was no reason to doubt him: he was as eager to get to China as Miss Tozer. He was as concerned for his own neck as much as for Bradley Tozer's.

"Righto, we start first thing in the morning. Now shall we join the Countess?"

We got back into our planes and with me in the lead taxied up the long road towards the big house behind the trees at the end of the valley. The field workers watched us go, still standing there unmoving among the bright blooms like iron effigies in a graveyard. I don't know why the graveyard image came to mind, except that I knew Ruritania was dead, gone forever.

We taxied in through a wide gateway in high stone walls covered in climbing roses. There was a lawn set in the middle of the circular driveway, ragged and unkempt, nothing like an English lawn. The Countess stood at the top of the steps that led up to the terrace stretching across the front of the house; she gestured at me to park the planes on the lawn. We lined them up facing the house, climbed out, took our baggage and went up the steps. Miss Tozer carried the hessian-wrapped box in which was her father's ransom; Sun Nan, looking like a valet, carried her suitcase and his own. The Countess, arms akimbo, fur shako cocked jauntily, waited for us at the top of the steps. Two young men stood with her, one on either side. They were brawny, muscular chaps, good-looking in a coarse way, bulls in trousers: studs, I guess you'd call them today.

"These are my companions, Michael from Roumania, Georgy from Bulgaria," said the Countess. "The border also runs down the middle of my bed."

End of extract from O'Malley manuscript.

CHAPTER 3

1

"We must get out of here," said Eve. "At once."

"How?" said O'Malley. "Fly the Baron's machine on one wing? We need him, Miss Tozer. The further we get on this trip, and I'll admit we haven't got far, the more I think you need an extra man on hand. If anything happened to me—"

"Don't talk like that!" Then she gestured an apology, leaned against the lower wing of Kern's plane. "I'm sorry. I'm tired—worried—"

The Countess had welcomed them into her house, every gesture a grand one. The house was big but she obviously saw it as a palace and did not realize her gaze was astigmatic with illusions. She produced a silver bell from a pocket and rang it; servants came with a shuffling run. They brought small dishes of jam made from rose leaves, served it to each of the guests with their own long silver-handled spoon, then handed them tiny blue glasses of a fierce-tasting brandy. Eve coughed over hers, but the Countess took no notice of her. Eve had begun to appreciate that the Countess was ignoring her.

The Countess herself had shown Kern to his room. The Roumanian and the Bulgarian took O'Malley to his. Eve and Sun Nan were left with a sullen servant who jerked his head, left them to carry their own bags, and led them up to the first floor to rooms that smelled as if they had been locked up for years.

Eve had been in her room, exhausted but too restless to lie down, when she had gone to the windows and seen O'Malley down on the straggly lawn inspecting the dam-

aged Bristol. Wanting advice, comfort, anything that
would sieve the mess of fears and doubts that clogged her
mind, she had impulsively gone down to join him.

"Mr. O'Malley—"

"Would you mind calling me Bede? While you're Mr.
O'Malleying me I keep feeling we should shake hands
each time we meet."

She smiled, suddenly liking him for the first time. Or
perhaps it was just that she felt safe with him, at least for
the time being. They had got off on the wrong foot somehow; she had recognized that he had been trying to make
money out of her, trying to sell her the aeroplanes for
more than they were worth. He was a liar, too, though his
lies so far had been told in her cause. She suspected he
was one of those men who would always have an eye to
the main chance, but only if it did not require too much
effort, the sort of man with enough cunning intelligence
and bravado to be a crook but not enough dedication and
too much residue of ethics to be a good one. A possible
rogue but not a bounder.

"Bede, we can't stay here. I saw the Countess looking
at you and the Baron—"

O'Malley grinned, looked up at the big house, rose-
pink in the rose-pink sunset. "I wonder if she has any
ideas of turning that bed of hers into a League of Nations? Don't worry," he added hastily. "I'm not getting
into it. But I think we'd better keep our eye on the Baron.
I think he's been in more beds than I've been in pubs."

She didn't want to discuss the Baron's weakness or
whatever one wanted to call it. Instead she looked down
through the wide gateway (there were no gates, she noticed) to the long narrow valley. Those rose fields were a
lake of blood and cream; the white road ran through it
like a causeway. The workers were coming up the road,
heading for a row of black tents and painted carts just
outside the walls of the garden. The still, warm air was
heavy with the smell of roses; the smell was heavier, sick-
lier, than any she could remember. But then her boy-

friends had brought her only bouquets, never fields of roses.

The workers had stopped in the middle of the road, were staring in through the gateway at her and O'Malley. They were clustered tightly together, silent and motionless; there was a menace about them that was difficult to define. She shivered, looked away from them and back at O'Malley. She heard herself say, "Do you think she is a—" she couldn't remember using the word before—"a nymphomaniac?"

"The Countess? Cool her down and I suppose you could call her that."

She did smile again, surprised at what she was finding in him. "Then we shall just have to see that she remains cooled down. With her Roumanian and her Bulgarian. My God, two men on tap all the time! Be careful, Bede."

"You be careful, too." He sobered, looked up at the house. "There's something, I don't know, *mad* about this place."

"I've felt it, too, Not just *her*, but everything. The house itself—it's crumbling to bits, did you notice? My bed was made up, but I don't think it has been slept in for years. The sheets are as clammy as—as a shroud." The sun went down behind the mountains, dusk bloomed under the walnut trees beside the house. Out on the road the dark figures, still together like a black cloud, drifted towards the tents and carts, silent faces turned back towards the intruders. She shivered again, even though the air still had a furnace-breath to it. "Are you superstitious?"

"No," he said emphatically. Too emphatically? she wondered; as if to comfort her. "I think we're in superstitious country, but I don't believe any of it. The Countess is no vampire, if that's what you're thinking. Not with those teeth. They're so perfect they have to be false."

"Countess Dracula? I wasn't even thinking of that." She knew she was being foolish. The long flight, the terror of the storm, the heat of the valley, had weakened her intelligence; her father, she thought, would have chided her more strongly than Bede O'Malley had. She straightened up, looked at the splintered strut, the trailing wires and the shreds of canvas on the wing of the plane. "Do you really think you can fix this?"

"I talked to Michael, the Roumanian boy-friend. In sign language," he explained as she looked puzzled. "He doesn't like us, is suspicious of us and he'll be glad to see us gone. So he's willing to help. He can get me some canvas. I don't know where, probably tarpaulins or something like that."

"What about the ailerons? Will you be able to get those to work?"

He grinned again. Her mood had lifted a little: they were talking about practical things, problems that had nothing to do with superstition. "We'll know that when I try to get the machine into the air."

"I'll take it up to test it. You don't have to take all the risks, Mr. O'Malley."

"We're back at Mr. O'Malley again. Look, Miss Tozer—"

"Eve."

He looked at her carefully for a moment, then nodded. "Righto. Eve. You hired me to get you to China. I'm going to do it, risks or no risks. Shall we have no more argument about it?

She capitulated at once, something she knew she would not have done in other circumstanecs. But she had looked up at the house again, seen the Countess standing in a window watching them with a steady stare, and once again she wanted to be gone from here as soon as possible. The damaged Bristol, when it was repaired, would have to be test-flown before they could continue their flight and she knew that Bede was a better pilot than she would ever be. She was not lacking in courage, but she was not foolhardy.

"All right. No more arguments about the machines."

"Righto." But he, too, had seen the Countess at her window. He took Eve's arm protectively, led her towards the house. "You take care of yourself. I'll take care of the aeroplanes."

"You're a kind man, Bede." She knew she sounded surprised, but couldn't hide it.

"Only in self-defence," he said deprecatingly. "It's another name for chivalry."

"You're not the cynic you try to be."

"I could be by the time we get to China."

The Countess had told them dinner would be at nine o'clock. Eve had a bath in a bathroom that seemed in itself to be a museum. Its walls were all mirrors, peeling, scabbed and cracked, so that Eve, looking into them, saw herself leprous and deformed. She wondered what the Countess's bathroom was like, if the mirrors there were new and flattering. A giant ceramic stove stood in one corner; but the flue above it had the middle neatly sawn out of it. Only when Eve went to run water into the bath did she discover there were no taps, nor even pipes in the bathroom. It was a museum of pieces that did not work, probably never had. But while she was pondering what to do, two women servants, silent and sullen, arrived with cauldrons of hot and cold water. They kept coming back till the huge bath was filled almost to the brim. Then they brought her towels, threadbare as a beggar's shirt.

Eve bathed, put on a clean blouse with her only skirt and went down to dinner. The dining room suggested delusions of grandeur; or perhaps the grandeur had once been warranted. Eve had no way of knowing who had dined here in this high-ceilinged room with its tall cracked mirrors, walls lined with peeling green silk and its gold velvet drapes faded to a jaundiced yellow; Hapsburgs, Coburgs and Hesses might have sat in these carved, high-backed chairs, the *Almanach de Gotha* come to dinner with exotics from further east. The table was set for a formal dinner, but the napery was frayed and thin, the wine glasses chipped, the monogrammed plate cracked. The food was so bad that even Oliver Twist would have had second thoughts about a second helping.

Eve thought the Countess was vulgar, but grandly so;

which made her different from other vulgarians Eve had known. O'Malley and Kern sat on either side of their hostess; Eve was at the opposite end of the table flanked by Michael and Georgy. Sun Nan sat between O'Malley and Georgy, odd man out in every way. When they had first entered the house, Eve had explained that Sun Nan was a business associate of her father; the Countess had appeared not to be listening, but when they had come in for dinner a place had been set for the Chinese. But the Countess continued to ignore him, as if he were as remote from her as his homeland itself.

She was dressed in pink chiffon that seemed to Eve not so much a dress as a series of veils (to be discarded one by one for the lovers?). Her face was made up in the style of motion picture vamps Eve had seen, the eyelashes thick with mascara, the full lips too heavily painted. She wore a tiara and a diamond-encrusted gold cross that hung down on a gold chain between the firm heavy breasts under the chiffon. She had once been startlingly beautiful, was still good-looking but coarsened; it was impossible to guess her age, but she was still vital and sensual. Eve looked at her hands, often the giveaway of a woman past middle age, but they were as smooth as a young girl's. But no young girl would have had the time and experience to have accumulated the diamond rings that made an icy blaze of her fingers.

"You like my roses?" The four corners of the room were thick with the blooms in huge urns; the all-pervading scent had begun to sicken Eve. "I live for them. When I was a young bride—" She smiled coquettishly at O'Malley and Kern; then her belly laugh reduced the coquetry to a joke against herself. "Some years ago, let us say, I travelled down with my husband to the Valley of Roses near Karlova. It is where they distil the attar of roses, the most beautiful of perfumes. I told my husband I wanted my own Valley of Roses. We came back here and he planted those fields for me. My roses bloom later than those of Karlova, but even so they are almost at an end. So sad—I hate the end of summer, of my roses. I retire to my bed for the winter." She smiled, said something in the tongue that Eve did not understand, and Michael and Georgy smiled and nodded. Then, still smiling, she said in English, "My husband died from the prick of a rose thorn."

"Handing you a bouquet, I hope," said Kern, and Eve saw O'Malley roll his eyes.

At once the Countess reached for Kern's hand, stroked it. "I hate Germans, my dear Baron, but you are different."

"My dear Countess," said Kern, his voice still quiet but stiff with pride, "I am still a German, different or not."

But before he could draw his hand away, there came the sound of music from outside, beyond the garden walls, the lively vibrancy of violins and the jingling of tambourines. The Countess straightened up, dropped Kern's hand, dismissing him, and turned to O'Malley.

"Ah, my gipsies! Do you dance, Mr. O'Malley?"

"Only the minuet," said O'Malley drily. "And not at dinner."

"Ah, the English are so staid! We should all dance whenever we have the opportunity. Dance and make love!"

"Oh, we do that," said O'Malley. "But not at dinner."

The mascaraed eyes looked baleful for a moment: she could hate the English too, Eve thought. Then she dismissed O'Malley. "My gipsies will be gone soon—they come only for the summer, for the gathering of my roses. My army, I call them. Then we are left alone, aren't we, my sweethearts?"

She looked down the table at Michael and Georgy. Eve was aware that the mood of both of them had changed when the Countess had clutched Kern's hand. They were taut, jealous twins; she wondered if they were ever jealous of each other. But she knew they hated Kern: he was being favoured by their mistress, he was also a German.

Georgy said something in a harsh voice and the Countess's smile disappeared as if she had been slapped in the face. The black-rimmed eyes flashed and she answered in

a voice that was as harsh as the Bulgarian's. At once he
stood up, slamming his chair back, bowed to Eve and
marched out of the room. The Countess watched him go,
then tilted her head to listen to the music and smiled
again at O'Malley.

"Will you dance with me later, Mr. O'Malley? I shall
teach you the *horo*. It is livelier than the minuet, stirs
one's blood."

"Delighted," said O'Malley, undelighted. "But only if
Michael and Georgy don't object."

The Countess's eyes suddenly seemed as hard as the diamonds on her fingers. "If they objected they know what
would happen to them."

Abruptly she turned her head away from O'Malley,
looked at Sun Nan, recalled him from China or wherever
he had been in her mind. He had sat stolidly ignoring the
tension between the Occidentals, chewing on his *kebab*,
now and again unembarrassedly pushing his dental plate
back into position as it slipped on a tough piece of lamb.

"Miss Tozer said you are in business, Mr. Sun. The
opium business?"

Even Sun Nan looked surprised at the question. Eve,
watching him closely, saw him tightening his defences. He
was not going to dance the *horo*, actually or metaphorically, with his hostess.

"My master grows it."

"Do you smoke it?"

"No. It is not good for one who needs his wits about
him."

"It's not always best to have one's wits about oneself.
Dreams are more comforting. Don't you think so, Miss
Tozer?"

Eve had always had dreams; but her only opium had
been her own imagination. "Only if they're attainable."

"Americans!" said the Countess, dismissing Eve and a
nation. "Always so practical-minded."

"One has to be," said Eve, daring to argue, "if one believes in the future."

"Who believes in it?" The Countess looked back down

the table, blinking her eyes as if to adjust their focus, as if she had dropped Eve right from her vision. Then Eve realized she was not seeing her at all, was staring into space and time. "The past is all one can believe in. It was the only reality, wasn't it, Baron?"

Kern, the hated but different German of a few moments ago, did not shy at suddenly being on the Countess's side. "It is all we have to believe in."

"I am a Guelph. I can trace my lineage back ten centuries. But I have no children. So what else is there but the past?"

"A Guelph?" Eve noticed Kern sit up. She had watched him watching the Countess, sensed that, whatever the Countess's feelings about Germans, he could not resist her sexuality. His balls have no intelligence, she thought, and saw her Boston grandmother have a fit of the vapours at such a thought crossing a young lady's mind. "Then you are a German, too."

"Too many generations ago, my dear Baron. I am spread among half a dozen nationalities." She tilted her head again. "Ah, the music! Let us go and dance!"

It didn't matter to her that dinner was only half-finished. It didn't matter to Eve, either: the food was inedible. The Countess rose up, veils floating like pink mist about her, and went out of the room between Kern and O'Malley, a hand on the arm of each. O'Malley looked back as he went out the door, winked at Eve. He, she thought, has his intelligence in the right place.

Eve pushed back her chair. Michael, eyes still on the door through which his mistress had disappeared, suddenly thought of his manners, but Eve was moving away from the table by the time he got behind her chair. Sun Nan, who had never pulled back a woman's chair in his life, rose and followed Eve, sucking his teeth back into a comfortable position.

"I haven't thanked you for getting us safely through the storm."

"Luck, Mr. Sun, that was all it was."

"Good fortune favours only those who deserve it." He suddenly smiled. "We must be deserving."

He could be likeable; but she couldn't forget the reason they were together. Nor could she forget that he had been smiling only a minute or two before he had knifed George Weyman. "Just pray that good fortune stays with us. Goodnight, Mr. Sun."

She went up to her room, locked the door. She avoided the hole in the once-thick carpet where she had already tripped, opened the doors of the tall wardrobe. She had tried to open it earlier but had failed; now she struggled with the doors and suddenly they jerked open. The wardrobe was full of gowns, dank-smelling, cobwebs encrusting them like grey lace. On a shelf above the gowns were a dozen hats, some wide-brimmed with huge feathers resting on them like nesting birds, others high-crowned with crêpe-de-Chine roses that had faded to the colour of bone. The bottom of the wardrobe was thick with rose petals rotted to an evil-smelling brown humus.

She slammed the doors shut, went quickly to the open windows and gulped in deep breaths of fresh air, trying to clear her nose, her lungs, her mind of the smell of decay. She leaned against the sill, overcome again with the weight of omens. Then she became aware of the music, so lively as to be mocking in her present state. There were no sour notes in the scraping of the violins: sweet and gay, punctuated by the thump and jingle of tambourines and the thin piping of a flute, the music came up to the house in a light, swift-running surf of sound. Voices shouted in rhythm and beyond the garden wall she saw the flash of shadows dancing against the red glow of a fire.

She shut the windows quickly, but just as quickly opened them again. She undressed, got in between the sheets that she had aired by turning back the bed before she went down to dinner. The mattress was cold, smelled of mould; but she was too exhausted now to care. She fell asleep, heard shouts for help in her dreams but didn't recognize the voices, felt helpless and turned away. Then someone tapped on the bedroom door (in her dreams or in reality?). She wakened, eyes and mind glazed with sleep. She waited, floating up into full consciousness, but the knock wasn't repeated. Outside the walls the music had stopped. There was silence but for the thinner music of crickets, to which no one ever danced.

She got up, went to the windows. The clouds had gone and the moon rose over the mountains like a yellow cheese, decaying as it climbed higher. The road now was a silver lance laid on the breast of the dark fields: all the roses were colourless in the night. The aeroplanes down on the lawn were like giant prehistoric birds: still half-drugged by sleep, she waited for them to fly away, leaving her stranded here. Then she saw the movement on the lawn. The Countess and Kern came out from the shadow of the damaged Bristol. They stood close together, then the Countess put her arms round Kern's neck and kissed him passionately. Then she left him, floating up the steps in a mist of veils, running as lightly as a young girl into the black shadows of the house. Kern looked up, saw the pale nude figure of Eve at her window, clicked his heels and bowed, then followed the Countess into the house. Eve waited, but there was no sign of O'Malley. She felt relieved, as if his non-appearance was some expression of loyalty to herself.

She went back to bed, but couldn't go back to sleep. She heard occasional movement in the house, but couldn't tell where: the sounds floated rootlessly, as if the house were no more than an empty shell. Head restless on the pillow, eyes unfocused, it seemed to her that the shadows in the room were moving, rootless as the sounds. All at once afraid (of what, she didn't know; but that was the fearful thing), she sat up in bed, wanting protection. Then she thought of her gun in its case, still down in the cockpit of her plane. She had thought of bringing it into the house with her when they had arrived, but already disturbed by the Countess's demeanour, not wanting to offend her by carrying a weapon into her house, she had left the gun in the plane, then had forgotten about it. She felt she must now go down and get it.

She put on her blouse and skirt, unlocked her door cautiously and, barefoot, went silently down the dark stairs and out through the front doors on to the terrace. She crossed the lawn, feeling the dew on her bare feet, clambered up into the cockpit of the Bristol, felt around, then dropped back to the ground. And almost fainted as the man came up from under the bottom wing and stood beside her.

"If you're looking for your gun," said O'Malley, "someone has pinched it."

"What are you doing here?" Her voice was a choked whisper; she leaned against the fuselage, trembling. "Have you been here all the time?"

"Only since the Countess and our German friend went to bed. We'll have to have a word with him in the morning. If he's going to act like a stud bull all along the way, we can do without him."

"Why are you sleeping out here?" She saw the heap of his sleeping-bag beneath the wing.

"I checked on the guns while everyone was busy dancing out there. The Vickers and Lewis guns are still there, but yours was gone. I decided I didn't want anyone tampering with the machines."

"Do you think they might?"

"I don't know. But I wouldn't try to guess at anything that might happen around here. Those gipsies would cut our throats if the Countess gave the word."

Then they heard the scream, long drawn out, dying away to nothing. There was utter silence then: even the crickets had stilled. Eve felt O'Malley's hand on her arm, was glad of it even though his grip hurt her. They waited for lights in the house, but none came on. The house remained dark, floating in its shadows, obscure against the faint glow of the moon now hidden by clouds.

"It could have been a night-bird," said O'Malley, but Eve noticed his grip on her arm hadn't relaxed.

"I'm afraid, Bede. I've never been afraid before—not like this."

"Go back to bed. Lock your door. I'll be down here if you want me."

"I wish I had my gun. I killed a man with it once." She sensed rather than saw his surprise, and explained: "He was going to rape me."

"I don't think the Countess would allow rape in her house. She wouldn't understand the necessity for it."

The light, dry remark was meant to reassure her, to take some of the tension out of her. But the real comfort was in the warm pressure of his hand on her arm. "Goodnight, Bede."

2

When the sun came up the gipsies were already in the fields, waiting to pick the roses while the dew was still on them. They moved up and down the rows, sacks at their waists, stripping off the blooms almost brutally, oblivious of the beauty amidst which they walked. They were singing, but their song had none of the gaiety of last night's *horo* music; it was slower, the women's voices harsh with melancholy, one of the sad Turkish songs brought to the region centuries before. Kern, standing at the window of his bedroom, listened to it and felt it reflected his own mood. Last night had been a mistake, his balls had betrayed him once again.

He dressed and went down to breakfast. It was yoghurt and fruit, much less than he was accustomed to; he looked for a servant, but no one answered the silver bell that he rang. He drank two cups of acorn-coffee. He sat on at the table, waiting for the Countess or Eve to put in an appearance; then he heard the voices outside on the lawn and remembered what had to be done to his aeroplane and that he had promised to help. He still had to learn not to expect everything to be done for him. His depression increased as he went outside: he hated work, always had.

O'Malley, Sun Nan and Michael, the Roumanian, were already at work on the damaged Bristol. He went down to them, apologizing for being late.

"We have to rebuild part of the front of the wing." O'Malley, intent only on the job, ignored the apology. "Michael not only dug up some canvas, he got me that cane couch and chairs."

"You must have been up early." Kern saw the rolled-up sleeping-bag on the lower wing of O'Malley's own plane. "Or didn't you go to bed?"

"Both," said O'Malley cryptically. "Now do you mind stripping down those chairs and couch?"

O'Malley, expecting no argument or ignoring the possibility of it, turned his back and gave instructions to Sun Nan and Michael. Kern had never taken orders from any but his superiors; but in his melancholy mood this morning he recognized the war was over and who had lost it. He was a paid working man now, if not of the working class.

He began to strip the cane couch, handling the hammer and pincers awkwardly. He barked his knuckles, drew blood on a finger, and was glad when the Countess came out of the house. She was dressed as she had been yesterday, but she wore a hip-length blue kaftan instead of the red tunic. There was no sign of the short dagger-like sword and he wondered if it was hidden beneath the kaftan. O'Malley, sweating, marked with grease, looked down at her as he stood up on the cowling of the Bristol.

"We could do with another helper, Countess. I wonder if Georgy would mind?"

"Georgy is no longer with us."

Kern saw Michael straighten up as if he had been hit in the back. He and Sun Nan had been laying out the canvas, stretching it and measuring it. He dropped the canvas and looked at the Countess with puzzled, frightened eyes. Dammit, thought Kern, he understands English!

"I want Michael," said the Countess. "I have a chore for him."

She went back up into the house. Michael hesitated, then he followed her, stumbling once as he missed his footing on the steps, as if he hadn't been looking where he was going. Only when they had both disappeared did it strike Kern that the Countess had not even looked at him, that last night's love-making might never have happened. His mood turned from melancholic to sardonic; he felt the first relief of laughter at oneself. Junker to worker, Don Juan to stud stallion, all in one night.

"What happened with her last night?" said O'Malley.

"Is it any of your business, Herr O'Malley?"

"I think it is. I have to get us out of here and I want to know what complications might stop us."

"There will be no complications."

"Did you hear that scream during the night?"

"There was a scream? I wasn't sure I hadn't dreamed it. I woke up, but our hostess wasn't in bed with me. Then I went back to sleep."

"I heard it," said Sun Nan. "It was the Bulgarian."

"How do you know?"

"His room was right above mine. I explored the house this morning. The Bulgarian is in his room, lying on his bed, with the Countess's sword through his chest. Miss Tozer's gun, in its case, was lying beside him. I took it down to my room."

"Jesus Christ!" O'Malley said. "How bloody inscrutable can you Orientals be? Why didn't you tell us before?"

"It is no concern of ours. Getting to Hunan is our only concern."

O'Malley sighed deeply, then looked at Kern. "If Georgy had that gun, it was to blow your balls off, Baron. The Countess must have got to him first. In future, when you get the urge, take a cold shower instead. At least till we get to China."

"Don't lecture me, Herr O'Malley," said Kern coldly; then gestured at the cane he had stripped off. "Will that be enough?"

"It'll do. Now we'll need some hot water, so we can bend it into the shapes we'll need. We still haven't any varnish for treating the canvas."

"There are tins of it in the stables at the back of the house," said Sun Nan. "I explored there, too."

O'Malley sighed again. "I could almost like you, Sun, if you weren't such a murderous bastard."

"I am only that through circumstances," said Sun Nan. "It is just a question of survival."

He and O'Malley went away to get the varnish and hot water. Kern was left alone with the planes. He stroked a wing, as he had stroked the flesh of the Countess last night: the war years had been the one real passion of his life. Not the killing, that had been incidental, but the flirting with death, his skill against that of the enemy pilot, his luck against the bullet of darkness.

Eve came hurrying down the steps. "Where are the others?"

"Round the back of the house. What's the matter?"

She was white and strained, her hands bunched in nervous first. "I saw them carrying Georgy downstairs—"

"We know," he said gently. "The Countess, or someone, killed him last night."

"She said something to me just then—the Countess—" She made an effort to calm herself. There was the bone of determination in her, he noted: there was also the jelly of fear, but that was understandable. He had seen heroes vous fists. "I saw them carrying Georgy downstairs—" did she mean by that?"

Kern had no answer. He had loved women, had found them as necessary as food and drink, but he had never understood them nor tried to. Illusions were also necessary, for the proper enjoyment of love-making.

O'Malley and Sun Nan came back, followed by two servants carrying a large vat of hot water. Eve volunteered to stay and help and O'Malley gave everyone a task. They worked all through the morning, with no further sight of their hostess. They did catch a glimpse of an ox-drawn cart moving away through a side gate; the back of it was heaped high with roses, like a hearse, and two cloaked and hooded figures sat on the seat of the cart. It disappeared into the shadows of the forest that ran back to the mountains behind the house. It was O'Malley who remarked that the cart seemed to have turned off on to the Bulgarian side of the border.

By lunchtime O'Malley had repaired the broken framework of the wing and shaped a new strut out of a piece of ash Sun Nan had brought him.

"Where did you get it, Sun?"

"It is better not to ask."

O'Malley and Sun Nan had smiled at each other, fellow rogues. Kern, seeing them, had felt unaccountably jealous of the Englishman. *He is a friend of both Miss Tozer and the Chinaman now.* And felt put out, though he had never cared for friendship in the past.

A bell rang inside the house. They all looked at each other, then decided it was a summons to lunch. "I'll stay out here with the machines," said O'Malley. "Just in case."

"I'll send something out," said Eve. "What would you like, Bede?"

"Anything. It's worse than school food, but I'm hungry."

No places were set for Michael or Georgy at the luncheon table. Was the Roumanian also to be eliminated? Kern wondered. The Countess ignored Eve and Sun Nan, chatted only to Kern all through the meal, once again as amorous as she had been last night. Her hand kept touching his, her eyes never left him: she was inviting him to bed all through the cold fish, the over-cooked vegetables, the pulpy strawberries. Then at the end of the meal she rose from her chair and said, "You will leave my house, Miss Tozer."

Eve, cup of coffee half-way to her lips, turned her head in puzzled surprise. "When?"

"Now!" The Countess was quietly mad today. Has she been smoking opium? Kern wondered. Her voice had a dreamy quality, the screech of anger in it only to be imagined. But she hated Eve for some reason, there was no mistaking the venom of her feeling. "At once!"

"That is impossible, my dear Countess."

Kern stood up. No clicking of the heels, no bow to her: the time for manners was past. Last night this woman had talked of *us*, joined them in pedigree. *Are you born?* she had asked, the question of the aristocrats; and he had said yes, he was born, that like hers his family was in the *Almanach de Gotha*. Last night he had not thought she was mad, only eccentric: he had made love to girls with much less intelligence. But they were no longer *us*, he knew where his duty lay. All true aristocrats did.

"Miss Tozer cannot leave here till my aeroplane is ready. We have to leave together."

The Countess gave him a hurt look, said softly in German, the language they had used last night, "You don't have to go, my dearest. Who else will take Georgy's place?"

God in Heaven, why had he got into her bed? He answered her in German, "There is Michael."

"He is not born. A peasant."

"All right then, I shall stay," he lied, and smiled: the charm lay on his lips like cyanide. "But let Miss Tozer stay, too. At least till tomorrow morning."

"No. She is the cause of my unhappiness. If she hadn't brought you, my dearest, Georgy would still be alive." "It was lunatic logic, unanswerable. "She must go now! You will see to it."

It was an order, as if she were talking to the dead Georgy. She turned and swept out of the room, not quickly but almost as if floating, the blue kaftan swirling out in a slow flare as her body turned. Kern shrugged, baffled.

"What did she say?" Eve put down her cup with a rattle. "Why does she hate me so?"

No explanations were valid in a madhouse. "You had better pack your bag, take it out to the machines."

"But why?" Eve persisted. "Did she talk to you about me last night?"

"No." Only *us*: as if the war and everything that had been lost with it had never happened. "Please go and pack your bag. We may all have to camp by the aeroplanes tonight."

He went outside, told O'Malley what had happened. "The Countess came out a moment ago," said O'Malley. "Almost walked over me as if I didn't exist. She's gone down to the gipsy camp. They've finished the rose harvest, I gather. I can't see any more blooms."

"How soon do you think you can finish the wing?"

"If you and Sun can fit the canvas and paint it, I can work on the new ailerons. If we worked right through and provided the varnish dries . . ." He looked up at the sky, cloudless and hot. "Perhaps we can get away at first light. Or earlier, if we have to."

While they were talking, the Countess came back through the big gateway. She was hatless and her blonde hair, let loose, hung down her back like a young girl's. She must have looked like this, Kern thought, when her world was still real and golden.

"Come with me, Baron."

"Later, Countess." He tried to sound gentle, charming: anything to prevent another outburst from her. "I must help my friends if they are to leave."

"You will be staying?"

Behind her back he saw O'Malley nod. "Yes," he said.

She smiled at him, went on up the steps, drifting through the brilliant yellow light into the purple shadows of the great open doorway. Kern looked at O'Malley.

"Why did you nod when she asked if I were staying?"

"You're our passport. You have to keep her happy in bed while we get the machines ready."

"And if I refuse?"

"You can't, Baron, not really. You're a man of honour above your navel. That's the part I'm relying on. You——"

He stopped. Kern looked back over his shoulder. The gipsies had come to the wide gateway, were slowly filtering in and moving round the walls of the garden. Some of them squatted down, others leaned against the wall and the climbing roses; there were no children, but some women had come in with the men. They stood arrayed against the walls like giant black beetles, the sun glinting on beadwork on the women's dresses, on the men's pruning knives, as on an insect's elytra. They made no sound, not even whispering among themselves.

"I could mount the Lewis guns again," said O'Malley without preliminary, "but that might have them on us in a rush."

Then Eve and Sun Nan came out of the house, Eve carrying the hessian-wrapped box, Sun carrying his own and Eve's bags and Eve's gun-case. They pulled up sharply at the top of the steps when they saw the gipsies. Then they came down and across to the aeroplanes.

"Put your gun into the cockpit without any fuss," O'Malley said quietly. "Then we'll get to work as if they're not watching us."

Eve asked no questions. She was once again the cool, self-possessed girl Kern had met two days ago; at least on the surface. She did what O'Malley told her, then listened patiently, ignoring the silent watchers, while he explained to her, Kern and Sun Nan what he wanted them to do.

"The canvas has to be stretched tight, that's the main thing. Good old George." O'Malley looked at Sun Nan as he said Weyman's name; but the Chinese's expression didn't alter. "He thought of everything—there are some clamps in the tool kit. The tricky bit is going to be getting the ailerons to work. I'll take over your machine, Baron, when we leave. Just in case my work isn't as good as I hope it'll be."

"You will not," said Kern. "This is my machine, Herr O'Malley. I shall fly it."

The two men stared at each other, then O'Malley said, "Have it your way. I'll do my best to make it safe."

They worked all through the hot, stifling afternoon. Several times they rested, sitting beneath the wings of the planes, gazing across at the watching gipsies. The latter had not remained motionless, some of them moving out through the gates but always coming back; and they were no longer silent, but occasionally murmured among themselves. But there was still a dark menace to their patient watching. Out in the camp someone played a flute, but the sound of it was not lively, was only a file against the nerves of the four people working on the crippled plane.

By sundown the canvas had been fixed on the main section of the wing and the varnish applied. O'Malley was still having difficulty in fitting the new ailerons; each time he got into the cockpit and worked the controls, the flaps didn't move in unison when they were supposed to. Independently, they worked only intermittently.

O'Malley, dark as the gipsies with grease and sweat, appeared at last to be losing his optimism. "I'll work on them all night, but you'll still be taking a risk, Baron, when you take her off in the morning."

"It won't be the first time I've taken a risk. You know that."

"We each had good, trained mechanics in those days. It was a different sort of risk."

"All risk is a matter of one's luck." The silver bell rang in the house. He smiled drily. "She calls. I'll see you get some food."

He washed, changed his clothes, looked at himself in the mirror: not what he would have worn to a tea dance, but he was presentable. Lovers these days in Europe wore what they could afford; and after all, he was a travelling lover. He would be travelling tonight or early in the morning, though the Countess would not know that. He packed his bag, put it under his bed. Then he went down to dine with the Countess, just the two of them, *us*, the born, sitting at the long table with its frayed cloth, chipped glass and air of touched, hopeless nostalgia.

The Countess didn't demur when he asked if food could be sent out to Herr O'Malley and Herr Sun; he didn't mention Eve, but knew the two men would share with her. Aware that no extra place was set, he wondered where Michael was. As if reading his thoughts the Countess said, "The peasant has gone away for a while."

"Like Georgy?" He tried to put it delicately, but he had to know.

She smiled, the secret smile of children and the mad. "No, Michael may come back. But only if you should go."

The food in his mouth turned sour. But she was still smiling, more openly now: he was her favourite, the properly born lover. He swallowed, returned her smile, tried desperately to remember the sort of lovers' banter they had engaged in last night. Anything to keep her in good humour.

Before they went up to bed he excused himself to say goodnight to "my friends." He went out quickly, not wanting her to accompany him. The gipsies had retreated from the garden, but some of them still squatted and lounged in the gateway, silhouetted against the fires of their camp behind them. O'Malley and Sun Nan were working by the light of two oil lamps they had scrounged from somewhere, and Eve was up in the cockpit of O'Malley's plane.

"What is Fräulein Tozer doing?"

"Loading my forward gun, just in case. I'll get her to do the same on yours. Later on, if those chaps on the gate doze off. I'll mount the Lewis on my rear cockpit."

"Who'll fire it for you?"

O'Malley looked at Sun Nan. "I can take you in my machine now the weight is down—the tanks are nearly empty. You'll be a bit uncomfortable, but I shan't do any fancy flying, so you shouldn't fall out. Can you fire a machine-gun?"

"Of course."

"Silly of me to ask. Is there anything you can't do?"

"I can't cook," said Sun Nan.

O'Malley grinned, then looked at Kern. "We should be ready to go by midnight. There'll be enough light, unless the moon clouds over." The night was bright, the blue shadows under the trees almost as sharp-edged as they had been during the yellow day. "We'll go straight down the road for take-off."

"How are the ailerons?"

"I think I've at last got them working. There'll be only one way of knowing, I'm afraid."

Kern nodded, unperturbed by the prospect: rather, excited by it. "I may not be able to be here by midnight, I shall have to wait till the Countess is asleep."

He went across to say goodnight to Eve. A belt of ammunition in her hand, martial and unromantic against the moonlight, she looked down at him. "I hope the Countess is not making things too difficult for you, Baron."

He smiled up at her: how much easier it would be to be charming to her than to the woman who waited upstairs in the house for him. Out of the corner of his eye he saw the light go on in the Countess's bedroom. Eve saw it, too.

"You don't have to do it, Baron."

"Entertaining a lady is not a chore, Fräulein." He waited for her to ask him to call her Eve; but was disappointed. "In the present circumstances I don't know of any other way of dealing with our hostess."

"There is another way!" She slammed the ammunition belt into the gun. "But I don't suppose even in this country, whichever one we're in, it would be considered legal."

He went up to join the Countess, in more ways than one, walking stiffly, in more ways than one, the duty lover. He felt suddenly degraded, wished for a gun instead of the weapon that the others had delegated for him.

The Countess was waiting for him, naked, her hair loose as it had been during the day. Lush is the word for her, he thought; and, betrayed again by his conscienceless crotch, decided he had had worse duties to perform. She welcomed him to the bed as if he had been long lost. The room, facing west, was like a hothouse, not yet cooled off from the afternoon sun. Roses were in vases and bowls all round the room; it was as if they were in bed in a roofed-in garden. The perfume she wore was as thick as that of the flowers; he felt overpowered by the smell of flesh, sex and flowers. He was in danger of being drugged: he had to keep his wits about him, to stay awake when all this was over.

Unlike some women he had been with, she was more lucid in bed than out of it. While they rested she talked of life before the war. "I was welcome at both courts, my darling, in Bucharest and Sofia. I was a favourite of Ferdy, dear sweet man." Kern remembered that his father used to refer to Tsar Ferdinand as Foxy Ferdy. "We used to go to Euxinograd—I was always the one who wore the most daring bathing costume. In Bucharest I was a friend of Marie's before she became Queen." She was silent for a while, staring up at the ceiling; he looked up at it, saw for the first time that it was decorated with painted roses. "Ah, dearest, do you think we were wise in those days? Thinking it could last forever?"

"No," he said, knowing he and his kind in Germany had been guilty of the same folly. "Go to sleep."

"No." She turned towards him, the present, all that she lived in when she wasn't mad. "Not yet."

It was after midnight before she slept, but she slept soundly, exhausted. He slid quietly out of bed, took his clothes and went down to his own room. He dressed quickly, took his bag from under the bed and went downstairs. The others were waiting for him, already in their planes, Sun Nan cramped high in the rear cockpit of O'Malley's machine behind the remounted Lewis gun.

"We thought you'd fallen asleep," O'Malley said irritably.

"It wasn't intentional on my part that I'm late," Kern said just as irritably.

O'Malley got out of his plane. "Some of the gipsies are still awake—they're just outside the gates. The engines will have to fire first time and we can't fool about. You go first, then Miss Tozer, and I'll bring up the rear."

"Where do we head for?"

O'Malley gave him a bearing. "I've taken a star-shot. That will take us to Sofia, I hope. We're a long way past Belgrade, so there's no point in turning back. I've checked the tanks—with luck we'll just make Sofia. But you'll have to nurse it all the way, so don't waste petrol climbing."

"Is there an aerodrome at Sofia?"

"There's a military aerodrome on the outskirts."

"We'll arrive there in the dark. How do we find it?"

"That's what worries me. We could sit here till first light, just hope the Countess doesn't wake. We'll do that," he said, making a sudden decision. "If the light goes on in her room, we'll start up and take-off. Good luck, Baron. I hope these bloody ailerons hold up. Treat them gently. Like a woman—if that's not too indelicate a way of putting it."

It was three-thirty in the morning, still dark, when the light went on in the Countess's bedroom. At once Kern, awake but only by an effort of will, sat up straight in his seat. He saw O'Malley jump down from his own plane and race across to grab the propeller of his machine.

"Contact!"

O'Malley swung on the airscrew, swung again. The engine coughed, then took. Kern opened the throttle and the silence of the night went in an exploding roar. He glanced up, saw the Countess at her window, her arms waving; he knew she was screaming, but he couldn't hear her. He swung the Bristol round, the air-stream whipping back at him, and saw O'Malley running away from Eve's plane as she gunned her engine. Sun Nan was standing in front of O'Malley's plane, both hands on the propeller, waiting for the Englishman to jump up into the cockpit and take the controls. But there was no time for Kern to see any more.

The gipsies were coming thorugh the gateway, knives flashing, some of them with old-fashioned long-barrelled rifles, all of them yelling silently in the thundering roar of the planes' engines. Kern aimed the Bristol at the gateway, rolled it forward as fast as he dared. The gipsies fell away from the scythe of the propeller and the Bristol was through the gates before they could recover and fling themselves at its wings. He went down the long straight road, slowing down when he had passed the gipsy en-

campment to look back at the gates. He saw Eve come
through in her plane, two men clinging to a wing. Her
plane slewed, but didn't go off the roadway; the men fell
off and she straightened up and came down the road after
him. Then the third Bristol came through, Sun Nan standing up in the rear cockpit firing the Lewis. Two men were
clinging to its lower wing: Kern wondered if their extra
weight would prevent the plane getting airborne. But he
couldn't wait any longer to see. Eve was right behind him
on the road, waiting for him to take-off.

He moved the stick back and forth, kicked the rudder
bar: everything *felt* all right, if a little stiff. Then he
looked down the road, a blue-white strip stretching away
into the blue darkness. He pushed the throttle forward,
felt the plane begin to roll. He couldn't remember the
road's being bumpy when they had taxied up it yesterday;
now the Bristol seemed to be bouncing every few yards.
He held it straight, feeling his stomach beginning to
tighten as he waited for the speed to build and the moment of knowing to come. Then through the seat of his
pants, as the plane hit an extra large bump and went up,
he knew the moment had come. He pulled back on the
stick, keeping the nose up, trying to look both sides at
once as the wings took the strain.

He was staring at the wing above his head, waiting for
the canvas that he and Sun Nan had so laboriously
stretched and stitched to start coming away from its
frame; but no, it held, looked solid and dependable, rode
the 60-miles-an-hour currents of air and kept lifting him.
Then it was time to bank, to pick up the bearing for Sofia, somewhere south-east in the darkness.

He kicked gently on the rudder bar, watching the upper
wing again as the turn put pressure on it. His whole body
seemed to have contracted; only his hands and feet, his
tools of trade, were relaxed. The scream of the engine
sounded louder than he had ever heard it before; the slipstream seemed to have become a tornado wind. Everything was going to fall apart: he looked up, waiting for
the upper wing to fly off into the laughing skull of the

moon. The ailerons suddenly stiffened; he felt the pressure. They were going to go just so far and no further: he was going to slip into a stall. He struggled, pushing the controls; then abruptly the ailerons responded again. He completed the turn, felt sweat on his face that was suddenly like ice in the slipstream.

He looked back and saw the second Bristol, then the third, come up off the road, ghostly birds in the moonlight. He set course for Sofia and the daylight beyond the edge of the turning world.

3

Somewhere close at hand there was the sound of a banjo being played not too expertly: someone was going heavyfooted down a long, long trail a-winding. "Who's that playing the banjo?" said Bradley Tozer.

"The General," said Colonel Buloff. "He heard an American playing it when we were down in Shanghai last time and bought it from him. And a book of instructions how to play it."

"I didn't know the General ever went to Shanghai. Or anywhere else, for that matter."

"He goes incognito. To choose his latest girls. He changes them every six months. That was how he met me. My wife was running the Blue Delphinium Tea Rooms in Szechuen Road. You may have heard of it?"

"Afraid I haven't But then I've never been a tea drinker."

"Not even in China? Of course, my wife didn't serve only tea. One has to make a living."

Tozer had never met Colonel Buloff in Shanghai, but he had heard vaguely of him and his wife. He had come out of Russia, a cavalry commander in one of the White Armies, had spent a year in Harbin with all the other exiles, then had arrived in Shanghai where he had discreetly advertised his services as a military adviser to any war-

lord willing to hire him. Shanghai then was over-stocked
with out-of-work military advisers: British, American,
Russian, Australian, war surplus looking for another war.
No one, it seemed, had wanted the services of Colonel
Buloff, and his wife had kept them by running her tea
rooms and brothel.

The banjo strumming went on: General Meng was now
trying to keep the home fires burning. Tozer said, "What
has happened to my servants? I had three with me when I
was captured."

Buloff shrugged, stoked his red walrus moustache. He
was thick and squat, with a face to match, and Tozer
wondered what sort of figure he would cut on his horse
with his short thick legs. "Unfortunately, I think they are
dead. I shouldn't worry. You can get others when you are
released."

"That's not the point——" But Tozer gave up the argument before starting it. He felt sick at the thought of the
murdered servants; two of them had been with him for
years. For the first time he felt the blade across his own
throat. He got up from the bed, went to the window and
looked out. Kite-hawks hung in the heat-hazy sky, sullen
and watchful. The yellow-brick palace fell down in terraces towards the town that stood half a mile away from
the hill on which the palace stood. Partridges strutted on
the terraces, moving off in startled flight as soldiers or
palace staff appeared, but returning as soon as the ground
was clear again. On the terrace immediately below Tozer's
window a peach tree threw a pool of shadow, its fruit
hanging like yellow grenades from the drooping branches.
"Will he really kill me, Colonel, if my daughter doesn't
arrive in time with the statue?"

It had been the Colonel, accompanied by half a dozen
soldiers, who had come to the inn in the town and abduct-
ed him. He had shouted at the innkeeper as he had been
hustled out in the middle of the night, but he knew now
that the man would have turned a deaf ear to his pleas to
get in touch with the American Consul in Changsha. The

American Consul was a hundred miles away and General Meng was just up the hill here.

"I don't know, Mr. Tozer. But I fear he may. He's a very superstitious man, you know. Since that pair of statues was separated, he believes nothing has gone right for him."

Tozer looked at the mirror on the wall, saw his pessimism as clearly as the stubble on his cheeks. "I'd like a shave."

"I'll send one of the girls. Of course, I'll have to send one of the guards, too. Can't have you trying to take the razor for your own use." He smiled, gold gleaming like a small reef in his mouth. He was quite one of the ugliest men Tozer had ever seen and the American wondered what his wife was like.

"Is your wife here with you?"

Buloff nodded, widened his smile into a bonanza. "I'll ask her if she would like to shave you. She complains she has not enough to do while she is here."

"Does she still run the Blue Delphinium?"

"Of course. One never knows how long this job of mine will last. I, too, could have my throat cut some day. We might even die together." He laughed, belly bouncing up and down. He was dressed in riding breeches and wore a loose white silk blouse over them; he looked pregnant. "But the same thing might happen to me in Russia. At least here I am being paid."

He went out, walking with a wide-legged strut as if he expected a horse to appear between them at any moment. Bradley Tozer stood closer to the mirror, felt the stubble on his chin and cheeks, then felt his throat. He didn't know why he should expect to be killed by a knife, but somehow a bullet seemed too clean and quick for a man of General Meng's taste. He had heard stories of the General's cruelty: a few survivors, minus hands or eyes, were witnesses to what Meng could do to those who crossed him. "God damn him!" said Tozer, and the mirror's image mouthed an echo; but he knew the curse was just a whistle into the wind. Somewhere outside the banjo

strummed on, the General on his way to Tipperary. Tozer
wondered where he had learned the soldiers' songs, unless
they were in the book of instructions. The last thing one
could say about General Meng was that he was sentimental. Superstitious, yes, but not sentimental.

It was ten minutes before the door opened again and
the Colonel's wife and a soldier came in. The soldier was
one of thousands Tozer had seen in his years in China: an
automaton with a gun, dressed in a uniform that would
have gone unnoticed in a dozen armies. But Madama Buloff would have gone unnoticed nowhere. She was younger then Tozer had expected, no more than in her
mid-twenties; but she was big, God damn it, she was big.
Tozer himself was six feet tall, but even in her flat-heeled
sandals she topped him by two inches. She was built in
proportion, a green silk-clad mountain; she wasn't blub-
berly fat but was built of firm solid flesh. Her gown, tight
as a green skin, was slit up one side: a white tree-trunk of
a leg showed when she moved. If there had been less of
her face she might have been beautiful, but Tozer felt he
would have needed at least another ten feet of perspective
between them to appreciate her. He wondered what she
and the Colonel looked like together in bed. Their love-
making must sound like a cavalry charge.

"Sit down, please." He had expected a booming bugle,
but her voice was soft and small; not a little girl's voice,
but far too small and gentle for someone her size. "Shall I
shave your upper lip? You would look more handsome
with a moustache."

Despite himself, he felt flattered; then remembered she
was a brothel-keeper. "You don't have to flatter me,
Madame Buloff. I'm not looking for a girl."

She produced a razor, began to strop it with a professional jerk of her wrist. "Don't let's be cheeky, Mr. Tozer.
I'm the one with the razor."

He looked in the mirror, then surrendered. "Okay, let's
try a moustache. I can always shave it off when I leave
here."

"If," she said, and smiled. She *was* good-looking, he decided, even if her smile seemed to have more and bigger teeth than he had ever seen. "I'm only teasing, Mr. Tozer. The General's bark is worse than his bite. He is treating the two girls I brought him as if they were his daughters. Well, not his daughters," remembering why she had brought them.

She went on talking while she shaved him with delicate professional skill, comforting him to the tinny antiphon of the General's banjo. He was now attempting "Over There," a labored effort that would have sent the dough-boys marching the other way. Tozer, lying back beneath the massif of Madame Buloff's bosom, began to nurture an idea.

"How much does the General pay your husband?"

The razor rested, blade edge-on, against his throat. "What business is it of yours?"

"How much does he pay for your girls?" He swallowed, his throat rippling under the razor.

She stared down at him a moment, then went on shaving him. Then: "He pays my husband too little. And too little for the girls, too."

"Have you ever thought of going to America?"

She had already lathered his face twice: she did so again. The soldier came forward curiously, but she waved him back. He was a small man and she towered over him. "I hate the Chinese," she said to Tozer. "We Russians cannot stand them. America? Yes, I have thought of going there. But what could my husband do?"

He hadn't really thought. "A man of his ability—anything. I would pay you and him ten thousand dollars. With that you could build yourself a new life."

"Do they have tea rooms in America?" She began to scrape the lather from his face: he had never been shaved so closely.

"Not like the Blue Delphinium. But if that's the sort you want—well, American men like girls." He was offering to stake a brothel-keeper; but then his grandfather had dabbled in the opium trade. "You could start a tea room in New York."

"What is your city?"

"Boston. But they don't have tea rooms there, not ones with girls." Or so he believed. When a young man he had always gone to New York for *his* girls.

"What will we have to do for this ten thousand dollars?"

"Help me escape from here."

The razor rested against his throat again. The banjo was being tortured once more: there was no place like home, plunked the fumbling fingers of General Meng. "The price is too little, Mr. Tozer," said Madame Buloff. "Shall I come again tomorrow and shave you even closer?"

CHAPTER 4

1

Extract from the William Bede O'Malley manuscript:
Once upon a time the Balkans were volcanoes where the
people, rather than the mountains, used to erupt. Communism has spread like fire-foam over the passions that
used to flame there. I still wonder, all these years afterwards, if the Countess managed to die in time not to be
extinguished by conformity. But the morning we left her
front lawn I should not have blamed Sun Nan if he had
put a bullet through her. Though I could not hear her
above the roar of the engines—and those three Rolls-
Royce Falcons were threatening to blow out those garden
walls—I knew she was screaming for our blood. And the
gipsies, no doubt tired of picking roses, would have given
it to her.

By the time Kern and Eve had got through the gates,
the gipsies had decided their last chance for a couple of
victims was Sun Nan and I. They came at us from all
sides, looking suicidal in the moonlight, black vampires
with knives and guns instead of fangs. I couldn't fire the
forward gun; I would have blown Eve right off the road
in front of me. Sun Nan, strapped in on top of the extra
tank in the rear cockpit, hampered by the straps and his
own portliness, could only swing the Lewis gun in a narrow arc. I had told him not to shoot anyone unless it was
absolutely necessary. He was firing back over the tail and
to either side of it, but unless the gipsies ran right in behind us none of them was going to be bowled over.

They came at the wings from both sides, knives glittering: they were going to stab the big bird from the sky to

113

death, rip it to pieces. There were half a dozen men across the gateway now. I hated to do it, but there was nothing else for it. I gunned the engine and drove the machine straight at them. I had come in the gateway at less than ten miles an hour, knowing there was less than a foot to spare at each end of the wings; I had caught a glimpse of Kern and Eve going out, both of them taking it cautiously until they were through and out on to the road. There was no time for caution now. I aimed the Bristol at the middle of the gateway, trusting that the moonlight had brought on no temporary astigmatism.

I went through the gates at 30 miles an hour, one wing brushing a gate-post. The men across the roadway stood their ground till the last moment; then they dropped flat or dived aside. A man was hanging on each side of the lower wing; if they had been on the same side I'd never have made it through the narrow space. I kept the machine going, glancing to see how the unwelcome passengers were making out. They were running, feet barely touching the ground, scared of hanging on, scared of letting go. Charlie Paddock was the world's fastest runner that year: he wouldn't even have tasted the dust of those two fellows. I began to laugh, sadistically I guess. I increased the speed: I was approaching take-off rate. They were barely touching the ground now; but didn't have the strength to haul themselves up on to the wing. Sun Nan was still shooting back over the tail; then suddenly he stopped, his gun empty. And at that moment the gipsy athletes decided they had had enough: better to fall arse over gipsy at ground level than from a great height. They suddenly let go, as if they had cued each other. They fell behind, tumbling over and over in the dust. The machine, all at once relieved of the extra weight, was straining to be airborne. I lifted the nose and went up into the smiling stars. I looked back: there were two black crosses on the blue-white road.

We made Sofia with about two minutes' petrol left in the tanks. The dawn obligingly came up, the colour of roses, and we flew over the city and found the aerodrome, a primitive one. Arriving so early had its advantages: there were no officials to ask awkward questions. A sergeant and a soldier, speaking German to Kern, sold us petrol. A bribe of five pounds helped. They didn't recognize the money, but Kern told them it was legal tender anywhere in the world, the pound sterling of His Majesty King George the Fifth. The good old days, eh?

We dismantled the Lewis gun and packed it away again. Sun Nan got back into Eve's machine and we took off into bright daylight and a cloudless sky. It was like that all the way to Constantinople: or Istanbul, Stamboul, New Rome, Byzantium, give it any name you wish. It was Constantinople when we got there, still being fought over as it had been for centuries, if only with words at that time.

The Allies were in occupation, backing the Sultan Mehmet the Sixth against the Nationalists and the general we now know as Kemal Ataturk, but who was then known as Mustafa Kemal. We flew in over the Golden Horn, saw the British warships in the Bosphorus; then we went looking for an aerodrome. We should have flown on, found a quiet unoccupied field somewhere. But we needed petrol.

The aerodrome was under British military occupation. As soon as we landed we were surrounded by Tommies: they wore pith helmets against the fierce sun and suspicious looks against us. We climbed down and I tried my friendliest smile.

"Major O'Malley." Even in those days I was not in favor of using your rank once you'd left the services; but it never failed to impress, especially when you found yourself in a military situation again. While in Rome do what the legions do. "Who is your CO?"

The sergeant gave me only a quick glance, but looked long and hard at the girl, the Chinaman and the dandy who could be a Jerry, then at the three Bristols, then back at me. "You some sorta flying circus, sir?"

"You might say that, sergeant. Now you can take us to

your CO and we'll see what sort of funny questions he has?"

The Commanding Officer was Johnny Silversmith, all moustache, pop eyes and bonhomie just as he had been when I had seen him last the night before the Battle of the Somme.

"Gad, O'Malley—it's you! Jolly marvellous to see you, what? Stayed on in, y'know, when the show was over. Didn't fancy peacetime, all those bloody trade unionists, votes for women, all that. Who are your friends outside? Gather one of them is a Jerry, that right? Not very welcome here, y'know. Going to China, are you? Jolly long way. Care for a snort?"

"Not now, Johnny. The question is, where can we buy some petrol and get on our way? We're rather pushed for time."

"Where are you heading?"

"Adana, straight across the country."

"Out of the question, old chap. Blighter named Mustafa Kemal has got all of Anatolia in a turmoil. They'd shoot you down, what? Couldn't have that, not to a friend from the Fusiliers. Afraid I'll have to hold you here till we get you permission to fly on. But you'll have to go the long way around. Smyrna, Cyprus, that way. Have to get permission from the Greeks for you to land at Smyrna. Awful bore, I know, but that's the way it is."

"How long will that take?"

"Two or three days, perhaps a week. Have to go through channels, y'know. The Greeks are rather slow at answering our signals. Blighters don't bother to learn English, y'know. Think they would, if they want to be on our side, what?"

I felt my heart sink, for Eve; but I was angry too. At bloody wars that never knew when to end, at victors who always wanted that final bit of territory, winners who would never accept horizons. "Are we under arrest or can we go to a hotel?"

"Oh, a hotel by all means, old chap. Can get you into the Perapalas. I mean——" His red face turned purple with his flush. "I mean, unless you would prefer one a bit cheaper. Rather plush, y'know."

"That's what we want," I said, sure that Eve wouldn't want anything less than plush. I knew that was what I wanted, having slept for two nights in a sleeping-bag under the wing of an aeroplane. "The plushest."

"I'll get you some transport. Awfully sorry about this, old chap. Still teaching Johnny Turk a lesson, what? Blighters will never learn. How does your friend feel? The Jerry, I mean."

"Oh, I think he's learned. Some of them are intelligent."

A staff car, piled with the four of us, our baggage and a driver, took us into the city. We climbed the hill of Pera through narrow thronged streets where Allied uniforms stood out amongst the crowd, Janissaries at a shilling a day and an issue of Wild Woodbines. New smells assailed us, thick and sharp: roasting coffee, goat's dung, garbage, sweating people: it was a change from roses. We came to the Perapalas, a grand hotel such as they don't make any more.

"It will cost you a fortune for the four of us," I said.

Eve hadn't spoken all the way into the city. She lifted herself from her depression, looked at the hotel and shrugged. "It'll do."

We went on in, escorted by what might have been a dozen eunuchs who rushed to grab our bags. The interior was all red plush, marble and aspidistras, a stopover for passing sultans: I felt at home at once, Mehmet O'Malley. Kern nodded approvingly and even Sun Nan lost some of his inscrutability.

"Don't all look so damned—*comfortable*!"

We looked contrite, forgiving Eve her snappishness. Her father was inching, day by day, towards having his throat cut; and we looked like squandering some of those precious days in this five-star seraglio. I had looked around the foyer and high-class whores seemed to be as numerous as the aspidistras. One or two of them looked at us, but didn't appear particularly interested, dismissing us as three men not in their price bracket or already in tow to Eve. Which we were, gradually growing more and more committed to her than those whores would ever know.

"I'll hurry things up," said Kern.

A delegation of some sort had just arrived on the Orient Express, diplomats with wives and mistresses and servants, politics on a summer treat: there were junkets even then. Kern pushed his way through them, and two minutes later came back with the manager, a squat page-boy and four eunuchs. We rode up in style in the open lift, while the delegation looked up at us, the scruffy, travel-stained foursome, and wondered which defeated they had overlooked in their dunning for reparations. I was beginning to feel like Kern.

We were shown to four suites, the manager bowing us all the way. Today, when hotel managers have a Caesar complex, it is almost impossible to imagine how far they could bend over in those days without falling over or, somehow, losing their dignity. "It is such a pleasure, Herr Baron—ah, it is like a reminder of the old days—"

We dropped off Eve and Sun Nan at their suites and I followed Kern into his. The manager wished us a pleasant stay, told us he was always at our command and withdrew, bent over like a pederast's victim. The page-boy was the last to leave, after the four bag-toting enunuchs.

"I remember when you came to visit your uncle, sir. You were much younger." He spoke German and I understood just enough of the language to catch the gist of what he was saying. "He was a fine gentleman, your uncle."

"I must visit his grave," said Kern.

He put his hand in his pocket, but the page-boy waved a hand. "Please, Herr Baron. Your uncle always paid me well." I could see now, smooth and unlined though his cheeks were, his eyes looked as if they had peered through a hundred years of keyholes. "Have a pleasant stay, sir."

He went out and I said, "How did he knew you when you were a boy? He only looked about sixteen himself."

"He's closer to forty-six, I should say. He's a midget. He used to spy for my uncle."

"Who was your uncle?"

"Baron Von Wangenheim. He was an uncle by marriage. He was our ambassador here before and during the war. He was responsible for the Turks coming in on our side."

"He was also responsible for getting us in here ahead of the crowd downstairs—am I right?"

"In a manner of speaking. He is buried out at Tarabya. I must visit his grave if we are delayed here."

I walked to the window, looked out at the Golden Horn turning to brass under the sinking sun. Down there the Genoese had flourished, merchants who had warded off their rivals the Venetians, the Pisans, the Florentines; they had been succeeded by the French and Dutch; then by the English. There had been the Turkie Company, then the Levant Company. The men who had run those companies had been virtual kings, subject only to the Sultan: I longed for a man like Harborne or Barton, someone I could go to and ask for free passage for the four of us. But those days were gone forever. It might have been possible even six years ago to find someone in authority to give one a passport to wherever one wanted to go; but not now, not in 1920, I had to go through channels, through stupid Johnny Silversmith, some oaf at GHQ, the obstinate bloody Greeks who wouldn't learn English—I hit the window-sill with a fist. "Christ, we've got to get out of here! And quick!"

"Unfortunately, neither of us has any influence. I am my uncle's nephew here in the Perapalas, but outside I'm afraid I'm no more than a bloody Hun."

There was nothing to say to that. I left him, went along to my suite, had a bath and changed into my one suit. When we went down to dinner everyone looked at us again. Kern, Sun Nan and I were the only men in lounge suits, Eve the only woman not in an evening dress. The

head waiter, all apologies to Kern, put us in a corner behind an aspidistra. We could have been some of Mustafa
Kemal's Anatolian peasants having a night out, only toler-
ated because the head waiter wasn't sure that pretty soon
the peasants might not be running the country.

Eve was still subdued, but made an effort to be part of
the conversation. "We'll have champagne. Don't raise
your eyebrows—I'm not trying to put on a stiff upper lip.
In a hotel like this my father always ordered—orders—"
just the slight slip, the correction of tense, was the
measure of her pessimism "—champagne. He'd want me
to do the same. What would you like?"

It was no use looking at me or Sun Nan, one a beer
man, the other a green tea connoisseur. The drink waiter
stood by, bored and supercilious: obviously he thought we
should be drinking no better than *arak*. Kern turned to
him. "When I was here with my uncle Baron von Wangenheim in 1912 you served us a champagne I still
remember, a Krug. I've forgotten what year it was, but as
Dom Perignon once said, it was like drinking stars."

The drink waiter, who evidently hadn't been told who
Kern was, suddenly beamed. "The Krug 1904, sir. There
is still some left."

"We'll have it," said Eve.

The dinner was excellent and even I appreciated the
champagne. At last I sat back and looked around the
restaurant. A small war was going on not a hundred miles
from here, but nobody in the big room looked as if they
knew of it or cared. The delegation were at tables in the
middle of the room, the men smug and indifferent behind
their shirt-fronts, the women showing enough bare shoulders and bosom to have had them shot if the Moslems of
Anatolia had seen them. Some Turks in white ties and
tails sat at a corner table, stiffer even than the delegates
behind their starched shirts; those damned shirts were the
forerunner of jeans as the uniform of the conformists. The
Turks were accompanied by three of the whores who had
been in the foyer this afternoon; the whores were dressed
more modestly than the women who had arrived from Eu-

rope. A party of handsome young French officers had four whores at their table: good-looking, well-dressed girls who kept shooting triumphant glances at both their colleagues with the Turks and the women with the delegates. There were about a dozen British officers scattered around the room, none of them with a woman and all of them looking enviously at the French; and there were three Greek officers who, judging by their expressions, were with their wives. The rest of the diners were all civilians: diplomats, rich businessmen, politicians, and the assorted women who go with those assorted classes. A Hungarian orchestra was playing "tzigane," and the waiters flew and swooped like penguins on speed pills.

Johnny Silversmith, red-faced and red-tabbed, came to our table. "Hope you're enjoying yourselves. Marvellous spot, y'know. Don't ever want to go home."

"Have you heard from the Greeks?"

"Yes, actually. Their senior liaison chappie is over there at that table, the one with the fat wife. Speaks English, actually. Saw him this evening when he came up from Smyrna. Afraid it's bad news, old chap. He said no, not a chance of your being allowed to land there. You look like being stuck here. Unless you want to go up through Russia, across the Black Sea. Can't help you there, I'm afraid. Don't know any Russians, what?"

I was just drunk enough to say, "Is there anyone here who would take a bribe?"

His eyes popped. "I say, old chap, that's hardly a decent question, is it? You mean, on *our* side?"

"Yes," said Eve: champagne or desperation had had its effect on her. "A hundred pounds, two hundred if you like. Just to fill up our machines and turn a blind eye while we take off."

Silversmith knew we were offering *him* the bribe. I had no idea what his financial circumstances were, except that during the two years I had been in the army with him he had never given any hint that he had any money. And if he had stayed on in the army, the chances were that he knew he could not get a job if he had left it.

He stared at me and suddenly I had the sickening recognition that those blue pop eyes were honest. "I must say I'm disappointed in you, O'Malley. You must think I'm a damned Wog or something."

He turned on his heel and marched off to rejoin the officers he had been sitting with on the other side of the room. I looked at Eve. "I think I queered our pitch. He's not going to trust us from now on. Not even if we decide to head north across the Black Sea."

"You're not to blame entirely," said Eve, and sounded more dispirited than at any time since we had left London. "I offered him money. I misread him, too."

"One should always read a man's bank account," said Sun Nan, Confucian in his cups, "before trying to bribe him."

"Bloody funny," I said, and didn't apologize to Eve for swearing in front of a lady.

The Hungarian orchestra was playing a Strauss waltz. Everyone else in the room became gayer, even the Greeks with their wives; the whores laughed as if they were enjoying themselves, instead of just being paid; the delegates and their women joked and hummed, heads swaying in time to the music I suddenly wanted to be sick, not from drinking too much but just out of sheer bloody misery.

Kern drank the last of the champagne. "It tastes even better than I remembered. But I was young then and all you really have when you're young is a thirst."

"Christ," I said, "don't *you* start playing Confucius."

"Try and be a gentleman, Herr O'Malley." His patience annoyed me but, dimly in my misery, I knew he was right. I was acting like a boor. "My uncle was a great diplomat. Here in this very room he gave me some advice. In every war, he said, there is always someone who thinks he is on the wrong side."

I looked at Eve. "It certainly is a night for pithy wisdom. What do we have from the United States of America? There's nothing from England, I'm afraid. We are absolutely out of wise sayings tonight, pithy or otherwise." Drink, even the best champagne, can make a fool of the wisest man: how's that for a wise saying? "I think I'll go to bed."

"I think we all should." Eve rose.

We all went out, every eye in the room following us. I saw Silversmith at a table with three officers, all younger than himself; he nodded at me, not *to* me, and said something to the chaps with him. I suddenly hated him, wanted to shout to him why we had to be on our way in a hurry. But my tongue was already a yard long, flapping in the breeze like a windsock. We went on out to the lift. There were a couple of whores, well-dressed and modest, in the foyer. I looked at them, felt a surge in the crotch but did nothing about it.

On our floor Eve and I said goodnight to Kern and Sun Nan and I walked her to the door of her room. "I saw you looking at those girls downstairs, Bede. I shan't mind if you want to go down and join them. You can put them on my bill."

"You're too broad-minded. Or you're like me—so darned tired and miserable, you're saying things you'll be sorry for in the morning."

After a moment she nodded, leaned her head back against the door. "What do we do, Bede?"

"I don't know. I'll have to look at the maps. Russia is out—they're still fighting in the Crimea. The alternative is to fly back to Athens through Salonika, then down to Crete and across to Egypt, then through Palestine and Mesopotamia. That's supposing Colonel Silversmith lets us get away at all."

"How long will that route take us?"

I tried to picture the distances in my mind. "It'll add three or four days, at least."

Her eyes glistened. I then did a surprising thing, to her as well as me: I kissed her cheek. "Go to bed, Eve, and try to sleep. I'll have something worked out by morning."

She opened her door. "I'm sorry I suggested the girls downstairs. You're too nice for them."

"Not really," I said modestly.

I went along to my own suite, undressed and stood at

the window in my pyjamas. I could see the warships drawn up near the Galata Bridge; further out in the stream there were other ships, like basking sharks in the moonlight. Half a dozen British soldiers went home somewhere down in the narrow streets, exhorting the Turks to keep their sunny side up; there was a shot, a yell and the singing abruptly stopped. I leaned out of the window, but could see nothing; just heard another yell, then the sound of galloping heavy feet. Some Turk, sunny side very much down, had taken a pot-shot at the foreigners. I was suddenly sympathetic to him, on his side, the wrong side, in the war.

There was a knock at the door. I went to it in my pyjamas, opened it. The midget page-boy and a young British officer who looked vaguely familiar stood in the corridor. "Major O'Malley," said the page-boy in his piping voice, "may I introduce Lieutenant Hope? May we come in?"

I wasn't accustomed to luxury hotels: for all I knew, page-boys went about all the time introducing young officers to male guests in their pyjamas. "What is this? You've knocked on the wrong door, I'm afraid."

Lieutenant Hope looked blank, then actually blushed. The page-boy giggled, shook his head. "Major O'Malley, it's nothing like that. May we come in?"

They came in. The page-boy looked up at me, no longer giggling. "Major O'Malley, my name is Ahmed. I understand you have three aeroplanes, two of them armed, out at the military aerodrome."

"We'd like to buy them," said Lieutenant Hope.

"We?" I looked at the two of them, the four-foot-nothing Turkish midget and the thin six-foot British officer.

"We shall pay one thousand pounds sterling for each of the three machines," said Ahmed. "We should like them tonight."

"Is this some sort of practical joke? Did Colonel Silversmith send you up here? This sounds like his drunken sense of humour—three gins and he was always ready to act like a bloody schoolboy—"

"It's no joke. I know what you mean about the Colonel—" I recognized Hope now; he had been one of the officers sitting with Silversmith when we had left the restaurant. "I'm in his unit. Dreadful man when he's blotto."

"If you're in his unit, why are you offering me three thousand quid to buy our machines? You know he's virtually impounded them. What are you going to do with them?"

"We'd like you to deliver them to the Nationalist forces up in Anatolia, to a place called Malavan. There is a Greek army up there, out-numbering Mustafa Kemal's men about eight to one, and the Greeks also have aeroplanes. They caught the Turks in retreat a couple of weeks ago, in the gorges, and almost massacred them. Unless those Greek machines are put out of the sky, Mustafa Kemal can't think of counter-attacking."

"Just who are you, Hope? A Turk?"

"No, I'm Welsh, actually. Caradoc Dylan Hope, from Llanelli." Now I could hear just the faintest lilt in the otherwise English public school voice; and the way he pronounced Llanelli was further proof that he was what he claimed. "I'm not fighting for the Nationalists nor am I a spy for them. Ahmed here is the one who does all the spying."

"Years of experience," said Ahmed, pride lighting up his middle-aged infant's face.

I was more intent on Hope than on the self-acknowledged spy. "If you're not fighting and not spying, what *are* you doing?"

"I'm a sympathizer, I suppose." Baron von Wangenheim's man who turned up in every war, the one who thought he was on the wrong side. "We're being bloody beastly to the *real* Turks, the ones up-country, not the supporters of the Sultan down here in Constantinople. I fought against the Turks at Gallipoli. One had to admire them as fighters, absolutely magnificent. I don't think they should be made to rub their noses in their own shit, which is what the peace treaty is making them do. I suppose when I'm trying to say is that I'm glad we won the war, but I don't enjoy being a bloody conqueror. Some people do, Colonel Silvermith for instance, but not me. If you'll sell those aeroplanes, I can guarantee you'll get them away tonight. I'm the duty officer as from midnight."

"If we take off, how can you be sure we'll head for Malavan?"

"Where else can you head for? If you fly back to Greece or down to Smyrna, the Greeks will grab you—they are looking for warplanes, too. Same thing if you head across towards Russia. The thing about an aeroplane is that sooner or later it has to land to refuel. Better to land where you will be welcome, and paid three thousand pounds into the bargain, than land somewhere where you could lose your machines and finish up in jail."

"You appear to have thought of everything. Are you by any chance related to Lloyd George?"

Hope smiled. "No. But I have the devious Welsh mind that you English say we all have."

"We can't sell you the machines, that's out of the question. We have to take them on to China."

"Would you hire them?"

"For how long?"

"I don't know. Perhaps only a couple of days, perhaps a month. The Greeks have six machines up there. They have to be destroyed."

"What sort of pilots have you?"

"Excellent," said Ahmed, the proud Turk.

"Not really," said Hope. "They're very inexperienced. There is only one who's actually flown in combat."

"We could lose the machines before they'd been in the air five minutes" But I knew I was hamstrung, that he had me by the balls, as they say now. I looked at Ahmed. He might be a spy for the Nationalists, an agent authorized to spend money to buy aeroplanes, but he was still a hotel page-boy. "Go and get Miss Tozer and Baron von Kern."

"And the Chinese gentleman, too?"

"No, he won't be necessary."

Ahmed left us and I turned to Hope. "What do you get out of this? Are you on commission?"

He flushed, but kept his sudden temper in hand. "You bloody English are all the same! You think everything is a matter of trade."

"Not all of us." I knew now I had misread him. I was having trouble with the peace-time soldiers. "I apologize. You really are committed to this chap Mustafa Kemal?"

He gestured vaguely. "I don't know if I'm *committed*. But I think they deserve a chance to start afresh. Turks are not the most likeable blighters—they can be pretty cruel and they did some frightful things to our prisoners. But perhaps we think that because we're applying our own standards. Present day standards. We forget things we used to do. Tying Indian sepoys to the mouths of cannons and shooting shells through them, that wasn't exactly civilized. You English have very convenient memories."

"You were saying *we* a moment ago. I've seen some Welsh rugby players you couldn't call exactly civilized."

He smiled again, recognizing I didn't really disagree with him. "The trouble is, after wars we always seem to back up the reactionaries we've just beaten."

"What if our machines should be used against our own chaps?"

"That worries me a bit. Let's hope you only come up against the Greeks."

He might be Welsh, but he had all our English prejudices.

The door opened and Ahmed ushered in Eve and Kern, both in dressing-gowns. I noticed his more than hers: it was green silk with a monogram on the pocket. I suddenly realized I was still wearing just my pyjamas, striped flannelette from the Army and Navy Stores, and I looked around for my trench-coat, my only dressing-gown.

"You're modest enough," said Eve. "Why did you send for us?"

I explained the situation. "I've told Lieutenant Hope we can't sell the machines, that we need them to get us to China. However——" While I had been talking to Hope an idea had been growing, the sort of wild scheme that blooms out of the seed of desperation. "If you agree, Eve, we can rent them two of the machines with the Baron and me as pilots. Are you willing to do some more fighting, Baron?"

"Of course." Somehow he made it sound as if I had insulted him by asking.

"Good. It's your decision, Eve. We can get the three machines out of Constantinople tonight. If the Greeks are in the air tomorrow, we could take them on then. With a bit of luck we could be on our way to China again by the day after tomorrow."

"Mustafa Kemal would have to agree to your flying the machines," said Hope dubiously. "He might not like it, I mean using mercenaries. They have an awful lot of pride, Turks."

"Why shouldn't we have?" Ahmed stretched himself to his full height; I wanted to laugh, but was sensible enough not to. "We are a proud people. We had an empire once."

"The Janissaries were mercenaries in a way. They were Christians, too, to begin with."

"They were the Sultan's men," said Ahmed. "I shouldn't make the comparison to Mustafa Kemal if I were you, Major O'Malley."

There was something unreal to being lectured in diplomacy by a baby-faced midget in a fez and a page's uniform. I looked down at my pyjamas, beginning to wonder if I wasn't sleepwalking.

Eve had listened expressionlessly. Now she said, "What if you don't have any luck? What if you and the Baron are shot down?"

"That is the chance we have to take," said Kern. "Herr O'Malley and I have taken the same chance before."

She shook her head angrily. "You mustn't be killed——"

"Nobody's going to be killed," I said, "At least not us."

She knew what I meant: her father could have been

there in the room with us. I had never met him, knew virtually nothing about him, but gradually he had become a presence to me. I am not even sure that at that time I was determined to save his life: more, I think, to save Eve from grief that might destroy her. One thing I did know was how much she loved him.

"All right," she said reluctantly.

"We fly just two machines," I told Hope and Ahmed. "Whether we down the Greeks or they get us, whether we do it tomorrow or it takes us a month, Miss Tozer must be allowed to fly on the day after tomorrow for Malavan. That's the bargain."

The Welshman and the Turk, the unlikely allies (or were they? I wondered), looked at each other. Then both nodded. "Be out at the aerodrome of two o'clock. I'll have your tanks filled. We have some Turks working for the army out there—they'll get the machines ready. Ahmed will provide a car to bring you out."

"What about you? Won't you be court-martialled if you let us get away?"

"Possibly," said Hope, and smiled. "But in some parts of Wales it is still an honour to be kicked out of the army." He shook hands all around. "I may have to open fire on you if you're discovered, but I'll try and have our chaps shoot over your heads."

"I'll be surprised if they do," I said. "Especially if they think we're Turks."

End of extract from O'Malley manuscript.

2

They left the hotel at one o'clock in the morning. Ahmed and a one-eyed night porter came up to collect them and their baggage, took them down a flight of back stairs.

"What about the hotel bill?" Eve asked. "I should pay—"

"It will be paid tomorrow." Ahmed had changed from

his page-boy uniform into striped trousers, a black coat and a black homburg. He looked to O'Malley like a mini-diplomat, an ambassador to San Marino, Andorra or some other mini-country. "The night clerks are in the pay of the British. They would be on the telephone at once if you went down and paid the bill. It will be paid, Miss Tozer."

The car waiting for them in the side street was a pre-war Mercedes. "My uncle's car!" Kern exclaimed.

"Yes." Ahmed beamed. He was a secret agent, but he was also a true grand hotel man: he had a sense of occasion. "Would you care to drive, Herr Baron? I have a little difficulty in reaching the pedals."

He rode in front with Kern, while Eve sat between O'Malley and Sun Nan in the back. The latter had asked no questions when wakened and told they would be leaving in the middle of the night. He had already become fatalistic about the fact that they would not reach Hunan in time and he had gone to sleep at once, depressed but able to turn his mind off as easily as he had turned off the light. His life had not been uneventful, not without its dangers, and he had discovered that fatalism was as good a sleeping pill as any.

"Even if we do not reach my master in time," he said, as he settled in beneath the baggage, "I shall tell him it was not for want of trying."

"If he harms my father," said Eve, "I shall kill him. You can tell him that, too."

With Ahmed giving him directions Kern drove them out of the city, opening up the car when he reached the outskirts. The warm night cascaded past their faces, taking some of their weariness with it. The stars were yellow with the heat of the day gone and the day to come; the moon was low, as if eager to be gone into another night. They almost ran down a herd of goats sleeping by the roadside: goats and goat-herd started to their feet, bleating after them into the whirling dust. Then they turned up a slight hill and Kern, at Ahmed's instruction, brought the car to a halt.

"Now we walk," said the midget. He had talked to O'Malley on the drive out, giving him instructions on which direction to take off, what bearing to take for Malavan, what to look for when approaching the town. "Our men will swing over your propellers for you. When you get to Malavan there will be trucks lined up on either side of the field. It is not an airfield, but it is smooth enough for you to land on. They will switch on their lights as you fly over."

They left the car and climbed the slight rise of the hill, through rocks where clumps of lilac, thyme and some stunted mastic grew. Eve sniffed the mixed perfumes, clearing her nose of the cloying memory of roses. They scrambled over a broken stone wall and O'Malley, the history student among them, wondered if the wall had been built to keep out other invaders. But they were not invaders: they were *escaping* from Byzantium.

They went down the other side of the hill, watching for the British guards. Four men materialized out of the shadows behind the hangars. They said nothing, just took the bags and led them to the parked planes.

One of the men patted the wing of O'Malley's plane. *"Peki."*

"He says everything is all right," said Ahmed.

They got aboard. Once settled in her seat Eve felt an excitement take hold of her; not a frivolous excitement, but a pumping of adrenalin that brought her wide awake, banished her weariness. They were on their way again, racing towards her father. Suddenly there was a warning hiss from the Turkish mechanics and they vanished back into the shadows of the hangar. Eve slid down into the cockpit, hoping Sun Nan and the others had done the same. She heard a guard coming along the perimeter, whistling softly to himself. He had a musical whistle and was proud of it: she heard him do a double trill. He stopped by the front of her plane and she heard the clump as he dropped his rifle butt to the ground. Then he lit a cigarette, the match flaring for a moment in the darkness. He stood there by the plane, leaning on the lower wing, while Eve held her breath and felt the sweat beginning to run on her.

Then she heard the guard scraping his boot-heel on the hard ground as he ground out his cigarette butt. She heard the clink of metal as he slung his rifle over his shoulder again; he said aloud, "Foock 'em all," then went trudging off down along the perimeter. She waited, then eased herself up straight in the cockpit again, fretting now to be away.

O'Malley sat up in his cockpit, turned to look at Ahmed crouched on top of the tank in the rear cockpit. When the guard had come along, the midget had been standing on the wing of the Bristol giving O'Malley last-minute instructions. There had not been time for him to jump down; O'Malley had grabbed him by the collar and hauled him into the rear cockpit. Now O'Malley said, "When you get there, who takes us to Mustafa Kemal?"

Then he heard the shouted order somewhere up the perimeter, a shot, then the sound of running feet. Something had gone wrong; some other guard must have discovered the Mercedes. Lights went on in a long shed further along the perimeter; a door was flung open and men ran out. The Turks came running out of the hangar, grabbed the propellers of the planes. O'Malley's engine was the first to burst into life: he forgot all about Ahmed as he checked the controls. The little man struggled to get out of the cockpit, but his legs were too short to reach the wing. O'Malley yelled at him, gesturing to get back and down in the cockpit. Then the plane swung round, began to roll, and Ahmed, clutching his homburg, hunched down as best he could on top of the tank in the cockpit.

Eve waited while the man in front of her plane wound the propeller, then swung it. The engine coughed and she resisted the temptation to add more throttle, not wanting to risk flooding it. The man swung the propeller again, and again the engine just coughed, then died. O'Malley's and Kern's planes were already beginning to roll, their engines obliterating the silence of the night. The man in front of her shouted, but she couldn't hear him nor would have understood him if she had. He swung again on the propeller, working desperately; the engine spluttered, died, then abruptly took. The man fell back as the propeller whirled. He kept running backwards, holding his side, then suddenly he fell over and lay still. Eve stared at him, puzzled, then horrified as she realized he had been shot. Sun Nan hit her on the shoulder, shouted at her. Something hit the rim of the cockpit and zipped past her ear. With even colder horror she realized the soldiers were shooting at *her*.

She pushed the throttle, every muscle tight as she told herself not to rush the engine. It wasn't running smoothly, it didn't seem to be firing properly; but it had to do as it was, it had to get her and Sun Nan off the ground. The three planes went down the dark field side by side, gathering speed quickly, bouncing as they hit bumps but keeping their noses straight. Bullets puffed the ground around them; several went through the canvas of the fuselage and wings; if Lieutenant Hope had given any orders to fire high, his men were either ignoring them or were bad shots. Eve felt the nose of the Bristol beginning to lift and she eased back the stick. The engine missed a beat and so did her heart. Then the plane was climbing, they were out of range of the bullets and a moment later she saw the city away to her right, the domes of the mosques reflecting the last of the moonlight, the minarets glowing faintly like candles that had swallowed their own flames. She saw O'Malley bank his plane, Kern follow suit; she did the same, fell in behind them. They headed south-east towards Anatolia and the war.

O'Malley had set their speed exactly right. Almost on the dot of two hours' flying, the instruction Ahmed had given him, they saw the dark trench in the plain below that was the Malavan gorge. It led them straight to the line of hills where the town sprawled on the lower slopes. They flew in low over the town, banked and came back. And at once two lines of light flared at the southern end of town, out on the plain. O'Malley took them down to the makeshift flare-path, put them down neatly between the waiting trucks on the wide field.

Eve cut her engine, sat back. She was suddenly, overwhelmingly, exhausted. It took a tremendous effort to haul herself up and out of the cockpit. She stumbled as she stepped on to the wing; Sun Nan, who had already climbed down, grabbed her and helped her to the ground. She felt weak, helpless, womanish. But somehow she dredged up a sediment of strength and straightened up. She wanted none of them to fuss over her because she was a woman.

Then she saw O'Malley lifting the bundle down from his plane. She went across to him, her legs weak, as he laid Ahmed out on the ground. "He must have fainted. We're lucky I didn't lose him. He wasn't strapped in."

Ahmed blinked his eyes, sat up slowly as a group of officers came out from behind one of the trucks. The lights were switched off and one of the officers said in English, "Pardon the darkness. But the Greeks could be within artillery range. We'll know in a minute or two."

"Do we wait?" said Eve.

"A woman?" The officer peered at her in the starlight. "Nothing was said about a woman."

Ahmed, still on the ground, said something in Turkish. The officer looked for him, found him, snapped something in reply. Then he looked at O'Malley. "Did you kidnap this man? He is supposed to remain in Constantinople. He is no favourite of the General's."

"We wouldn't be here if it weren't for him," said Eve. "Why is he out of favour with your General?"

"He once worked for the Germans." The officer was obviously not happy at having to deal with a woman. "Who are you?"

"I own the machines. Why are we waiting here?" Eve was too tired to be diplomatic or even feminine.

"If the Greeks are in range and open up, you will have to take the aeroplanes up again." They all waited, looking in the direction of the officer's gaze. Then: "They must know they're out of range. But they will have their machines over here at sunrise to see what has been happening here."

"What time is sunrise?" said O'Malley.

"Another two hours. Will you be ready to fly then?"

O'Malley looked at Kern and the latter said, "Of course."

They were escorted to a truck and driven into the town. There were people in the streets, brought out by the roar of the planes as they had swooped overhead, but no lights showed. The truck pulled up outside the largest house in town; as they went inside. Eve smelled roses in the garden through which they passed. Two tall guards stood at the front door, men with fierce moustaches and fiercer eyes; dressed in slashed black coats, blue trousers and high boots, they had a musical comedy air to them. But when they stepped together, barring the door, there was no play-acting about them.

The officer who spoke English said something to them. They stared at the foreigners, then reluctantly stepped aside. As he ushered the newcomers into the house the officer said, "They are the General's own bodyguard. They are Lazzes, from the mountains near the Black Sea."

Eve and the others were not kept waiting, though Ahmed, now recovered from his faint, looked as if he wished he were still in Constantinople. They were shown at once into a large room that once might have been a salon but was now a battle-room. Maps instead of pictures decorated the walls; a long conference table ran down the middle of the room. At the end of the table a tall handsome man in uniform rose from a high-backed chair. He didn't come forward to meet the foreigners but waited till they were brought to him.

The officer introduced them in Turkish, then Mustafa Kemal said in French, "Welcome. I apologize for not speaking English."

Eve said, putting every word carefully as if she were taking it out of a dictionary and laying it on the table in front of him, "I speak only schoolgirl French. But Major O'Malley and Baron von Kern speak it."

Mustafa looked at Kern. "You are German?"

"Yes, General." He straightened up, clicked his heels. But Eve noted that the German had not called the Turk *mon Général*. "I flew with Hauptmann Boelcke and Rittmeister von Richthofen."

Mustafa studied him for a moment, his mouth tight with disapproval. Then he looked down at Ahmed, standing fearfully in the background. He said something in Turkish that had a searing bite to it. He hates Germans, Eve thought with dismay. She glanced at Kern, but there was no expression on the Baron's face. He stood stiff and straight, impregnable, or seemingly so, against the feeling that Eve could suddenly feel emanating from the half a dozen other men in the big room.

Mustafa said something else in Turkish to the officer who had brought them to the house, then turned back to Eve and smiled. His charm was heavy-handed, but it was obvious that he didn't hate good-looking women. Eve was all at once glad of her looks, dusty and wind-swept though they might be, but she was also glad she was not a German.

"You will be my guest in this house, mademoiselle," while the machines are being used against our enemy." Then he looked at Sun Nan. "Does the Chinese also fly? No? Then perhaps he is a gunner?"

"No," said O'Malley, deciding he and Kern, the two who would have to do the flying, were being left in the background. "If we are going to take up gunners in the Bristols, General, you will have to supply them. And we shall have to make the decision quickly, because I have to take some extra tanks out of the rear cockpits. Do you have any experienced gunners, men who have flown in two-seater fighters?"

Mustafa Kemal gave him a hard look. "I have the rank on you, Major. You will speak to me when I ask you to."

"With all respect, General, I don't belong to your army. My rank is one that doesn't mean anything—I'm a civilian pilot, as is Baron von Kern. If the Greeks come up this morning and our luck holds, I hope this will be no more than a one-day contract."

"I am fighting for the future of my country, Monsieur O'Malley." If O'Malley made no claim to his rank, Mustafa Kemal was not a man to use it. "I shall decide whether your contract is for one day or not. You will leave when I say you may."

Exhausted herself, it was only now that Eve saw that Mustafa too, was haggard with fatigue. Ill, too, perhaps; she saw his hands shake and he hid them by clasping them behind his back. She had seen the advantages of power, but it had been the power of wealth, that of her father and her grandfather. She had once, as a child, overheard her father say that there would always be men who would bend their knee to money. Now she was seeing another sort of power, witnessing the disadvantages of it. She had joked in London about her father's thinking he owned China; now she was seeing a man who hoped to own Turkey. But the effects of that ambition were plainly evident, he had been bombarded by defeat and disappointment.

"I own the machines, my General." She was meticulous about the address: she did not want to antagonize him any more than he had been. "You should be talking to me about what use is to be made of my aeroplanes."

She had turned her head away from O'Malley, so she did not see his reaction to being put in his place. But Mustafa's reaction was not encouraging. He stared at her and she saw the sweat glistening on his broad forehead. He was ill, there was no doubt of it.

"Madamoiselle, I have respect for women and in the new Turkey there will be a place for them. But not in war, not now. You are my guest and will be treated accordingly. But those machines are mine now and I shall use them how and when I deem fit. They became mine when you accepted the midget's offer to help you escape from Constantinople." He looked at Ahmed. "Did you make any other offer?"

"No, my General." Ahmed's French was as good as his

English and German. He was the complete spy: Eve wondered how many other languages he spoke. But she noticed that he was afraid; he was tainted with his association with the Germans, Wangenheim and his nephew. But she was pleased to see that he was not ingratiating: the tiny knee was not bent. "But I did promise them that they could fly on as soon as the job was done."

"You had no authority to make promises." Mustafa looked back at Eve. "I need the machines, mademoiselle."

"For how long, my General?"

Mustafa shrugged, a concession. "That remains to be seen."

"Do the Baron and I fly them?" asked O'Malley: the aeroplanes had to be protected as best they could be.

"You will not attempt to fly off with them?" Mustafa Kemal smiled, no more than a spreading of the thin lips under the dark moustache. "Of course you won't. Mademoiselle Tozer and the other machine will be our hostage, shall we say? But then I take it you are gentleman of honour?"

"Not really," said O'Malley, speaking for himself; he could not bring himself to butter up this arrogant man, half-way to being a dictator if he should win his war. "But the Baron is."

"I have difficulty in believing Germans. Ever since I met the Kaiser. A most deceitful man."

"One doesn't judge Turks by the Sultan down in Constantinople," said O'Malley, surprised at himself defending the German.

Mustafa looked at him, then at Kern. "There is no comparison, is there, Baron?"

"None at all, General," said Kern, bony with pride. "I don't defend the Kaiser. But I don't criticize him, either. If he had won the war, I should have thought he was right in what he did. It is the duty of an officer to believe in his commander."

There was a murmur from the officers in the background. Mustafa said, "Even when he has lost the war?"

"Even then," said Kern, and nobody in the room could be sure that he did not believe what he had said.

Mustafa nodded. "I am impressed, Baron. I should hope for the same devotion from my men." But he did not look at them; and Eve, acutely aware now, knew that he had some enemies in the room. Or anyway some whose faith was not as strong as his. "You and Monsieur O'Malley will fly the machines. Without gunners. I don't think my men are experienced enough in that sort of fighting. They might fire the wrong way and shoot your heads off—and then I would lose the machines." He smiled again. "And now, madamoiselle, perhaps you will have coffee with me while the machines are prepared?"

O'Malley and Kern were escorted out by several of the officers. Eve was left in the room with Sun Nan and Ahmed, Mustafa and a man who came in the door as the others left. He was dressed in the same garb as the two Lazzes at the front door, but he looked even fiercer than they and wore a bright purple coat instead of a black one. A long-barrelled rifle was slung over one shoulder and a jewelled curved sword hung from the red sash at his waist. He is medieval, Eve thought, one of Saladin's men.

"My friend and chief of my bodyguard, Colonel Osman," said Mustafa. "Unfortunately he speaks nothing but Turkish." He said something to Osman and the latter smiled extravagantly under his extravagant moustache and made some reply. "He paid you a compliment."

"What was that?"

"He said he would like to take you to bed."

"In America men take that as a compliment to themselves," said Eve. "Tell the Colonel I am not flattered."

But Mustafa was not interested in acting as interpreter, especially in front of Sun Nan and Ahmed. He shouted an order and at once the door opened and a young officer stood there. He gestured at the Chinese and the midget, and the officer led them out of the room. Though summarily dismissed, both Sun Nan and Ahmed left with dignity.

"You will not harm Monsieur Sun Nan?" said Eve.
"He is very necessary to my trip to China."

"He will not be harmed."

"And Monsieur Ahmed? I shouldn't want him harmed,
either."

"You are a demanding woman, madamoiselle."

"If, as you say, there is to be a place for women in the
new Turkey, you will find they will be demanding, too."

Mustafa smiled, once more trying his heavy charm. He
had been successful with women, but he was never completely at ease with the educated ones; there would always
be traces in him of the provincial upstart from Salonika.
"You are fortunate Colonel Osman cannot understand
what you just said." Osman flashed his many-toothed
smile, the idiot grin of the uncomprehending. "I think he
would cut your throat instead of taking you into his bed.
He is a very old-fashioned Moslem."

An orderly brought thick coffee and small sweet cakes
and honey. Mustafa drank only the coffee, but Osman
wolfed down cakes and spoonfuls of honey that smeared
his thick moustache. Eve sipped the coffee, disliking its
thick sweetness, and ate a cake. She was watching Mustafa
closely as he kept wiping his face with a handkerchief.
Once he shivered violently and the cup rattled in its saucer in his hand.

"Malaria," he said, as he saw Eve watching him. "This
is a harsh country of ours. When I win our war, that will
be only the start of my struggle."

"If you don't win, what happens then?"

"Certain of my friends will cut my throat. Before my
enemies can do it. They call me Kemal, which means perfect. But not everyone thinks I am." He put down his
coffee, the cup rattling once again in the saucer. "Let us
go and wait for the Greeks."

"You are sure they will come this morning?"

"They will come. They are winning at present and in
wars the winning side is always predictable. That's the
only hope for those who are losing."

They walked through the town, Eve, Mustafa, Colonel

Ogman and the two bodyguards. It was the shank of the night, the air motionless, the heat a country-wide blanket. Eve remembered a night earlier in the summer in Kwei-chow when she had gone tiger hunting with her father. It had seemed dangerous then, but she had been excited by the prospect rather than frightened. But this was a different sort of hunt: Bede and Kern were going hunting men. And she was afraid for them.

They came to the edge of town, stood in the waning moonlight looking east for the new day. A mosque stood behind them, its minaret a flagless mast. Eve wondered if Mustafa was fighting for Islam, but supposed not; he did not look a religious man. He took something from the pocket of his tunic and she saw his hand fidgeting with a gold amulet of some sort. At least he was superstitious, which was some encouragement. She was looking for weaknesses in him, something that she might play on if she had to plead for the release of their aeroplanes.

The planes had been brought up from the fields, were parked in the dusty square just across from the mosque and beneath some scrawny plane trees. Kern was supervising the draining of petrol from the spare tanks of his own and O'Malley's machines; O'Malley had dismantled the Lewis guns and was now loading the Vickers guns on both machines. Sun Nan and Ahmed stood off on the edge of the square, their guardian officer with them. O'Malley went across to Sun Nan, spoke to him, then came over to Eve. Kern followed him.

"I've told Sun Nan that if the Baron and I should be shot down, he is to see you get to Hunan."

He spoke with the casualness of a man who had gone out far too often on a flight like this. She tried to keep the apprehension out of her voice. "Be careful, Bede. And you too, Baron."

"We shan't beat the Greeks if we're careful," said Kern. "We might save the machines and ourselves, but we'd still have to go up again tomorrow. And perhaps the next day and the next. We can't afford that sort of delay."

"What are they saying?" Mustafa sounded patient, as if

he appreciated that this might be some sort of farewell. "Please speak in French."

"If the Baron and I are shot down, General," said O'Malley, "we want Madamoiselle Tozer and Monsieur Sun to be allowed to fly on today."

"No promises," said Mustafa. "If your machines are shot down, I may need hers."

"But her father's life is in danger! She must be in China by a certain date—she will tell you how it is—"

"I don't want to hear." The amulet clinked in his fingers. "I am sorry for whatever troubles Madamoiselle Tozer has. But my country comes first. Good luck."

In the east the sky began to pale, the night dying. The edge of the world began to take shape, nightmare country coming out of the darkness. Bare hills, rocky slopes that grew nothing, dry river-bed, ruins left by an earthquake: Eve wondered why anyone should fight over such territory. Strips of cloud turned red, like blood-stained bandages: the morning was ominously quiet, as if death had already touched it. O'Malley put out his hand to Eve.

"Good luck," said he, who needed it.

Kern kissed her hand, clicked his heels. "We'll shoot them down. Sixty-three machines shot down between the two of us—what chance do the Greeks stand?"

"Sixty-four," said O'Malley. "I still claim you."

They were still speaking in French and Mustafa said, "I am impressed. Shoot down another three each today. There are only six of them. The Greeks are in for a surprise on this dawn patrol."

The two pilots walked across to their planes. Eve watched them, suddenly cold in the heat of the early morning. Had it been like this for each of them every morning of the late war? The dawn patrol: the phrase had a death-ring to it, a hint of men going blindfolded to a firing squad.

3

The two Bristols took off into the growing light, lifting the blood-red sun over the rim of the hills with them as they climbed. O'Malley led the way and Kern followed him as they climbed steeply to get height before the Greeks appeared. They headed east, into the sun; the great red ball and the two tiny black crosses drew together, moths into the biggest flame of all. Kern kept his face averted from the blazing sky, saving his eyes. He looked south and west, where the Greeks should come from, but there was no sign of them. They were late, if they were coming at all, either cockily confident or inexperienced. He hoped they would be the former: shooting down novice pilots was too easy, somehow dishonourable.

At 12,000 feet they levelled off, sat like eagles in the shining galleries of sky. The air was much cooler up here and Kern was glad of his flying suit. He felt the weariness slide off him with the sweat that had swamped him on the ground. But it was more than just the air that was invigorating him. He had felt like this on other mornings, but now the feeling was heightened, there was almost a sexual edge to it.

Did the suicide feel like this in the moment he put the gun to his temple? Once, long ago as a child, he had tried to hang himself: he could not remember now the reason, except for desire at what was his world then. His English governess had cut him down, scolded him but had not told his parents, had berated him for how selfish and ungrateful he was that he did not love his parents and the world they had made for him. Yet now he wanted to die because that world was gone. The English governess, as the English so often were, had been right: he had not been properly grateful for the Germany of those days. He had had plenty of time to think about that fact in the past two years; but an honourable way of dying had not

presented itself till now. He wondered if he would be
properly grateful for the next world, if God was a Junker,
as his father had always claimed.

He came back from the past, saw O'Malley waggle his
wings and point. Coming out of the south-west, flying at
no more than 5000 feet, were five aircraft in V-formation,
with a sixth plane riding a couple of thousand feet above
them. Well, there was at least one experienced pilot
among the Greeks; Kern had flown in such a pattern himself on the Western Front. He moved in beside O'Malley
and the two Bristols banked to come down out of the sun
on the unsuspecting Greeks. He remembered a story his
uncle, the diplomat, had told him, of how every year the
storks flew south from the rivers and marshes of Russia,
Poland and Roumania and how every year the eagles
waited for them here in the skies of Anatolia. The eagles,
his uncle had said, might have a bloody battle but they always won.

Kern recognized the planes now, four SE$_5$'s and two
Sopwith Camels. He opened his mouth in a shout as he
began to dive, tasting the wind and the irony: two British
planes, one flown by an Englishman, the other by a German, hurtling down out of the sun to shoot down six
British aircraft given by the British government to a
British ally. He shot a glance across at O'Malley, wondering if the Englishman was capable of appreciating irony,
but he was too intent on the target below. Kern looked
into his Aldis sight, forgetting irony, regret for a lost
world, everything but the kill.

He opened the throttle, going down faster than
O'Malley. The wind tore at him, pressing his goggles
against his face, forcing his lips back into savage, humourless grin: it was the frenzy of another sort of love-
making, one you could never explain to a woman. He
could feel the plane juddering as it built up speed in the
dive; a screeching storm blew past him, deafening even
through the earmuffs of his helmet. He saw the Greeks
begin to scatter, turning frantically as they sighted the enemy (who could he be? The Nationalists had no aero-

planes!) coming down out of the sky above them. An SE5 was suddenly in Kern's sight, desperately trying to bank and climb to get height. Kern put his finger on the gun-button, pressed, saw the pilot throw up an arm. That was what he always hated, the sight of the pilot or gunner actually being hit: the kill should always be impersonal, just the machine going down. He saw smoke bloom out from the fuselage, a red-streaked black flower. One more down: 33 kills.

He pulled back on the stick, eased off on the throttle as he saw the ground quickly coming up at him. He was out of practice, he must have pulled out too sharply; he was being forced down into his seat, a heavy weight, that of his blood, his bones, his flesh, was being shoved down into his stomach. His eyes began to glaze over, the world went grey, his jaw was forced open, he knew he was going to faint. And die.

But the souls of men, sometimes, die more easily than their bodies. His hands held the spade-grip of the stick as the plane quivered, threatened to split apart; then the nose came up, the quivering slid out through the tail-assembly. His eyes cleared, his stomach lightened and unwound, he closed his aching jaw with a bite that snapped his teeth together. Then he saw the shreds fly off his top wing as the high-flying Greek, the one riding high above the V-formation, came in behind him, guns blazing. Again his hands and feet worked of their own accord, wanting him to stay alive.

He opened the throttle again, climbed into a half-loop, did a half-roll and came down again in a dive on top of the Greek; he might be out of practice but he felt a thrill, knowing he had done a perfect Immelmann turn that the Greek pilot hadn't expected. The SE5 was there in his sight, a sitting duck: he pressed the button and the bullets went into the plane, fifty or sixty of them, blowing pieces off it as if it were coming apart a square inch at a time. The Greek rolled to starboard, went down in a spin; Kern went down after him, keeping him in sight all the way. Smoke and flame began to come out of the SE5; it went

down, a flying pyre, and hit the ground in a deep wadi; a
tree of smoke suddenly grew out of the depression, a black
oak above the dead Greek. Kern went in through the
smoke, only 50 feet above the ground, looked up as he
began to climb again. He *was* out of practice, was doing
foolish things this morning: he should never have lost so
much height. But the pilots above him must be inexperienced: none of them had followed him down. Then he
saw why. There were three remaining Greek planes
(O'Malley must have downed one) and they were too
busy concentrating on O'Malley to worry about the Bristol coming up at them from below.

O'Malley was twisting and turning, diving about the
sky in a marvellous exhibition of flying. Kern held the
controls between his knees while he changed the drum on
the Vickers; he continued climbing, keeping wide of the
dog-fight, hoping O'Malley could survive till he could go
in and help him. Then the gun was reloaded and it was
time to rejoin the fight.

He had climbed above the other four planes. He saw
O'Malley do an Immelmann, the professional in him admitting that it was every bit as good as his own. O'Malley
came down on the tail of a Camel, put a burst into it and
the Camel suddenly flipped over and went tumbling down
in a spin, smoke trailing from it in long streamers, a discarded bouquet falling out of the shining sky. Kern picked
out an SE5 that was closing in on O'Malley; the Englishman seemed unaware of it. The German took the Bristol
down in a shallow dive; but the Greek had seen him coming, climbed steeply to his right. Kern went after him, but
this pilot was a good one. The two planes drew each
other about the sky in steep banks, rolls, climbs and
dives; Kern felt the blood rolling in his head, his intestines
twisting, it was far too long since he had done anything
like this. Then suddenly the SE5 was only 30 yards in
front of him, big as an airship. He pressed the button and
once again he saw the pilot in front of him throw up an
arm. He went over the top of the Greek as the latter's aircraft slipped away in a dive. He felt again the sickness

that had hit him previously; suddenly he did not want to kill these men; he was the one who should die. This was not his war; it was beyond him to be a mercenary. He looked down, saw the SE5 in the last few hundred feet of its dive; from 4000 feet up he imagined the scream of its engine, the prayers of its pilot, but he looked away in the moment before impact. He began to climb again, all at once feeling lost in the sky he had thought he knew so well.

He saw O'Malley still twisting and turning, trying to avoid the last of the SE5's. The second Camel stood off, circling around the invisible globe in which the Bristol and the SE5 wove their invisible pattern. Twice O'Malley did a beautiful manoeuvre, came down on the tail of the SE5; each time the Greek got away from him. Then Kern saw O'Malley peel off, realized why the Englishman hadn't got his kill: his gun was jamming. The pilot of the Camel must have come to the same realization at the same moment: he decided to join the fight. He flipped over awkwardly and came down on the Bristol; O'Malley took evasive action, but now both Greeks were coming at him. He climbed steeply, saw Kern, waved frantically to him, banged his fist on his gun.

Kern, hating what he had to do, rolled his plane over and went down in a screaming dive. He saw the Camel go under him, saw the frightened face of the pilot look up at him; but he hadn't pressed the button, he went by the Camel with only feet to spare and he was still diving, no help at all now to O'Malley. He pulled back on the stick, abruptly angry with himself; he pulled back too sharply, felt himself black out. But again his hands had saved him; the plane climbed out of its dive and the black fog turned grey, then was gone. He looked up, seeing nothing for the moment; then saw O'Malley, gun working again, shoot down the last SE5. That left only the surviving Camel.

Kern, still climbing, saw the pilot of the Camel pull away as O'Malley, hungry it seemed for another kill, banked to come in at him. The Camel's turn was too shallow; it left it right in O'Malley's sight. But again the Bristol's gun jammed; it went in over the Camel, almost taking off the top wing; the Greek fluttered away as if his plane had no weight. Kern saw O'Malley gesticulating at him to go after the Camel; but he knew that he couldn't. The Greek pilot knew nothing about fighting in the air: he was a complete novice, should never have been sent on this patrol. He put the Camel into a steep dive, high-tailing it for home, and Kern let him go. O'Malley flew up alongside him, only thirty or forty feet away, and threw up both hands in exasperation.

They went down together, landed and rolled up towards the square in front of the mosque. They had been in the air only three-quarters of an hour, but it was now bright daylight, the morning already hot. For the first time Kern, as he came in to land, saw that the town was the close rear echelon of a considerable army force. Trucks and artillery ringed the town, barely out of sight in shallow wadis; sandbagged machine-gun emplacements were placed strategically on the hillsides; infantry were dug in in a wide circle below the town; a regiment of cavalry was camped on the far side of the mosque. Mustafa Kemal was not the sort of general who remained a long way behind his troops.

A crowd of townsmen and soldiers thronged the edges of the square as the two Bristols came to a stop and cut their engines. Kern, already sweating in his flying suit, got down as O'Malley came across to him.

"Why the hell didn't you shoot down that Camel? Has your gun jammed, too?"

"No." He wasn't going to explain, not now with Mustafa Kemal and the Turkish officers coming across to them.

"Then why, for Christ's sake? We'll have to go after him—"

Then Mustafa had arrived, took the hand of each of them and shook it warmly. "Magnificent! You were true professionals—you made them look like beginners! But why did you spare the last one?"

O'Malley looked at Kern, who said nothing. Then he said, "Our guns jammed, General. It happens sometimes."

"You must find him and destroy the machine. While they have one aeroplane and pilot left—"

"He was a novice," said Kern. "He knew nothing about aerial fighting."

"What has that got to do with it?" Then Mustafa seemed to become aware of the tension between the German and the Englishman. "Don't you believe in killing novices, Baron? Is that why Germany lost her war?"

Kern saw Eve with Sun Nan and Ahmed on the edge of the group of officers. Behind them the men of the town and the soldiers pressed closer, their faces still bright with the excitement of what they had just seen in the air above them. They had just witnessed a new type of war to them; somewhere behind the mosque the cavalry horses whinnied, but no one heard them. People pressed in on Kern, bruising him with their enquiries if not their fists. All his life he had been accustomed to the privacy of his class. One did not declare one's principles to a crowd of strangers.

"I refuse to answer that, General."

The pride and arrogance of the two men seemed to push everyone else back. The brightness faded from the faces of the onlookers; they did not understand what was being said, but they recognized the oldest war there was, the clash between two men. Eve took a pace forward, but O'Malley put an arm in front of her. Kern was grateful to the Englishman: Eve was the only woman among a thousand Moslem men here in the square. He did not want her on his side at this moment.

Mustafa said, the French rough on his tongue with Turkish anger, "You forget your circumstances, Baron, if not your place. I want that sixth aeroplane destroyed."

"Then someone else does it. This is not my war, General."

"Tell me where their airfield is," said O'Malley. "I'll refuel and go looking for the machine."

"No," said Mustafa, his voice too definite. He wishes for privacy, too, Kern thought, he has more to lose than I have if I refuse his order. "Your gun is jammed. Baron von Kern will destroy that sixth aeroplane. None of you will leave here till he has done so."

"General—" Eve pushed against O'Malley's arm; but Mustafa paid no attention to her. Colonel Osman growled angrily and the closest ranks of soldiers and townsmen looked at her in amazement. What was the world coming to, that a woman should expect to speak in a council of men? There were rumours that Mustafa Kemal planned certain freedoms for women, but no one here in Anatolia believed them.

O'Malley said, "May we talk to the Baron, General? No one doubts his courage, you saw how he fought up there. If he doesn't want to go after that machine, I'm sure his reasons are good ones."

Don't plead for me, Kern said silently. He didn't look at O'Malley, but at Eve behind him. He could see the distress in her face, the realization that they might have come to a full stop in the race to save her father. But whose life was the more important, that of Bradley Tozer or the unknown young Greek pilot? A man's life was of no less value because he was nameless. Of course, all the men he had killed in the war had been nameless, but that had been different. He had been fighting for something he had believed in, still believed in. But this war . . . He was not the sort of German who joined foreign legions, the misfits who worked off their frustration in what they liked to call adventure.

"If I can find the machine on the ground, I'll destroy it," he said. "But if the pilot takes to the air, I shall come back."

"I don't understand you, Baron." Mustafa was a proud, vain man, but no so stubborn that he did not recognize the value of a compromise; the thing to be done was to get this German back into his aeroplane and off the ground while the crowd, among whom, he was sure, there were some doubters of himself, was still here in the square. "War is war. I'm sure the Greeks recognize that as much as we do."

"Perhaps not all of them. They were more renowned as philosophers than as warriors."

"I'll get your machine refuelled and your drums reloaded," said O'Malley, eager to have Kern airborne before dialectics got in the way again. "Ten minutes."

The crowd stirred again, fell back to the edges of the square. They had not understood the argument, but they understood some sort of resolution had been reached. Kern gave his flying suit to Sun Nan, knowing he would be doing no high flying on this sortie. The crowd murmured appreciatively as he and Mustafa Kemal walked across to the aeroplane where O'Malley had two mechanics refilling the tanks. It was good to have allies, even a single German.

"You must understand, Baron," said Mustafa. "I am fighting more than one war. I have as many enemies inside my country as I have outside it. But someday Europe will be grateful that I kept Turkey for the Turks."

"I understand your patriotism, General. It's endemic with us Germans, a disease, our enemies call it. But I have a confession to make and I ask you to keep it to yourself. I have suddenly grown sick of killing men."

"You are fortunate your war is over, Baron. I can't afford myself the luxury of *not* killing them. Good luck, I hope for your sake the Greek pilot does not attempt to get off the ground. But I want his machine destroyed—while they have even one aeroplane they have an advantage over me. Destroy it. Otherwise, I promise you, your party will not leave Malavan."

Kern got into the Bristol and O'Malley, inspecting the upper wing, said, "We must have done a good repair job. Everything held together. How were the ailerons?"

He hadn't really noticed; but they must have worked perfectly. "I did as good an Immelmann as I've ever done."

"Good enough. I got four grenades for you—that's the best I could do at short notice. Strafing may not be enough."

"I've never ground-bombed before. I must learn to throw straight."

"Well—" O'Malley looked at him. "Don't do anything bloody silly. Good luck."

Kern took off, climbing steeply into the bright hot morning. Major Arif, the officer who had first met them last night, had given him an approximate co-ordinate of where they suspected the Greeks had their air base. He checked the map spread out on his knee, looked for landmarks, saw the Greek trucks and artillery and horse wagons camped in depressions among the hills, then found the long twisting road he was looking for. He knew the Greeks had no air-craft guns, so he did not have to fly high, just high enough to be beyond the reach of accurate rifle and machine-gun fire. There seemed to be movement down on the ground among the trucks and artillery, but he took no notice of it. He was intent only on getting done the job that had to be done.

Five minutes' flying: he must be approaching his target. War had suddenly become so swift: he thought of his father who had taken weeks to reach Verdun, only to die within hours of his arrival, of the Hittites who had marched through these hills at a snail's pace. He was grateful that he had so little time to think. He went down low, risking fire from the long convoy of marching men and artillery coming up the road; he wanted to come in on the airfield without warning, before the pilot had time to get his machine off the ground. It was always good military tactics to do that; but now it was also philosophical tactics. The machine, not the pilot, had to be killed.

The troops below, expecting to be gunned, were diving into the rocks and bushes on either side of the road. Some of them were firing at him; bullets thumped into the Bristol's belly. But he didn't climb above the fire, knowing in a moment he was going to go over the ridge ahead of him and come down on the village where the Camel should be parked. He raised the nose of the Bristol a trifle, went over the rim of the ridge with only feet to spare, and there was the village below him, the Camel parked in a field by a row of houses at the edge of it.

He had been wrong in not expecting the Greeks to be waiting for him. He had not yet reached the village when the machine-guns opened up on him. He went through a chain-fence of fire that tore strips off his wings, snapped wires, sent splinters flying off his propeller. He felt a sharp tug on his thigh, thought he actually *saw* bullets coming up through the floor of the cockpit at him. The fury of the reception disconcerted him; he was over the Camel, having fired only one long burst into it, before he thought of the grenades in the string bag hanging from the hook on the instrument panel. He went up, banking sharply, knowing he was making himself a bigger target to the machine-gunners below but determined to get the job over and done with. Or his life over and done with: he felt the taste of suicide again.

He came back in, the Vickers blazing. He pulled the pin from a grenade with his teeth, held it in the same hand that clutched the stick. On the edge of his vision he could see the machine-gunners, a dozen guns placed to catch him in their cross-fire. He went in as low as he dared. Bullets tore into the Bristol, threatening to take it apart; but all he was aware of now was the Camel on the ground ahead of him. He saw the bullets of the Vickers machine-stitch the ground towards the Camel; then he flung the grenade straight down when he was some distance short of the grounded plane. His guess at the parabola the grenade would describe was perfect: at 120 miles an hour he scored a bull's-eye on the Camel. He pulled back the stick and went on up in a steep climb away from the pursuing bullets. He looked down, saw the Camel burning, smoke enveloping it. The job was done.

He continued climbing, set course for Malavan. His thigh was paining him and he put his hand on it and felt the blood. The cockpit seemed to be full of holes; the wind was coming in at him from all angles. The engine stammered, ran rough, and he knew something in it had been hit.

He flew over the hills, nursing the plane. Then he looked down and saw the convoy still moving up the road, the long line being thickened and lenghtened as more trucks, artillery and horse wagons came down out of the depressions in the hills and joined for the attack on Malavan. Kern suddenly felt very tired and wondered how much longer he would need to fly before the plane ran out of fuel and he crashed, ending everything.

4

"The problem is," said General Meng, sitting back in his chair, running a loving hand over his hair, "we don't even know if your daughter is on her way here with the statue."

"Can't you send a wireless message?" Bradley Tozer ran a hand over his own head, but worriedly, not lovingly. He had lost track of the number of days he had been held captive, but he knew that the deadline must be getting close. He was being treated with politeness and consideration, almost as an honoured guest in the tradition of Chinese hospitality; but he knew now that he was going to have his throat cut, be beheaded or be shot if Eve did not arrive here at Szeping in time. "Send a man in to Changsha, have him send a message to my daughter at the Savoy Hotel in London."

"Ah, the Savoy!" said Colonel Buloff, slurping up the watery fruit salad his wife had made. "In Moscow and St. Petersburg we used to hear about that marvellous hotel from our diplomat friends. I applied once to be our military attaché in London, just so that I could dine at the Savoy. But they said I was not diplomatic enough to be a diplomat, as if that were necessary."

Meng smiled. "Are you not happy with the food and accommodations in my *yamen*, Colonel?"

"It couldn't be better," said Madame Buloff who, if no

cook, was a better diplomat than her husband. "Everything is relative."

"Not in a brothel, surely." Tozer had heard nothing further from the Buloffs on the possibility of his escaping and had given up hope that they would help him. "General, why don't you send a wireless message?"

"A copy of every message that goes in or out of the cable office in Changsha goes to that dog Chang. If my message was allowed to go through and your daughter replied to it, he would know where to intercept her. We shall have to be patient, Mr. Tozer."

Tozer looked across the table at Madame Buloff. For the past two days he had been allowed out of his room and brought in here to dine with the General and the Buloffs. Madame Buloff had persuaded Meng to let her do the cooking ("To keep me occupied," she had said) and though Tozer thought she must be the worst cook south of the Arctic Circle, her Russian-style meals had been a change from the *kua mein* that had been his sole dish since his capture. Even with the thought that one might be dead in ten days, or so, one could grow God damned tired of noodles and red peppers. But even if she couldn't cook, Madame Buloff might still have her uses.

"Why not send Madame Buloff back to Shanghai to dispatch a cable to my daughter?"

"You are beginning to sound desperate, Mr. Tozer," said Meng.

"I am concerned for my neck. But I also want to relieve you of the misfortunes that have befallen you since you lost your statue."

"That is the Chinese side of you speaking. It must be a relief to you not to be one hundred per cent American, as so many of your countrymen boast they are."

"I am from Boston, General. Good manners are as natural to us as they are to you." And we don't cut our guests' throats, at least not physically. Metaphorically yes, but then only if they are from New York.

"Would you like to go back to Shanghai, Madame Buloff?"

Madame Buloff, losing patience with her own cuisine, drank the last of her fruit salad. "I should not like to go alone. Perhaps my husband could accompany me?"

"I need your husband here. What good is a military adviser who is far from the military action?"

"There is no action at the moment." The Colonel removed fruit salad from his moustache with a big yellow handkerchief. "We could be back in four or five days. We could pick up the train at Fengsham."

"You forget, Colonel. The train isn't running. It was on your military advice that my men blew up the railway line."

Tozer, despairing once more, went back to finishing his fruit salad. God damn China! Suddenly he hated the country, with all its factional fighting. Why couldn't it get together, be a United States like America? He said snappishly, no longer Bostonian polite, "You *tuchuns* are going to ruin China, General."

Meng shook his head, unoffended by the remark. He understood the American's nervousness and made allowances for it. "The *tuchuns* will always rule China. Our country is too big ever to be ruled by one man or one government. Colonel Buloff's Tsar found that out. His successor will find the same."

"I hope so," said Colonel Buloff and crossed himself, making a strenuous effort to look devout.

"But who will succeed you?" Tozer said to Meng.

"I have sons. A couple of dozen, I am told. I don't intend to die for many years yet, Mr. Tozer, and by then I shall have a favourite son. Perhaps one of Madame Buloff's girls will be his mother. Colonel Buloff can be his godfather, if the boy should decide to become a Christian. Though Christ knows why he should do so, if you will forgive me making a sacrilegious joke."

Tozer knew the power of the *tuchuns,* the war lords. Any good businessman did; for many years they had been the business men's best customers. They were military officials, with rank equal to that of a major-general; they were supposed to be subordinate to their province's civil governor, but there were very few *tuchuns* who paid even lip service to that situation. They had always been powerful of their own right and he was a rare one who was not ambitious to widen both his powers and his domain. General Meng had taken over this wide area of southern Hunan and ran it as his own province. He controlled the farms, the shops, even had his own bank. But he had no cable office.

The General stood up, looked at himself in the big mirror at the end of the room, was satisfied with his looks and the possibility of his immortality. "I must practise my music. Do you sing, Mr. Tozer? Perhaps you could accompany me with the words to a song I am learning. "Apple Blossom Time in Normandy."

"I haven't sung since I was at college."

The General looked disappointed. "Well, stay and drink tea to finish off your meal. I understand Madame Buloff does make very good tea. Was that a typical Russian meal, Madame?"

"Yes," said the cook proudly.

"Then I understand the reason for your revolution."

He went out, leaving both the Buloffs fuming. Tozer looked after him as he paused for a final look at himself in the mirror. You son-of-a-bitch, Tozer thought, you'll probably make some joke when you have my throat cut. Or play some farewell tune on your God damned banjo.

"We have to leave here!" Buloff's voice was a growled whisper somewhere down in his chest. "He's insulting us now!"

"All three of us?" said Tozer. "My offer still stands if you can get me away."

"How do we get away?" Madame Buloff removed a kettle from a small spirit stove on a stand beside her, poured water into a teapot. "This is Russian tea, Mr. Tozer. I hope you like it."

"I shall have to think." The Colonel sat back in his chair, hunching his shoulders and lowering his brows; thinking, with him, seemed to be a physical exercise. "We have no transport, that's the difficulty. Just horses and horse wagons, that's all. We should be caught before we had gone a dozen kilometres. The General's cavalry would catch us."

"Not if you broke the legs of the cavalry horses," said Madama Buloff, pouring tea.

"I couldn't do that!" Even the Colonel was horrified. "I am a cavalry man!"

If anyone gets me out of here, Tozer thought, it is going to be Madame Buloff. I'll be paying ten thousand dollars to a potential horse maimer, but I'll gladly do it, may the SPCA forgive me.

"You shouldn't have blown up the railway line," said the Colonel's wife. "You're worse than the Bolshevists, you're always blowing up things. Your tea, Mr. Tozer."

Tozer took the cup, wishing it were a good cup of coffee. "How far is it to Fengsham?"

"Eighty kilometres," said the Colonel. "I couldn't walk that far. I am a cavalry man. My legs are not made for walking."

They were not made for riding, either. "What about bicycles? I have seen some of the soldiers riding bicycles."

"I couldn't ride a bicycle," said the Colonel's wife, all 250 pounds of her.

This is getting ridiculous, Tozer thought. From another room there came the sound of the General practising his banjo: he was picking his way through the apple orchards of Normandy. "Well, for Christ's sake, come up with *something*! You're the military adviser, Colonel—give us some advice!"

Buloff hunched down again in his chair, sipped his tea, dropped his brows till they hid his beady eyes. There was silence for a while, broken only by the plinking of the strings in the next room. The General had enjoyed Normandy: he was going through it again, withering the blossoms. Tozer drank his tea, thinking now of a good whisky and soda such as he used to have at the Somerset Club before Prohibition had been introduced. Boston seemed a long way away, but suddenly he wanted to go home to it. Madame Buloff, little finger raised delicately, sipped tea and dreamed, perhaps, of being a slim, petite girl in Boston, New York, Normandy, anywhere at all but Russia or China.

Then the Colonel said, "There will be trucks coming up here next week from Shaoshan, bringing rice the General has had to buy. Perhaps we could commandeer one of those. But once we get away from here, we still have to pass through Governor Chang's territory. And he knows I work for the General."

"We'll worry about that when we meet up with Governor Chang," said Tozer, unworried for the Colonel.

In the next room General Meng had begun struggling with a new song. "Ain't We Got Fun," said his stumbling fingers. Syncopation was not his strong suit.

CHAPTER 5

1

Extract from the William Bede O'Malley manuscript:
My eyes seemed to be rolling on ball-bearings of grit and, with the headache I had, if I had been capable of one clear thought it would have been like a lance to a boil. It was God knew how many hours since I had slept; and then only for a couple of hours. In my sleeping-bag in the rose garden on the boundary between Bulgaria and Roumania: in another world and another century, it seemed. I am not susceptible to premonition, yet something told me it was to be some time before I could lie down in comfort for the long, dreamless sleep I craved.

"Are you all right, Bede?" Eve said.

"First rate." I tried to push the sand-hills to the back of my eyes. I was trying to keep up her spirits by disguising how worn out I felt, but I had given her the wrong answer.

"You really enjoyed that fight up there, didn't you? Shooting down those men."

"Jesus Christ, Miss Tozer—" I went back to the formal note so that I could swear at her; I tell you, my mind wasn't working at all well that hot Turkish morning. "Do you want to get to China or don't you?"

"Don't you swear at me, Mr. O'Malley, or you'll get as good as you give."

We were ready to be at each other's throats; but if we had literally done that, I think we'd have both fallen down in sheer exhaustion. We were saved from further snarling by Sun Nan, pouring oil on troubled waters like Confucius on one of his more rhetorical days.

Tom Selleck and Bess Armstrong head a star-studded cast in *High Road To China*—a tale of adventure, intrigue, and romance.

Tom Selleck plays O'Malley, a pilot and war hero running a broken down flying school to try to make ends meet.

Bess Armstrong is Eve Tozer, a globe-trotting millionairess who enlists O'Malley's help to locate her father.

Jack Weston is O'Malley's trusted sidekick and ace mechanic who keeps both their planes and their lives running.

Wilford Brimley portrays Bradley Tozer, the heiress's father, a success-ful munitions inventor who has disappeared somewhere in the Far East.

Robert Morley is Bentik, Tozer's partner who also wants to find the missing millionaire, but for his own, more deadly, reasons.

As a flyer during World War I, O'Malley earned an ace's rank, but since then has fallen on hard times, and bad liquor.

When first approached by heiress Tozer, O'Malley is reluctant to accept her offer, but eventually decides to help her locate her father.

Soon all three are airborne (Selleck, Weston, and Armstrong) taking the fastest way possible to the Far East, or as the title calls it, "the high road to China."

Their journey across two continents is soon interrupted when they enter the domain of Suleiman Khan.

After a slightly unfriendly introduction...

...they are soon made dinner guests of the Waziri leader Suleiman Khan (Portrayed by Brian Blessed).

Suleiman Khan (Brian Blessed) and his mistress Alessa (Cassandra Gava).

Next stop Katmandu...

...and the village where they hope to find her father.

Upon arriving in China, after many death-defying encounters on both the ground and in the air, there is finally time for romance.

"Does bad language show the true man—or woman? Harsh words never solved any problem."

"Jesus Christ!" I said again; then gave up and looked down at Ahmed standing in the plump shadow of the Chinese. "What do we hear from Omar Khayyam?"

"Omar Khayyam was Persian, not Turkish," said the midget.

"Wrong country. Sorry." I really was exhausted, felt I was going to fold up at any moment and slide down beneath the wings of my machine. We were standing between my aeroplane's and Eve's, trying to catch some of the shade from the upper wings. Mustafa Kemal and his officers had retreated to the entrance to the mosque, stood there in the blue shadows discussing war while a *muezzin* leaned from the balcony of the minaret above them and called the faithful to prayer. The *muezzin* had been trying for some time to catch the ear of the faithful but had only just now succeeded in doing so. I have no doubt that the men of Malavan were a religious lot, but it was not every day they had a war right above their roof-tops and they had forgotten Allah while they had watched the aeroplanes. But now they were going into the mosque, though not Mustafa and his officers. Like us, they were waiting for Kern to come back.

"If he doesn't destroy the aeroplane," said Eve, changing the topic, if only slightly, "what do we do?"

"We still have a few days in hand."

"We might need them later. We still have a long way to go."

I wanted to swear again, not at her, but just because I was too tired for any real answers. Then I heard the machine, sick as a bronchial cow, and saw Kern coming up from the south-west. He was at a fair height, but not too high for me to detect at once that he had a very sick engine. Mustafa Kemal and the officers came out of the shadows of the mosque entrance; the late-comers among the faithful paused before going in to their prayers. The *muezzin* had either finished his call or interrupted it; he stood on the minaret balcony and, like the rest of us, looked up at the approaching plane. Coughing and spluttering, its note ragged against my apprehensive ear, it came gliding down. He was going to make it, he had enough height to glide in if he had to, but he could not have gone on flying for another minute.

He put the plane down and the engine died before he had a chance to cut it. The Bristol stopped just short of the square; two donkeys tethered to a pole outside a house brayed and kicked in fright. Kern climbed out, leaned against the wing. Tired though I was, I was the first to reach him. I had run across, pretty certain that Mustafa and his officers, careful of their dignity, would not hurry.

"Did you get the Camel?" He nodded, and I nodded back in satisfaction: at least now we were free to go . . . "What's the matter with the machine?"

"I ran into a lot of fire." Then the others had reached us. Eve put a hand on his arm and he smiled at her. "I am all right, Fräulein."

"You're not! Look at your leg—" She turned to Mustafa. "General, do you have a doctor—?"

Mustafa nodded, but wounds could wait. "Did you destroy the aeroplane, Baron?"

"Yes, General." Kern was pale. He was as exhausted as I was, perhaps more so: emotion and a bullet had also taken their toll of him. "But that is unimportant now. The Greeks are moving up to attack."

"You're sure?"

"General, I have had as much experience of war as you. I know the preparations for an attack when I see them."

Mustafa took the rebuff, but only because he was a professional soldier dealing with a man he recognized as another professional. "How far down the road are they?"

"About fifteen to twenty kilometres."

"They won't attack before late afternoon then, not in this heat. Perhaps they had not intended to attack till tomorrow morning, but they will know you have given their game away."

He snapped some orders to the officers around him and they all left in a hurry, leaving him with only Colonel Osman and the two bodyguards. The *muezzin* had disappeared from his balcony and the last of the townsmen had gone into the mosque. The soldiers around the edge of the square were dispersing under orders from the officers; only some children and a few women remained pinned against the glaring yellow walls of the houses like impaled blackbirds. It seemed to me that the bright hot morning had begun to shimmer with tension.

"You will get the machines ready again, Monsieur O'Malley. We shall need them. In the meantime, Baron, I have sent for a doctor. Will you be able to fly again?"

Kern was holding his thigh with a tight hand, but all he said was, "If I have to."

I said, "We have fulfilled our part of the bargain, General. Our contract was to destroy the six machines—"

"I made no contract. You were dealing with the midget." Mustafa gestured at Ahmed, dismissing him as if he were no more than an irresponsible schoolboy and I had been a fool to make any deal with him. "Your machines will still be very useful. Have them ready."

"We need sleep—"

"We have mechanics. They can repair and service your machines."

"Motor mechanics for lorries and cars. They wouldn't understand an aero engine."

Suddenly he lost his temper. The sweat stood out on his brow and he trembled. "God curse you! I am not concerned for you and your damned machines and whether you fly on to China or wherever you are going! I am fighting a war to save my country—and the machines will be flown to help me win it! Whether you fly them or my own men do, does not matter—they will be ready to fly this afternoon!"

He turned and stalked off, the two bodyguards marching with him. Colonel Osman put his hand to the curved sword at his waist, drew it half out of its scabbard, then slammed it back in. The gesture was enough. Then he, too, stalked off, his long slashed coat swishing like an angry woman's skirt.

"What are we going to do?" Eve's voice was a thin plaint: she sounded on the verge of hopelessness.

"I'm going to get some sleep," I said. "I'm too bloody tired to care any more." Which was suddenly the truth. Lately I had begun to have little respect for the truth, philosophizing that humanity preferred the alternative, any alternative, and a good liar was a better man to listen to than a true gospeller. But that morning I was too tired for lies or philosophy. I could see that I had hurt Eve, but I was even too weary to apologize. "Here comes the doctor, Baron. Get your leg fixed, then get some sleep."

"And when you wake up?" Eve snapped. "What then?"

"Ask Confucius." I waved a hand at Sun Nan. "He's sure to have something to cover the situation."

The doctor, a tiny man with broken teeth, broken French and a small Gladstone bag, took the limping Kern by the arm and led him to the shade in the entrance to the mosque. I got my sleeping-bag out of my plane, looked about, saw a straw-roofed opensided shed at the rear of the nearest house and headed towards it. Then I stopped and looked back at Eve. "It's almost seven-thirty." It was hard to believe: the morning already felt fully baked, done to a turn. "Ask one of the officers to wake me at two o'clock. That will give me a couple of hours to work on the machines before the Greeks attack."

"Goddamn you, O'Malley, how can you be so—so resigned?" Where was the cool lady from Boston?

"Easy. I had four years training for it while you were just filling in your time spending money." And where was the cool gentleman from Oxford?

We stood there on either side of a minefield of abusive words. Sun Nan, picking his way delicately, said, "I think we should find a place to sleep, Miss Tozer. Perhaps there is a good hotel here."

"In a place like this?" Ahmed, a grand hotel man, looked at the stupid Chinese. "Still, I'll find you an inn or something. I am beginning to think this was all a dreadful mistake. Baron von Wangenheim never treated me like this."

He had reached the end of the road as a secret agent, but he was still a good page-boy. He raised his hat to Eve, gestured for her to accompany him and led her and Sun Nan off into the town to find a hotel that might not come up to his standards but would suffice in the circumstances. Eve, on the point of collapse, glanced back at me. There was an opaque glaze to her eyes, as if she had suddenly drowned in hopelessness.

"Eve," I said, as gently as I could, "if something happens, if the Greeks attack, come back here. The Baron and I will get you away, I promise."

She was carrying the hessian-wrapped box under her arm, as she had been ever since we had arrived here. She looked at it, then held it out to me. "Would you look after this for me, Bede?"

There was no reason why she should have given it to me. But I recognized the gesture for what it was: I was exhausted, but not entirely numb to nuances. She was telling me she was still relying on me, despite our differences, to get her to China. I took the box. "Try and sleep. Ahmed will wake you when it's necessary."

"The least I can do," said Ahmed, and led them off. They made a ridiculous trio, with tiny Ahmed, homburg stuck squarely on his head, almost running to stay ahead of the longer-striding Eve and Sun Nan. But I couldn't laugh. They were only a small corner of a much larger picture that couldn't be laughed at.

I crossed to the straw-roofed shed, spread out my sleeping bag and lay down on it, careful to anticipate which way the shade would move. I folded my jacket and spread it over the wooden box: I was probably committing Taoist sacrilege, but Lao-Tze was my pillow and I was glad of him. I slept as soon as I laid my head on him.

A soldier woke me at two in the afternoon. I rolled over, damp with sweat, and looked up at him uncomprehendingly; he gave me a big yellow-toothed smile, but looked no more intelligent than I must have. Then full consciousness came back and I sat up. Kern lay beside me on some army blankets, still asleep, a hand resting protectively on his thigh. I could see the bulge of bandages under his trouser-leg and there were flies holding a meeting on the dried blood on the cloth. I brushed them away; he stirred, but didn't wake up. He looked vulnerable, his handsome face cobwebbed with more than pain: doubt perhaps? I wondered why he had come here to sleep beside me; he wouldn't have done so, if he had known he was going to expose himself so much in sleep. I turned away: I've always felt you should respect the sleeping as much as the dead. They are entitled to their secrets.

I stood up, feeling giddy, felt even giddier when I looked out at the square and beyond it to the distant hills trembling in the heat as if an earthquake were rushing on the town. The one consolation was that the Greeks would not attack. War in high summer in certain regions has a certain civilization to it. Or it did in those days.

I rolled the hessian-wrapped box up in my sleeping-bag, took it across and stuffed it into the cockpit of my machine. I knew it would be safe there. Moslems are harsh on thieves and I guessed Mustafa Kemal might be the harshest of them all.

Even with the help of two mechanics from the transport pool, it took me almost three hours to repair Kern's machine. One of the petrol feed pipes had been badly dented but, miraculously, not broken; fuel had been getting to the engine only in a trickle. Another bullet had clipped a bearing and a connecting-rod had gone through one of the cylinders. The propeller was chipped and splintered, but it wasn't necessary to replace it with the spare one we had brought. I had the uncomfortable feeling that other emergencies lay ahead of us, that the road from here to China was going to get rougher and rougher.

I had just finished, once again wishing that George Weyman was still with me, when over in the shed I saw Kern sit up. Streaked with grease, uncomfortable in a total skin of sweat, I walked across to stand beneath the now-slanting shade of the roof. The sun was getting low and I wondered if the Greeks would attack in the next half-hour. If they did they would come right out of the face of the sun.

Kern stood up, taking all his weight on one leg. "It is just a flesh wound—the bullet went right through." He leaned on a rough walking-stick the doctor or someone had given him. There were sweat-stains in the armpits of his shirt and some dirt on his face, but he made me look as if I had just come out into the open after ten years down a coal mine. The aristocrat's look, I guess. And now he was awake the look of pain or doubt, whatever it was, had gone. He stared towards the distant hills, now becoming more solid and seemingly closer, as if the sun, now beyond them, was pushing them towards us. "Do you think the Greeks will come this evening?"

"I don't know. Their artillery might give us a pounding during the night—depends how much ammunition they have. But I don't think they'll send their infantry in before dawn. I hope not."

"We should move the machines from here, in case they do start shelling during the night."

"I'm having all the tanks filled." I nodded towards the three Bristols; the mechanics had brought up a truck and were filling the tanks from several big drums. "Once we take-off we're heading for Aleppo."

"In Syria? The General won't like that." He shook his head. "He won't trust us alone in the machines. He'll probably send someone up with us to make sure we put down where he tells us to."

"Whoever he sends up will have to straddle those spare tanks in the rear cockpits the way Sun Nan did when we got away from the Countess. A nice steep bank and they'd fall out."

He wasn't shocked. "I don't believe you are that callous, Herr O'Malley."

I knew I wasn't: at least up to a point. "I might be if it were just my own life I was thinking of. I'm still not quite sure if Miss Tozer would want us to kill someone to save her father. She told me she'd once killed a man who tried to rape her, but she seemed squeamish about what we had to do this morning."

"Are you experienced in women, Herr O'Malley?"

"I've had some experience of their bodies." What man ever admits to less? The proud cock crowing. "But I'm a virgin when it comes to their minds."

"Most of us are." It was an admission I didn't expect him to make. But he was no longer the man who had passed up the tea dance in Constance to fly to China with us. That amateur gigolo would have admitted no ignorance of women. Nor would he have spared novice fighters in the air.

"Do you feel up to walking? Let's go and find the hotel where Miss Tozer is staying. A bath might make us feel better."

We found the hotel without trouble. It was the only one in town; in those days there were not many travellers in Anatolia who could afford to stay in a hotel. The bath was a hollowed-out-rock in an out-house, an ancient tub worn smooth by time and countless bare arses. Alexander the Great might have bathed in it on his way through to the Cilician Gates and the Battle of Issus. O'Malley the Least soaked in it on his way to China, came out refreshed, the long-dormant Oxford imagination spiced by the bath-salts of history. Kern got into it, keeping his wounded leg out of the water. Like any fourteen-year-old I was gratified to see that he, the ladies' man, was no better hung than I. We never grow up, not down there in the crotch.

Eve and Sun Nan had already bathed. We had dinner in the hotel. Ahmed sat at the table with us, two cushions on his chair, and made the hotel-keeper raise his standards about four classes. The roast goat was tough but edible; the wine was rough but not lethal; but the dessert was sweet and tasty. "What's this called?" Eve asked.

"Kadin Göbegi," said Ahmed. "In English it would be called Lady's Navel. My apologies, madamoiselle."

"Have you tasted it before, Baron?" Eve said, face straight.

"Not in Turkey," said Kern, face equally straight.

Then we all laughed, even Sun Nan, and all the tension of the day had gone. We heard a lot of movement outside in the street, but we shut the world out of the dining room for an hour or two. Nobody came to disturb us, too busy with their preparations for tomorrow's battle. Then at ten o'clock Mustafa Kemal sent for us.

As we went down the main street with our escort we saw the reason for all the movement we had heard: the town was being evacuated. People were stacking their belongings on wagons and trucks, on bicycles and donkeys and camels. It seems to me I have been watching the same scene now for fifty years: the world is always on the move, someone is always fleeing: do their feet spin the world, turning it into a tread-mill? And why do the stacked belongings of all refugees always look the same: does misery come in job lots?

There were no loud voices, just a nervous murmur and the occasional crying of a child that would be immediately hushed, as if the fleeing townsfolk feared they might be heard by the Greeks somewhere out there in the hills in the silent, still night. There were few soldiers; we learned later they had already moved down to forward positions in the wadis below the town. No lights showed and all the figures were just black shapes in the gloom; one had to read in the slump of shoulders or the stillness of a crouched figure what despair we were passing through. A man came out of a shop carrying a sewing-machine, placed it carefully in a donkey-drawn wagon, covered it with a blanket; then he picked up two small girls, threw them carelessly into the wagon and went back into the house to decide what other treasures he should take with him. Three women came down the street, each carrying a mattress on her back: "Whores," Ahmed whispered to me and didn't explain how he knew their trade: they were not the only ones taking their mattresses with them that night. An old man and woman had already begun their flight, pushing a baby-carriage ahead of them; they must have been among the wealthy of the town to have afforded such a luxury, yet it contained only a big brass coffee pot and a few odds and ends; one wondered what had happened to the baby that had been wheeled in the pram when there had still been sap and hope and laughter in the couple who were now too old for any of that. We came to Mustafa's headquarters and, selfishly, I was glad to turn my back on the silent misery.

Mustafa Kemal must have slept for a few hours. He certainly looked fresher, more vital, than he had this morning. Or perhaps the thought of tomorrow's battle was just the adrenalin he needed. Later, when he became Kemal Ataturk, I would read that he would ·become quickly bored with inactivity.

"The aeroplanes are ready, I am told. And you have filled the petrol tanks, Monsieur O'Malley. Where are you planning to fly to?"

"Always be prepared, General. It's an old Boy Scout motto."

"It is an old trickster's motto, too. Don't try any tricks, m'sieu." There were half a dozen other officers in the battle room, including Colonel Osman. I don't know if all or any of them understood French, but they all nodded threateningly as if they all agreed with what their General had said. Colonel Osman bared his teeth and I waited for him to bare his sword, but the dental threat was enough. Mustafa did not look at them, just stared at me to make sure his message had sunk in, which it had, right to the bone. Then he went on: "You and the Baron will take-off an hour before dawn and bomb the Greek artillery positions. I have had my ordnance men make some bombs. They are rough and they weight only two kilogrammes each, but they will be effective enough if you aim them properly. You will carry a dozen bombs each and you will take one of my men in each machine to aim and throw the bombs for you."

"We can't do that, General." I tried to argue calmly, to dispel the idea that I had any tricks in mind. "We could never get the machines off the ground with all that extra weight—"

"Then you will have to drain some of the weight out of your petrol tanks—that's the only solution, isn't it?" He sounded reasonable, as if trying to help me solve our problem; but I knew it had already been solved before I had voiced it. "You shouldn't be in the air for more than twenty minutes—"

"We'll have to find the artillery positions. We could easily miss them in the dark—"

"We know exactly where they are. We have had spies come in from their lines. There will be no cloud, so the area will be moonlit. You will follow the main road to a certain point where there is a village. North of there, behind the ridge that runs up from the village, is their artillery."

"What if their guns open up before we take-off? How can you be so sure they won't put down a barrage before dawn? They could blow our machines right out of that square—"

"Monsieur O'Malley, in the war neither side can afford to be as extravagant as the Allies and the Germans were on the Western Front. Your generals, both sides, wasted shells as if they were men. This is a more economical war, m'sieu. They will open fire with their artillery just before their infantry attack at dawn."

"Then will you let Madamoiselle Tozer take-off? Her machine mustn't be damaged, she must be allowed to fly on to China, with or without me and the Baron."

"No," said Eve, and behind Mustafa the officers looked at her in amazement. How was a woman allowed to speak in a council of men? Allah must be sleeping. "I have an alternative proposition, my General."

"You are fortunate, madamoiselle," said Mustafa, smiling. "I am the only man on this side of the table who would ever listen to a proposition from a woman. A military proposition, that is."

"Allow Monsieur O'Malley and Baron von Kern to take-off with full tanks but no passengers. Let them drop the bombs themselves. Could you get the machines into the air with the extra weight of the bombs, Bede?"

"Just. But it's worth a try."

"How could I trust them?" Mustafa was still smiling; he was not taking Eve seriously. "They might even drop the bombs on *me*."

"Monsieur Sun Nan and I shall stay here with my machine as your hostage. Can you see the ridge from the town, the one the Greek guns are behind?"

"Not at night." He was beginning to take her seriously now: "But if the bombs were dropped in the right place, the explosions would silhouette the ridges."

"As soon as they have dropped all their bombs—and you will be able to count the explosions—let me take-off in my machine. Let me join them and let us fly on. I *have* to get to China—my father's life depends on it—"

Some of the officers understood what she had been saying. They looked at Mustafa, measuring him for the future: and he knew it. I learned a long time later he had a weakness for women: it was said that Fikriye, his cousin, selfish, unstable, a mind as empty as a balloon, could always get closer to him than any of his generals. To give in to this *foreign* woman now would be a weakness: to trust any foreigner at all, but particularly a woman, was a sign of insanity. But luck was on our side. He had the arrogance of the great man who has no time for the opinions of lesser men. He looked at me.

"Can you be trusted to bomb the Greeks? Scout's honour?"

"Scout's honour, General." We smiled at each other and at the small attempt at humour. If I had to stay around forever, became Air Marshal of his two-machine air force, I would never be close to him. I doubted if any man would ever be close to him: he had locked out trust. But he trusted us that night and I would never know how much effort it had taken. "We destroy those guns."

He nodded. "You had better get some sleep. Where will you fly on to?"

"Aleppo."

"Fly high then, in case the other side tries to shoot you down before you cross our border." He came round the table, kissed Eve's hand, shook hands with me and Kern, but ignored Sun Nan. The latter stared impassively ahead, face as bland as if he were alone in the room. "Good luck. I shan't be here to see you take-off. I am going down to join my men in the forward positions. But Colonel Osman will be in the square with Madamoiselle Tozer, just in case you forget your Scout's honour, Monsieur O'Malley." He said something to Osman, then turned back to us. He was trusting us, but only up to a point: "The Colonel has my permission to use his own discretion towards Madamoiselle if your bombs are not dropped on the right positions. I warn you, he is a man who believes in simple justice, the simpler the better. Especially towards women. Goodbye and good luck."

He waved a hand, dismissing us, and we were all escorted out of the room. We were taken back to the hotel. The streets were deserted now; the evacuation had been completed. The houses stood dark and empty, doors shut like a last defiant barricade against the Greek invaders. A wandering donkey came trotting down the street, braying hoarsely and mournfully, a farcical requiem for the dead and empty town. Eve stumbled on the cobblestones and I took her arm and was surprised at the tension I felt in it. We walked in silence, even the loquacious Ahmed appreciating that none of us wanted conversation at this moment.

The hotel-keeper had fled with the other townspeople. We went into the dark hotel, leaving our escort at the door. Ahmed clambered up into a chair in the narrow foyer; he was barely discernible in the moonlight coming through the open doors. His tiny legs stuck straight out in front of him; his homburg rested on his knees. He looked up at us: in the gloom he looked like a child playing at being a grown-up.

"I am sorry I brought you here. Perhaps it would have been better if you had stayed in Constantinople."

"No." Kern had said virtually nothing in the past half-hour. He seemed in some sort of pain, whether from his leg or from some discovery of himself, I couldn't work out; but he would not have admitted it if I had asked him. Every time I felt the barrier between us crumbling (and I had built as much of it as he had), I would catch a glimpse of the Prussian he still was and I would draw back. "That might have meant killing the English."

"Your uncle would never have had those qualms," said Ahmed.

"My uncle was a diplomat, not a soldier. They never have to pull the trigger. Goodnight, Fräulein." He bowed his head to Eve, but didn't click his heels this time; he *was* in pain, favouring his wounded leg. "I shall see you in Aleppo."

He went upstairs, leaning heavily on his stick. I looked at Sun Nan, who had said nothing at all in the last half-hour. "If the Baron and I don't come back from our sortie, Mr. Sun, it's up to you to see that the General lets you and Miss Tozer get away."

"He doesn't recognize me." He seemed to be having trouble with his teeth; his voice was a constant hiss. "I'm a Chinaman. Mustafa Kemal and your friend Mr. Weyman would have made a good pair."

"I doubt it. But you'll just have to get yourself recognized. The General will be down at the front, so you'll be dealing with Colonel Osman. He'll recognize you ahead of any woman."

We went up to our rooms. I said goodnight to Eve at her door; the darkness pushed us close. "Take care, Bede."

I felt for her hand, lifted it to my lips; I was more awkward than Kern would have been, but perhaps I was trying to say more. "Don't think about us in the morning. Think about your father."

Her fingers pressed mine. "I do that all the time. But—"

Then she stopped. I waited expectantly for her to kiss me; she was so close I could feel her breath on my cheek. But she didn't. She just pressed my fingers again, opened her door and went quickly inside.

I took a long time to go to sleep. I was falling in love,

almost against my will; I had always thought of myself as a natural bachelor. Not a swinger, as they call them today; I can't remember that species back in those days. All I wanted was to remain uninvolved. Selfish, I know; but in the punch-drunk world of 1919-20 I preferred no responsibilities other than just myself. There were a lot like me. We felt no pity for ourselves and I know I'd have laughed till it hurt if someone had called us the Lost Generation. It wasn't a matter of doing one's own thing, which suggests a certain rebellion. Most of us conformed to the patterns of society, didn't go in for radical politics, couldn't make up our minds whether to take sex seriously or lightly but never discussed it among ourselves. All we did was not vote, not get married, not become involved. And now I was falling in love with a rich girl who, if and when we rescued her father, would pay me £500, give me a return ticket to London and drop me out of her mind like last year's fashion style. *Go to sleep, O'Malley, you're dreaming the wrong sort of dreams.*

Ahmed woke me and Kern at 3:30. He had made us some coffee and toasted some bread in the hotel's kitchen; we ate the toast soaked in honey. We left him at the hotel door, shaking his tiny hand that grabbed two of my fingers with surprising strength.

"Good luck, gentlemen. Perhaps some day, when my country is free, you will be heroes to the Turkish people."

Modesty made us ignore that. Or anyway me: I don't know that Kern had any modesty. "You had better go back to Constantinople. Little heroes like yourself are likely to get trampled on up here."

"Perhaps I should come to London, work at the Savoy. Is there a place for little men in England?"

"You could go into politics."

Kern said, "If you get back to Constantinople, go out to Tarabya and put some flowers on my uncle's grave. He should be remembered."

"I remember him, Baron. He was a great man."

I was the outsider: defeat sometimes binds men together more than freedom does. The real war for Ahmed was the one that had been lost. The Hotel Parapalas would never be the same again.

Kern and I walked down through the deserted town. "How's the leg?"

"It will be all right." His stick tapped a hollow note on a cobblestone, the skull of the empty room. "If I had no legs I should still fly out of this place."

Our aeroplanes were ready. We loaded the bombs aboard, stacking them wherever we could in the front cockpits. As I started up my engine, I looked across at Kern, but he was staring straight ahead. I had the feeling he had said all his goodbyes, forever. And was angry with him. If he wanted to commit suicide, and I had seen the death-wish in some of his flying yesterday morning, that was all right with me. But not in *our* aeroplane. He should wait till we were within sight of Hunan, till there was no need of a third machine, or even a second.

We took off into the tail-end of the still, hot night. The moon was up; the hills looked as soft as blue mud in its radiance. We flew over the wadis where the Turks were dug in; I waggled my wings as a farewell to Mustafa Kemal. The road ran on into the hills and we followed it. We turned above the village that was our marker, flew up behind the ridge that ran down towards it. The Greek guns, a dozen of them, were lined up on a narrow road just below the crest of the ridge. For accuracy with our bomb-dropping we had to go in as low as we dared. We could only guess how close we were to the rough, undulating ground; in the moonlight there was almost no perspective. I went in, hoping my wheels would not scrape against some unsuspected outcrop of the ridge.

I took a bomb, wrenched out the safety-pin, held it over the side and dropped it. I was climbing to go over the top of the ridge when Kern came in behind me and dropped his first bomb. Then I came back, the second bomb in my hand. As I did the guns opened up, not firing at us but at Malavan, the target they were not supposed to hit till daylight. They were going to get as many shells off as they could before our bombs put them out of action. If, indeed, we could do that. As I dropped the bomb I saw the tracers coming up at me from the unseen machine-guns.

End of extract from O'Malley manuscript.

2

Eve, Sun Nan, Ahmed and Colonel Osman, with two soldiers bringing up the rear, had just come into the square when they heard the first shell. All the men dropped flat. Eve, the sound of the approaching shell unrecognized by her, looked around her, bewildered. The shell went overhead with a loud whine and landed on the mosque. Eve, her legs suddenly wrenched from under her by Sun Nan, saw the minaret fold, a candle that had suddenly melted; it disappeared into a rising cloud of smoke and dust. Another shell landed on a house; a donkey died with a hoarse scream of pain. Then a third, fourth and fifth shell hit with explosions that deafened her. Still flat on the ground, choked by dust and acrid smoke, her body trembling on the trembling earth, she heard Sun Nan yell into her ear, "We must take off!"

She scrambled to her feet as another shell landed in the square; pieces of shrapnel whirred dangerously close to her. She ran towards the Bristol, clambered up into the cockpit. She looked back, saw Sun Nan struggling with Colonel Osman who was trying to hold him and draw his sword at the same time. Ahmed, crouched in a tiny ball, bounced away as the struggling men fell over him. Then she saw Sun Nan's hand go up with the knife in it and then Osman fell away, his sword falling to the ground as he clutched his arm. She could hear nothing for the din of the falling shells, but she saw him jerking his head angrily at the two soldiers who could not make up their minds whether to run away or obey their colonel's order. Sun Nan backed away, coming towards the plane. Eve yelled at him, but her voice was lost in the thunder of exploding shells. The barrage had moved down towards the centre of town, or so it seemed; then she heard the whine of another shell and the mosque disappeared in a tremendous black explosion.

She jumped down from the cockpit, ran round and grabbed the propeller—then remembered she had neither switched on the engine nor set the throttle. She was panicking, her intelligence and reflexes pounded by the constant hammering of the shells as they exploded; the barrage was working its way back up to this end of town. She raced back round the wing, clambered up to the cockpit; then saw Sun Nan go round on the far side of the plane and grab the propeller. She waved, saw him swing on the propeller, saw it whir as it took first time. She revved the engine too quickly, but it didn't choke or flood. She swung the plane round, feeling it bump over the chocks; Sun Nan came round on the blind side, shielded for the moment from the two soldiers who were now raising their rifles to their shoulders as Colonel Osman screamed silently at them. Explosions lit the early morning; smoke and dust swirled like a violent storm. Sun Nan clambered up on to the wing, fell into the rear cockpit.

Another shell, its whine lost in the roar of the engine, landed ahead of the plane as it gathered speed for take-off. Out of the corner of her eye, through the drifting smoke, Eve saw Ahmed, short legs moving ridiculously fast, a tiny farcical figure, running desperately for safety; then she had gone through the smoke and dust, miraculously missing the shell-hole, was in the clear and rising into the air. She pulled the nose back, rising steeply, suddenly afraid that they would meet a shell in mid-air. What had happened to Bede and Kern? Why were the guns still firing?

Then she turned in a steep bank, flew back and saw that the barrage had abruptly stopped. The two soldiers lay flat in the middle of the square, dead or wounded; but Colonel Osman stood with his fist upraised and she could almost hear and understand the curses he was flinging up at her. She climbed higher, looked down the road towards the distant hills, peering into the lightening darkness for O'Malley and Kern, praying for them to appear. Then she saw the Very light, saw the two planes in its glow; she swivelled round and smiled back at Sun Nan as at a friend. He waved a hand, then she heard his voice through the speaking tube.

"The sun is rising," he said, Confucius at 4:30 in the morning, "out of China as it always does."

She looked ahead. He was right: there was a faint glow on the horizon, even if China was a long long way beyond it. She looked at her compass, set the plane on the course O'Malley had given her and flew south-south-east. The other two Bristols caught up with her and they flew slant-wise across the warp of the rising day, leaving behind them a war that would go on for another two years. But Eve was too young in experience, too relieved at being able to fly on to the rescue of her father, to think about the possible end to a war that didn't really concern her. And the men, the Englishman, the German and the Chinese were, perhaps, too experienced. They were accustomed to the continuum of war; only the geography changed.

Four hours later they landed in Aleppo, where a French officer demanded to know where they had come from. O'Malley, lying again as smoothly as ever, said they had come by way of Smyrna and Cyprus. Eve, her looks as smooth as she could make them in the mirror of her compact, smiled her most feminine smile and tried to make her schoolgirl's French sound like a courtesan's purr. Kern and Sun Nan stayed silent, which was probably just as well since the French officer looked sceptical of what had already been said to him.

"Mademoiselle—" He was lean and ugly, dyspeptic from a lifetime diet of froeign lands. He had fought the war for La Belle France at long distance and now he was tired of empires, they weren't worth a pinch of camel *merde*; he wanted to go home to Amboise, fish in the Loire and never have to speak to another foreigner. "I am old enough to be your father, perhaps even your grandfather. Don't flirt with me. And you, sir, sound like a first-class liar. I'll give you half an hour to refuel your machines and then take-off and don't come back. The petrol will cost you double the local price, half to the Syrian who will sell it to you and half to me, and you will pay in cash. Francs, preferably."

"I have only American dollars or English pounds," said Eve.

"English pounds, then," said the officer. "The Arabs trust it more than the American dollar. Bon voyage."

"I'm surprised you can spare the sentiment," said O'Malley.

The Frenchman shrugged and walked away. "Would you prefer good riddance? Pay the Syrian. He will give me my share."

The Syrian, wall-eyed and leering, arrived in a broken-down truck with a dozen drums of petrol, all marked French Army. As they watched him fill the planes' tanks O'Malley said, "Do you realize we weren't paid for what we did back there in Turkey?"

"Do you want to go back for it?" Eve said tartly, annoyed at how mercenary all soldiers and ex-soldiers seemed to be.

"No need to," said O'Malley just as tartly. "We'll bill you for it when we get to China."

Eve walked away. They were beginning to get on each other's nerves. Kern and Sun Nan virtually never spoke to each other; she could not bring herself to relax in conversation with the Chinese; since that day on the grass beside the airfield in Vienna the German had not started a conversation with her. He had changed and so, it seemed, had Bede O'Malley. She suddenly felt pressures bear in on her, like the heat, and she wanted to weep. But she would not have been Bradley Tozer's daughter if she had.

Half an hour later they were airborne again. The day was hot and they flew high to avoid the air pockets that bounced up from the bright earth. They passed over the green-brown serpent of the Euphrates; Eve looked for the Garden of Eden, but the tree of knowledge of good and evil was just a leafless skeleton half-buried in a lake of silt. Half an hour out of Baghdad five Royal Air Force Bristols joined them, their leader coming in close above the strangers and looking down at them suspiciously. Eve waved and the RAF leader waved back, but she noticed that each observer in the RAF planes kept his hand on his Lewis gun. Then Baghdad came up ahead of them and, still escorted by the RAF, they went down across the Tigris, over the red and brown sails of the trading boats hung out like shark fins to dry in the sun, and landed at the RAF aerodrome.

The leader of the RAF flight got out of his plane, pulled off his helmet and came across to Eve as she and Sun Nan dropped to the ground. "Good God, a woman and a Chinaman! I say, this is a surprise! You were jolly lucky my chaps didn't give you a burst or two—they're just itching for a scrap. Are your guns loaded?"

"Not mine," said Eve. "But Major O'Malley's and Baron von Kern's are."

The latter two had arrived by Eve's plane. The flight commander squinted in the glare. "O'Malley? From 24 squadron? I say, we flew alongside you chaps over Conteville for a couple of weeks. I saw you shoot down a couple of Boche."

"Small war," said O'Malley, "and small world. Are we welcome here or not?"

"I should jolly well say so! My name's Treloar, Dicky Treloar. I'm the CO here." He looked barely old enough to be the captain of a school.

O'Malley introduced Eve, Sun Nan and—"Baron Conrad von Kern. He flew with *Fasta* 11, von Richthofen's crowd. He shot down thrity-two of our chaps."

"Did you, by Jove! I say, I hope you're staying overnight—our chaps will love a chin-wag with you. Where are you heading? China? I say!"

Not all the RAF officers had their CO's boyish enthusiasm. There was a certain amount of awkwardness when the newcomers were introduced into the mess. They were still learning how to deal with the Arabs, over whom they had a mandate which the bloody Wogs didn't seem to appreciate. Most of them had come straight from school into the RAF and there had been nothing in the curriculum of either establishment that had taught them the proper social graces towards a Hun who might have shot down some of their friends, an absolutely smashing Yank girl who actually flew her own machine, and, for God's sake, a bloody Chink. Treloar took the visitors round, but they were greeted for the most part with that wary cordiality that Eve always thought of as an English welcome.

The oldest man in the room, in his mid-thirties, took drinks from a tray carried by one of the Arab mess orderlies and brought them to Eve and O'Malley. Sun Nan stood on his own in one corner, eyed suspiciously by both Englishmen and Arabs. Kern, leaning on his stick, was being cautiously polite to the ebullient Treloar.

"I'm Durant, the intelligence officer," said the older man. He was balding and running to fat, already resigned to being middle-aged. "I noticed you have some bullet and shrapnel holes in your machines. Did you run into a spot of bother?"

"Do you want the truth?" said O'Malley, sipping the warm beautiful English beer.

"That's what intelligence is all about." Durant smiled. "So they tell me."

O'Malley looked at Eve. "Go ahead. I'm too good a liar."

Eve told Durant the truth of what had happened and where they had come from. "I hope you're not going to hold us."

"Of course not. But you're not going to get out of here lightly tonight. The chaps will keep you up till all hours, wanting to hear all about it. They're itching for a scrap, y'know. We have some here who were too late for the show in France, got there when everything was all over. I think they'd trade off a few of our machines to the Iraqi rebels just to have someone to scrap with."

"Don't they ever grow up? Eve looked around at the schoolboys yearning for someone to shoot down and kill.

Durant glanced at O'Malley, who waved his glass, disowning Eve.

"One thing an intelligence officer learns, Miss Tozer, is that there is no intelligence about war. But if these chaps were home, what would they be doing? Creating hell in some other way, probably."

"Being a woman, I am not impressed by your argument."

"And she has a Magnum .375 out in her machine," said O'Malley, "if you want to take your argument further."

"You shoot, Miss Tozer? What's your favourite game?"

"Men," said Eve.

Over dinner she watched the reserve of the officers towards Kern slowly break down. He, too, seemed to relax: he is the old hawk (or the German eagle?) among the fledglings, she thought. O'Malley got up and went to join in the conversation at that end of the table; the air there vibrated with dog-fights sketched with words and swooping hands. Drinks were called for and a toast was drunk to someone or something: Eve waited for the glasses to be smashed against the tin walls of the mess, but the RAF was short on glasses and everyone restrained himself. Sun Nan sucked his teeth, freeing his plate of the last of the bully-beef-and-potato pie, and drank what the English thought passed for tea. He was as bored and irritated as Eve, but he hid it better.

Eve excused herself and all the fliers stood, impatiently polite, as she left the mess. Sun Nan followed her. They walked across to the tents they had been allotted. The moon was not yet up and the stars blazed without competition; they had the same brilliance that she remembered of Mexican stars. The night was quiet, the air so still she seemed to be moving through a vacuum. Then behind her in the mess someone started to play a piano and some unmusical voices began to sing: "Not much money/Oh but honey/Ain't we got fun."

"Mr. O'Malley and the Baron will have thick heads in

the morning," said Sun Nan. "You should go back and stop them."

"Do you think they would listen to me? I'm afraid they don't have the same strength of purpose as you and I, Mr. Sun. Not about getting to China."

"We can't afford to go on losing time. We are only half-way there. I noticed the box with the statue in it is not in your tent."

"How do you know? Do you mean you went into my tent and *searched* it?"

"Yes. That statue is as important to me as it is to you, Miss Tozer."

"Why, you—!" But Boston held her back: one didn't swear in front of the lower castes. Her grandmother didn't believe anyone, gentleman or lady, should swear even in front of the Irish, let alone a Chinese. "Don't ever do that again, Mr. Sun, or you won't reach China alive!"

He knew it was an empty threat: she would never use the Magnum .375 on *him*. "If I don't reach there, Miss Tozer, how will you find where your father is held prisoner? Where is the box?"

"It's held in the squadron office. At least there it has a guard on it all the time." She heard the back-down in her voice. Over in the mess Kern had begun to sing some rollicking song in German; one or two voices joined in haltingly and the pianist vamped his way through it with loud thumps. She suddenly felt deserted, tried for some defiance: "I have to protect it against you as much as anyone else, Mr. Sun!"

"Why should I want to steal it? I need you to get me home to China and my master."

But she didn't believe him, refused to be logical: no one could be trusted. She went into her tent, went to bed and tried hard to fall asleep. The party in the mess went on for hours: *everyone* there now sounded like a schoolboy. When at last she fell asleep she feld *old*, annoyed beyond measure by her two pilots who had no sense of responsibility towards her, who only wanted to get drunk on the boastful memories of dog-fights over the Western Front.

In the morning she was surprised to find O'Malley and Kern already at breakfast in the mess when she went in. They both looked pale and sick, their plates of sausages and fried eggs pushed away from them, their faces buried in big mugs of coffee.

"I hope you enjoyed your party."

O'Malley looked at Kern. "The lady from Boston has a vinegary tongue this morning."

Kern barely moved his head in a nod; he looked the sicker of the two. "Perhaps she has a right to."

"No." O'Malley kept his head very steady, didn't shake it. "We were entitled to last night's fun. I would remind you, Miss Tozer, that when the Baron and I bombed those guns outside Malavan, so that you could get away, *that* was no party. It was one of the damnedest, hellish shows I've ever been in. You are very lucky to have us here at all, hangovers or not."

She had thought and slept too long on her vexation to be instantly and contritely apologetic. "All right, you will be paid a bonus."

O'Malley put down his cup, stood up carefully. "Rich bitches are always the worst sort," he said, and walked out.

There were no officers in the mess, just Eve, Sun Nan and Kern. The latter said very quietly, "I think, Fräulein, that you have no idea of the weight of responsibilities. From what little I know of you, you have had a very soft life. You are very fortunate, Fräulein. I hope it continues that way for you. As for the rest of us, we are not so hopeful."

He, too, stood up carefully and, leaning on his stick, walked out of the mess. Eve looked down at her hands, which had clasped of their own accord. Then she reached for her handbag, took out a cigarette and lit it. Without looking at Sun Nan she said, "Add your bit, Mr. Sun. I deserve it."

"You do," said Sun Nan, never one to favour a

woman. "But Major O'Malley and the Baron have said it all."

When it was time to take-off, Eve collected the box from the squadron office and walked across with Treloar to the waiting Bristols. They had been refuelled and the RAF mechanics had repaired the bullet and shrapnel holes in the wings and fuselages. Treloar, carrying his head on his shoulders as if balancing it so that it wouldn't fall off, said, "That was a frightfully good binge we had last night. Pity you didn't stay for it."

"I was terribly tired. I went to sleep as soon as my head hit the pillow."

"Afraid if I put my head down this morning, I couldn't get it up again. They're jolly good drinkers, your friends. Especially the Baron. Never thought I'd like a Hun, but he's absolutely first class."

"And Major O'Malley?"

"Oh, one of the best. You're jolly lucky to have him flying for you. We could do with chaps like him back in the service, y'know. Sort of inspiration to the younger chaps," he said, the schoolboy veteran. "Well, I have to take a patrol out. Be some shaky take-offs this morning, I should think. Good luck."

Durant was with O'Malley and Kern. Perhaps he was a veteran of many parties: he looked bright-eyed, ruddy, nothing like the two walking wounded he was talking to. "You have a choice of two routes from here. You can head south to Basra, then round the coast to Bandar Abbas. But then you'd have to take your chances on where you could pick up petrol from there on—and Karachi is beyond your range, even with the extra tanks you're carrying."

"What's the alternative?" O'Malley hadn't looked at Eve as she approached them, though Kern had inclined his head and Durant had given her a polite salute.

"Isfahan, Kerjand, Quetta. Kerjand is a pretty small place, but it is at the end of a lorry road and you'll get petrol there. We use it ourselves when we're ferrying machines through to the Frontier. You'll just have to be careful on the last leg, though—the Mahsuds and Wazirs have been giving our chaps a rather rough time lately, shot down several of our machines. But if you stay high, you should be all right. Should be rather a nice little jaunt, actually. Well, jolly good luck. Absolutely splendid party last night, wasn't it? Pity you missed it, Miss Tozer."

"So I'm told."

Eve went across to her machine with Sun Nan and Durant looked after her. "She an absolute pip, isn't she? I envy you, you lucky blighters."

"An absolute pip," said O'Malley, voice absolutely flat. "Well, we'd better get started. I wonder if we could take-off without using the engines? I feel as if someone removed the top of my skull during the night."

They took off into the brassy morning. They flew for four hours over monotonous earth and through a monotonous sky. Eve began to long for the sight of a cloud to give her some perspective, some idea that she was actually travelling through the vast burning day. She looked across at O'Malley a couple of times, but deliberately or not, he was not looking in her direction. She flew on through an emptiness that began to have no dimension, that was as much mental as physical.

They landed at Isfahan, flying in over the old capital of the Persians and looking for the airfield rather than at the monuments of the past. The shadows of the planes crossed the dome of the Blue Mosque; the fliers looked down casually at it only as a landmark; they were on the right track. They refuelled, ate the bully-beef sandwiches and sweet biscuits the RAF mess orderly had given them, bought cups of sweet thick coffee from a vendor in the bazaar on the edge of the airfield, and prepared to take-off again.

Their conversation had been both terse and desultory. The crowd in the bazaar came across to stand around them, staring with that frank curiosity that assaults the European. "They had a king here in Persia once," said O'Malley, "who ordered twenty thousand pairs of his enemies' eyes to be brought to him. Probably fed up with all this staring."

They took off again and Eve was glad of the distance that separated her from O'Malley in his plane, thankful that she had not bought the Vickers Vimy bomber where the four of them would have been cramped into a confining space and atmosphere that would have worn them out. She took off her helmet, let the slipstream blow through her hair; let it blow, she imagined, through her cluttered, unhappy mind. Then, fearful of sunstroke, she put her helmet back on and tied a scarf over the back of her neck.

They hit turbulence and the machine bounced up and down, taxing the engine and making it gulp fuel. In the rear cockpit Sun Nan was sick, hanging his head over the side and banging his chin on the rim as the plane bumped its way through the rough air. Then the turbulence ceased, the engine settled back into its steady rhythm and they flew on over the old caravan roads that marked the desert below like the graffiti of ancient travellers. A caravan of camels, a hair-thin shadow on the glare below, moved with the slowness of historical time across the arid land.

They landed at Kerjand in the late afternoon. From the air it looked to Eve like a dozen other towns and villages they had passed over: several mosques, a few larger whitewashed houses, and the rest a jumble of brown mud huts that looked as if they had grown, rather than been built, out of the surrounding countryside. Mountains backed the town and irrigated fields gave a green tinge to the otherwise harsh brown landscape. The air began to turn cool as the sun went down and Eve realized they were in high country, that she might be glad of the warmth of her sleeping-bag.

Soldiers surrounded them as soon as they landed. None of them could speak English, but they made signs that the newcomers were welcome. O'Malley produced some boards to lock the ailerons, then pegged down the machines for the night. Then he and Sun Nan went into the town to buy some food.

"We'll have to sleep beside the machines," he said before he left. "I suppose these soldiers can be trusted. But just in case, we'd better take turns in staying awake tonight."

Left alone, Eve and Kern turned to the tasks O'Malley had given them. As each day passed she had noticed his gradual assumption of leadership. At times she felt some resentment of the off-handed way he gave orders and she saw Kern did not always take too willingly to them. But O'Malley always seemed to be gone before she or Kern could voice any rebellion; and she had to admit that whatever he told them to do was always sensible and necessary. She just wondered why Kern, who had had more experience of leadership than herself, who must have been bred for it, did not rebel more.

She supervised the evil-looking trader whom the soldiers had brought out from the town to supply petrol. He also sold them water and Kern had lit a fire and was boiling the water before putting it into their bottles. Most of the crowd had drifted away as dusk crept out of the desert, but some remained, squatting in a circle around the three planes. Eve was aware of the acrid smell she had noticed in Baghdad and Isfahan, of camel dung, urine and the dry burnt air; she was also aware of the smell of herself and wished passionately for a bath and a change of clothing. Then she thought of her father, imagined him being held in some filthy louse-ridden dungeon, and abruptly forgot about herself.

"I should not like to live in the desert." Kern stood up, easing his leg, and looked around him. "I like trees and grass and the sight and smell of water. That is one of the reasons I prefer the Bodensee to where I used to live near Koenigsberg. The country there was not as attractive."

"When you go back to Germany, what will you do? I can't see you spending the rest of your life going to tea dances."

He made a faint gesture, a shrug of the hands. "The army was to have been my life. But there'll be no army in Germany now. Not one I should want to serve in."

"You can't waste your life."

"How American you are," he said; then smiled wanly. "But we Prussians were like that, too. My father was always telling me that one's life was no more than a course of duty. Perhaps it was as well that he died at Verdun. Fräulein, when we reach China and have rescued your father, would you sell me this machine I am flying?"

She hadn't expected him to become so positive so abruptly. "Why—I don't know. Perhaps. What would you do with it?"

"I don't know—yet. Perhaps become a flier for a warlord like Herr Sun's master. Or go to America and be a stunt pilot. Storming the cow-shed, is that what they call it?"

She laughed, glad of the release it gave her. "They call it barn-storming. I can't see you doing that, Baron. Barnstormers travel all over the country, to small towns, country fairs. You'd be a long way from tea dances at Constance."

"The tea dances were a diversion, Fräulein," he said, smiling; but both his voice and smile were stiff. "A way of filling in time. How will you fill in your time when we have rescued your father and you have nothing else to do?"

It was a rebuke she recognized. She had never thought of her own life as a course of duty. It had been more a pursuit of pleasure and her father had encouraged her in it: he had never been an American Junker. Dancing at the Myopia Hunt Club ball; going on hunting trips to Mexico and East Africa; boating at Bar Harbor; playing tennis at Palm Beach: and she could still go back to it, it was all there for her to take again. Americans had lost nothing in the war, except lives.

"You may have the machine, Baron. As a gift."

He shook his head. "I was also taught never to accept charity, Fräulein. I shall buy it with the money you pay me."

She was losing contact with all three men, becoming the outsider in what she had thought of as her own party.

She had tried earlier, when they had first landed here, to re-establish her relationship with Bede; but he had given her no opportunity, too busy, it seemed, with practicalities to worry about personal feelings. All at once she wished for the end of this trip, the quick rescue of her father, the paying-off of these men who expected too much of her.

O'Malley and Sun Nan came back with some roasted goat and boiled rice. They ate it without relish, followed with a bar each of stale chocolate they had bought in the RAF mess at Baghdad. A coffee vendor had followed O'Malley back from the town bazaar and they bought cups of the thick liquid from him. "There was some fruit in the bazaar," O'Malley said, "but we decided against it. So far we've been lucky—no tummy trouble."

"It must be the only thing that hasn't happened to us." Kern stretched his leg out in front of him, wincing slightly.

"Shall I change the dressing on that for you?" O'Malley said.

Eve knew that she should have volunteered to act as nurse; but O'Malley had beaten her to it and she had the feeling she was being pushed further and further out of the men's circle.

"I'll get some hot water." She rose hurriedly, before her offer to help could be refused.

O'Malley said nothing, but she was aware of him looking after her as she went across to the petrol trader who was just about to drive off, bought some more water from him, paid extra for an old kerosene tin in which to boil it and put it on the fire. She studiously avoided looking at the men, conscious of the awkward way she had put the kerosene tin on the burning camel dung: she who was never allowed into the kitchen of her grandmother's home in Boston. She was beginning to appreciate how really useless she was in everyday matters. When it came time to lift the tin of boiling water off the fire she almost fell into it.

"Let me do that," said O'Malley behind her; and she was annoyed that it was he who had volunteered to help

her in her helplessness. Why couldn't the damned Chinaman have come to her aid? But Sun Nan, replete with
rice, his dental plate appreciating some civilized food at
last, was sitting with his back against a wheel of one of
the planes, contemplating with an air of superiority the
staring Persians.

"You'll have to take off your trousers," O'Malley said
to Kern. "Perhaps Miss Tozer had better take a walk."

"I've seen men without their trousers before."

"Stop boasting," said O'Malley.

It was the sort of stupid remark that crops up like
weeds in the spoiled ground of ill-feeling, one that could
have been swept aside by a laugh or just ignored. But
Eve, already too sensitive, reacted by abruptly walking
away. She got her sleeping-bag out of her plane, crawled
into it and turned her face away from the men. She closed
her eyes, but her mind remained wide open to all the
doubts, vexation and temper of someone discovering for
the first time that she did not belong. Then her belly
began to rumble and she knew she would have to get up
and relieve her bowels. The roast goat, the rice, something was having its effect on her.

She crawled out of her sleeping-bag and walked round
her plane and out into the darkness. She heard the footsteps behind her and she spun round, suddenly frightened.

"Where are you going?" O'Malley said.

She noticed he was carrying his service pistol, the first
time she had seen him with it. "I'm going to the lavatory,
if you must know."

"I'd better come with you. There are some rocks over
there."

"I don't want you to come—damn it, I'll be all right—"

"Miss Tozer, I know you must feel embarrassed, but
you'll just have to get over that. I'm not allowing you to
go wandering off in the dark on your own."

"You're not *allowing* me?"

"No."

Then she felt the cramp in her stomach and she had to
hurry for the rocks some distance away. When she came

out from behind them he was waiting for her, whistling softly to himself.

"Tummy trouble?" he said. "There's some stuff in the medicine box that should help. If you have to go again during the night, let me know. One of us will come over with you."

"I'll take my turn at guard."

"No, you won't. You'll get as much sleep as you can. I want you flying that machine tomorrow."

"Mr. O'Malley, you appear to have got the idea that *I'm* working for *you*."

"Not at all, Miss Tozer. You're the one who's paying all the bills."

"Is that what's worrying you? My money?"

"Not if it's not worrying you." He was infuriatingly bland; all at once she hated him. "Take that medicine."

He left her and went across to say something to Kern and Sun Nan, whose sleeping-bags were side by side. She got back into her own bag, mercifully fell asleep, but had to get up twice again during the night. When she woke the third time it was daylight, though the sun was not yet over the mountains behind the town. She looked at her father's watch, thought it had stopped, then realized she had not put it forward at all as they had flown east. She had the sudden depressing feeling, brought on by her weakened physical condition as much as anything else, that she had made no time at all in the race to save her father.

O'Malley stood over her. "How do you feel?"

"Weak."

"Feel up to flying on?"

"Of course." She struggled out of her sleeping-bag, felt giddy but managed not to sway. "I'll be all right."

He looked hard at her. "Righto, it's up to you. I shouldn't have any breakfast. Take some more of that medicine."

He didn't speak to her again before they took off. They climbed into another hot sky, headed east again. Eve rode in her aloneness once more, hating O'Malley, hating all men: something she had not thought herself capable of. Hating all but her father: she looked ahead of her into the shimmering distance, longing to see him again.

They struck more turbulence and she had to give up self-sympathizing (she was honest enough to admit that to herself) and concentrate on flying the bucking plane. She was glad she had had no breakfast; she had nothing in her to throw up and her bowels, too, seemed empty. All three planes rose and fell like gallivanting kites. Then she heard the missed beat of her engine, felt the nose of the plane drop as she gunned for extra power and it did not come. The engine coughed, spluttered, died; then stalled and slipped over in a spin. She lost all sense of orientation as the sky, earth and horizon whirled round her; the wind shrieked past and she felt the plane shuddering, threatening to fall apart. She worked desperately to bring it under control, trying to do what seemed to be a dozen things at once.

Then the engine started up again, she gunned it, heard it stop, then catch once more. She went with the spin, trying to widen it, hoping she still had enough air in which to work. She felt the rudder bar respond, she pulled on the stick. They came out of the spin no more than 300 feet from the ground; a steep hill was immediately in front of her. She dragged back on the stick, opened the throttle and took the Bristol up over the top of the jagged-edged hill with only feet to spare. She continued climbing, but she could feel the engine was as sick as herself, knew she was not going to reach Quetta.

O'Malley flew close to her, staying just far enough away not to be hurled into her by the continuing turbulence. She gestured at her engine, then pointed downwards. He waved to signify he understood, then flew on ahead of her. They were over very rugged country; the ground below looked like a vast rubbish dump of huge rocks. O'Malley kept looking back at her and when she turned and looked back she saw that Kern was shepherding her from above.

The engine was labouring, barely giving her enough

speed to remain airborne. Once she looked back over her shoulder and saw Sun Nan's face pale and frightened behind his goggles. Then she saw O'Malley point ahead, dip the nose of his Bristol and go down towards a narrow strip of bare yellow ground between two long-spined ridges. As O'Malley went down, Eve's engine began to die on her and she followed him down.

O'Malley went in over the narrow open stretch, came up in a steep climb, looked back and waved his arm frantically in a negative gesture. But it was too late: Eve couldn't get the nose of her plane up again. At 100 feet the engine suddenly cut out altogether. The sudden silence almost distracted her from the task ahead; she had to fiercely focus her concentration. The ground rushed up at her, an inverted avalanche: she saw rocks, bushes, a dry watercourse, wind-rippled yellow sand. She was leaning back on the stick, holding up the nose by sheer willpower; she felt it begin to dip and she knew she did not have enough air-speed. Then the wheels hit, bounced, and she was struggling to keep the plane on an even keel as it raced over the rough ground. She heard a bang, then the machine skidded sideways, tilted to port and she hunched down, waiting for them to be flipped upside down. But the starboard wing dropped again, the plane bumped along a few more yards, then came to a halt in a cloud of dust.

It took her half a minute to regather her strength and get out of the cockpit. Even then her legs buckled and she had to half-sit on the wing to prevent herself from slumping to the ground. Sun Nan was still sitting in the plane and she left him and stumbled away to look up at O'Malley and Kern circling above her. O'Malley came down low, swooped overhead and gestured at the ground. At first she didn't understand what he wanted; then abruptly her cool reason came back to her. He wanted to know if he and Kern could land without damaging their planes.

She began to run around, shouting for Sun Nan to come and help her, looking for a smoother stretch of

ground than that which she had had to take. She found it
a hundred yards from her own plane, a narrow strip of
hard ground littered with some rocks beneath the cliff of
the eastern ridge. It took her and Sun Nan fifteen minutes
to remove the largest of the rock, it would have taken them
a couple of hours to remove them all. Then, sweating, exhausted, driven into the black holes of their shadows by the
vicious punch of the blazing sun, they stood and waited
for O'Malley and Kern to come in.

O'Malley came down first. His machine bounced and
the starboard wing came down close to the ground; but he
managed to control it and he completed the landing,
swung the Bristol round and taxied it back to park it close
to Eve's. Then Kern brought his down, experienced a
similar bounce and tilt to O'Malley's, brought it under
control and swung round, came back to join the other two
planes.

"My engine just—*went*," Eve said; then looked at her
plane for the first time and saw the extra damage. "I've
blown a tyre, too. That could have bent the wheel or axle."

O'Malley looked up and around at the ridges: forbid-
ding, bare of all but odd patches of spiky scrub, a dead-
hot world. "Mr. Sun, give the Baron a hand to mount the
Lewis gun on my machine and his. Get the water-bottles
out of the cockpits, dig a hole in the shade of the wings
and put them in it. Load your Magnum, Miss Tozer, and
keep it near you, just in case."

"Where are we?" Kern, without his stick, had hobbled
across to join them.

"I don't know for sure. I think we could be in Waziristan—we've been flying long enough to have got that far.
If we are, then we'd better watch out."

While Kern and Sun Nan began to mount the machine-
guns on the rear cockpits, O'Malley went across to Eve's
plane. She followed him, kept silent while he inspected
both the damaged wheel and the sick engine. He kept
equally silent, seemingly ignoring her. At last he jumped
down from examining the engine. "We'll have to change
that tyre, but fortunately the wheel seems all right. But

the engine is going to take me some time. The cylinder heads look as if they overheated. And the plugs are oiled up to billy-ho. That's my fault. George told me to change the oil every twenty hours' flying. I'll have to change mine and the Baron's while I'm at it, otherwise we could have the same trouble."

"How long will we be here?" She did her best not to sound critical of him for not attending to the maintenance of the planes.

"Two hours at least, perhaps more." He looked up again at the surrounding ridges. "If we don't have any visitors, if our luck holds, we should be out of here by midday at the latest."

Kern and Sun Nan worked at changing the burst tyre while O'Malley got to work on the engine. It was less than half an hour before the visitors arrived. Eve, sitting in the shade of the wing of Kern's plane, her gun resting in her lap, was staring up at the ridge on the far side of the narrow valley. Lost in thoughts about her father, she was seeing nothing; then something moved in her gaze, something solider than heat-shimmer. Was it a rock that had shifted? She stood up, narrowing her eyes against the glare, wondering if she had imagined the movement.

Then the top of the ridge came alive. The tribesmen stood up, a long frieze of them spread along the skyline, rifles held straight up like tiny exclamation points. O'Malley dropped down from Eve's plane, raced to his own and jumped up into the rear cockpit, straddling the extra tank and swinging the Lewis gun round in the direction of the men on the ridge. Kern jumped up into his plane, did the same with his Lewis gun. Sun Nan came across, stood beside Eve. Out of the corner of her eye she caught a glimpse of him, was surprised to see that he looked calm and unafraid, nothing like the sick, frightened man who had ridden behind her in the ailing aeroplane.

"Maybe they won't attack us," she said.

"There's more coming," said Sun Nan and pointed.

They were coming up the valley, appearing like dark

shades out of the shimmering haze, riding above a billow-
ing surf of dust that made them look more spectral, a
hundred or more horsemen, their rifles plainly evident,
their leader carrying a long bright sword over his shoulder.

3

Kern watched the horsemen approach with a mixture of
apprehension and admiration. He had always been excited
by the sight of massed riders on the move; he would
have been a cavalryman had he not unexpectedly discovered the joys of being a flier. These men coming up
towards them out of the quivering haze had none of the
shining dash of a lancers regiment, but they were still a
thrilling sight, cantering close together, the horses with
their heads high, the riders as easy in the saddle as if born
to it. He kept his finger on the trigger of the Lewis but
wondered if he would be able to shoot at the horses when
the time came.

The horsemen came to a halt no more than twenty
yards from the parked planes. Dust swirled, then settled;
men and horses became solid, real. There was the jingling
of stirrup and bridle-iron and the horses slubbered; all the
sounds he remembered and loved. But they were the only
sounds. The tribesmen, dressed in dark turbans, tunics
and pantaloons, most of them bearded, their eyes ringed
with kohl, sat their horses and stared at the foreigners.
Then one of them, the man with the long bright sword,
rode forward on a jet-black stallion. He looked shorter
than the men behind him, a wiry man with only half a
nose and a caved-in-cheek, a half-dead face but for the
bright blue eyes gleaming out of their rings of kohl. He
wore pink Bedford breeches, expensive riding boots, a
purple shirt, a yellow leather waistcoat and a black turban.
His waist was circled by a gun belt, with a holstered pistol on his right hip and a sheathed knife on his left. He

looked at the three planes and the four foreigners, then he nodded to Kern.

"Don't be a wise guy, Jack," he said in an American accent. He slid the sword into a scabbard hanging from his saddle, took the pistol from its holster and aimed it straight at Eve. "You let go one round from them guns, I'll shoot the dame. Okay?"

Kern looked across at O'Malley, shrugged and took his hands away from the Lewis. O'Malley followed suit. Eve had been holding her own gun ready, but on a nod from O'Malley she lowered the butt to the ground, held it by the barrel.

"Who's the boss here?"

"I am," said Eve, and Kern almost laughed at the comical look on the man's shattered face. "You're not an American, surely?"

There were angry murmurs from the riders and even the horses moved restlessly. The leader, without turning round, held up his hand and snapped an order that silenced his followers. Then he looked at Kern. "Tell the woman to keep her mouth shut. Which of you guys want to say something?"

"What do you want to know?" Kern said. "The lady is our boss, as you asked for. But if you won't talk to her, then perhaps Herr O'Malley or I can accommodate you."

"*Herr* O'Malley? You German?"

"I am. Baron Conrad von Kern."

"A Fritz, eh? Where you heading?"

"China."

The leader shook his head. "You was. Not no more, you ain't. Okay, get down. Don't try no fancy tricks with them guns."

"Where are you taking us?" Eve said.

The leader looked at Kern again. "Tell her to shut up, for Crissake, or these guys gonna cut her tongue out." He shouted an order and four men dismounted and brought their horses forward. "Okay, get aboard."

"What about my box?" Eve looked at O'Malley, then

shut up abruptly as one of the dismounted horsemen pushed her roughly.

"Is someone going to stay here and look after our machines?" O'Malley shook his head at Eve, then looked at the leader. "If not, I'd like to tie them down."

"Jesus!" said the Wazir. "Don't you bastards know when you don't hold no cards? Get up in them saddles before I shoot the goddam lotta you!"

Kern was hampered by his injured leg but still managed to mount with the ease of the practised rider. Eve did the same, swinging easily up into the saddle. One of the tribesmen took her gun from her, looked at it admiringly. But the leader snapped his fingers and the man reluctantly handed it to him. The leader examined it, then looked at Eve.

"You use this?"

"I once shot a man about your size with it."

Kern had to admire her spirit, even if in the circumstances it was foolhardy. The leader lifted the gun to his shoulder and took aim at Eve. Everyone was suddenly quiet; even the horses seemed to stand stock-still. Eve stared at the leader, but didn't flinch. Kern tightened his grip on the reins of his horse, tensed, ready to fling himself and the horse at the leader. But at the moment he moved his feet to dig his heels into the horse, the leader lowered the gun, grinned a broken-toothed smile and said something to his followers. Some of them laughed, some nodded, but all of them relaxed.

"You got guts lady. That's the only thing saved you. Us Pushtun, we admire guts. But keep your mouth shut from now on or you gonna get shot by your own gun. Or maybe have your throat cut. Okay, you other guys get aboard."

Sun Nan had to be helped up into the saddle. He rolled dangerously and almost fell off the other side of the horse; Kern rode close to him and pushed him back into the saddle. All the tribesmen laughed, but there was no flicker of expression on the face of the Chinese. There had been no attempt to search any of the men. Kern saw that O'Malley was not carrying his service pistol, but he wondered where Sun Nan had hidden his knife.

O'Malley was not too ungainly in mounting, but once in the saddle he proved to be no rider. Kern was surprised. He had come to look upon the Englishman as almost one of his own class: not quite, but almost: O'Malley was not *born*. But he was educated (Oxford, no less: that meant something, even to a German), he was an officer, a distinguished flier: one naturally assumed he would be able to ride, as any gentlemen could. But as they cantered away, surrounded by the tribesmen, O'Malley wobbled in the saddle like a rag doll. The four Waziri who had given up their horses remained behind with the planes.

The long line of men along the top of the ridge had disappeared. It was ten minutes or so before the horse party picked them up. They turned out of the narrow valley up a steep-walled wadi, the horsemen stringing out in single file with the leader at the head and the four prisoners immediately behind him. The horses were reduced to a walk, picking their way up a rocky trail. Then suddenly they were joined by as many tribesmen on foot, all with rifles or long knives. They fell in on either side of the long file, looking curiously at the prisoners but saying nothing.

Half an hour's slow riding brought the party to a small town running up the wide flat crest of a ridge. Mud huts clustered together within a long walled rectangle; at each corner of the walls was a guard tower with narrow-slotted parapets. Guards stood up behind the parapets as the party approached and waved their rifles in greeting as the men on foot broke into a run and rushed ahead shouting and waving their long knives. As they approached the town Kern saw the huge heap of white rocks to one side of the road. He was immediately opposite the heap before he recognized that the rocks were skulls, a great mound of grinning welcome. He saw Eve turn her head away and he put out a comforting hand.

The party rode in through a tall gateway between two

further guard towers, into a square that ran from wall to wall across the flat crest and from which the town climbed back to a fourth wall that seemed to be the summit of the hill. An almost impregnable fortress, thought Kern, except to aerial attack.

Everyone dismounted and the horses were then taken outside the gate again. O'Malley and Sun Nan, stiff and sore, were bending their legs and rubbing the insides of their thighs. A crowd came down out of the town, flowing like black honey out of the honeycomb of houses, spilling into the square, buzzing with excitement. Kern and O'Malley moved close to Eve, both suddenly aware of the atmosphere the crowd had brought with them. These people, for whatever reason, hated foreigners.

"English!" A white-bearded old man spat at Kern, and the German wondered if there would be any dividend in his explaining that he and Eve were not English. But another look around told him this crowd would never listen to explanations: many already had their knives in their hands.

He and the others were led up through the narrow streets of the town. The crowd and the noise pressed in on them; the sun beat down from above; Kern had the feeling they were being reduced to nothing. His wounded leg began to ache, but he did his best not to limp. Several times Eve stumbled and he and O'Malley grabbed her and held her up. Sun Nan, round face glistening with sweat under his bowler hat, his black coat folded neatly over his arm, seemed oblivious of the crowd pushing in on him, striding through them as if they were bushes on an overgrown track.

They came to a larger house, were taken into it and shoved roughly into a side room. The floor was tiled, covered with richly-woven rugs that Kern knew would have been prized back home in Germany but here seemed to be only part of the rough furniture of the room. The door of the room was left open and four tribesmen, rifles slung over their shoulders, hands resting on the knives in their belts, lounged in the hallway outside, staring in at the prisoners and occasionally saying something to each other that, though Kern didn't understand the words, was obviously full of malevolent amusement.

"We're not going to talk our way out of here," said O'Malley.

Eve had slumped on a rough, straight-backed chair, taken off her shoes and was rubbing her feet. "You should have flown on, there was no need for you and the Baron to have come down—"

"Tosh," said Kern, though he felt like saying something much stronger. He was not afraid, but all at once he was angry at the smirking men in the doorway. It had been part of his code that prisoners should always be treated with respect. He turned on the men, snapped in German, "Get your dirty, leering faces out of here and shut that door!"

The tribesmen did not understand his words but they understood his tone. One of them drew his knife and advanced into the room, snarling something in his own tongue. Eve cried out and started up from her chair; O'Malley said something under his breath and Kern heard Sun Nan give a soft hiss. The Wazir stepped right up to Kern, but the German held his ground. The knife came up in a quick thrust, paused, then the point of it pricked Kern's throat. He didn't blink, but stared into the angry eyes only a foot from his own, feeling the heat of the man's body, smelling his breath and the stink of him.

"You got guts, too, Fritz. Just like the dame." The wiry, little man stood in the doorway, amused but not malevolently so. He said something to the man with the knife and the latter, with a final snarl at Kern, reluctantly stepped back. "You folks better come eat with me. I don't want you to die on me. Not of starvation, I mean."

He had a laugh that was almost a cackle. He jerked his head at the four guards, who moved in and grabbed the prisoners, pushing them roughly out of the room and along a narrow hall into another, larger room where food was set out on a wide cloth on the rug-strewn floor. The leader waved Kern and the others to places around the meal, then sat down on cushions at the head of the spread cloth. He had taken off his Bedfords and riding boots and wore white pantaloons and boat-shaped slippers decorated in silver and gold. The sleeve of his shirt kept sliding back and Kern saw that he wore a thick silver bracelet. He still wore his turban, as did the half a dozen other men, two of them old and white-bearded, already seated around the meal.

"Okay, help yourselves. No knives and forks here, just fingers. That's *chaple kebab*—watch the chili in it. Gonna burn your mouth out, you ain't careful." He took a large ball of the ground meat, bit into it and nodded appreciatively. "Okay, gimme the lowdown. Who are you, what you doing with them airplanes? And I don't want the dame to answer. She's lucky she been allowed to eat with us. My pa here," he nodded at one of the white-bearded men, "he'd make her wait and she'd just get the leftovers. So who the hell are youse?"

O'Malley told him; then said, "May we ask who you are?"

"I'm Suleiman Khan." He munched on another meatball, followed it with a mouthful of flat round bread. "They used to call me Solly when I was in the States. I worked around the race-tracks at Saratoga, Belmont Park, places like that. I led in Sweep, he won the Futurity and the Belmont Stakes, 19-owe-9, 1910. Me and the nigger boys. Pushtuns like me, I was the only one around there, I was just one step up from the nigger boys. The dame's an American, ain't she? She got nigger boys working for her?"

"Am I allowed to answer that?" Eve said.

The men had been listening with only half an ear to the conversation they didn't understand. Now they abruptly stopped eating, some with their hands half-way to their mouths, and looked at Eve, then at Suleiman Khan.

"For Crissake, lady," said he, "you wanna finish up on that heap of skulls outside the gate? Now bow your head right down to the ground like you was apologizing to me, then shut up, for Crissake."

"Better do as the man says," said O'Malley.

Eve looked around her, saw the glowering bearded faces, then bent over till her forehead touched the floor. "I'll bet you're enjoying this," she muttered to O'Malley.

"What she say?" said Suleiman.

"That she bows her head to all men and apologizes for the squeaking parrot that is her tongue."

"She said that? Hey, that's not bad." Suleiman conveyed the apology to the other Waziri. "Okay, they accept. Tell her she can straighten up."

Eve sat up, made an angry face at O'Malley. The Wazir next to Eve suddenly raised his hand to slap Eve across the mouth, but O'Malley reached across Eve and grabbed the man's wrist. He smiled at him, then glanced at Suleiman. "Tell your friend that I'll slap my own woman when I think she needs it."

Suleiman looked at each of the four prisoners in turn, then he said something and the man beside Eve jerked his wrist free of O'Malley's grip. Eve folded her own hands in her lap and stared down at them. Kern, mouth burning from a piece of chili he had inadvertently bitten on, looked across at Sun Nan who, self-contained as always was daintily eating his way through a meatball, being careful of the chilis.

"Not that I got any time for nigger boys meself." Suleiman went on with his conversation as if there had been no interruption. "Us Pushtun we got no time for Hindus, either. Most of them, they too dark. You ever see a Hindu with blue eyes like mine? You oughta hear my pa, hear him tell where us Pushtun come from. From Kais, that's who, and he come right down the line from Afghana, son of Jeremiah, son of Saul, the first king of Israel. That's why most of us got names outa the Bible. I'm Suleiman, my pa's Yakub, that's Adam, Ibrahim, Yusuf, Isa. Used to make me laugh seeing them swells at Saratoga and Belmont and Pimlico, strutting around like they owned the world and most of 'em couldn't tell who their great-granddaddy was. But us, we know who we born from."

He's *born,* thought Kern: the *Almanach de Gotha* began to look as much a late-comer as the *Berliner Tage-blatt*. He sucked in cooling air, sure that his mouth was blistered. "Why did you go to America?"

"I stowed away on the wrong boat outa Australia. I took some camels out there for my pa, there's a lot of Afghans up there in the north of Australia trading around all over the place, and then I went down to Brisbane and stowed away on a boat I thought was going to Calcutta. It was going to California—I didn't speak English too good, them days. There was nothing in California but a goddam earthquake—I got off the boat the day San Francisco fell down. So I bummed me way across to New York State, got me a job around the racetracks. One thing I could do, I could always handle horses. Except the son-of-a-bitch done this." He touched his smashed face. "I run smack into his hoof."

"What brought you home to Waziristan?"

"I killed a guy." Suleiman bit into another meat-ball, wiped his mouth with the back of his hand. "I come across to France when war broke out, I was with the 81st Mule company. There was a lieutenant kept riding me all the time, so I waited till Armistice Day and I cut his throat, sorta to celebrate the end of the War. Then I bummed me way home across Europe, Turkey, Persia, all through there. Them breeches I was wearing, they was the lieutenant's. The boots, too, Nice fit."

"You became chief pretty quickly, didn't you?" said O'Malley; then added with a hasty grin, "I mean that as a compliment."

"I had to prove meself," Suleiman cackled, but added no explanation.

Kern said, "What are you going to do with us? We don't add to your stature as leader, do we?"

Suleiman looked at him out of the corner of his eyes, over the broken, sunken cheek. "You see that pile of skulls we passed when we come in? A guy named Babur, he come through here on his way to India hundreds of years ago. Used to cut off all the heads of his enemies, pile their skulls up, sorta head count, you know what I mean?" He cackled again. "Pushtun *maliks,* that's a chief, they still do it. The more skulls, the bigger chief you are. I ain't been back here too long, but I added my lot to that heap out there. There's nearly fifty English soldiers' skulls on the heap, but you wouldn't know 'em. All skulls sorta look alike. I think the dame's gonna be sick."

Eve, pale, spat some food into her hand, looked around, then dropped it into a bowl of scraps behind her. She nodded when Kern asked her if she was all right, but the look she gave Suleiman almost got her a smack across the mouth from the tribesman beside her. He looked at O'Malley, who said, "I'll deal with her later, chum."

"She been brought up too soft," said Suleiman. "My ma, when I was a kid, she used to sing me to sleep. A lullaby, that what you call it? You know what she used to sing to me? All the names of the guys my pa and my grandpa had killed. I used to go to sleep counting all them dead guys like you count sheep."

"I'd like to think you were pulling our leg," said O'Malley, "but somehow I don't think you are."

The blue eyes seemed to pale in their rings of kohl: all at once Kern was reminded of the Countess. But Suleiman wasn't mad: "I ain't kidding, Jack. We gotta get the English outa our country and you gonna help us, by Christ!"

"How?"

"You gonna fly them airplanes and you gonna bomb the English!"

"Here we go again," said O'Malley softly; then louder: "First, we have to get them back in the air. I was working on them when you, er, interrupted me."

"How much work you reckon you gotta do on 'em?"

"Three or four days."

Kern saw Eve lift her head and a look of pain passed across her face, but she said nothing. Time was running out: the horizon beyond which lay China was getting no closer.

"Okay, we can wait," said Suleiman. "I'll get our guys make some bombs for you."

"You can't throw just any sort of bomb out of an aeroplane."

"Don't worry. Our guys, they'll make you any sort you want. I'll take you down, you give 'em your order."

When the meal was finished Suleiman took O'Malley and Kern down to his bomb-makers. Accompanied by half dozen guards, they walked down through the narrow streets of the town. Kern could hear a continuous tap-tap in the dark caves of shops they were passing. Peering into the gloom he saw men beating at silver and copper sheets with tiny hammers.

"What do you do with all that silver-work?"

"They take it down to the big towns, Kandahar, Quetta, places like that. Nobody comes through here no more, not since the English put in new roads for their trucks. But there's stories been handed down, Genghis Khan and Tamerlaine, they come through here. This was on the big caravan road from Bokhara, Samarkand, Meshed, places like that. But that's all finished now, the good old days, the world's been spoiled. I'd have liked to been alive then." The smashed face seemed to crumble further, the piercing blue eyes softened. Even murderous villains are dreamers, Kern thought. And worlds are falling apart all over the world. Then Suleiman looked at Kern, his eyes sharpening again. "But this is still better than what you got, eh, Fritz?"

Anything is better than what we have: the good old days were gone forever in Germany. "Possibly."

They came to a row of shops that had been knocked into the one small factory They went into its dimness, glad of the coolness after the concentrated heat in the narrow, crowded streets. The dozen men working at the benches and the small forge stopped what they were doing, looked at the foreigners, then at Suleiman. The latter said something to the oldest man, a tall tribesman with a grey beard and oné eye blinded by cataracts. While the discussion was going on, Kern looked around him, then at O'Malley. The latter gestured at one of the workers, took from him a rifle the man was working on. "Lee-Enfield .303. It looks a pretty good copy."

"It's good enough," said Suleiman, breaking off his conversation with the elderly man. "They can make anything. We got Mauser pistols, Springfields. Look at that, a Webley .455—you tell the difference from a real one?"

"Where do you get the originals to copy from?"

"Steal 'em. Take 'em off English soldiers we kill. So far we ain't been able to get any machine-guns, not till now. But now we got your Lewis guns we can copy."

"I apologize for not bringing a couple of howitzers with us."

"What are you planning to do?" said Kern. "Wipe out the British Empire?"

"You guys tried it, didn't you, Fritz? You blaming us for trying? No, all us Pushtun want is to get all foreigners outa our country. We'll do it. We the biggest tribal society in the word, you know that? Us Waziri, Afridi, Mahsuds, Durran, Ghilzai—all we gotta do is stick together and ain't nobody gonna beat us."

"Do you want to be another Genghis Khan or Tamerlaine?"

"Me?" Suleiman cackled, shook his head. "A stable-boy from Saratoga, Belmont Park, places like that? A corporal in the 81st Mule Company?"

Kern saw his point: corporals did not rise to be great leaders. Back home in Germany corporals and sergeants were leading their tiny rebellions, but in the end, if the Germans responded to rank again, it would be the generals who would win. Then, and only then, Germany might be worth living in again.

"Will Herr O'Malley and I be flying for you or some other *malik*?"

"Me, of course." Suleiman wasn't going to take modesty to ridiculous lengths. "There are two cantonments you gotta wipe out for me. When that's done—well, it's none of your business. The first place you gotta bomb is Fort Kipling."

"Will you let us go after we've done both bombings?"

"Sure. After you taught some of our young guys how to fly your airplanes."

"You mean you're not going to let us take the machines with us?"

Suleiman shook his head. "Did King George let the Kaiser take everything home with him? Don't be stupid, Jack."

"What if we refuse to do what you ask?" said Kern.

"These guys make very good knives, too. All their own work, no copies. Like this one." He took a curved blade with a decorated silver handle from his belt. "Not bad, eh? I'd cut your throats with it, you wouldn't feel any pain before you were dead. Waddia say then?"

"With a cut throat it's very difficult to say anything," said O'Malley. "We'll bomb the contonments and train you an air force."

Kern and O'Malley were taken back to Suleiman's house, put in the same room again with Eve and Sun Nan. A heap of cushions had been brought in and four low-slung *charpoys,* the native beds. Suleiman was at least going to give his prisoners a degree of comfort before he cut their throats.

"He's going to do that, don't you agree, Baron?" said O'Malley.

"I should think so. I don't think we are dealing with an honourable man here, not like Mustafa Kemal. What's the matter, Mr. Sun?"

Sun Nan was smiling to himself, shaking his head. "You hypocrites from the West. Why is a man dishonourable because he wants to cut our throats? We came here uninvited. Your countrymen, Mr. O'Malley, are at war with him and his countrymen. Why should he be hospitable towards us?"

"Perhaps it is that we are not accustomed to having our throats cut," said Eve.

"I thought it was the custom all the time on Wall Street." Sun Nan did a good job of looking genuinely surprised.

"Bolshevik propaganda," said O'Malley. "I didn't think the Middle Kingdom would fall for it."

Kern said, "Herr O'Malley, will you really need three or four days to repair the machines?"

"No. But we may need that much time to think up some way of getting out of here. How are you feeling now, Eve?"

Kern had been aware of the tension between Eve and O'Malley. But the latter's voice this time seemed properly solicitous and Eve seemed to recognize it. Still, her own tone was wary: "My tummy's settled down, I think. But I don't know how long it will stay that way if I have to go on eating food like they gave us at lunch."

"You'd better try and eat it, get your strength up. If we get out of here at all, we may have to do it on foot."

"You saw the country when we were flying over it— we'd never survive on foot. Not in this heat."

"Perhaps we could steal four horses."

"The way you and Mr. Sun ride?" Eve smiled wanly; the mood between her and O'Malley was improving. "No, if we get away, it's got to be in the aeroplanes."

"Then we'll have to spin out time while we think up some scheme."

"Can we afford four days?" Kern asked.

"Not really. But in the meantime we all have to keep our eyes and ears open." O'Malley looked at Sun Nan. "Have you ever been in a situation like this before?"

"Once," said Sun Nan. "My master and I were captured by General Chang."

"How did you get away?" Eve said.

"We cut the throats of our guards with their own knives."

"I asked for that," said Eve. "But this is no time for jokes."

"It is the truth, not a joke. You and the Baron were soldiers, Mr. O'Malley. You know we are not going to escape from here without someone being killed. It will be better if it is them and not us."

Kern saw Eve pale as she realized that Sun Nan was

deadly serious. Had she really shot the man who had tried
to rape her? One couldn't ask a lady such a question. But
shooting in self-defence and premeditated murder were totally different. He knew that even he, the killer of men in
the air, might have qualms when it came to killing a man
in cold blood at close quarters.

4

"How will I get away from my guards?" said Bradley
Tozer.

"I shall leave you the razor," said Madame Buloff.
"You can cut their throats."

They were walking on one of the terraces below the
palace. A guard, chewing on red peppers, stood under a
tree watching them with a languid eye. The air was still
and from somewhere down near the town there came the
constant sound of a gong being hit, a slow sonorous beat
that somehow was the sound of such a hot sultry day.
Tozer could see the sun shining on the rice paddies, turning the fields into huge sheets of glass: human flies
crawled across the panes. A water-wheel, powered by a
plodding buffalo, spun slowly, spilling buckets of shining
light. What am I escaping from? Tozer all at once wondered. This was all so peaceful, far removed from the talk
of murder.

"We're not sure exactly what day the trucks will be arriving with the rice. We shall wait until one of them is un-
loaded, then take that. It will go faster."

"How many trucks will there be?"

"Four, perhaps five. They are old ones that the General
stole from one of the Shanghai companies. Jardine
Matheson, I think."

"Good." There would be a certain pleasure in escaping
in one of his competitors' trucks; he hoped they would be
as good as the ones owned by Tozer Cathay. "Can you or
the Colonel drive?"

"No. You will have to drive." She stopped, staring out over the plain below them. She was wearing a brown silk *cheong-sam* and a big coolie's hat; she reminded him of a baobab tree he had seen in Africa. He wished he were not so tall himself; he would have been glad to stand in the shade of her. "If we can steal enough petrol, perhaps we can drive all the way to Shanghai."

Tozer said, "Do you really expect me to cut the throats of the guards?"

"Why not? I can't see any other way of getting away from them. It will be quicker than garrotting them."

They could have been discussing her dreadful cooking, one recipe against another. But then she was an experienced escapee: for all we knew, she may have left a trail of cut throats all the way from Moscow to Harbin.

Then she said, "The alternative would be to poison the General. I could do that while I am preparing the meals. The difficulty will be finding a slow poison that will kill him in his sleep. We should not want him to die at the table."

Poisoning would be better, much less messy. Tozer Cathay sold poisons: anything that made a profit, his father had always said. But for the life of him, literally, he could not remember a slow one.

She patted his arm, a remarkably gentle gesture considering her size. "Leave it to me. We shall escape from here. The Colonel and I guarantee it. You guarantee the twenty thousand dollars?"

"I offered ten."

"I have found out how much you paid General Chang for the statue that General Meng wants back. Is your life worth only what you paid for the statue?"

"All right, twenty thousand." He had always been known as a hard bargainer; but he had never had to bargain for his life before. "You'll be a big success in the United States, Madame Buloff."

"You mean big because of my size?" She smiled, patted his arm again; he began to feel like a client at the Blue Delphinium tea rooms. "I am only joking, Mr. Tozer. I intend to be a success. Perhaps I shall have a chain of tea houses right across America. I can see them now. All white with an orange roof and a little tower on top. And a wide variety for the customers to choose from."

"Tea or girls?"

She smiled again, patted his cheek this time. "Both, Mr. Tozer. Ah, here come my husband and the General!"

The group of horsemen, a couple of dozen of them, came trotting along the road that ran through the rice paddies. A gong sounded in the palace and, though he saw no immediate movement, Tozer felt the great brown ant-heap come alive. He had been surprised at the size of Meng's *yamen*. It stretched for a hundred yards on either side of its main gates, a monument that Meng had built to himself on top of what, the *yamen* of the previous warlord, had been no more than a modest barracks.

Guards and servants appeared on the terraces; the guard under the peach tree threw away his red peppers and straightened up. The Lord of the Sword ran his palace as he ran his army: there was no place but the grave for slackers. By the time the party of horsemen had come up the road and in through the palace gates the somnolent scene had changed to a busy one: guards paraded, servants moved to and fro as if in the middle of spring-cleaning. Tozer smiled to himself and wondered if the Lord of the Sword was fooled by all the activity that greeted his return. He was limited by his own Occidentalism: he had suppressed too much of his half-caste mother. He would never know how much one Chinese could fool another.

The tweed-capped Mongolian guards had led the horse party. They swung down, held the General's and Colonel Buloff's horses while those two dismounted. Tozer watched the Colonel, was surprised how easily the squat Russian slid out of his saddle; with his short legs he might have difficulty in getting *on* a horse, but coming up the road he had looked what he claimed to be, a cavalryman. Tozer, all at once, began to have confidence in the Buloffs. They might be opportunists, brothel-keepers, even crooks; but it wasn't luck alone that had enabled them to flee the Bolsheviks. Besides, they were his only hope.

General Meng, dressed in a blue uniform and riding boots whose gleam was only faintly dulled with dust, his gleaming hair protected under a peaked cap, nodded for Tozer to follow him as he strode into the cool halls of the palace. "I may have a skirmish or two on my hands, Mr. Tozer. The dog Chang is having trouble in Chang-sha and the word is that he is blaming me. He is sending some of his troops out this way."

"Will he attack here? Your palace, I mean."

Meng took off his cap, sat down, looked at himself in a mirror. A girl appeared from behind a curtain, stood behind him and began to stroke his hair with a brush. Another two girls came in, took off his riding boots, began to wash his face, hands and feet. Bradley Tozer, regretting that American women never seemed to have this much consideration for their menfolk, sat down on a chair opposite the General.

"Let me go, General, and I'll go straight down to Shanghai and buy you two, three, as many aeroplanes as you want and you can blast hell out of General Chang when he arrives here. You said Chang was looking for aeroplanes. You can get in first."

Meng smiled. "You know as well as I do, Mr. Tozer, that there are no aeroplanes in Shanghai just for the asking. They would have to be brought from America or England. And that might take weeks, even months. Where would you be all that time? Still in Shanghai, still looking upon yourself as my prisoner, still promising to return my statue to me when your daughter arrives back with it? As the English so vulgarly say, not bloody likely."

"Like you, General, I am a man of my word."

"Like me, Mr. Tozer, you are a man of your word when it pleases you to be. It is the only way to survive. Honourable men are only revered by their descendants. The rest of us take advantage of them."

Tozer was surprised by such honest cynicism. But then his dialogues with war-lords had been few and far between until he had met General Meng. Too, Meng had read him correctly. Once he got to Shanghai he would not hang around buying aeroplanes for the Lord of the Sword. He would be on a fast boat out of China.

Meng dismissed the girls, looked at himself again in the mirror, spoke to Tozer's reflection: "I am not going to defeat Chang with just flying machines. One needs good fortune, Mr. Tozer, and you still possess my good fortune. You have less than a week to return that statue to me. Chang and his dogs may be here before then. If they are, I shall have to kill him and you, and hope that will appease the gods who have deserted me. Now shall we go in to supper? I've persuaded Madame Buloff to take a night off from her cooking, so we should have a civilized meal. I think I shall have to send her back to Shanghai before she poisons us all." He smiled at Tozer. "I have never had a food-taster before. The old Emperors used to have them and I believe some of your kings in the West had them."

"We never had kings in America."

"Your Presidents never had food-tasters?"

"Poison has never been the American way. We shoot our Presidents or vote them out. Even capitalists are not poisoned by their cooks."

"Then you will have built up no immunity." The Lord of the Sword smiled again, this time into another mirror. "You can be my food-taster, Mr. Tozer."

CHAPTER 6

1

Extract from the William Bede O'Malley manuscript:
Two days passed and nothing presented itself that offered
any hope of escape. I would look at the surrounding hills
and mountains, remember Kipling's stories of the British
officers and their trusty sepoys coming to the rescue: but
where was the Empire now when we needed it? Playing
polo, no doubt, and sticking bloody pigs down around
Poona. I would think of my father out in Tanganyika, sitting there in his stiff collar and ever stiffer prejudices, sure
that he was making the world safe for Englishmen and,
just incidentally, the natives.

I would look up at the sky, hoping for a sight of an
RAF patrol, the aeroplanes that Durant had told us were
always being shot down by the Waziri: but all I saw were
the cruising kites dropping bird-lime on *our* machines.
Optimism ran out of me with my sweat and each time we
passed the mound of skulls outside the town I began to
get light-headed, as if my own skull was being cleaned
and scoured ready to be added to the heap.

God knows how many bony heads were there in that
macabre monument. A thousand, two thousand? I
wouldn't know. I can never guess at the size of a crowd
when it's alive and its heads are shouting and moving
around. Or even in a church, just nodding off to sleep. I
couldn't *see* at least half the skulls: they were piled high
in a great pyramid of sightless eyes and mirthless smiles.
They grinned at us morning and evening as we rode past
and I noticed that the tribesmen who accompanied us always kept their eyes averted. I began to wonder who had

been the real victors. But I didn't want my skull grinning
out at Suleiman and his followers. If that was victory, I'd
rather be a loser.

"Thank God we are civilized in Europe," said Kern.

"Yes," I said, thinking of all those young men dying as
they walked up the hill on that July morning four years
ago. "At least we bury our skeletons."

Eve and Sun Nan were kept in the town, but Kern was
allowed to accompany me down to the machines. Suleiman accepted my word that I needed Kern, an expert
mechanic, to help me. In the country of the blind the
one-eyed man is king . . . So it is in the country of the
non-expert. Suleiman had men who could fashion rough
works of art in silver, forge swords and knives that Shef-
field wouldn't have been ashamed of, make copies of guns
that could kill just as effectively as the originals. But none
of them knew anything about Rolls-Royce Falcon aero
engines. And even if he had never so much as changed a
spark plug, Kern *could* fly an aeroplane and that, I reck-
oned, would suggest to these tribesmen a certain expertise. After all, entire nations have elected as their
presidents men whose only expertise was in their gall. The
United States was about to do so that coming November,
though none of us knew it just then.

Kern had taken to wearing his silk scarf round his head
as a turban. Suleiman, cackling like an old crone, had
shown him how to wind it. I had no hat and didn't fancy
having my head wrapped in a turban, though Suleiman
offered me one; but I had to protect my head somehow
from that sun that beat down on us each day. Going
down through the town I saw a pith helmet for sale on
one of the stalls in the bazaar; I bought it for a shilling
and only when I was about to put it on did I see the
bloodstains on the dented crown and the name, Hourigan,
in faded ink on the underside of the brim. I wanted to
give it back, but the stall-owner had no time for a dissat-
isfied customer: a sale was a sale. I gingerly put on the
helmet and, when I passed the mound of skulls, wondered

if the late owner, Private, Corporal or Sergeant Hourigan, was grinning out at me.

We rode down the winding track through the hills each morning, half a dozen tribesmen riding guard with us. I was becoming accustomed to the gait of the horse, though a rough hill trail is no place to learn to sit a horse properly. When we got out on to the flat of the narrow valley the guards made us break into a canter and on the morning and afternoon rides of the first day I bounced up and down so much I feared for both my testicles and my head, the ones to be crushed and the other to fall off. But on the second morning I had gained confidence and a little of the horse's rhythm.

To give myself time to think of ways of escaping, I had stripped the engines as far as I dared; to go too far might mean not being able to reassemble them. We went down to the machines in the early morning and worked till about eleven o'clock; then the guards took us across to some caves in the steep cliff that fell down from the eastern ridge. We lolled there in the comparative coolness, eating the food they gave us, dozing off. Kern and I occasionally talked about the only thing we had in common, the Western Front, while the guards eyed us suspiciously but said nothing. Then around three o'clock in the afternoon they would take us back to the machines and we would go through our pretence of working on the engines.

Suleiman had come down the first day and taken away both Lewis guns. "A couple months and I'm gonna have a machine-gun company. Next time the English come up here I'm gonna knock the shit outa them."

"The English have come up here?" I tried to make the question sound casual.

"Coupla times. That's when I guess we collected that hat you wearing. Nice fit?"

"A little tight. Or perhaps dead men's hats never fit the living. History bears me out, I think."

He was ugly enough, but he was frightful when he grinned. "The guy wore that hat, he didn't mean nothing to history. Just some poor son-of-a-bitch didn't even know what the Raj stood for."

"You could be wrong about him." Unreasonably, the nonbeliever in the Empire, I felt I had to defend the dead Hourigan. "Perhaps they gave him a medal for dying. He could be a hero back home in Dublin." I hadn't the faintest idea where Hourigan came from: I said the first Irish place name that came to mind.

Suleiman shook his head, still grinning. "You wear his hat when you go to bomb the English. The Irish would like that."

"You learned a lot around that racecourse at Saratoga."

He shook his head, stopped grinning. "No, Jack. I learned more in the eighteen months I was in France. Didn't you and Fritz?"

I looked at Kern. Neither of us had an answer that would put the cocky little Wazir in his place. He grinned at us once more, mounted his horse and rode off back to the town, his followers carrying the dismantled Lewis guns with them.

Riding down the third morning we passed, as we had each morning, the rough yards outside the town where the horses were kept. I looked back, tried to remember them as I had seen them yesterday and the day before. The scene had been the same: a hundred or more horses in the yards and only three or four men to look after them. There were four large yards, two on each side of a mud-walled hut where the horse attendants ate and slept.

Half an hour later Kern and I were working on Eve's machine. The hessian-wrapped box was still in the front cockpit. Possibly because there were no guns mounted on Eve's plane, none of the Waziri had bothered to climb up and search its cockpits; the only machines that concerned them were Kern's and mine. Suleiman had inspected the forward-firing Vickers, but hadn't suggested I should try to dismantle those; all he had done was to take away all our ammunition. But the statue in its box, more valuable than any of the guns, was still where it had been when we had left Waddon aerodrome. On the floor of Eve's cockpit, tucked up hard against the petrol tank under her wicker seat.

"If we could get out of Suleiman's house and down to those horse yards, do you think we could race him and his cut-throats down here to the machines?"

"No." With his face darkened by grease and dirt and sweat, his head wrapped in the scarf, he could have passed for a Wazir. "You and Sun Nan can't ride well enough to come down that path at a fast pace. Not at night. And I presume you mean for us to try and escape at night?"

"When else?" But I saw his point. "Then somehow we have to get Sun Nan down here at the machines waiting for us."

"How? And what about yourself? Herr O'Malley—"

"Baron, do we have to be so bloody formal out here?" I waved a hand at the wilderness that surrounded us. If he and I were going to die here, if our skulls were going to grin forever at each other on that great mound outside the town, it should not be as two men who had always addressed each other as if reading from visiting cards.

"Bede—" He smiled, put out his hand and I shook it. "Bede, our only way of getting Sun Nan down here is to convince Suleiman Khan that you need a second man in your machine to bomb the English."

"That doesn't appeal to me at all, bombing my own countrymen."

"Would you consider me a filthy Hun if I volunteered to do it? I wouldn't enjoy it any more than you. But after all, I have done it before."

Then I heard a faint drone. But our guards had heard it first. They were already on their feet, shouting at us, running towards us with their rifles raised threateningly. I looked up at the blindingly brilliant sky, but before I could catch a glimpse of the plane or planes, I was hit in the back by a rifle butt. A second guard flashed a knife at me. I skipped away from its sharp point, started running towards the caves. Kern, still hampered by his leg, hobbled after me, with the tribesmen shouting at us all the way.

We stumbled into one of the caves, three of the guards coming in with us and pushing us back into the shadows. The other three Waziri took the horses into neighbouring caves. If the plane or planes sighted the valley at all and came down to inspect, all they would see would be three abandoned Bristol Fighters.

We waited there in the dimness, staring out at the yellow-white glare framed in the entrance. Here in the cave we couldn't hear the drone and I began to wonder if the pilot or pilots had flown on and not seen the Bristols. Then suddenly, with a roar that startled us, two aircraft zoomed past low above the three Bristols. With the suddenness of their coming and going, just swift streaks in the glare, it was impossible to identify the planes. But I knew they must be RAF; who else would be flying around in this Godforsaken wilderness? But then the RAF pilots were probably asking the same question about the three machines parked out there in the middle of the deserted valley. Durant, in Baghdad, had said he would wireless ahead to Quetta to expect us; but perhaps these planes were based somewhere else and knew nothing about us. They could have come from one of the cantonments that Suleiman wanted us to bomb.

I edged towards the entrance, but one of the guards aimed his rifle at me. I stopped, leaned back against the rock, gestured that he was the boss. But I was close enough now to get a clear view of the two planes when they came back again. They were RAF De Haviland 4's, each with a pilot and observer. Then they were gone from sight, but I heard them going up in steep climbs.

I looked at Kern and he nodded. The guards watched us closely, as if expecting us to burst out of the caves and run—but run where? We would have a dozen bullets in our backs before we had gone twenty yards.

Then we heard the planes coming back. One went over, too high for me to see it; then I heard the second plane coming in to land. The pilot throttled back, then he rolled into sight beyond the cave entrance, pulled up beside the three Bristols and cut the engine.

We had a clear view from the cave. I saw the observer stand up in his cockpit, take hold of his Lewis gun and look quickly around him. The pilot jumped down and crossed to the Bristols. I saw him walk quickly round them, then abruptly stop and look down at the ground. He had seen our footprints in the yellow dust. He shouted something to his observer and at once the Lewis gun was swung round and pointed straight at the mouth of our cave. Christ, I yelled in my mind, he's going to blast us out of here!

I heard the pilot shout, "Come—"; but the rest of it was lost in the rear of the second DH4 as it came back less than 100 feet above the ground. Then I felt the barrel of the rifle pressed against my cheek. I didn't turn my head, but out of the corner of my eye I saw the Wazir, a young handsome bastard who couldn't have been more than eighteen or nineteen, shaking his head at me. Swivelling my eyes, I looked the other way: Kern was in exactly the same situation, a gun pressed against his head. The third tribesman had knelt down and was aiming his rifle at the two RAF men. I felt the sweat turning cold on me and I got a sudden blinding headache, the first I could ever remember having. The Wazir squeezed off a shot, the cave reverberating with the crack of it.

Then the Lewis gun opened up. The first burst tore into the cave, hitting the roof and showering us with dirt and splinters of rock. Careless of whether the gun against my head went off, I fell over and rolled towards the back of the cave. If I was going to be killed, I didn't want it to be from a British bullet. The bullets continued to thump into the rock; the RAF man was giving us the whole bloody drum. Bits of rock were flying everywhere; a spent bullet dropped on my back and burned me through my shirt; the air was thick with dust. Coughing, blinded, I rolled myself into a ball, tried to crawl back into the great dark rock womb.

Then abruptly the shooting stopped. I rolled over on my back, wiped the grit and dust from my face, looked out at the entrance. The dust cleared slowly, the glare appearing again like a yellow sun coming out from behind a brown storm-cloud. Two of the Waziri were stretched out; even through the drifting dust I could see they were dead. The third one was sitting against the wall, his head back against the rock, staring out through the entrance. Then all at once he fell over and I realized he was dead, too.

I sat up; and so did Kern. "You all right?" I spat out dust with the words.

"Yes." He stood up, limped to the front of the cave. I saw him outlined against the glare, then suddenly he leaned against the rock as if he had been hit and had only just realized it. "Oh, mein Gott!"

I scrambled to my feet, reached him as a Wazir from the neighbouring cave came running at us, covering us with his rifle. I saw the DH4, the pilot slumped over the lower wing, the observer hanging half-out of his cockpit. Then I heard the approaching roar as the second plane came back down the valley. He was too low; he should have stayed higher. He came back at the same low altitude as before, making a run along the base of the cliff so that his observer could rake the caves with his Lewis. I fell down again, Kern and the Wazir following suit. I heard the stutter of the Lewis and I lay there in the open praying that his line of fire would be too high. Then I saw the tribesman behind the rock outside the other cave.

He had his rifle resting on the rock and was taking careful aim as if he were on range practice, as if he were aiming at a stationary target instead of one going past him a hundred yards away at 100 miles an hour. I know this sounds as if I'm making it up, but I swear it is true; ask any old soldier, if you know any, who served on the North-West Frontier about the marksmanship of the Pathan snipers. That Wazir got off two shots while the bullets from the Lewis gun stitched a line only three feet above his head. I saw the pilot suddenly slump in his cockpit, just as I had seen other pilots do in other skies;

the DH screamed up as if it were trying to climb vertically. The observer was struggling frantically to sit down in his cockpit: as if it were going to make any difference. The aircraft slipped sideways in a half-roll and, engine still roaring, went straight into the side of a ridge and exploded with a bang that, in memory, still hurts my ears and eyes.

"Jesus Christ!"

I jumped up. But the Wazir lying on the ground beside me was quicker. He backed off, covering Kern and me with his rifle, while his two companions came running towards us, one of them going into our cave to look at the three dead men, then coming out almost at once. They were shouting at us and at each other, their eyes wild in the rings of kohl; I thought they had gone insane, were going to kill us then and there. One of them, the youngest, raised his rifle and pointed it at me, his finger curling on the trigger.

I'll never know where I got the coolness to do it. Perhaps in the moment before you know you are going to be dead you get a calmness that accepts it. I'd been faced with death before; but never this close. Not to be able to see the man's finger about to squeeze the trigger.

I looked directly at him, then waved a hand towards the Bristols. "Suleiman Khan won't like it," I said.

If I could have spoken his language I couldn't have said any more. I was looking straight down the barrel of the gun only ten feet from me, right into those dark-rimmed eyes. He was young, his beard wispy: perhaps it was his youth that saved me. He was still young enough to be afraid of his leader, the *malik* Suleiman Khan. If he killed me and Kern his own head might be added to the mound of skulls outside the town. They were different days then, young men were put in their place. Sometimes I'd like to see a mound of skulls outside Fort Lauderdale.

He lowered his rifle, glared at me with hatred, then spun round and went back to the caves where the horses were still held out of sight. I wanted to collapse where I stood, but somehow managed to stay upright.

"Jolly good, Bede."

I looked at Kern and grinned weakly. Then I looked
back towards the distant ridge and the burning pyre of the
crashed DH4; then closer, at the two dead RAF men in
the machine parked by our Bristols. "Poor blighters.
We're to blame for that. We should never have attempted
this stupid bloody flight—"

He shook his head. "Don't say anything now, Bede.
Tomorrow you'll realize we were no more to blame than
we were for all those English skulls on that heap outside
the town. Those fliers out there were fighting these chaps
long before we got here."

He was right, of course. The four dead RAF men, if
the dead ever think of blame, would not have cursed me.
Soldiers of the king, and queen, had been fighting and dying in these hills for years before I was born, before even
my father was born. One can't blame oneself for the
wages of empire: only emperors can do that.

The horses were brought out of the caves. The three
dead Waziri were thrown across the saddles of their
horses; the three survivors seemed to take particular care
that each dead man was on his own horse. Kern and I
were ordered to mount. The youngest Wazir rode across
to the aircraft; when he came back he had the heads of
the two RAF men dangling from the back of his saddle.
They were both young men: fair-haired, blue-eyed, handsome and horrible. I turned away, looked at Kern, knew
that each of us was as white and sick as the other.

We rode back to the town: five live men, three corpses,
two heads: a macabre party. When we passed the mound
of skulls the Wazir carrying the two heads dropped behind; Kern and I didn't look back. We rode up through
the narrow streets followed by a murmuring, threatening
crowd; two women suddenly screamed and ran after us,
clutching at the bodies draped over the horses. By the
time we reached Suleiman's house the crowd was pressed
in against us like dark mud trying to engulf us: the faces
that looked up at us could have been suffering the agony
of their own dying instead of screaming hate at me and

Kern. We were thumped, scratched, spat upon as one of the guards pushed us ahead of him into the house. The door was slammed shut, shutting out the bedlam of the crowd; we could still hear them, but we were safe. For the time being, anyway.

Suleiman, in his gold-and-silver slippers, came into the hallway as Kern and I were pushed into the side room where Eve and Sun Nan were waiting to hear what had happened. I had just finished explaining when Suleiman came into the room.

"You bomb the English first thing tomorrow morning," he said without any preliminary. "One of them airplanes has gotta be flying."

I knew there was no use arguing any further. The crowd was still outside, the shouts of the men and the wailing and screaming of the women beating against the shutters like a storm of demented birds. Our only hope of staying alive was to do everything Suleiman asked. He had suddenly become our only protection.

"I'll fly the machine," said Kern. "You can't trust Herr O'Malley to bomb his own countrymen."

"It ain't only me's gotta trust him." Suleiman must have been the shrewdest stable-boy they ever had around Saratoga and Belmont Park; I don't know why he didn't make a fortune there, either as a better or a professional nobbler. "You gotta trust him, too. He don't bomb the English, you ain't gonna be alive tomorrow night." He drew his finger across his throat, something I thought only Tom Santschi and other motion picture villains did. "You seen those guys' heads they brung up from the valley? You wanna look like that?"

I looked at Eve. She was pale, but that was all: no wobbling at the knees, no sign of the vapours. She couldn't help acting like a rich bitch at times, spoiled by her father's money; but she was a thoroughbred, an absolute pip, as Durant had said. I was still annoyed at her attitude towards Kern's and my relaxation in the mess at Baghdad, but I had lost none of my admiration for her. Nor was I any less in love with her.

"I'll bomb the cantonments," I said. "But if you keep me and the Baron here to teach your chaps to fly, will you let Miss Tozer and Mr. Sun fly on tomorrow morning? Miss Tozer has to be in China in another four days. Her father is being held prisoner, just as you are holding us. He'll be killed if she's not there in time."

"You gotta pay some ransom or something?" The blue eyes looked at Eve with sudden interest; evidently he was the sort of Moslem who would listen to a woman if she had money. "How much?"

"I don't know until I get to China." Eve didn't bat an eyelid; she lied as well as I might have done myself. "The money is in a bank in Shanghai."

"How much money would your pa pay for you?"

"My father isn't in a position to pay anything. You forget, he's a prisoner, too."

"You got any other family? Your ma, someone like that?"

"Nobody. There are only my father and I and we have both been kidnapped. The bank would not pay out money for either of us without authorization. And my father and I are the only two who can authorize payment."

"Kinda funny, ain't it?" Suleiman cackled, grinning horribly. "Okay, I ain't promising anything. I might let you go, I might not. We'll see after Fritz or O'Malley comes back from bombing the English."

"I'll do the bombing," said Kern. "I'm a better flier than Herr O'Malley, as he will admit. I shot down twice as many machines as he did on the Western Front."

"That so?" Suleiman looked at me.

"Thirty-two to sixteen," I said, and hoped I lied as well as Eve just had; I know I must have looked unhappy, making such an admission. "The Baron is far more experienced than I am."

"I'll take Mr. Sun with me as my bombardier," said Kern. "Then you need have no fears about whether the English will be bombed."

"I fought the English in the Boxer Rebellion." Sun Nan added his bit; I couldn't be sure, but he looked a better

liar than any of us. "I have waited a long time for revenge."

Suleiman nodded appreciatively. "That's the first com-
mandment of *Pukhtunwali*, the way of the Pushtun—revenge. We call it *badal*. You want some revenge, too,
Fritz?"

"Yes," said Kern, and had the grace not to look at me.

"Okay, you fly one of them airplanes at daylight tomorrow. You gotta be there before they send up airplanes to
bomb us. We got some maps—I'll show you later where
you gotta fly to."

He went out, closing the door. The noise of the crowd
had stilled, but when I went to the window and looked
out through the half-opened shutters I could see there was
still a mob in the street, staring sullenly at the house in
which the infidels were held.

Sun Nan was pouring tea for the four of us. A large
brass samovar had been brought in and placed on a table
in the corner of the room. There were thick china cups
that looked as if they might have come from some looted
English mess; and a plate of *nan*, the flat round bread,
and another of small cakes covered with honey and nuts.
Kern and I had arrived back from the death and horror
down in the valley in time for afternoon tea.

"You have a choice," said Sun Nan. "Green tea, which,
naturally, I think is the best. Or what Suleiman Khan
calls English tea." He gestured at a small teapot, which
had some sort of regimental crest on it: probably another
looted relic. "But you may not think it is English. The
tea, buffalo milk and sugar are all boiled together. So he
tells me."

I grimaced. "Green tea, please. What's that coat-of-
arms on the samovar?"

Kern had been examining it. "It is one of the Russian
Tsars. Alexander the Second's, I think. My grandfather
had one like it. He was the Prussian military attaché at
the court at St. Petersburg."

"How did Suleiman get it? The Pathans never had anyone in St. Petersburg." Though Suleiman, like all his

tribesmen as I've since found out, called himself a Pushtun, I couldn't get out of the habit of the English usage:
Pathan. "Unless one of the Tsar's relatives came through
here, down from Samarkand?"

"Some of those skulls outside town could be Russian."
Eve sipped green tea, little finger daintily crooked, a
proper Bostonian doing her best to accept a situation that
no Bostonian would consider proper. Not unless the skulls
were those of Bolsheviks. "I wonder what of ours Suleiman will keep in his house as a souvenir of us?"

"He has your gun," I said, taking the tea Sun Nan
handed me. "But when we leave here tomorrow morning
we're going to take that with us."

"We? All of us?"

"Yes. What I have in mind might be a hundred-to-one
chance, but it's all I can think of. And I'd rather die running than standing still."

End of extract from O'Malley manuscript.

2

The faint skirling of the pipes had gone on all night, a
keening that had a universal sadness. Eve found that she
was not untouched by it. The lament was for the three
Waziri who had died, not for the two RAF Englishmen,
but gradually she had become depressed by the thin sad
music, felt sympathy for the unknown mothers or wives of
the dead tribesmen. In the morning their fathers or brothers might want to kill her and Bede and the Baron and
Sun Nan, but tonight, in the darkness of the world and
the spirit, she understood and felt the pain of those who
had asked the piper to play.

She had slept only fitfully on the uncomfortable *charpoy*, dozing off and coming awake suddenly several times.
The fourth time she came awake the three men were
standing by the window. The shutters had been closed
and locked from the outside, but moonlight filtered in,

enough to illuminate the three men as they stood close together.

"What's going on?" she whispered as she sat up.

"Suleiman will be coming for us soon," said Kern. "It should be daylight in another hour."

"How long do you think from the time you leave here till you come back?" O'Malley asked. "Eve and I have to be ready to move."

He called me by my first name again, Eve thought. And was glad: she needed comfort, if only in the tone of a voice.

"Forty-five minutes at least." Kern unwound the silk scarf that he was once again wearing round his neck. "You had better take this. It is easier to garrotte a man with a scarf or stockings than with your bare hands."

"What twist do I use?" said O'Malley. "An Immelman turn?"

Both men smiled at each other, a joke among professionals; except, Eve thought, neither of them has made a profession of strangling men to death. She was shocked to realize she was not shocked by the grim little joke. The fear of one's own death coarsened one. If she got back to Boston alive she would tell her grandmother one didn't survive with civilities. Her grandmother, safe among the civilities of Beacon Hill, would tell her to forget such heresy.

There was the sound of footsteps in the hallway. O'Malley, Kern and Sun Nan went back to their beds; Eve lay down again. The door was unlocked and Suleiman and three guards came in, two of them carrying oil lamps.

"It's time, Fritz." Suleiman was dressed as he had been the first day they had arrived, in his purple shirt, yellow waistcoat and the dead American officer's Bedfords and riding boots. The long sword hung in a scabbard at his belt. "You keep the dame company, O'Malley. She talks too much, but she's a nice bit of flesh. I seen worse than her around Saratoga."

"Horses or women?" said Eve.

Suleiman gestured to O'Malley. "See what I mean? Talks too much. Okay, Fritz, let's go. Here, I want you to wear this. So when you fly over the English, they'll think you a Pushtun. That oughta scare the hell outa them. A Pushtun can fly."

He picked up the silk scarf that O'Malley had dropped on the end of his bed, handed it to Kern. "Wouldn't it look better if I wore a real turban?" the German said. "I'd be honoured to wear it."

"Next time, Fritz. The English ain't gonna be close enough to you to tell the difference."

Kern wound the scarf round his head, tucked in the end. In the flickering light of the oil lamps he looked a brother to the Pathan. He looks cruel and handsome and romantic, Eve thought; in other circumstances she knew she might have been infatuated with him. He turned to her, clicked his heels, kissed her hand. "We shan't be long, Fräulein."

"Good luck, Baron. Your turban suits you."

"Thank you. Herr Sun, shall we go and bomb the English?"

"A pleasure," said Sun Nan, voice hissing a little, and fixed his bowler hat carefully on his head.

"One things you guys got," said Suleiman. "You civilized."

"It'll come to you, too," said O'Malley.

"Sure. When we get rid of the English."

Suleiman led the way out of the room, the door was locked again and Eve and O'Malley were left alone. Eve, intent on doing anything to avoid a feeling of helplessness, of doing nothing but just sit and wait, went across to the samovar and lit the small oil lamp under it. O'Malley said nothing, just watched her. She was aware of his gaze. She had been stared at by men ever since she had turned fifteen, but for the first time she felt uncomfortable.

At last she handed him a cup of green tea. "There's still some of that awful flat bread. And some honey."

"We'd better eat some. We're going to have to do some heavy running to get down to those horses."

"Do you really think we can get away?"

He shrugged, sipped his tea. "You make a good cup of tea."

"My grandmother taught me. She has always thought the Boston Tea Party was a mistake. She would have preferred it if they had thrown coffee into the harbour. She never drinks it."

Suddenly he smiled at her and just as suddenly she smiled back. Then she sat down on the low *charpoy* and began to take off her stockings. Her skirt slid back above her knees and when she looked up he was watching her.

"Suleiman was right. You are a nice bit of flesh."

He was still smiling and she couldn't take offence; not that she wanted to. "I think you'd be a cad and a bounder, given half the chance."

"Not really. Not unless I was encouraged. Why are you taking off your stockings?"

"I'm not encouraging you, if that's what you think."

"Have you ever been made love to by a poor man?"

"I don't know. Depends what you mean by making love and what you consider poor."

"A proper lady's answer. You win. What am I supposed to do with these?"

She had handed him the stockings as she stood up again. "Bede, use them. The Baron said a scarf or stockings was best for—you know."

He took the stockings, tied them together, rolled them into a silk rope and tested the strength of it. She watched him, trying to keep from seeing it round a man's throat. "It'll do. When we get to Shanghai, I'll buy you another pair. The best a poor man can buy."

I like him: he can be so nice. "Don't let's fight again, Bede."

He took her left hand, felt the third finger. "Do you have a chap waiting for you in America?"

"No. No one special—rich or poor." There were men waiting in Boston, at Bar Harbor, in Palm Beach, to dance with her, take her sailing, try to make love to her.

But no one special. "The only man I'm thinking of right now is my father."

He squeezed her hand, dropped it. "Of course."

Later he said, "How much longer do we have?"

She took out her father's watch, held it up to the growing daylight filtering through the shutters. "Five minutes, I should say."

"Righto, you know what to do as soon as we hear the Baron."

Outside the town was coming awake. The skirling of the pipes still went on, but very faintly now, as if the piper was exhausted or half-asleep. A cock crew, was answered by another. Some shutters were slammed back against the wall of the house next door, the day begun with a bang. A voice called out, gruff and whining with sleep: Eve didn't understand the language but she knew some lazy so-and-so was being told to get out of bed.

Then she heard the sound of the aeroplane. She looked at O'Malley and he nodded. He slipped behind the door, his hands held wide apart as he stretched the silk rope between them. The plane came up over the town, flying low; in the dim daylight Kern had done a marvellous job of picking out the right street. He brought the Bristol in just above roof-top; the sound of it was a bombardment in itself. It swooped over the house and as it did Eve started to thump on the door and scream at the top of her voice.

As soon as the plane had passed overhead she stopped screaming (she must not be heard by the people next door, she suddenly realized) but continued to bang frantically on the door. There were hurried footsteps in the hallway, an angry shout, then she heard the key being turned in the lock. She stepped back into the room; the guard came in and advanced towards her. She saw O'Malley come out from behind the door, his hands held high; the noose went round the Wazir's throat and was pulled tight. He dropped his rifle and clutched at the rope; his eyes popped and his mouth fell open. Eve watched him die, unable to take her eyes off him: it seemed to take forever.

Then O'Malley stepped back, loosening the noose and the tribesman dropped to the floor. "Jesus! There are better ways of killing a man than that!"

Then he snatched up the dropped rifle, grabbed Eve by the hand as Kern came back from the opposite direction. They heard the roar of the engine, then of the bomb: it hit the house. The top floor must have gone in the blast: the ceiling of the room cracked and began to cave in above them. They ran out through the doorway and stumbled into a thick fog of dust and smoke. O'Malley fell over something, dragging Eve down with him. She fell on him, heard him gasp and curse. She rolled away, coughing as the dust and smoke bit into her throat, and saw the second guard, knife in hand, coming at them.

She felt something beneath her hand, a piece of masonry; she picked it up and hurled it at the Wazir as she struggled to her feet. Then the rifle went off almost in her ear. Deafened, she saw the tribesman lurch back, sit down and fall over. O'Malley had fired from the hip; she saw him nod his head in satisfaction. "*That's* a better way to kill a man!"

Kern must have done an incredibly sharp turn. He was already coming back down the street, again just above the rooftops. O'Malley flung himself flat, pulling Eve down with him. The second bomb sliced through the top front of the house. There was another tremendous explosion and everything seemed to fall in on them.

"Too close, you bloody Chinese fool!" O'Malley yelled, then began to cough on the smoke and dust.

Eve, bruised, cut, unable to believe she was still alive, scrambled to her feet. O'Malley sat amidst the rubble, head between his knees as he coughed as if trying to bring his lungs up. She hit him on the back, helped him to his feet. The front door was wide open; or rather, the whole front of the house was wide open. But they couldn't leave just yet.

O'Malley, still coughing, dragged the dead Wazir further back along the wrecked hall. "Strip him!" he spluttered, then stumbled over the debris back into the room

where the first guard lay. Eve began to tear off the clothes
of the dead man. She pulled on his pantaloons over her
skirt, wound his filthy turban round her head. But when it
came to putting on the bloodstained shirt, she couldn't
face it; she dropped it and pulled on his tunic over her
blouse. As she finished O'Malley came out of the side
room, dressed like herself.

"The Pushtun Twins. Come on!"

"I want my gun first!"

She found it in the big room on the opposite side of the
hall, a room that hadn't been touched by the bombs. The
Magnum .375 lay on a table, beside the four boxes of ammunition she had brought with her from London. She
grabbed the gun and two boxes of ammunition, while
O'Malley yelled at her from the doorway for God's sake
to get a move on. They went out of the house into the
street as Kern and Sun Nan came back a third time. The
street was full of fleeing, shouting, screaming Waziri, all
running up the street towards the hill behind the town.
Eve felt it was like plunging into a thick turgid sea: one
couldn't swim with the current. She kept her head down,
afraid of being recognized; kept hold of the back of
O'Malley's tunic as he forced his way down through the
running tide of people. She almost fell, felt something soft
beneath her, looked down and saw she had trodden right
over an old woman who had fallen to the ground. The
Bristol went over with an ear-shattering roar; the crowd
fell back against the walls on either side and for a moment
the street was comparatively clear. They ran on, down
towards where the third bomb had exploded at the bottom of the street.

They ran into a swirl of smoke and dust, came out into
the square at the bottom of the town, kept running
towards the gates in the wall. Eve was gasping for breath,
her knees were buckling, she knew she was going to collapse into the dirt long before they reached the horse
yards. But O'Malley was dragging her along, shouting encouragement to her, shaking his rifle furiously, like a
good angry Wazir, at the Bristol as Kern brought it back

again and Sun Nan flung another bomb at the guard tower on the wall above the gates. The tower disappeared in the explosion and O'Malley and Eve ran in under it and came out into the open, the horse yards only fifty yards ahead of them.

The horses were screaming and rearing, galloping madly round and round the yards. Oh God, Eve thought, how are we going to catch them? Then, still running, blinded by dust and exhaustion, her lungs burning like a fire inside her, her legs ready to give out, she saw the two horse-guards trying to calm the two saddled horses outside their hut. O'Malley saw them at the same time. He slapped her hand away from his tunic and raced ahead.

One of the guards turned as O'Malley reached him. Blinded though she was, Eve saw the look of surprise on his face as O'Malley hit him with the butt of his rifle. The guard went down, falling under the horse. O'Malley grabbed the reins, flung them at Eve and ran round to take on the second man. His horse was rearing, screaming shrilly in terror; he didn't see O'Malley at all. He went down without knowing what had hit him. O'Malley slung his rifle over his back, grabbed the reins of the rearing horse and tried to mount. Eve, already mounted, swung her horse in beside the panic-stricken bay, forcing it against the yard fence. The Bristol had flown off, but the horses in the yard were crazy with terror; the saddled horse outside the yard seemed as if it were trying to get in with them. O'Malley was never going to be able to mount it, let alone ride it.

"Take mine!" Eve yelled.

O'Malley didn't argue. He grabbed the reins of Eve's horse. She kicked her feet free of the stirrups, grabbed the reins of the rearing horse and swung herself across into its saddle. O'Malley somehow swung up into the saddle of the calmer horse, pulled it away as Eve tried to quieten her mount. The horse, a big bay stallion, reared again; but fortunately it didn't buck. It suddenly took off, running blindly. Straight back towards the gate of the town.

Eve struggled desperately, pulling with all her strength

to get the stallion's head down. They went in under the shattered gateway at full gallop, the horse's head tossing wildly, Eve fighting to master it. They raced across the square and for one awful moment Eve thought they were going to go plunging up the crowded street she had just left. Then the horse seemed to sense it was going to get nowhere running into the crowd of people ahead of it. It veered away, putting its head down, and in that moment Eve took control of it. She swung it round in a wide circle, riding it now, not fighting it, talking to it, and took it out through the gateway again at the gallop.

She saw O'Malley waiting for her. He swung his horse round, she caught up with him and they went down the narrow road that led off the ridge and down through the hills to the valley. As they did so, Kern and Sun Nan came back and bombed the mound of skulls.

3

Kern saw the great heap fly apart as a giant flower; petals of bone flew off in all directions. He lifted the plane, saw the two horsemen racing down towards the road. He wanted to zoom down low above them to express his delight at their escaping from the town; but, afraid of frightening the horses, he kept a discreet altitude. But he saw one of the riders glance up at him and he waggled his wings in encouragement. Then he looked back at Sun Nan, spoke into the tube.

"How many more bombs?" Sun Nan held up two fingers. "Save them. We may need them."

"I should like to drop them on Suleiman Khan."

When they had ridden down from the town and reached the planes, Suleiman had been like a schoolboy about to blow up his school. He was cackling and joking with his men and they all shared his mood. There were fifty or sixty of them and when they had come down on to the flat of the valley floor most of them had broken into a gallop and, yelling at the top of their voices, had charged up towards the aeroplanes. Despite his overall mood, Kern had once again felt a thrill as he had watched the massed party of horsemen stretch out at full gallop.

Suleiman must have been watching him. "You like horses, Fritz?"

"I was trained for the cavalry before I became a flier."

"Stay with us, Fritz. You'll get to fly airplanes, ride horses, anything you want." Suleiman was expansive in the early morning light, the dawn of a new day when the English were going to have the hell bombed out of them. "You can have the American dame, if you want her."

"It's an attractive thought," said Kern, but didn't specify which of the prospects appealed to him. "I'll think about it."

They had reached the aeroplanes. The horsemen had formed a circle round the three Bristols and DH4, as if to guard against any of the planes taking-off of its own accord. Kern and O'Malley had been brought back here late yesterday afternoon, the engines had been reassembled and the planes were ready to fly again. It had been decided that Kern and Sun Nan would take-off in Eve's plane this morning. If Eve and O'Malley did not manage to get away from the town, the German and the Chinese were to fly on, taking the statue in its box with them. Even if Eve's and O'Malley's lives were lost, Kern was still to try to save Bradley Tozer's life.

He felt the weight of the responsibility that had been given him, but he had not tried to shirk it. But it made him cold and aloof to the grinning banter of the Waziri leader. "You sound pretty toffee-nosed this morning, Fritz. You ain't getting any ideas you gonna double-cross us or something?"

"I'm going to bomb the English for you. That's all you've asked me to do."

Suleiman looked at him suspiciously, then at Sun Nan. "How about you, Chink? How you feeling about what you gonna do?"

"All I wish is to get home to China. I shall bomb anyone."

"You high-class, Chink. I never seen a high-class Chinee before, only guys work in a laundry."

"There are several hundred million of us back home in China. All of us can't be laundry workers. Some of us are pushed up to be, er, high-class Chinee."

Suleiman cackled; he was in such a good humour this morning he could take a joke against himself. But the biggest joke is to come, Kern thought, and you won't be laughing then.

The bombs had been brought down last night by four tribesmen who had stayed to guard the planes. During the night they had either buried or otherwise disposed of the headless corpses of the two RAF men; Kern had noticed there were no circling carrion birds in the morning virgin sky. He and Sun Nan got up into Eve's plane and the bombs were handed up to them. Kern was surprised at the finished look of them; they might almost have come direct from an armament factory. Krupps would not have suffered by employing some of these Pathan bomb-makers. Providing, of course, that the bombs went off when they hit their target.

"You're sure the bombs will go off?"

Suleiman, on his black stallion, was on eye-level with Kern. "They gonna go off all right." He wasn't cackling or grinning now. "All you gotta do, you drop 'em. And then you come back here. You don't, the dame and the Englishman, their heads gonna be on that heap outside town before the sun gets up there." He pointed straight above his head.

"Oh, we'll be back."

"It is a promise," said Sun Nan. "We shall drop every bomb on its proper target."

And they had. Now there were two bombs left. Kern took the Bristol up till he could see down over the sharp-ridged hills to the valley. The sun was up, throwing everything into sharp relief. He saw the horsemen down by the planes congeal together and start riding at full gallop back towards the road that led up to the town. Suleiman had heard the bombing and knew he had been double-crossed.

Kern took the plane down, straight at the horse party as it came up the track. He raised his hand and behind him Sun Nan let go the first of the two bombs. It hit the track ten feet in front of the leading horsemen, sending up a black mushroom that obscured them. He banked, came back, saw that at least half the Waziri had got through and were still hurrying their mounts up the narrow track. The last bomb landed right in the middle of the file of horsemen. But when he looked back he saw there were still half a dozen tribesmen on their horses, still heading up towards the town. One of them looked up and waved his rifle defiantly.

Kern climbed higher, looked for Eve and O'Malley, saw them coming down the track no more than half a mile ahead of the climbing Waziri. He went down as low as he dared without frightening the horses, pointed frantically down the track. He saw them slow, then abruptly swing their horses off into a narrow wadi. The sun struck across the top of it and he saw them pull into the deep shadow of it. The half a dozen Waziri went past the end of the wadi and as soon as they had, Eve and O'Malley were on the track again. Kern circled above them, saw them thread their way through the corpses of men and horses where the last bomb had dropped, then quicken their pace as they came down towards the floor of the valley. They stretched out as they reached the flat, raced for the planes. Kern swung up in a wide bank, looked up towards the distant town and saw the horsemen, half a dozen of them, coming back down the track.

He went down low above the parked planes, waggling his wings and pointing in the direction of the town. Eve was already in one of the Bristols and O'Malley was cranking the propeller. They both waved to Kern, but he had no way of knowing whether they had understood his warning. He climbed higher and flew back up over the ridges.

The Waziri had already passed the two spots where Sun Nan had dropped the bombs. They were riding like the hillmen they were, pushing their horses down the winding track with reckless disregard for themselves or their mounts. They were led by a rider in a yellow waistcoat and purple shirt.

Kern swung back towards the parked aircraft, expecting to see the propeller swinging on one of the Bristols. But O'Malley was still struggling to get the airscrew moving. Suddenly he ran across to the other Bristol; Eve scrambled down from the cockpit of the first plane and followed him. Kern flew low over them, banked sharply and came back along the valley. As he did so he saw Suleiman and his men come down on to the valley floor. He continued straight at them, no more than four or five feet above the ground. The riders came towards him incredibly swiftly. They were going to meet his machine head on: again he tasted suicide, heard Sun Nan's yell in the Gosport tubes. At the last moment he lifted the nose, caught a glimpse of the horsemen as they abruptly pulled away, three of the horses plunging headlong as their legs snapped beneath them. He climbed steeply, looked back and saw the lone horseman in the yellow waistcoat, sword strident in the morning sun like a visible scream of rage, still galloping full tilt towards Eve and O'Malley and the still earth-bound Bristol.

Kern banked, came back, but he knew he was going to be too late. Then he saw O'Malley suddenly step back, saw the puff of smoke from the engine and the sudden circle of shimmering light where the propeller had been. O'Malley ran round the wing on the blind side of the plane from the rapidly approaching Suleiman. The Wazir was no more than forty yards from the Bristol, still racing at full gallop as if he intended to run straight into the plane, his sword held high in a frightening, splendid, useless challenge. Then Eve stood up in the cockpit and aimed her gun at him.

The little man fell out of his saddle only ten yards short of the plane. His horse swung to one side, just missing the tail-assembly, and went galloping off up the valley. Eve sat down again in the cockpit. O'Malley swung up into the rear cockpit. A moment later the Bristol was moving down the valley, then climbing into the face of the sun. Kern looked back at Sun Nan, raised his hand in triumph and the Chinese smiled and nodded vigorously, anything but Orientally inscrutable.

Kern took his machine round in a wide circle, came back to fly in beside Eve as she levelled out. When he looked back he saw the two surviving horsemen riding towards the abandoned Bristol and the DH4. Lying between the two planes, his yellow waistcoat fading out in the growing glare of the sun, was Suleiman Khan, Pushtun *malik*, collector of skulls, corporal in the 81st Mule Company and stable-boy at Saratoga, Belmont Park and places like that.

4

"Madame Buloff hasn't poisoned us yet," said General Meng. "No offence meant, Madame. It is just that my humble Chinese stomach is not accustomed to the richness of Russian cuisine."

If Madame Buloff was offended, she didn't show it. "I only wish I could serve you caviar, General. Next time you come to Shanghai I shall serve you the most sumptuous meal you have ever tasted."

"I cannot wait," said General Meng. "Now would you be so kind as to taste the dishes, Mr. Tozer? Don't be afraid. You have survived so far."

Bradley Tozer, not looking at the Buloffs, tasted the food. He knew he was not going to be poisoned; but that didn't make it taste any better. If Madame Buloff intended to offer meals in her chain of tea-rooms-cum-brothels across the United States, she would soon put herself out of business. A man's ardour would soften if he had to take bismuth before climbing into bed with one of Madame's girls.

He had told her that the Lord of the Sword had become suspicious that he might be poisoned; she had told him not to worry. "I still have not found a slow poison. I'm sure the Chinese have such a poison, they are so advanced in disposing of people, much more than we Russians. But here in the General's palace they prefer quicker methods." She gave pantomimic illustrations of shooting, throat-cutting and head-chopping; with her bulk she looked frightening in all methods. "Do not worry, Mr. Tozer. When I find the right poison, I shall let you know."

"But how will I avoid tasting it?"

"Oh, you will have to taste it. But we can pump your stomach out before it kills you. Grigori Rasputin showed me how to do it. He was my lover, you know."

"Oh, really?" Tozer wasn't accustomed to such confidences from women.

"Of course I was not his only mistress. He was a devil, that man."

"So I've heard."

But his idea of a devil and hers were different. "He was a monk, but he was always jumping into bed with women. He had the stamina of six stallions. But he saved me."

"What from—hell?" He had a vision of the virile monk indulging in some evangelism while rebuttoning his cassock.

"No, food poisoning. He laid his hands on my stomach and cured me. But afterwards, when everyone had gone, he pumped my stomach out with tubes. You will be safe, Mr. Tozer. I shall do the same with your stomach."

But so far she had not come up with anything that would kill General Meng in his sleep. Time was running out and Bradley Tozer, the food-taster, had lost his taste completely.

The meal began. It was no better than any of Madame Buloff's other meals. Later General Meng invited Tozer to walk with him on the terrace. They went outside, began to stroll up and down, the two Mongolian guards watching from a distance. They walked under the peach tree and Meng reached up and plucked a fruit.

"One treasures the peach—it is the symbol of longevity for us. I eat at least one a day. It is one of the few good things about this part of the country—that the peach grows so well."

"Would a peach guarantee me a long life?"

"In the circumstances, I doubt it." Meng changed the subject, as if embarrassed at having to deny a superstition, one that didn't fit in with another. "Once, as a boy, I went with the English botanist Wilson into western Szechuen. We climbed mountains and he showed me flowers I had never seen before. I should like to go back there, be the *tuchun*. I should build myself another *yamen* and surround it with peach trees. I shan't, of course. One can't choose one's kingdoms any more."

"One can in America. A business kingdom."

The Lord of the Sword smiled. "Perhaps I shall come to America and be a *tuchun*. Where would you suggest?"

"Texas," said Tozer, trying to think of some State that deserved a *tuchun*. "But why don't you become war-lord of all China?"

"No one man can ever rule China. Those days are gone. No, I am happy to be lord of what I am. Domains can become too big, Mr. Tozer. So many of your Western kings fell because they never recognized that fact."

He paused by the terrace wall and gazed out over the countryside. In the evening light it seemed that nothing moved. Tozer had often been aware of this utter stillness that could descend on the Chinese landscape, as if the farmers and whatever travellers were passing by had made themselves invisible, had surrendered the countryside to its own pattern of light and shade and soothing tranquillity. But he knew it was all illusory. Under the soft dusk-blue peace was the volcano of hundreds of millions of human beings.

"The dog Chang's forces are no more than twenty miles down the road. Several regiments, my spies tell me."

"Will he attack?" Tozer felt a lift of hope: perhaps he could escape in the heat of the coming battle.

"Not with so few men. He will need treble that if he hopes to beat me. But perhaps he is just flexing his muscles. In other circumstances I should go out and cut his regiments to pieces."

"But not now?"

Meng smiled again. "The circumstances are not propitious, Mr. Tozer. What if my fortune should be as bad as it has been since I lost my statue? I might even lose my own life."

"I shouldn't want that to happen," said Tozer politely.

"You are a charming man, Mr. Tozer. I do hope I don't have to kill you."

The Buloffs came strolling along the terrace, hand-in-hand, a two-tiered monument to marital devotion. Buloff stood on tip-toe and his wife leaned down: his lips met her cheek in a kiss. "These Russians," said General Meng. "They have no sense of modesty in public."

"In America brothel-madams are the most modest of women in public."

"I should not have thought you would know any."

"Only by repute, General."

The Buloffs reached them and Madame Buloff put out a hand and stroked Tozer's upper lip. "Your moustache is coming on, Mr. Tozer. In this light it looks almost full grown. Doesn't it suit him, General?"

"Let's hope he has enough time to grow it fully."

Madame Buloff ran a finger along Tozer's cheek. "But you need another shave. I shall give you one tonight before you go to bed."

"I shouldn't want to tear you away from the Colonel."

Buloff beamed, waved a generous hand. "My wife has

dedicated her life to attending to men's pleasures. But I am *her* only pleasure. If you know what I mean."

"How quaint," said the Lord of the Sword, suddenly Puritan-prim. "Goodnight, Mr. Tozer. Don't forget to pray."

He walked off, followed by the two Mongolian guards, and Madame Buloff stared after him. "I should *love* to shave him."

"Now, now, my pet." The Colonel stroked her as if she were about to run amok. "We shall be out of here by to-morrow evening." He saw Tozer look sharply at him and he added, shrugging, "I hope."

An hour later Madame Buloff came to Tozer in his room. By now the guard no longer bothered to come into the room with her while she shaved the prisoner; the door was kept open and he remained sitting on his stool in the corridor outside. Madame Buloff began to lather Tozer's face.

"I can find no poison, so we have to go back to our original plan. You will have to dispose of the guard, then join us down at the truck lines."

"How do I dispose of the guard?"

She drew the razor's blunt edge across his throat. "How else? I do like your moustache. You are a handsome man, Mr. Tozer."

"I am not a client, Madame Buloff."

She smiled, towering over him, massively seductive. "It would be free, Mr. Tozer. I have never sold myself."

"You would find me a disappointment after Rasputin and the Colonel."

"I think you must have been a stallion when you were young."

"I was just a virgin quarterback. All American," he added, not wanting to downgrade himself too much.

She finished shaving him, patted his cheeks with cologne. "I love the smell of men after they have shaved. That was one of Grigori Rasputin's drawbacks. He never shaved or bathed. It was like being made love to by a rubbish dump. Here."

She wiped the razor, folded it and slipped it down the front of his shirt. It rested against his chest, making his skin tingle, as if the blade were open and he was only a tremor away from suicide.

CHAPTER 7

1

They flew all that day, trying to make up lost time. Eve was annoyed that in all their preparations, even though they had been hasty, they had overlooked an item that had suddenly become important: a calendar. As they flew the second leg of the day's flight, with O'Malley now at the controls of his plane and she in the rear cockpit, she opened the school atlas and traced the route and the time that had already elapsed. They had four days to do roughly another 3000 miles. They could afford no more delays. The planes were beginning to show the effects of so much constant flying through such conditions and O'Malley had said they could expect to do no more than 900 miles a day in two legs and still leave him time each evening to service the machines. She closed the atlas, looked down at India. It was coloured red in the atlas, shaped like a crumpled ice cream cone. But there it was below, brown, blotched with green, stretching from horizon to horizon with no shape at all, teeming with people of a dozen hues, a vast joke on the cartographers.

They had landed at the first large settlement they had seen after leaving the valley and the dead Suleiman Khan. It had turned out to be one of the cantonments Suleiman had wanted bombed, Fort Kipling. It was a combined Indian Army and RAF station, its commanding officer Lieutenant-Colonel John London.

"Glad to hear Suleiman Khan is dead." London was a tall lean man with a hawk nose and bleached blue eyes; he looked like one of the Pathans he had spent his life fighting. "Given us a devil of a time. You'll have to stay here, of course, till someone comes down from Quetta or Peshawar to talk to you."

"Couldn't we fly on to Quetta?" O'Malley had said. "That would save them a trip and we're going there anyway."

London pondered a moment, "Good idea. Actually, the less we see of HQ wallahs, the better. They're a damned nuisance, actually. If you will forgive the language, Miss Tozer."

"Then we'll go on to Quetta?" said O'Malley. "Good. Now I wonder if I could have some of the RAF chaps remove the spare tank from my machine? From now on we should be able to pick up petrol fairly frequently."

"I'll telegraph Quetta to expect you."

But Quetta was still waiting. While both machines were being serviced and the RAF mechanics were replacing the spare tank in O'Malley's plane with a wicker seat, O'Malley had a quiet word with the others.

"We can't afford to get caught up in army red tape. I don't know what the German Army was like, Conrad, but the British Army thinks it invented red tape. They might pass us on right up the line to Delhi. I've looked at the map. We'll fly on to Multan. They won't have heard of us and we'll dream up some tale to satisfy them."

"Do you think we can?" said Eve.

"You disappoint me. You sound as if you're losing confidence in me as a liar."

"Not really."

The mood that had been re-established between them during the previous night and early this morning was still there. After all, if it had not been for him, she would probably have not got out of Suleiman Khan's house alive. Still, she had repaid the debt and saved both their lives, as he had told her, by shooting Suleiman. She had fired from the hip when she had killed the Mexican would-be rapist, but the shot that had killed the Waziri leader had been deliberately and calmly aimed. The act might haunt her dreams in the future, but she knew she would sleep tonight without any qualms about the dead Suleiman. She was too relieved at being still alive to feel any pangs of conscience about what she had had to do to survive.

Colonel London came to see them off. "What about your other Bristol Fighter up there in Suleiman Khan's valley?"

"It belongs to Baron von Kern," said Eve, looking at Kern; he brought his heels gently together and slightly bowed his head. "Could you have it held here and he will pick it up on his way home to Germany?"

"Are you going back to Germany?" London sounded surprised. "From what I've read, I thought it would be a good place to be away from."

"I left in a hurry, Colonel. I'll go back, if only to say *auf Wiedersehen* in a proper manner. I was taught always to do that."

"I'm sure," said Colonel London, embarrassed; he had been taught to do just the opposite, never make a show of farewells. "Well, I've had a signal back from Quetta. They'll be happy to see you, but then they want to pass you on to Delhi. You won't enjoy Delhi, not this time of year. Damned hot there. If you will forgive the language, Miss Tozer."

They had taken off, by-passed Quetta, landed at Multan and spent the night there. The commanding officer had hardly bothered to listen to O'Malley's story that they had flown up from Bombay and were on their way to Kabul to buy carpets—"Miss Tozer and Mr. Sun have their own import firm in America. Persian and Afghan carpets are very popular in America at the moment. President Wilson has several of them in the White House."

Colonel Kyne just kept looking at Eve as if he had never seen a beautiful woman before, just kept saying, "Jolly good, jolly good."

It was his adjutant, a captain with a light voice and limp wrists, who said to O'Malley, "Miss Tozer is frightfully scruffy-looking for a businesswoman, isn't she? Is that one of her old carpets she is wearing?"

"Is the Queen's Own Rifles stationed here?" said O'Malley.

Captain Le Quex's eyes narrowed and his wrists stiffened. "We are Skinner's Horse here, not bloody infantry." He flicked an invisible speck of dust from his immaculate self. "You're ex-RAF, I understand. They didn't dress up much in your squadron?"

"Oh, spick and span all the time, never went into battle without having our flying suits pressed. Actually, we had all our baggage pinched down in Jaipur. Miss Tozer, dressed up, would make the Colonel's eyes pop. Even more so than now."

"If you were staying longer, I could introduce you to my tailor. Marvellous chap, really, even though he's a *chee-chee*. But I'll see what I can do to tog you out. I'm frightfully glad to hear you care about appearances. One must out here, y'know."

"Balls," said O'Malley, "of style. That's our motto, all the time."

"Jolly good, jolly good," said Colonel Kyne, still staring at Eve.

Captain Le Quex fluttered around to get them togged out while O'Malley took Eve aside. "Would you mind spending some money on us? I'm afraid if we continue to look like this—" he and Eve were still wearing the clothes they had taken off the dead Pathans in Suleiman's house "—we may be picked up for vagrancy. Captain Le Quex, who I think is a dressmaker in uniform, says he can make us look respectable. He may even make us look as pretty as himself."

"I didn't think they had pansies in the army. Did you have them in the RAF?"

"I believe they did in bombers, all squashed together. It encouraged those sort of tendencies."

"I'm glad you were in fighters, Major O'Malley."

"So was I, Miss Tozer."

When they took off in the morning Captain Le Quex had outfitted them as if he had personally taken responsibility that they kept up appearances. He had produced tussore silk suits and pith helmets, with bright puggarees, for O'Malley and Kern; Sun Nan, in his black suit and bowler hat, was considered either presentable or beyond redemption. Three dresses, two skirts and two blouses had been obtained for Eve. Captain Le Quex waltzed round her as if he were the Multan representative of Paul Poiret, and sent them off into the heavens with his hands fluttering like birds in farewell.

They headed north, as if making for Kabul, then turned abruptly east and headed for Meerut. That town was only fifty miles or so from Delhi, but O'Malley hoped that word of their coming had not yet made its way up the chain of command to Delhi and HQ there would not know of them. They were fortunate: no one asked any awkward questions at Meerut, their planes were refuelled and they flew on. Eve, clean and fresh in a new blouse and skirt, felt her spirits begin to rise again. They would be there in Hunan in time to save her father.

They stayed that night at Guraka, a small station in the foothills near the Nepal border. Everything was going swimmingly: the planes were running smoothly, there was no friction between the four travellers, the officers at Guraka fell over themselves to be hospitable. They even got out maps and helped plan the rest of the trip.

"Right through to Hunan, eh? I say, what an absolutely ripping time you'll have. Wish we were coming with you. Look, this is your best plan. Fly on here to Samarand, that's just this side of Cooch Behar. It's one of the princely States, not as big as Cooch Behar, but jolly rich. The Rajah there, absolutely top-hole chap, plays a marvellous game of polo—plays a marvellous game of everything, actually. Frightfully keen on sport. Women, too, I'm afraid."

"He considers those a sport?" said Eve.

"Afraid so. Keep an eye on him, Miss Tozer. Anyhow, he has a fleet of Rolls-Royces, so you'll have no trouble getting petrol. Go on from there to Myitkyina—it'll be just about the end of your range, but you should try to make it. Then over the mountains, you'll have to fly rather high, to Yunnan. Have to find your own way from there, I'm afraid. But you have the Chinee with you, he should know the way. Was talking to him in the mess. Quite nice, isn't he, actually?"

"For a Chinee," said O'Malley. "The Boche is quite nice, too."

"Oh, rather. But then they can't all be beastly, can they?"

They left Guraka in the early morning, climbing on ramps of sunlight into the crystal-clear air. To the north of them the mountains sloped up towards the final barrier of the Himalayas; in the far distance Eve imagined she saw the white-silver shine of snow. India once again stretched out below them, here green and restful on the eyes after the harsh brown glare further west. They passed over rivers that glittered like gem-encrusted snakes on vast green lawns below. Further south monsoon-clouds rested on the horizon like grey-white buffalo waiting to charge.

They had been flying for just over three hours, rising and falling gently with the occasional up-draft as they flew over some higher hills, Eve relaxed and content to leave the piloting to O'Malley, when suddenly there was a tremendous bang in the engine. It seemed for a moment that the whole front of the Bristol was going to explode and fall off. There was a frightening clatter, as if everything under the cowling had come apart. The plane shook from propeller through to tail-assembly; the wings fluttered as if about to fly off on their own. Eve sat up, her stomach tight, able to tell even from the back of his head that O'Malley was as bewildered as she was. She felt the sudden helplessness of all aircraft passengers, just sat and could do nothing while the pilot tried to bring the machine back under his control.

Then, just as abruptly as it had happened, the noise and vibrating stopped. Eve let out her breath, only then realizing she had been holding it in. She said into the tube, "I thought we were finished then," and smiled at O'Malley as he turned his head and looked back at her.

"We still could be," he said. "The engine's conked out."

Then she realized they were riding in almost absolute silence. She snatched off her helmet, felt the wind in her hair, heard it in the wires. But could hear no engine.

"The stick's dead," said O'Malley. "Sit tight!"

As if she could do anything else. She looked over the side and ahead of them. In the distance she saw a white square, a green rectangle and a blue circle. The officers at Guraka had told them they would recognize Samarand by its vast white palace, its polo ground and its circular lake. But how far away was it? Six or seven miles? There was no altimeter in the rear cockpit, but she guessed they were somewhere above seven thousand feet. Could O'Malley keep the nose up, keep them with enough airspeed to prevent them from stalling, while they glided down to the distant polo field?

She heard the wind sighing, the whispers of men already dead, as it swept past the struts and wires. Occasionally O'Malley would dip the nose to give them more speed as they slowed, then lift it again and flatten out the plane. Eve looked across and saw that Kern and Sun Nan had seen their plight. But she knew they felt as helpless and frustrated as she did. Once again her life was in O'Malley's hands.

A polo game was in progress on the broad green sward between the lake and the palace. Spectators lined both sides of the ground; a line of cars was drawn up behind the crowd on the palace side of the field. Nobody seemed aware of the approaching silent Bristol; Kern was high above O'Malley and behind him. Players raced their ponies up and down the field, oblivious of the fact that their chukka and perhaps even their heads were about to be cut short by a non-player dropping in from the sky. Eve, staring at O'Malley's head, saw the field coming up, the polo ponies crossing and criss-crossing it in a swift maze of manoeuvres that seemed designed to do nothing but bring about a terrible disaster. Suddenly she wished for a klaxon, a bugle horn, anything. She reached for the gun resting by her side.

Then Kern came down in a steep dive, engine roaring.

He plunged by on their starboard side, went in low over the grass. The polo players scattered, leaving a clear space down the middle of the field.

O'Malley brought the dead Bristol down to a perfect landing. He let it roll the length of the field, keeping it steady. Eve glanced to either side, saw the startled onlookers, felt a frivolous thrill at the entrance they were making. Then she looked ahead beyond O'Malley. The plane was still rolling and she saw the rider, mallet on shoulder, sitting his horse in the goal-mouth dead ahead. Put the brakes on! she shouted silently to O'Malley. We're going to run him down! The plane slowed, rolled to a stop only feet from the polo player.

O'Malley stood up in the cockpit, leaned on the upper wing. "Terribly sorry about that, old chap. Couldn't be helped, I'm afraid."

"There had better be a good explanation." The Rajah of Samarand's black eyes mirrored his soul, which was also black. "My jails are always open for unwelcome strangers."

2

O'Malley turned to Eve, said quietly, "Remember what we were told at Guraka—the Rajah has an eye for the ladies."

Eve didn't hurry. She took out her compact and repaired her make-up. She combed her hair and straightened the seams in her stockings. The Rajah rode round to the side of the aeroplane and watched her performance without comment. At last Eve was ready to disembark. O'Malley was already on the ground waiting for her. He helped her as she swung down, standing aside so that the Rajah could observe the length of silk-clad leg that was presented to him. Then she turned round, pulling her blouse tight over her bosom.

By the time Kern brought his plane down there was no

question that they were all more-than-welcome strangers and there was no fear of their being jailed. The polo match was abandoned and the crowd began to disperse. The vast majority of them, peasants, servants, clerks and Untouchables, drifted away to the drudgery and misery that filled their day. The small minority turned to the diversions that they needed to fill their day. There were maharajahs, rajahs, nawabs and a nabob, colonel, captains and a judge: and their ladies, brightly-plumaged as birds in their Mysore silk saris and their Army-and-Navy crêpe-de-Chine. The women, more bored than the men, eyed the female newcomer as a diversion they could have done without.

The Rajah of Samarand escorted Eve across to the largest of the twelve Rolls-Royces parked at the side of the field. It was gold-plated, with two enormous gold headlamps; the steering wheel was ivory; the rear seats were two separate gold-plated thrones upholstered in crimson velvet. The other eleven Rolls-Royces were stock luxury models; O'Malley wondered if they had been bought as a job lot. He, Kern and Sun Nan stayed with the planes, but the other cars were filled with guests in descending rank and the whole convoy drove through the gates of the palace into the huge central courtyard. The distance of the journey was no more than two hundred yards.

Kern looked at O'Malley. "I haven't seen anything like this since I was in Vienna and my father took me on a shoot with the Emperor."

"You have seen nothing yet." A slim young man, still in polo togs, had stayed with them. He had been introduced as Prince Chitra, the eldest son of the Rajah. He had his father's black eyes but there was too much humour in them to suggest that his soul, too, might be black. "My father is dedicated to extravagance. He thinks it is a virtue."

Kern ventured an impolite question: "You sound as if you are not in favour of it?"

"I'm not. I'm a Communist." He smiled, leaning on his

mallet. "The only polo-playing Communist in the world, I should think. I should like to change things, but I'm afraid my father will live to a ripe old age. Our family does, unless they are killed. What is the matter with your aeroplane?"

O'Malley had the cowling off the engine. "A valve stem has cracked. I don't know yet what else is wrong. I'm afraid we're going to be stuck here overnight."

"You will be most welcome. I know my father will be overjoyed to have your lady friend stay with us. Is she experienced?"

O'Malley and Kern looked at each other. It was Sun Nan who said, "Miss Tozer has already shot two men."

"Jolly good," said the Prince, his smile widening. "My father is sport mad. It will be a new sport for him, trying to seduce a woman who shoots men. Leave your machine. We have a mechanic, specially brought out from Rolls-Royce in England, who will attend to it. Do you mind walking to the palace?"

O'Malley peered into the distance, said drily "I think we can make it. Were you educated in England?"

"Oxford, at Christ Church. My father was there at The House, too. We both played cricket for the University against Cambridge. I'm afraid that's *all* we did."

"I was at Trinity. I was studying rugger and beer-drinking—"

O'Malley and Prince Chitra walked on. Kern and Sun Nan followed, suddenly outside the circle: Prussia and the Middle Kingdom had nothing in common, least of all Oxford.

Inside the palace Eve had just had her hessian-wrapped box taken from her by a servant. "A treasure?" the Rajah asked.

"In a way, Your Highness. A jade statue that I am returning to its owner in China."

"Jade?" The Rajah's eyes lit up, eliminating the heavy-lidded stare that Eve had begun to find boring and too obvious. He was a handsome man, but he had vandalized himself: he was running to fat, debauchery marked him like an eczema. He was a man who had been corrupted by riches and power long before he had been born. He was the absolute son of his father, who had been equally extravagant and hedonistic. Sometimes the Rajah wondered what had gone wrong with his sperm that *he* had sired a son who, even if it was over the gold plate at dinner, professed to be a Communist, whatever that was. "I have the best collection of jade in India, possibly in the world. I am always looking for new pieces. May I see it?"

Eve hesitated, then took the box from the servant. But the Rajah took her by the arm. "Not here. In my private chambers. It is where I always do business."

He's ridiculous, thought Eve; but she let him lead her away, leaving his other guests gazing after them. And his wife, the Ranee: she sat among her ladies-in-waiting on the balcony of the *zenana* and saw her husband leading the new candidate for his bed along the terrace and into his chambers.

"Tell the head butler I shall be coming to the banquet tonight after all," the Ranee told a lady-in-waiting. "We must see that the new woman, whoever she is, is kept in her place."

The occasion, Kern, O'Malley and Sun Nan learned from Prince Chitra, was the culmination of the Rajah's annual sports week. "He always holds it in the middle of August, to test the English, he says. They can't afford to offend him and they have to come down from the summer stations and resorts in the hills. The other princes are poor relations—they can't afford to offend Father, either. You will be expected to take part in the last event of the programme, tonight after the banquet."

"What's that?" said O'Malley, threatened by a sudden vision of pig-sticking by moonlight.

"A roller-skating race, twice round the corridors of the palace. Two miles. Can you roller-skate?"

"I can ice-skate," said Kern.

O'Malley said he was a poor ice-skater, but Sun Nan said he could not skate at all. "A pity," said the Prince.

"You will have to attempt the race, I'm afraid. My father allows no non-starters."

The English visitors, the newcomers learned, were the officers of Farnol's Lancers. Kern, having bathed and changed, went for a walk round the vast courtyard of the palace and came upon an English officer and his wife doing the same exercise. They were a young couple, both fair, in love enough to make each of them beautiful in the other's eyes and good-looking as a pair to any outsider. Kern liked the Lockes at once, but, held back by his Germanness, was stiffly polite till he felt it was safe to be otherwise.

"It's another world," said Pamela Locke when Kern commented on the size of the palace. "Three hundred and one bedrooms, every one just too luxurious for words. We ladies have compared notes. Some of the older ones have been coming here for years, so one way and another we've managed to see every room in the palace."

"Even the Rajah's rooms," said Captain Locke. "Some of the ladies, no names, no pack-drill, have caught his eye and been invited into them."

"Some of them have seen his treasury, too," said his wife. "I'm dying to be invited."

"No jolly fear," said her husband and only half-jokingly put an arm around her.

Peacocks flared on the sun-browned lawns, fountains sprayed like silver images of the birds, a liveried servant went by exercising two cheetah on leashes: Kern knew there had to be a treasury in such surroundings and wondered what it contained. "Miss Tozer is seeing it now, I believe."

"I hope she realizes what that implies," said Pamela Locke.

"She is American," said her husband. "They do tend to be rather naïve."

"Miss Tozer is less so than most," said Kern.

The naïve American at that moment was standing in a huge room the like of which she had never seen before. It was a treasure cave, a warehouse of gems, gold, silver, ivory and jade: riches reduced to grocery level by their extravagant abundance. Everything was laid out on green baize-topped tables or on shelves round the walls; the owner of the treasures only had to step through the heavy brass doors to get instant satisfaction of his avarice. There were no windows in the huge room and the doors were guarded by two heavily-armed servants.

"A little fakir named Gandhi came to see me early in the summer," said the Rajah. "He asked me to give it all away, to help his poor brethren, as he called them. But what good would that do? There are hundreds of millions of them, all multiplying much quicker than my treasures can. They would all be poor again within a year."

Eve had never pretended to the principle of the equal distribution of wealth; such apostasy of the family faith would have been unthinkable. But here among these riches she felt uncomfortable, as if the diamonds had been rubbed roughly against her conscience. Her only protest, weak and shaming to her, was, "But what do you *do* with all this?"

"I possess it, my dear. That is enough. Will you sell me your jade statue?"

"You want to possess that, too?"

"Yes." In anyone else the Rajah's candour might have had a certain charm; but Eve had already guessed that his candour was only another manifestation of his power and wealth and contempt for everyone but himself. He had changed from his polo clothes and was dressed in a sky-blue silk coat over white silk trousers. His turban was pink crêpe-de-Chine over a lilac head-band and he wore a ruby ear-ring. Eve had never met a man she liked less, not even the Mexican rapist or Suleiman Khan. "It is the most beautiful piece of jade carving I have ever seen."

"What would you do with it?" She had begun by calling him Your Highness, but she no longer felt she owed him any deference. If he felt any offence at her own candour, he did not show it. Perhaps he took it as a sign that she was ready to fall into his bed. "Just leave it here among all these other things?"

"After a while, yes, I suppose so. I grow tired of my pleasures. Except beautiful women."

"No, I shan't sell it." Eve felt angry; her father's ransom was being reduced to a bauble. "I have to take the statue on to China with me."

"You can have any price you name." He picked up a diamond-and-ruby necklace. "This would be worth twenty times the statue."

He moved closer to her, put the necklace round her neck, spread it out on her bosom. She could smell the perfume on him, musky and suggestive. Everything about him was so obvious, she had expected something subtler. But perhaps he had never needed to be subtle.

She took off the necklace without even looking down at it, handed it back to him. "I told you, the statue does not belong to me."

He dropped the necklace carelessly back on the table. He waved at the room at large. "You may change your mind about it by morning. You may have anything you wish as your price."

"I don't have a price, Your Highness." Always be formal, her grandmother had taught her: it is the best defence of a young girl's virtue. "What about your wife? What would the Ranee say if she knew you were offering me so much?"

"My wife doesn't understand me. She never has."

She wanted to laugh: he sounded like a cartoon character from the Harvard *Lampoon*, to which her father subscribed. But there was no self-pitying note in his voice as was suggested in those cartoon captions: he wouldn't expect *any* woman to understand him. Which was in effect what she said: "Perhaps she expects more understanding from you, Your Highness."

He shook his head, arrogantly amused by her American innocence. "I don't have to understand anyone, Miss Tozer. My family has ruled this State for over a thousand years. We don't have to explain ourselves or to justify ourselves. We *are*."

Eve had no answer to such arrogance; such exalted

sovereignty was beyond her understanding. The dynasties back home, the Cabots, the Vanderbilts, the Mellons, were all at once reduced to nouveaux riches immigrant families. "I think I shall go and lie down."

"Do that, Miss Tozer. And think about my offer. I want that statue."

Later, in the early evening, Kern and O'Malley strolled on the wide outer terrace that looked down over the polo field to the circular lake. The sun had just set below a peacock's tail of cloud; the sky was aflame with colour. Down on the lake flamingoes formed their own pink mist on the golden water; ibis and heron rose in an explosion of pure white. Purple bougainvillaea hung down like cooling lava from the terrace and, below, the gardens blazed with flowers that made the earth a mirror of the sky. But sky, birds and flowers could not dim the glory that walked on the terraces.

Kern and O'Malley were dressed in white tie and tails that the valet assigned to them had produced without being asked. "His Highness insists that everyone dress for dinner, sahibs. He thinks it is a most admirable English custom."

"But how did you know our sizes?" O'Malley had asked.

"While you were bathing, sahib, I took your suit along to the wardrobe and compared the size. His Highness keeps hundreds of suits there for his guests, so that they need not be embarrassed. You and the Baron were not difficult to fit, sahib."

"Ready-to-wear clothing," said Kern. "My father must be spinning in his grave."

"I haven't worn tails since I was at Oxford." O'Malley admired himself in a mirror. "But I must say, I look jolly good. You too, Conrad. Let's go out and thrill the ladies."

But when they got out on the terrace they found they were only penguins among birds of paradise. The princes were resplendent in silk coats threaded with silver, their turbans every colour across the spectrum; their women floated beside them in saris that made them look like spectral reflections of their menfolk. The English officers were not to be out-done; O'Malley wondered what Captain Le Quex, the exquisite of Skinner's Horse, would have thought of Farnol's Lancers. They wore emerald green jackets with silver facings, green-and-gold sashes and tight gold trousers, and O'Malley closed his eyes. Not at the foppish elegance, but at a sudden memory of mud-covered, khaki-clad men lying in trenches in France.

"It's not fair," Pamela Locke said. "We English girls just can't compete with all this peacockery."

Kern looked out on to the polo field. At both ends, behind the goal-posts, crowds of villagers had gathered. They were too far away from him to discern them clearly and he hoped there were no eagle eyes among those spectators of this parade on the palace terrace. The avian image persisted: black, grey and dirty-white, they looked like carrion birds waiting for something to die.

Something was happening to him, he mused wryly: he was developing a social conscience. "What do all those people think of such a show as this?"

"They love it," said Captain Locke. "It's their entertainment, their escape, if you like. Back home our working class go to the music halls or the picture shows. Here, these people look at us."

You simple-minded man, Kern thought; but knew he had been like that himself only six short (no, not short: long) years ago. "Let us hope they always remain content just to look."

"Never fear," said Captain Locke. "The Raj is the best thing that ever happened to India and those people know it. They know it is us who keep despots like His Nibs in check."

"Hush, darling," said his wife. "Here comes the Ranee. Who's that with her?"

"My God," said O'Malley, "it's Sun Nan."

The Chinese, too, was in white tie and tails. Impassively dignified as ever on the outside, Sun Nan inwardly was both amused and awe-struck by what surrounded him. If only the Lord of the Sword could see him now!

Especially with the Ranee by his side; no concubine of the General's could ever equal the lavish splendour that enhanced the beauty of this Indian woman. She wore a skull-cap of diamonds that glittered with every movement of her head; a pendant hung down over her forehead, the centre stone of which was a blue diamond. She wore no necklace above her pale-blue silk sari, but when she lifted her hands diamonds caught the eye like a heliograph and each wrist was cuffed with the same gems. Sun Nan, a mercenary man, knew he was walking beside a fortune and he idly wondered if any of it would be available for taking back to China. Avarice began to nibble at him like lust.

"Gentlemen," said the Ranee when Kern and O'Malley had been introduced to her, "I have been talking to Mr. Sun. He tells me you must be away by morning."

O'Malley gestured down towards the polo fields where four Indians, supervised by the man who had been brought out from Rolls-Royce, were working on the damaged Bristol. "Your man tells us our machines will be ready for an early take-off."

"*My* man? I have no man, Major. Women don't, not in India. Isn't that true, Mrs. Locke?" Pamela Locke looked at her husband and the Ranee smiled. "I'm sorry. How unfair of me to ask such a question of you."

She moved on, leaving Sun Nan with the others. "What a charming woman," said Captain Locke. "An absolute charmer."

"Piffle." Pamela Locke drew on her gloves as if she were drawing on iron gauntlets. "She and Lucrezia Borgia would have made nice twins."

"Well—" Her husband looked foolish. "Perhaps. I don't know much about women, actually."

"I'll keep you that way." She took his arm. "Then you will always be safe."

They moved off and O'Malley looked at Kern. "Is that true? Safety from women lies in knowing nothing about them?"

"It's a principle I've never operated on. What about Chinese women, Mr. Sun?"

"Women are the same everywhere, Baron. None of us is safe from them."

Eve, like the men, had been dressed from the palace wardrobe. She had found nothing Western that she had liked; everything had looked like left-overs from the Durbar of 1911. Greatly daring, she had decided on a pink chiffon sari. The Rajah had sent in the necklace he had offered her this afternoon, but she had sent it back. She had guessed that she would be flouting custom enough by wearing the Indian dress; to wear the necklace would be to flaunt herself. She was only a mild rebel: there was still too much of the Proper Bostonian in her. As she moved along the terrace she knew she had done the right thing in refusing to wear the necklace. Her dress alone was causing enough comment: whispers grazed her like thorn-bush. One should not ape the natives, not even natives who had been to Oxford and were richer than any army officer and his wife could ever be.

A lady-in-waiting intercepted her and took her to the Ranee. "You look beautiful, my dear," said the Ranee, smile as sharp as her diamonds. "Are you supposed to be one of us or a *Red* Indian?"

Prince Chitra stood up, gorgeous in mauve silk; Lenin would have pleaded with him to embrace some other faith but Communism. "Now, now, Mother. I am sure Miss Tozer has dressed like this as a compliment to us."

"Or your father," said the Ranee. "I understand my husband wants to buy a piece of jade from you, Miss Tozer?"

"A jade statue, Your Highness. But it is not for sale."

"Have you anything else for sale?"

I don't have to stand for this, Eve thought. Then remembered that the Rajah's jails were always open for unwelcome strangers: perhaps the Ranee had her own quota of prisoners. Farnol's Lancers paraded by, but they were not the US Cavalry, not here to defend an American. "Nothing, Your Highness. As I told your husband."

"Will you sell the statue to me?"

"It is not mine to sell."

"It could be confiscated."

"That would be uncivilized," said Prince Chitra.

"I don't have the advantages of having gone to Oxford," said his mother, under-privileged under her diamond cap. "Enjoy our hospitality, Miss Tozer. Wear your sari with virtue—though pink is the wrong colour for it."

Then gongs rang all round the palace, a whole symphony of them: dinner was served. The guests lined up in pairs, over a hundred of them, and went down past rows of uniformed servants into the banquet hall. Kern, walking beside Sun Nan, looked at neither the princes nor the women but at the officers of Farnol's Lancers. Mein Gott, how beautifully the English could dress up tradition. They looked like fops, peacocks without balls, yet he knew, without ever having heard of them before, that the Lancers would be heroic and glorious in battle. For a moment he longed to be English, to join them.

"You look ill, Baron," said Sun Nan.

Kern was surprised: he thought he might have looked elated, ready to fight another war. "The heat, Mr. Sun. These are not the clothes for such a time of year."

"A long way from your tea dance at Constance."

"A long way from—where are we supposed to be going to?"

Sun Nan smiled. "That would be telling, Baron."

The table was a long one, 55 people on either side, the Rajah at one end, the Ranee at the other. O'Malley was on the Rajah's left hand, Eve on his right; Sun Nan on the Ranee's left, Kern on her right. There was no way of knowing who had decided on the seating arrangements; Kern wondered if it was some sort of insult to the other princes and to the English, putting them in their place by putting the drop-in strangers above them. The last shall be first . . . But he didn't think the Rajah or the Ranee would ever have read the Bible. He looked at the Ranee, a beautiful woman, and she gave him a look from under lowered lids. He wondered if she had ever read the Kama

Sutra, then looked down the table at her husband and decided she must have, plus any addenda. He began to feel the old feeling in his loins, something he hadn't felt since he had left the Countess Malevitza.

On the other side of the table Sun Nan was not looking at either the women or the men, but at the table setting. It was solid gold: candelabra, plates, cutlery, goblets. The table deserved a Lucullan feast, larks' tongues and the rest: instead they got brown Windsor soup, Bengal curry, roast beef and brussels sprouts, plum pudding. Only the wine was good, but Sun Nan had no head for it and he sipped it sparingly. There was an individual servant behind each guest and Sun Nan's man kept coming forward to replenish the wine, but the Chinese waved him away.

"You don't like wine, Mr. Sun?" The Ranee missed nothing.

"I do not have the head for it, Your Highness." He hissed a little but it was not with disrespect; he enjoyed the formality of titles, wondered idly what he would like for his own. But no one would ever call him anything but Sun Nan or Mr. Sun. He looked down the table, wondered again if he could take some of this palace's treasure with him. And felt drunker than the wind could have made him. "We live a spartan life in China."

"How foolish. To what end?" She turned to Kern. "Do you think we should all live a spartan life, Baron?"

"Only if one can afford it," said Kern, not having heard the question properly.

The Ranee laughed, a sudden peal that made her sound younger than she was: almost innocent, Kern thought, giving her all his attention now. The unintentional joke spread down the table; everyone looked at Kern, as if surprised that a German was capable of a joke. There had been a certain stiffness, but now everyone began to relax. Some even enjoyed the food, dreaming of home: sweat ran down their faces, looking like tears.

"You will be entering my roller-skating race, Major," said the Rajah at the far end of the table. "I call it my

Roller Derby. It doesn't matter if you don't win, all you have to do is finish. I always win, anyway."

"I never was competitive," said O'Malley. "Except in dogfights."

"I must learn to fly. There are so few things left to excite one." He spoke without sounding bored, even rather sadly. "So you are flying all the way to China with that statue?"

Why does he keep harping on it? Eve wondered; and began to worry.

"Perhaps we could get a statue like it," said O'Malley, "and bring it back for you."

The Rajah shook his head. "It would be almost impossible. That statue is priceless. I know my jade. I don't believe Miss Tozer really knows how beautiful and rare it is."

"Perhaps not," she said. "Mr. Sun is the expert."

Sun Nan at that moment, to his surprise, was discussing the jade statue with the Ranee. "It belongs to my master—he values it more than his life. Did Miss Tozer show it to you?"

"Oh no, I haven't seen it. Where is it—in her room?"

Sun Nan's face was blank. "Possibly. Miss Tozer does not confide in me."

"If, as you say, the statue belongs to your, er, master, why is it in Miss Tozer's possession?"

"Women are more careful with precious things," said Kern, knowing Sun Nan would not be capable of such an answer.

"I fear you are a ladies' man, Baron," said the Ranee, looking very much unafraid. "Like my husband."

Kern looked down the table at the gross sensualist at the far end, then back at the Ranee. "Not quite. There would be a difference."

"Yes. I think you are far too serious a man to be interested in just playthings. Is that because you are German?"

Why do they all think we are so humourless? "Not so long ago Germans enjoyed themselves as much as anyone.

Are all Indians interested in playthings? The people out-side the palace, for instance?"

"Ninety-nine point nine per cent of them are not," said Prince Chitra, seated one down from Kern, on the far side of a placid Englishwoman who had said nothing and ap-peared to have heard nothing. "But Mother and Father have never met them."

"The peasants love my son," said the Ranee. "They all think he is the Indian Prince of Wales. So far he hasn't told them he is a Communist."

"The Prince of Wales is no Communist," said the En-glishwoman, coming awake.

"Of course not, Lady Blackwood. No proper prince would be." She looked down the table, exchanged smiles with her distant husband, like formal notes from separate countries. "Well, I see my husband has finished his din-ner. We ladies have to retire. When you gentlemen have had your port and cigars, we shall meet you in the cor-ridors for the roller-skating. I hope you enjoyed your din-ner, Baron?"

"Excellent."

"Liar. But charming—I should like to know you better, Baron." She rose. "I noticed you admiring our plate, Mr. Sun. Perhaps we could trade your, er, master this dinner service for his jade statue?"

She left the table without waiting for Sun Nan's answer. The men were left alone at the long table; none of the splendour appeared to have evaporated with the women's withdrawal. The princes and the Lancers moved closer to the Rajah's end of the table, like a rainbow contracting. Cigar smoke began to drift through the room and the port passed from hand to hand in crystal decanters brought to India in the heyday of the East Indian Company. Kern noticed that only some of the princes declined the port; the rest of them became part of what could have been an English mess scene. The German smoked his cigar and sipped his port and once again wondered wryly if Farnol's Lancers would welcome an application from a former Uhlan officer. He had once belonged to a world like this, not as splendorous perhaps but just as companionable: his world had gone forever, but these English, and their Indian brothers, still had theirs. He began to feel depressed and envious.

At last the Rajah rose to his feet. "We have drunk enough, gentlemen. We must remain sober enough for our roller-skating. I take it you have all made your bets. Am I the odds-on favourite as usual?"

There were roars of laughter all down the table. O'Malley laughing politely, said, "What a swine!"

"Of course," said Captain Locke, also laughing. "But without frightful swine like him our job would be twice as difficult."

The English, thought Kern, must be the most successful fools in history. They sound like silly asses, but make asses of the people they use. If only we Germans could learn their skill of deception. But all we can deceive are ourselves.

The corridors had been lined with chairs and the women were already seated, dutiful spectators of their menfolk's schoolboyish pleasure. At least it was better than watching cricket; a detested husband might fall and break his leg. Some of them did not attempt to hide their boredom; others looked impassive; a few, the young wives, did their best to show their husbands they hadn't made a mistake in marrying them. Servants appeared with skates, began, as it were, to shoe their chargers. Kern sat down, feeling as if he had been turned into some sort of steed, and a servant knelt and buckled on the skates.

The corridor was wide enough for the racers to line up ten abreast. The floor was tessellated tiles, richly patterned: the competitors tried out their skates, gliding over legends in mosaic. Some were expert skaters, including Kern: others, including Sun Nan, wobbled dangerously, threatening to fall and crack their skulls. But the Rajah would allow no non-starters. He was the sort of host who believed the only welcome guest was one who did what he was told.

Sun Nan ventured cautiously away from the support of

his chair. He would not tell his master about this: the
General might introduce it as another form of torture. As
a boy he had once skated on rough wooden skates on the
frozen creek near his home; but that had been years ago
and his skating since then had been only political. Plump
and unathletic though he was, he had a good sense of balance and he managed to remain upright. But he knew he
was going to be one of the last to finish, if he finished at
all.

The racers were lined up, colourful as jockeys in their
silks. The Ranee dropped a scarf and the race was on.
The Rajah went to the front at once; Kern, following him
closely, was surprised at the agility of a man of such bulk.
O'Malley was lost somewhere in the ruck, a non-com-
batant who had somehow wandered into a charge of Farnol's Lancers. Sun Nan brought up the rear with an
elderly prince, both of them skating along with a sort of
prim decorum, like virgins on thin ice.

The corridors reverberated with the whirring of the
skates as the peacock flock plunged down them. The Rajah led the way round the first corner; hard on his heels
were Kern and Captain Locke. A Lancer came into the
corner too fast, cannoned off the wall and brought down
half a dozen other skaters; servants, hiding their smiles
and their malicious delight, hurried to pick them up.
Down another quarter-mile corridor, arms swinging, legs
pushing: past statues and friezes of Vedic gods, Indra
seemingly wide-eyed at what humans had finally come to
for earthly pleasures. Kern, tails flying behind him, his
stiff shirtfront turning limp with sweat, slowed for the second corner, went round close behind the Rajah, who was
grunting like a rutting buffalo. O'Malley was still back in
the ruck, beginning to think he was in a rugger scrum on
wheels: the princes and Farnol's Lancers were no gentlemen on skates.

By the time the first circuit had been completed, the
Rajah still in the lead and Kern skating closely on his tail
in the box position, Sun Nan was the length of a corridor
behind the field. The elderly prince, deciding he had paid

his debt to the Rajah's hospitality, had retired to a chair, where he sat too exhausted to respond to the enticements of the Asparas in the frieze above his head. Sun Nan skated on, past the ladies seated in the corridor that would be the winning stretch; they all gave him a polite clap as he went past, not even looking at him but continuing with their gossip. All except Eve, who let out an unlady-like cheer, as if she were at the Yale-Harvard game. Sweating, puffing, Sun Nan saw none of them as anything but a coloured blur. So that he did not notice that the Ranee was missing from among her guests.

He was a third of the way down the far corridor, skating along alone down what had become a dream-like tunnel, when he saw the Ranee coming out of Eve's room carrying the hessian-wrapped box. She stopped when she saw him bearing down on her, her face wide open with surprise under its diamond cap and sparkling pendant. She must have waited till the main herd had gone by; she had not considered the Chinese patience of the last straggler, plodding on regardless of when he might finish. She stood in the middle of the corridor, the box held on both arms like an offering; unable to pull up, he bore down on her, went past and took the box with him. He heard her scream, looked over his shoulder, somehow keeping his balance, and saw the two servants, armed with curved knives, chasing him, urged on by the shrewish screams of the Ranee.

He tried to skate faster, pushing his legs harder. He went down the long corridor, travelling so fast that he became dizzy. A frieze of gods, goddesses, elephant, tiger, serpents and dragons whipped by him like a motion picture meant to haunt him; his feet whirred over a thousand myths that would take their revenge. He saw the corner coming up and he knew he was going too fast, that he was not going to be able to negotiate it.

Then the armed guard from outside the Rajah's treasury, hearing the Ranee's screams, came round the corner to investigate. He was holding his sword straight out in front of him, ready for any emergency. White-tied, black-tailed, more formal than he had ever been in his life, the box held in his arms as if he were a butler delivering a package from the evening mail, Sun Nan went down the corridor at full speed and right on to the guard's sword.

3

Extract from the William Bede O'Malley manuscript:
"I am extremely sorry," said the Rajah. "I can't understand what your Chinese friend was doing with the box, unless he was trying to steal the statue. My wife said he had offered it to her for some gold, but she had declined it."

How do you call a Rajah a liar, especially in his own palace? "It was just an unfortunate accident. The Ranee told me the guard was cleaning his sword and Sun Nan came round the corner and ran right into him."

"The guard will be punished for being so careless, though it will be my wife's decision. She is in charge of the housekeeping."

He was having me on, I knew. But again, what could I say? The damaged Bristol engine had been fixed, we still had the statue in its box, and we were ready to leave in half an hour. There was no time to demand justice and I was not even sure that Sun Nan would have believed in it.

The guard, sword still red with blood, had been standing above Sun Nan, looking bewildered, as if he had just been abandoned, when I came skating down the empty corridor The race was over, won by Kern in a last-moment dash past the Rajah. There had been only one cheer for the winner, that from Eve; everyone else had sat in stunned silence, as if the Baron had tripped the Rajah and then skated over the top of him to victory. I had skated on, anxious to be absent from what I thought might be an awkward scene: odds-on favourites, especially princely ones, might not take too kindly to being licked on their own course. I had gone down the first long corridor, pretty sure that I would catch up with Sun Nan somewhere along the course; then down the second corridor, which all at once was strangely empty, though I don't think I remarked it at the time. Then I turned into the third and it, too, was empty. I skated down it, my skates whirring eerily, and I was half-way down it before I saw the two figures at the far end, one on the floor and the other standing over him.

"It was an accident, sahib," the guard mumbled when I reached him. He was still looking beyond me, down the empty corridor, as if expecting someone to appear to corroborate him. Still shocked by Sun Nan's death, I don't think I was aware then that the guard seemed to be speaking parrot-fashion, as if he had been coached what to say. Only later, like an echo, did I recognize the mechanical tone of his voice and became suspicious of those suddenly empty corridors. But by then it was too late to do anything, if anything could have been done at all.

I took the box from Sun Nan, having to prise his hands away from it. I told the guard to remain where he was, then skated back down the corridors to the far side of the palace. Don't ask me why I skated. Perhaps it was because I knew, even if only subconsciously, that I had half a mile to go; perhaps I was still stunned by what had happened and floated back on those whirring wheels along the empty halls. As I went down between the decorated walls, over the mosaic and under the gilded ceilings, moving along in the slow lope of a man in a dream, I knew we had just come up against the biggest handicap that had faced us since we had left England. Sun Nan had been the only one who knew the name of the man who held Eve's father captive, he had been the only one who knew our exact destination.

There was great commotion when I reached the members' enclosure and gave my news. The Rajah let out a roar and dispatched servants on the run. I sat down, took off my skates and handed the box to Eve.

"There's blood on it. Watch your sari."

"What was he doing with it?" Eve held the box away from her, as if it contained a bomb. She shook her head, bewildered and shocked. "Poor Mr. Sun."

She still hadn't realized the real significance of Sun Nan's death as it affected us. But Kern had: "When we get to China, whom do we ask for? Sun Nan's master? This makes everything almost impossible, Bede."

The commotion had died down, but everyone was still disturbed by what had happened. The evening had been cut short; the women were already retiring to their rooms. The officers stood around in groups, their bright uniforms at odds with their sober faces; they didn't know what to do, this was no place where they could respond with a military reflex. The princes had clotted into their own small parties, looking vexed and irritable; the party had been spoiled by an outsider, a Chinese at that. All at once I wanted to be out of here, on our way again. But, as Kern had said, where to?

"My father can have the guard executed for his carelessness," said Prince Chitra. "Do you want that?"

It was only then that I began to see clearly what I had seen dimly and uncomprehendingly twenty minutes before. "I don't think the guard is to blame."

"You have something on your mind, Major."

"I have a lot on my mind, Your Highness, but I think it had better stay there. We'll be leaving first thing in the morning. Can you arrange Sun Nan's burial?"

"Would he wish to be buried or cremated?"

"We never got around to discussing it. But I think cremation would suit him. That way a part of him, in smoke, may reach China."

"I doubt it. The wind never blows that way."

And now we were down on the polo field ready to take-off. We had been driven from the palace to the machines in two Rolls-Royces, another journey of two hundred yards. My legs ached from last night's skating, my eyes were gritty from lack of sleep. My nerves had begun to stretch, something that had not happened to me since France. I was beginning to feel the rack of responsibility. Up till now all I had really had to do was keep the aeroplanes flying; now, suddenly, I was the navigator, without a compass or bearing. Yet somewhere there to the east was still the destination that had to be reached within the next two days.

There was movement back at the palace. Farnol's Lancers were going back to their stations, their women to the hill resorts; cars were taking them to the nearest railway station. The princes were leaving, driving away in their Rolls-Royces, Daimlers and Lanchesters; somehow I had expected them to depart on elephants, lolling back in luxurious howdahs under silk canopies. The peasants and villagers stood in thin crowds at the ends of the polo fields watching the exodus; it was impossible to tell whether their silence was born of sullenness or indifference. Perhaps it was just the debilitated stillness of the real poor. Though I had no money, I was just as much a stranger to real poverty as the princes.

"I hope the statue has no ill-luck attached to it," said the Rajah. "I should hate to think of your machines being plagued by it."

"We shall have to risk that."

"Goodbye, Miss Tozer. I am sorry your stay ended so tragically." He had all the right words, but somehow he sounded like the guard had last night. Except that he was totally unconcerned, rather than bewildered as the guard had been. "I had hoped we'd get to know each other better."

"You would have been disappointed," said Eve: no Your Highness, I noticed.

He smiled, cocooned in his ego. "We'll never know, shall we?"

We took off into the humid, cloudy morning; a pink-and-white cloud of heron and flamingo took off from the lake with us. The palace fell away below; I suspected the Rajah would have forgotten us before we were out of sight. Samarand slid by beneath the wings: green fields, ramshackle villages, jungle; looking back I saw the palace

disappear into the haze like a mirage. There is no Samarand today and I sometimes wonder if it was already
beginning to disappear while we were there. The Rajah
and the Ranee are both dead and buried somewhere on
the French Riviera among the new extravagance. I don't
know what happened to Prince Chitra. The Communist
countries have champion ice hockey, football and basket-
ball teams, but so far I don't believe they've raised a polo
team. Unless Chitra gave up his ponies and took to the
water. Farnol's Lancers are gone, too, and all the splendid
elegance of its officers is now found only in museums,
fading under gathering dust and dimming memories.

We flew on. It was strange to look across from Eve's
machine and see Kern flying alone in the other Bristol.
Something was missing from the sky, the third aeroplane
and the fourth person. We had never really known Sun
Nan, never would have known him, but suddenly I missed
him. And not just because without him we were, almost,
flying blind.

Then India was behind us, though we'd never have
known. Fliers today can recognize frontiers in certain
parts of the world by guard towers, barbed wire fences
and cleared no-man's land; but generally speaking, then
and now, fliers are the last free wanderers. You can't
draw boundaries on clouds. We flew over green tangled
hills, then saw the great river up ahead that we knew was
the Irrawaddy and came down to Myitkyina. Despite the
rich greenness of the countryside, the map here was
coloured red. British officers greeted us warmly while the
Burmese serviced our planes. I had a vision of my father
out in Tanganyika, playing host to visitors while the locals
ran around doing the work. Yet I knew that once we
crossed those mountains up ahead of us I would miss the
Empire.

"Into China, eh?" said Major Horler, the OC. He was
old for a major, a small, fierce-looking man who had
grown frustrated in the outposts of Empire, seeing that
the sun never set, keeping up standards by dressing for
dinner every night, being English in the only way he knew

how and hardly given a thought by the English back home. "Must be jolly interesting there."

Even then China had its mysterious appeal to those who hadn't been there. Now we were so close I was beginning to have my own expectations waver into doubts. Beyond the mountains the map was no longer red. I looked at the school atlas: the cartographers, their prejudices showing, coloured China yellow.

"I envy you, y'know. Rather dull here. The Burmese are very placid. I've hardly seen a shot fired in anger since I came out here. Missed the whole show in France, y'know."

"Never mind. Another war may turn up."

"Afraid not. Not out here." There were stirrings in the years ahead, but you can't hear the future, not when your world is as small as his was and as content. "Well, good luck in China. You on holiday or business?"

"Business. Miss Tozer travels in shoes. Marvellous market in China. Hundreds of millions of feet."

He smiled, unfooled. "I like that. Well, it's your business, O'Malley. But remember—China isn't India. The English won't be there to help you out."

We climbed out of Burma, over the hills where the red turned to yellow somewhere under the green blanket of jungle, headed for Yunnanfu, or Kunming as it is called now. For one reason or another, political, sentimental or just plain vanity on the part of some conqueror, places all over the world are always being renamed. But history mocks the changes, because no one can change that. That was one of the few memorable things I retained from reading History.

We flew at 18,000 feet and it was chilly up there. I kept watching Kern and talking to Eve, careful that neither of them suffered from lack of oxygen. Aeroplanes had gone a good deal higher than our altitude in 1920, but fliers still knew very little about the effects of the lack of oxygen. I had known pilots on the Western Front who had blacked out when they had taken their SE5's to their ceiling of 22,000 feet; yet all I had felt at that height was a beautiful, but I suppose dangerous, feeling of exhilaration. That afternoon, over the Yunnan hills, we flew through air that was more than just elements; it was sheer light, clear, shining and cleansing. There are still regions of sky like that somewhere round the world, but I don't know where and I'm too old now to go seeking them. I'm only glad I appreciated them when I knew them.

"What's that river down there?" I asked Eve through the tubes, just to make sure she was still alert.

She looked at the atlas. "The Mekong. Never heard of it. Is it important?"

"Not to us."

I looked at the petrol gauge, decided we had better start saving petrol and waved to Kern that we should start going down. Our only extra tank on each plane now was the gravity tank on the upper wing and we were going to have to squeeze every drop out of the tanks to get us to Yunnanfu. I was relieved when I saw the lakes coming up ahead that told me we were within range of the city.

There was no aerodrome, but there was a field on the outskirts of the city that looked small enough. It proved to be a training ground for the troops of the local military governor. We were surrounded as soon as we had cut our engines. We might have been Lindbergh landing at Le Bourget, only no one had heard of Lindy then. Soldiers and citizens rushed at us like grey water about to plunge down a drain.

It was my first experience of the ignorance of the Western eye when confronted with a mass of Orientals: they all looked alike. Beauty is in the eye of the beholder; and so is prejudice. We look for ourselves in the strangers we meet and when we don't recognize the familiar we pretend to a superiority. The crowd, as far as I was concerned, had one face and not too bright at that.

It was then that Eve sprang her surprise: she spoke a smattering of Chinese. It was what I later learned was Mandarin and many in the crowd didn't understand her, though frowns on the faces of some of them showed that they were puzzled by this foreign woman who spoke the language of the officials. The officials were impressed: they always are when you address them in their own tongue, as if you have offered them personal flattery. Or a bribe.

They told us we could stay the night on the field, there was petrol available and that we should have to pay taxes to the governor. They would accept English pounds or American dollars: the mainland Chinese in those days had no xenophobia towards foreign money. The taxes were two hundred dollars, asked for without a blink of a slanted eyelid.

A chow-vendor appeared, set up his soup and rice pans and let everyone know he was in business by shaking chopsticks up and down in a bamboo cylinder. We bought soup, rice and eggs and green tea; again I regretted Sun Nan's absence, that he wasn't here to have his loose plate chomping on his native food. I thought we might have been summoned before some senior officer or even the governor; but higher authority seemed content to let us remain undisturbed, so long as there were soldiers there to keep an eye on us. And the crowd to do the same.

Darkness fell and the evening turned cool. We were at 6000 feet, an altitude for the sleeping-bags even in summer. We went to bed surrounded by the soldiers and the crowd; our bedroom was wall-papered by grinning, curious faces. Eve, lying beside me under the wing of her machine, said, "Do you think we'll find my father, Bede?"

Yunnanfu was not a large city, but somehow in the last few hours I had become aware of the vastness of China. Perhaps it was the unfamiliar faces that, to my eye, looked like the one face; perhaps it was being surrounded by a language, in voice and on the signs around the field, that was totally incomprehensible; perhaps it was just the fact of being European in a country that cared absolutely nothing for us. We were in the Middle Kingdom, the centre of the world; we were late-comers to civilization, cave dwellers with aeroplanes. We were absolutely without authority, there was no reason in their world why they should be concerned about one of their war-lords and his captive foreign devil. Sun Nan suddenly began to look like a dearly beloved friend, his death deeply grieved.

But I couldn't confess all those doubts to Eve. "We'll fly on to Changsha and start looking from there. All we know is that your father bought the statue from General Chang in that city."

"What if General Chang just takes back the statue? He may not care about my father."

"Eve, all we can do is hope. We've got this far and it hasn't been easy—but our luck has held."

"Not poor Mr. Sun's."

Poor Mr. Sun: it was as if he had been one of us, someone on our side. "That may take some explaining when we finally meet his master, whoever he is." I reached out, patted her through the quilting of the sleeping-bag; not very intimate, but what can you do when there are several hundred spectators standing around your bed? "Go to sleep, Eve. We still have tomorrow."

Tomorrow came up on fire: the horizon was charred black under the red ball of the sun. Geese flew low over the lakes of flame, a dark ghost of a boat sailed under a pall of smoke that reason told me was only rising mist. In the morning light the soldiers' faces were bronzed and their shadows long enough to be threatening. During the night the crowd had disappeared, bored at last with the foreigners.

We were about to take-off when the governor of the province arrived. Seems he had been out of town last night, otherwise he would have greeted us then. He was all smiles and politeness, but he was looking at the machines as much as he was at us. My spirits sank as the sun got higher: we were losing valuable time out of our last day. For all we knew Bradley Tozer might already be dead. Was the deadline for the delivery of the statue sunrise or sunset?

The governor was proud of his English, learned, he

told us, from American missionaries. "Where do you fly to?"

"To Shanghai." Eve was developing a nice talent for lying. "We work for Tozer Cathay. Perhaps you have heard of the company?"

"Of course. My automobile was bought from Tozer Cathay." It stood in the background, a Model T Ford. He looked at the planes again, then back at us. "You know, of course, our countryside is overrun with bandits? If you were forced down, I should have to send out my soldiers to rescue you and that would cost a lot of time and money."

"How much money?" Eve said.

"One thousand American dollars." A computer could not have answered quicker.

"Did you work that out on your abacus before you came?" Eve said.

"Naturally." He smiled. "Of course, it would be safer if you did not fly at all, if you turned your aeroplanes over to me for safe keeping—"

Eve was counting out dollar bills. "There you are. May I have a receipt?"

"Of course." He produced it from a pocket, already made out. The Chinese were the original bureaucrats and this fellow could have held his own with any of them. "You will have a safe journey now. I guarantee it."

We took off half an hour late. The morning was brighter now, more hopeful-looking, no sign of the shadows that had looked like ashes. We flew slightly north of east, pushing the machines along. It was almost ten-thirty, a great slice of our day gone, when we put down on the outskirts of Tuyun.

There was no bureaucrat to hold us up there or to ask for a bribe. Eve mentioned Tozer Cathay again and the soldiers patted the truck, another Ford, which had brought out the petrol drums to fill our tanks. We were in Tozer Cathay territory and I began to appreciate the American form of imperialism. The later Venetians must have felt the same way travelling Marco Polo's sales route.

We left Tuyun and headed out again on the same bearing. We flew over China, indifferent to what lay below us; we were in another dimension now, flying through and against time. During the stop at Tuyun we had all been quiet and sober, as if talking itself were a waste of time. Deep inside I had the feeling we were already too late.

It was three o'clock in the afternoon when we set down at Changsha. We saw the green-brown curve of the Siang River and the rice paddies stretching away on either side. The city stood above the river, junks and sampans crowded together like feeding ducks at the foot of it. There was no aerodrome; we landed in a field at the back of what turned out to be a school. We were no sooner down than kids converged on us, shrilling like tiny birds. They fell abruptly silent as we got down from the planes, staring at us as if we were gods. No, devils: no Chinese god would have our colouring.

"What do we do?" Eve said. "Ask the way to General Chang?"

It was a dilemma. Chang Ching-yao was our only lead to the man who had been Sun Nan's master; but why should he accommodate us? Why should he be concerned for the life of Bradley Tozer?

Then I saw the young man pushing his way through the crowd of children, none too gently but with a sort of affectionate roughness. He was taller than the average Chinese we had met, energetic and loose-limbed, as if he might go in for physical exercises. He was a little unkempt, suggesting appearances meant nothing to him; rather like teachers today and not the ones who had taught me. He was wearing a high-necked white jacket and blue trousers, both of them unpressed. He had alert eyes, but his stare at us was flat and cautious, even a little arrogant. He looked like a man who might have ambitions to be more than just an ordinary teacher. A headmaster, perhaps.

Eve greeted him, then spoke to him for a minute or two. Neither Kern nor I understood what she said, but I caught the word *Chang*. The teacher listened without comment or expression; but his hand flipped out and cuffed the ear of a whispering boy beside him. Then the teacher suddenly clapped his hands together, still without having spoken to Eve, and shouted something to the children. They retreated at once, not sullenly but with instant respectful obedience. It's hard for me to believe that those kids would grow up to be the parents of the Red Guard brats of a few years ago.

Then the teacher spoke to Eve. She listened carefully, then looked at us. "He says the situation in Changsha is not good. He wouldn't be surprised if General Chang's soldiers are already on their way out here to arrest us and confiscate our machines. There is a lot of unrest in the province and there could be civil war."

"Then we'll get out of here as soon as we can," I said, one eye on the lengthening shadows of the afternoon. "Sun Nan said that his master was the enemy of General Chang—that's our only clue. Ask him which war-lord would be Chang's worst enemy."

Eve put the question to the teacher. He stared at her a moment, then suddenly smiled and shook his head, as if she had made a joke he hadn't at first caught. He answered her and she turned to us looking irritated and disappointed. "He says General Chang is his own worst enemy."

"Christ Almighty, the last thing we want just now is aphorisms!" I spoke directly to him. "Tell us what generals would like Chang dead!"

Eve translated for me. The teacher stared at me, offended by my anger: I could see anger growing in his own face. But there was no time for polite exchanges, the day was running out. At last he replied, still not taking his eyes off me, and Eve said, "There are two men. General T'an Yen-kai and General Meng Chia-lien."

"Tell him about the statue and your father," Kern said. "They can't all be kidnappers. Tell him who your father is. They must have heard of Tozer Cathay in a city this size."

Eve hesitated, then started speaking. The teacher looked at her with new interest, none too friendly. He snapped something and I saw the shocked look on Eve's face. She said to us, "He wants to know why he should be concerned for an American capitalist, especially one like my father."

"Translate for me." I looked directly at the teacher. "We are not here to argue capitalism, Marxism or whatever you believe in. All we are concerned with is a human life, that of Miss Tozer's father. Wouldn't you be concerned for your father's life?"

Eve put it to him and he shook his head. "He says he has no love for his father."

"Christ!" I've never felt so frustrated; I was banging my head against the Great Wall of China. "Righto, tell him I don't care a damn about his father, either—no, don't tell him that! He's so bloody contrary, he might take offence. Since he is such an anticapitalist, ask him which of the two generals would be so materialist-minded as to prefer a piece of jade to a man's life."

Eve asked the question. The teacher considered it; then smiled drily. He evidently was not without a sense of humour. He said something, still smiling, and Eve gave it to us. "General Meng—he calls himself Lord of the Sword. He says the other general is concerned for the future of China, but General Meng is concerned only for himself."

"Where is he? Can we fly there?"

"Look—out on the road!" said Kern.

A road ran along the far side of the school, beyond the buildings. Three trucks were speeding along it, soldiers standing up in the backs of them. Some of the children in the background began to stir. The teacher looked over his shoulder, then back at us. For the first time he looked as if he might be helpful.

"Get into your machine, Conrad—I'll swing your prop for you. Eve, ask this chap how we get to General Meng—tell him to be quick!"

Eve babbled the question, looking beyond the teacher; the trucks were now out of sight beyond the school buildings. The teacher said something, Eve said "Thank you" in English and turned quickly back towards the planes.

"We head south! Hurry!"

While she clambered up into the front cockpit of our machine, I raced across and swung the propeller of Kern's. It took at once with the engine still warm. I jumped back and ran across to Eve's plane. Out of the corner of my eye I saw the trucks come out from between the buildings. I grabbed the propeller, pushed it up, then swung it down. It fired, whirled lazily, then broke into the shimmering fierceness that could chop a man's head off. If we had to, I was determined that we should drive the planes right at the soldiers.

I ran round the wing, clambered up into the rear cockpit as Eve turned the machine to head it down the field. Only as I slipped down into my seat did I see what was happening. The teacher was marshalling the children into a long line; holding hands, they formed a human fence in front of the trucks as they tried to drive straight through at us. Perhaps some of the children belonged to the drivers of the trucks. They screeched to a stop and soldiers tumbled out of the back of them, tried to force their way through the hand-holding children. In the middle of the human fence, like a master post, stood the young teacher.

Eve gunned the engine and we went down the field and climbed into the slowly-falling sun. Kern came up behind us and both planes turned south.

"How far?" I said into the tubes. "And where?"

"Szeping. About a hundred miles."

"We may not have enough petrol." I said it quietly, matter-of-factly: the day was nearly over and I had sunk into the resignation that admits defeat: we were never going to make it in time. I looked back at the school and the field. The fence of children had been broken; they had been rolled up into one tight bunch like rusted barbed wire. A tiny group of men, three or four of them, was moving towards one of the trucks: one of the men looked as if he could be struggling. "I hope that teacher doesn't get into trouble. Did he say his name?"

"Mao Tse-Tung, something like that."

End of extract from O'Malley manuscript.

4

"I shall hate having to kill you, Mr. Tozer," said General Meng. "I truly mean that. We have come to have a very pleasant relationship. We could have been friends."

With a friend like him, who needs . . . But the old witticism was too trite. He *was* the enemy and always would be; he would never be capable of friendship, never capable of trust and loyalty. "I don't understand how a man as intelligent as you, General, can be so primitively superstitious. Do you really think the return of the statue will change your fortunes?"

"Do you ever pray, Mr. Tozer?"

"No." He was a church-going Episcopalian, it was part of the family's image in Boston. But he could not honestly say he was a man who believed in prayer.

Meng looked at him as if disappointed. "Well, then, take the Roman Catholic Pope. He preaches the efficacy of prayer. Unless you are utterly cynical, wouldn't you believe that he practises what he preaches?"

Tozer knew some Boston Catholics who, he was sure, prayed only for votes. But they didn't necessarily reflect the Pope's faith. "I suppose so. But prayer is only superstition, isn't it?"

"Of course. But it doesn't reduce a man's intelligence to believe in it. There are Marxists in this country, a small core who will never amount to anything, who do not believe in the gods. But it is the gods, Mr. Tozer, who have kept this country together for more years than you Western barbarians can count. We fight among ourselves, but the gods keep us together when we are threatened from the outside. It will always be so."

"The fighting among yourselves could destroy you from the inside. What about the gods then?"

The convoy of rice trucks from Shaoshan had not arrived yesterday afternoon. Madame Buloff had come to him last night and given him the bad news. The convoy had been held up by troops of General T'an Yen-kai, who was on his way to do battle with General Chang Ching-yao. A small war was developing in the district and General Meng was doing his best to be neutral. He was not going to send *his* troops out to try and force a way through for the rice convoy.

Tozer, painfully aware of the razor inside his shirt, as if it itself were a wound, had handed it back. "I couldn't have used it anyway. I'm not a cut-throat, Madame Buloff. I might punch a man on the jaw or, if the worst came to the worst, I might shoot him. But I couldn't kill a man at such close quarters, not so that his blood ran on me."

"You are too squeamish, Mr. Tozer. Or perhaps you have never been really desperate. When the time comes, I don't think you will find you are quite so fastidious. Still—" She took the razor. "We had better pray for a miracle, then."

He couldn't see her on her knees. "Who taught you to pray? Rasputin?"

She smiled, opened the razor. "You are an insulting man sometimes, Mr. Tozer. Shall I trim your moustache?"

Now, today, Madame Buloff was somewhere in the *ya-men*'s kitchen, supervising this evening's meal. Colonel Buloff was marshalling General Meng's troops for action stations down beyond the town. The Lord of the Sword himself was sitting beneath a tree on the terrace with his intended victim. He had his banjo on his lap and occasionally plinked a string, a sort of musical punctuation.

"I'm afraid you will have to die at sunset, Mr. Tozer. Things seem to be getting worse for me instead of better."

"They *could* get better. What if General Chang and

General T'an eliminate each other? That would make you supreme here, wouldn't it?"

"You argue well for yourself, Mr. Tozer. I admire that, a man who won't give up. Of course, it won't do you any good. It's a pity, because I should have liked to continue our conversations. You have no idea how boring it is to try to converse with those Russians. They have only one point of view, their own."

"How are you going to, er, kill me?"

"I'm afraid it will be by beheading. I could shoot you, but I don't know that that would appease the gods. We Chinese invented gunpowder, but I don't think it was due to divine inspiration. I think they will prefer older methods. Gods tend to be conservative."

I'm out of my head, Tozer thought. This conversation isn't happening: I'm dreaming it all. But he was not looking out on the landscape of a dream: the sunshine was real. the buffalo-carts creaking up the road, the old men and children flying kites in the fields below the *yamen*, the guards standing at every corner of the terrace, ready for the outbreak of the small war twenty miles away. "If I tried to escape, you would have to shoot me to prevent it. That might offend the gods."

"Would you try to escape, Mr. Tozer?"

"I might." He had the bravado of the desperate.

"Then I could be forced to bring forward your execution. Would you care to die sooner, while I am sure you are still here as my guest?"

"Forgive the insult to your honourable mother, General, but you are a real son-of-a-bitch."

"Thank you for your respect for my honourable mother, but actually she was a bitch and I was glad to leave her home. No, Mr. Tozer, don't try to escape. Resort to superstition, like me. Pray for what you Christians call a miracle. Now would you care to accompany me in that American college ditty, 'The Whiffenpoof Song'?"

"I went to Harvard, General. I am not a Yale man."

"In China, Mr. Tozer, I'm afraid the difference is indistinguishable."

So much for American traditions and superstitions. Bradley Tozer, choking on the words, began to sing "The Whiffenpoof Song" in a cracked voice that was appropriately tuneless while the Lord of the Sword, equally unmusical, plinked his way through the melody. The guards on the terraces, turning deaf ears, stared away into the distance, their faces grimacing as if they were already war casualties. Far away in America the gods in New Haven and Cambridge were rolling in their sarcophagi.

CHAPTER 8

1

The end of the journey was near, if not yet in sight. London lay half a world away to the west; thinking back now Eve could not remember whether she had started the long hazardous trip with optimism or not. All she had been intent upon had been getting to her father and she had shut out of her mind, as best she could, the thought of whether he would be alive or dead when she reached him. Now, as they flew through the declining light of the last day, she forced herself to be optimistic. Never a religious girl, she had begun to pray desperately over the past couple of days. It was something her father might have called childish superstition; but she wondered if now he might have resorted to prayer himself. Her grandmother, the religious one in the family, had often told her: God was the last resort of the atheist.

She took out her father's watch. But it had stopped: 5:14. Yesterday afternoon or this morning? She couldn't remember when she had last wound it or looked at it. Was it an omen? Had it stopped this morning, had her father been killed at sunrise? She felt sick and fumbled to put the watch away in her pocket.

Clouds were building up, coming towards them out of the south. Hills rose and fell beneath the planes like waves in a static sea; villages perched on their crests like flotsam. Then the landscape flattened out into a wide plain. A railway line ran north and south, a dirt road following it like a pale astigmatic trick of the eye. Two trains were halted on the line and several trucks and dozens of horse-drawn wagons were pulled up on the road.

"Soldiers," said O'Malley's voice in her ear; she turned her head and saw that he was examining the scene below through binoculars. "They have some artillery pieces."

"Whose would they be—General Chang's or General T'an's?"

"Chang's, probably. They seem to be headed south."

They passed over other convoys along the road; then they were over what was seemingly no-man's land. Or the peasants' land, if the peasants meant anything in the impending battle. The rice fields spread out on either side of the railway line and the road, the water glittering through the rice stalks. A wind had sprung up and was passing over the fields in dark shadows. Peasants, wide-hatted, bent over as if beneath the wind among the crop; if fighting broke out, they would be among the first harvest. The planes flew on and the opposing troops came into view. A third train was halted on the line and a long convoy of trucks and wagons stretched down the road beside it. The war was gathering like a plague.

They flew on and at last O'Malley said, "I think we've come too far."

Eve, eyeing the petrol gauge, had begun to have the same thought. She signalled to Kern, banked and headed back the way they had come. As they passed over the southernmost convoy she saw puffs of smoke below, then suddenly realized the planes were being fired on. She was about to pull back the stick, to climb above the fire, when O'Malley shouted in her ear.

"Over there—to the west!"

She banked sharply, Kern following her and followed the road that ran at right angles to the railway line and the main north-south road. She was a mile short of the town when the engine began to splutter and she knew they had run out of petrol. There was no time to go looking for a field in which to land; the rice paddies stretched away as far as the eye could see. She put the nose down to give her air-speed, then lifted it again and held the plane flat as she went down to the road. Three ox-carts lumbered up the road ahead of her; she went in over the heads of them with only feet to spare. The wheels hit the dirt, bounced in the ruts, but she kept the machine on course. She let it roll up the road, let it come to a stop of its own accord. When she looked back Kern had brought his machine down behind her.

They all got out and Eve was surprised at how weak she felt. If this small town up ahead was Szeping, then this was the end of the journey.

"How's your petrol?" O'Malley said to Kern.

"Nothing is showing on the gauge. If we can't buy petrol here, this is the end of the line." He looked up towards the town and beyond it to the barracks-like palace on the hill. Its brown walls took on a yellow tinge under the lowering sun so that it stood out in sharp relief against the darkening clouds coming up behind it. He looked back at Eve. "I'm sorry. I should sound more hopeful."

"Well, I suppose we walk from here."

Eve got up into the plane again, handed down her gun and the hessian-wrapped box to Kern. Sun's blood on the hessian had dried to just a brown smear, indistinguishable from the other marks on the wrapping. His life-blood had become just another travel stain.

Peasants had begun to move towards the planes, coming through the rice fields in slow motion like wary water-birds. Just down the road a huge water-wheel eased to a stop as the women walking the tread-mill that operated it paused to stare at the newcomers; the ox-carts had drawn up behind the aircraft and their drivers sat motionless and watchful. The wind came across the rice fields, darkening the stalks, and raised dust along the road.

"They think we are part of the war," said Kern. He had seen the same look on the faces in Belgium and France; the flat, expressionless faces were suddenly made familiar and readable; they were the casualties whose names never appeared in any lists. "I hope no one else does."

Then there was the sound of galloping hoofs and O'Malley said, "The welcoming committee."

The half a dozen horsemen came down the road from the town and reared to a stop in front of Eve and the two men. The barrel-bodied European with a red walrus moustache quietened his restive horse and looked down at them. "Who are you? Are you fliers for General Chang?"

"No," said Eve. "We are looking for General Meng. My name is Evelyn Tozer—"

"Miss Tozer!" He said something in a foreign tongue that none of them understood. "You have the statue? Quick—we must hurry!" He said something in Chinese and two of the horsemen swung their mounts about and went off at full gallop back towards the town. "The General is preparing to execute your father now!"

Eve said weakly, "My father—he's still alive?"

"He should be. He is supposed to die at sunset, but the General has a bad habit of changing his schedules. Can you all ride?"

Three of the soldiers dismounted and handed over their horses to Eve, O'Malley and Kern. The soldiers stayed with the planes while the horse party turned and headed back up the road. They went through the town at the gallop, scattering people, flocks of geese and vendors wheeling hand-carts. Eve, riding one-handed, the other hand grasping her gun, felt light-headed, galloping full tilt through something she couldn't believe. She was a stranger to herself, totally unrelated to the real Eve Tozer of the gay, frivolous, absolutely secure life back home in the real world of Boston, Bar Harbor and Palm Beach. Even the gun in her hand, though it had been used to kill wild beasts and wild men, now seemed unreal. The one lucid thought in her head was that she would shatter to pieces if they reached the palace up on the hill and she found her father already dead. That would be the ultimate unreality that she could not face.

2

Bradley Tozer walked out into the yellow light on the terrace between the two tweed-capped Mongolian guards.

"I thought you should have my own men to escort you," said General Meng. "A last courtesy."

"I appreciate it," said Tozer, resigned now, unafraid and so no longer feeling any necessity for Oriental politeness. "But you are still a son-of-a-bitch."

"I have admitted it, Mr. Tozer—what more can I say?" The General's politeness was impeccable; he knew how to conduct a dignified execution. "I still regret this, you know."

"You're ahead of schedule. You said I had till sunset."

Meng nodded at the clouds thickening overhead. "I'm afraid the weather has let you down. If it rains, how shall I know when the sun has set?"

Tozer refrained from repeating his opinion of Meng's ancestry. "Who is going to cut off my head?"

The General gestured along the terrace to where a huge figure in red silk stood beside a guard who was just handing her a long broadsword. "Madame Buloff has the necessary physical strength, don't you think? She may not have the strength of purpose, but she is a pragmatic woman. Most women are when it comes to a matter of life or death. They don't believe in sentiment at a time like that."

Tozer caught the tone in the General's remark and pulled up sharply. "What do you mean by that?"

The Mongolians each put a hand on Tozer to push him along, but Meng shook his head and they let him go. "Mr. Tozer, did you think I didn't know you have been conspiring with her for all of you to escape?"

Tozer might have felt sick if he had not already been empty. "How did you know?"

"Madame Buloff must have forgotten that one of the

girls she brought up last time from Shanghai speaks English. I have had her eavesdropping on you. Not very polite or honourable, but then, unfortunately, one sometimes has to lower one's standards."

"You can't make Madame Buloff do this to me! Good God, man, have a little consideration—she's a woman!"

"What makes you think women are weaker than us men, Mr. Tozer? Is it that way in America? I am not a misogynist like Confucius. I believe in equal opportunity for women. Up to a certain level."

"What level is that?"

"Just below mine," said the Lord of the Sword with a smile. "Don't despair for Madame Buloff, Mr. Tozer. When I put it to her that it was your head to be cut off by her or the heads of both of you to be cut off by one of my men, she did not hesitate."

"What about the Colonel?"

"He doesn't know yet. His wife can tell him later, over one of her abominable meals. Shall we proceed?"

As they continued along the terrace they passed under the peach tree; a fruit dropped, hitting Tozer on the head and bouncing off. The Mongolians laughed and Tozer said, "Shut up, you yellow bastards!"

"They have no sense of occasion," said General Meng and bent and picked up the fallen peach. "An omen, I'm afraid, Mr. Tozer. But the worms will be at it before they are at you, if it's any comfort. How are you feeling?"

Tozer had suddenly begun to feel weak and dizzy, as if he had been hit by a rock instead of the fruit of longevity. But he said nothing, tried to keep his back straight, did his best to show *he* had a sense of occasion. A Proper Bostonian should die in a proper manner, even if there were no other Bostonians around to appreciate the effort. He wondered where Eve was, if indeed she knew what had happened to him over the past few weeks. And suddenly felt even weaker and dizzier, debilitated by love.

Madame Buloff looked at him apologetically as he pulled up in front of her. A chopping block stood at her feet, narrowed off at the top to provide a comfortable

resting place for necks shorter than Tozer's; he wondered
how many times previously the block had been used. A
wicker basket was placed beside the block, as if waiting
for the week's wash. Or head.

"I hope you understand, Mr. Tozer," said Madame Buloff, sounding gentle and considerate: she could have been
apologizing for one of her girls having infected him with
venereal disease. His dizziness had abruptly gone, but he
was light-headed, removed from himself and what was
happening to him. He looked at the sword, felt like suggesting they wouldn't need such a heavy instrument to remove the thistle-ball that now rested on his neck.
Madame Buloff said, "I shall be as delicate as I can."

"Handle it as you handled the razor, Madame."

"Will you kneel, please?"

He knelt down, put his head on the block. And at once
it became like a ball of lead; his brain began to swell,
bursting with imagination; he was suddenly afraid and he
wanted to cry out. But his tongue turned to wood in his
mouth, his blood froze and his limbs became iron. He
closed his eyes and said, "Dear God—"

Then General Meng said, "Wait! There are aeroplanes
about to land down on the road!"

3

Kern, later, would marvel at their extraordinary timing.
They had flown 8000 miles to arrive in what was to have
been the last moment of Bradley Tozer's life. It was the
stuff of melodrama, of the English adventure books he
had read as a child with his English governess. But the
war had taught him that melodrama was part of life, not
the invention of dramatists. Fate itself was contrived and
he believed in fate. His own destiny might yet be suicide
and that was only a melodramatic way of arriving at true
tragedy.

The tragedy of Bradley Tozer's beheading had been

averted. The reunion between father and daughter had been something the others, even the two extraordinarily garbed Mongolians, had decently turned away from. To cover the moment Kern handed the hessian-wrapped box to the handsome Chinese in the uniform and peaked cap.

"This is what you wanted, General." He clicked his heels, stood at attention; he respected rank, even when it was held by a swine like this. "Herr Sun explained how much it meant to you."

General Meng said something to the walrus-moustached man in riding breeches and what Kern recognized as a Russian officer's tunic. So far there had been no introductions and Kern wondered who the giant European woman in the red silk gown might be. Everything was so bizarre: the chopping block, the wicker basket, the guards in their tweed caps, the woman holding the long sword on her shoulder as if it were a parasol. This was the stuff of opera; he would not have been surprised if he had heard Wagner with Chinese overtones. He suspended both belief and disbelief, just waited to be informed.

The walrus-moustached man said, "I am Colonel Buloff and this is my wife. I am General Meng's military adviser and my wife is his, er, domestic adviser."

"Christ," said O'Malley and laughed; then shook his head. "Sorry."

Colonel Buloff looked offended. "General Meng wants to know where is his respected and loyal servant, Sun Nan."

"Dead," said Kern, and explained what had happened to the respected and loyal servant. His leg began to ache and he felt exhausted, no longer really interested in explanations. But he added politely, "Tell the General we all regret Herr Sun's death very much."

General Meng, when the news was conveyed to him, just nodded. He asked for no further details and Kern got the feeling that Sun Nan could be easily replaced. He was suddenly angry for Sun's sake: no one should be so expendable. But the General was unwrapping the box; he took out the statue. It was the first time Kern and

O'Malley had seen it. Neither of them was a collector and they both looked at it with a singular lack of feeling. A green jade man, looking a little peevish, sat on a green jade ox that seemed to be asking its rider for directions where to head. It appeared to Kern, no expert in the quality or carving of jade, a mundane ornament; he would have been more impressed if it had glittered with gems. But it was worth a man's life and that made it invaluable.

Eve and her father had walked to the end of the terrace, he with his arm round her shoulders. If there were tears, none of the others saw them; but the reunion was obviously an emotional moment for both father and daughter. Kern watched them as they came back, composed now; it seemed to him that there was already a change in their bearing and attitude. The present still threatened them all, they were on the outskirts of a war that was about to break out at any moment; but the Tozers both looked confident, almost complacent, secure in the past and future of Tozer Cathay. Kern was not to know it, but unconsciously Eve and her father, his neck now safe from the sword, had regained the aura of their wealth and influence.

Bradley Tozer was grateful to his rescuers, but he had never been a man who could express thanks easily. "My daughter has told me briefly what you have done to get her here. I don't know what fee she promised you, but I shall double it."

"Thank you, Herr Tozer. But money was not the primary object in our volunteering to help Fräulein Tozer. Is that not so, Herr O'Malley?"

"That is so," said O'Malley. "The thought of money never entered our chivalrous heads."

Tozer knew he had made a mistake; he looked uncertainly at Eve who said, "I don't think this is the time to talk of bonuses. You both know how much I owe you—"

She stopped and Kern saw her grip tighten on her father's arm. He took pity on her, the beginning of love: so far he had looked at her only sexually, but now, close to saying goodbye to her, he saw much more in her. "We aren't out of the woods yet. How do you get away from here if fighting starts between those two armies?"

General Meng and the Buloffs had been bystanders for the moment, but the Lord of the Sword was not going to be pushed into the background in his own palace. The statue held in the crook of his arm, already sure again of the gods' good graces, he said something to Colonel Buloff who translated for him: "The General would like to know what you saw from the air. How close are the forces of Chang and General T'an?"

"They will be fighting each other by tomorrow," said Kern. "They may start with their artillery tonight."

Buloff shook his bullet head. "They haven't had our experience in modern war, Baron. They use their artillery only in daylight—they are short of shells and they like to see where they are landing. Though the supply may have improved. I understand the armament manufacturers from Europe and America are in Shanghai trying to sell off, at bargain prices, what they had left over from the war in France."

"Jolly good," said O'Malley. "One hates to see waste."

Buloff had a short conversation with Meng, then turned back to Kern and O'Malley. The Tozers were excluded: not being armament merchants, they were ignorant in the ways of war. Buloff, tugging at his moustache, talked to the professionals: "The General fears that both Chang and General T'an will try to capture your aeroplanes. They can be used to observe the other side's positions, can direct the artillery fire. We have learned a lot from the war in Europe. It was very educational to the generals here in China. They have been fighting wars longer than anyone else, but they had got behind in technique."

"Glad we were able to help," said O'Malley drily; and Kern nodded cynical agreement. "We had begun to think that perhaps no one had gained from the experience."

"Do you have any suggestions what should be done?"

"We need the machines to get us away from here, to Hong Kong," said Kern; like O'Malley, but without knowing it, he all at once opted for the security of the Empire. "We need petrol."

"There is very little in the town—our supplies have been cut off. Excuse me, I shall talk to the General."

The tall Chinese and the squat Russian walked away along the terrace, the Mongolian guards following them. The sky was dark now and the first drops of rain fell with tiny explosions in the dust of the terrace. Madame Buloff, the General's domestic adviser, took on the duties of hostess.

"We must go inside." She smiled at them all, gracious and charming; she was obviously an experienced hostess and Kern wondered where she came from. "I shall have tea served."

They all followed her, Bradley Tozer still with Eve's arm tucked in his. The rain suddenly became a deluge; the world turned grey, then disappeared. Kern pausing at the door to look back, saw the town, then the aeroplanes, then the whole countryside blocked out by the steel-grey curtain that thudded on the tin roof of the palace like bullets. The start of the war, he guessed, had been postponed for a while.

Madame Buloff served tea and small sweet cakes in a room that had none of a woman's touch. Kern looked around him: it was sparsely furnished, almost stark but for the four big decorative mirrors on the walls.

"Madame Buloff runs the Blue Delphinium tea rooms in Shanghai." Bradley Tozer seemed to have no resentment towards the woman who had just been going to chop off his head. "She has been very good company while I've been here. Do you like my moustache, Eve? That was Madame Buloff's suggestion."

"It suits you." But Eve was looking at the Russian woman with a suspicious eye. I don't blame her, thought Kern. What sort of woman keeps a man company, cultivates his appearance, then stands ready to chop off his head? "What else do you do, Madame?"

Madame Buloff, pouring tea, handing round cakes, said, "I supply gentlemen with female companionship. All the General's girls come from my establishment. Your father is going to help me set up business in America."

Kern wouldn't have thought Tozer capable of blushing. But when Eve looked at him that was what he did. "Well, not exactly. I was going to pay Madame Buloff and her husband a certain sum to get me away from here. How she used it would have been her own business."

"You mean she was going to set up brothels? What would Grandmother say to that?"

"Your grandmother has never before queried how our money has been earned or spent. But the deal is off now. Madame Buloff voided the contract when she agreed to the General's suggestion that she cut my head off."

"I am disappointed in you, Mr. Tozer. You know I had no choice."

She's amazing, thought Kern. She was attractive, despite her size; he wondered what she would be like to make love to. One could not afford to be too acrobatic with her, otherwise you might wind up crushed to death . . . He looked away from her, to Eve, the girl he knew he could love if the circumstances changed. He began to think of America . . .

O'Malley, at the window, said, "I've become quite attached to those old Brisfits. I don't like the thought of anyone else flying them."

"Are you thinking of offering your services to those other generals?" Eve said.

"Not at all. The Baron and I have had enough of that sort of thing. Correct, Conrad?"

"Correct," said Kern, all at once and at last finished with war.

Then General Meng and Colonel Buloff came in. Meng still carried the jade statue, occasionally stroking it as if it were a pet. He took off his cap, looked at himself in two of the mirrors, then sat down, running a hand over his hair with the same fondness as he had stroked the statue. He looked around his guests, smiled and said something in Chinese.

"The General says you may have what petrol there is

in the town," said Buloff. "But you are to make sure you do not land behind Chang's lines. You are to crash the machines rather than have them fall into that dog's hands."

"We'll go down and bring the machines up now," said Kern. "Before the rain stops and they can see what we are doing. May we have some oxen or horses to pull the machines?"

He limped towards the door, his leg beginning to pain again. Eve came to him, put a hand on his arm. "Conrad—" It was the first time she had called him by his given name; he wondered if it meant as much to her as it did to him. But doubted it. "Conrad, let Bede go with the Colonel. You should rest your leg."

"When Bede shot me down—" He looked at O'Malley and smiled, admitting the other's victory on that day long ago; surprised that it pleased him to do so. "I was hurt worse than this. But I still flew the next day."

"I'll see that he doesn't put too much strain on it." O'Malley winked at Kern and the German knew that he understood it was better to be doing something. He felt a stir of real affection for the Englishman, almost love. He laughed, suddenly forgetting the pain of his leg, and the two men followed Colonel Buloff out of the room, O'Malley saying as they went, "Ask Madame Buloff about her brothels, Eve. I may invest some of my bonus in them."

They rode down through the rain, the horses having difficulty in holding their feet on the mud of the road that sloped down from the palace. The rain was not so heavy now, but it still effectively blanketed the countryside. They went through the deserted streets of the town, watched by silent shopkeepers and householders from doorways and windows. They are waiting for the war, Kern thought, and marvelled at their stoicism.

While Colonel Buloff dispatched some soldiers to get oxen and ropes, Kern and O'Malley examined the town's defence positions. "He knows his job," said O'Malley.

"His field of fire is about as wide as one could wish for. The question is, how keen are his chaps to fight?"

But Kern was looking down the road to where it disappeared into the rain. "If they come up this road, Chang's troops or the other fellow's, we're going to take-off right into their fire. They could be down there now, hidden in the rain."

They stood there, oblivious of the fact that they were soaked to the skin, visualizing from experience the soldiers creeping up through the rain, keeping to the sides of the road, guns at the ready for when the target came into view. Kern, suddenly aware that he and O'Malley would be part of the target, shivered, became aware of the clothes clinging to him.

"Cold?" said O'Malley. "We'd better get started."

Colonel Buloff and the soldiers came back with eight oxen and two drivers. Four oxen were hitched to each plane and Kern and O'Malley climbed up into the cockpits. Urged on by their drivers, the oxen began to haul the two planes towards the town. A soldier walked at each wing-tip, keeping the machines steady as they skidded in the thin mud of the roadway. The town, really no more than a large village, did not begin gradually as a ravelled edge of scattered houses. One entered it abruptly, as if crossing a causeway across the green sea of the rice fields to an island. There were the fields, then a wall of dykes, then the houses clustered together. As they passed the dykes, the rain suddenly cleared and Kern glanced across at the soldiers in the machine-gun posts. Then he saw them stiffen, crouch down behind their guns and start shooting.

He looked quickly back over his shoulder in time to see his tail assembly disintegrate under the hail of fire that hit it. Down the road, beyond the flying pieces of canvas, he saw the other soldiers and their machine-guns.

He crouched low in the cockpit, waiting for the bullets to come up the length of the fuselage and hit him in the back. He felt as defenceless as the one time he had been shot down, when O'Malley, the then unknown British pilot, had come down on his tail and caught him unawares. But even then he had had a chance: his skill as a pilot against that of his pursuer. But now he could do nothing. He felt the plane swivel, sliding sideways in the mud; instinctively he tried to correct it, but there was nothing left with which to guide the plane. The two soldiers had disappeared from the wing-tips; one lay in the mud of the roadway and the other had jumped sideways into the dyke. The driver had fled ahead into the protection of the houses; O'Malley and his machine were already there. Kern, miraculously still unhurt, continued to crouch down in the cockpit, feeling the Bristol flying to pieces about him.

There was nothing he could do. He could not jump out of the plane and make a dash for it; he would be dead before he hit the ground. The oxen, two of them hit by bullets, were still on their feet, still pulling on the ropes. The plane, slipping and sliding crazily on the muddy surface, somehow stayed on the road as the oxen, bellowing in fear, pulled it past the dyke, past the first row of houses and round the safety of a corner.

O'Malley, out of his own machine, rushed at the shattered Bristol. "Jesus, are you all right?"

Kern unwound, sat back, shook his head in disbelief at his good fortune and smiled at his friend, the ex-enemy. "One should not get into a dog-fight on the ground."

He climbed down and the two men stared at the now useless aircraft. O'Malley said, "Well, the other one is undamaged."

"It is going to be overloaded when we take-off. There'll be four of us."

4

General Meng stood on the terrace and looked out at the countryside, at the rice paddies glinting dully like smoky glass as the moon occasionally showed through the scudding clouds. He plucked a peach from the tree and ate it while he continued to stare out into the darkness. The Mongolians stood just behind him, sleepy, wishing their master would go to bed. It had been a long day and everyone else in the palace, including the foreigners, were in bed.

"What do you think, Tso? Kwang? Should we go back to the cooler places?"

The guards came awake as if they had been attacked; they had never been asked this question before. What had happened to the Lord of the Sword?

"Oh yes, master!" They thought of the yellow grasslands in summer where they could stretch out their horses at full gallop; the frozen rivers and lakes in winter, more beautiful than any rice fields; the high passes of the Altyn Tagh where the caravans could be ambushed and plundered. "Oh yes, master, let us go back!"

The Lord of the Sword munched on the peach, wondering how long he had to live. If he was to survive to be an old man, was it worth it to stay here in this humid territory where rice fields, feuding governors and encroaching politics hemmed him in in a way that could never happen on the steppes of Sinkiang? He moved to the wall of the terrace, flicked away the peach-stone and saw the aeroplane that had been hauled up the sloping road to the palace gates earlier in the evening.

Was that the way out? To pay the Englishman or the German to fly him out of here, leaving everything and going back to Turfan, a General but a penniless one because he could take little with him but his jade statues? He put that idea away at once. If he went back to Sinkiang, to Turfan and his mother's house he would go back in style, a rich and powerful *tuchun*. The twin statues of Lao-Tze were back here in their rightful place: it would only be a day or two before his fortunes would turn for the better. He would survive both T'an and the dog Chang, there would always be a place in China for *tuchuns* such as himself.

He turned to the guards. "Kwang, Tso, now is not the time. We'll go back some other year." A cloud passed across the moon; he did not see the disappointment that clouded their faces. "Get me the sergeant of the guard. Tell him to bring the foreigners here. And Colonel and Madame Buloff."

In one of the palace bedrooms O'Malley and Kern, still wide awake, lay on their beds and stared at the ceiling. An oil lamp, turned low, washed the bare walls with shadow and the reclining silhouettes of the two men.

"Do you think we are going to be able to take-off down that road?" O'Malley said.

Kern looked at the road with his mind's eye. The oxen had dragged the one remaining aeroplane through the town and, when darkness had fallen, had hauled it up the slippery mud of the road that led up to the palace. He and O'Malley had walked up and down the slope several times. The road was perfectly straight, about two hundred yards long, cutting diagonally down across the face of the bluff on which the palace stood. At the bottom of the slope it turned at right angles to be lost at once in the town. A two-storeyed house stood at the corner, ideally placed as an obstruction. If they used the road as their take-off path they would need to be airborne no more than half-way down the slope. Otherwise they would finish up in the upper storey of the house.

"The road will need to dry out," he said, remembering the slick treacherous-looking surface. "But our luck has been good so far."

"It'll be all over tomorrow," said O'Malley. "One way or another."

Kern nodded, understanding him. They had grown long-sighted with experience over the past two weeks. The future beyond tomorrow and Hong Kong, if they reached there, had the bland beige look of cold cocoa. There would be money in the bank for both of them, but that would be all. Kern knew there would once again be only the tea dances at Constance; for O'Malley there would be just more attempts to stretch Oxo into five- and six-sylla-bles on the blueboard of the unpredictable English sky. For O'Malley it would be like trying to write on water;

for Kern, trying to dance to an out-of-tune orchestra. Despite their intelligence, they were reluctant to be cured of the fever of adventure. At least during the past two weeks they had lived, even if sometimes on the doorstep to eternity.

"We could go to America, Bede. We could be stunt fliers."

"Or ferry clients along Madame Buloff's chain of brothels."

They smiled at each other: suddenly they had reached a point where they knew words were no longer necessary. Then they heard the tramp of boots in the corridor outside and the door was swung open. Six soldiers stood there, rifles held at the ready. In the background, guarded by four more soldiers, were Eve and her father.

O'Malley and Kern sat up, both abruptly apprehensive. "What's going on?"

"I don't know," said Bradley Tozer. "But it doesn't look good. Not at this hour."

The soldiers, none too gently, escorted them down through the corridors and out on to the terrace. Cloud completely obscured the moon now, but several soldiers carried oil lamps. Along the terrace, beneath the peach tree, General Meng, flanked by the two Mongolians, faced Colonel and Madame Buloff. He smiled a welcome as O'Malley and the others were brought towards him.

"Ah, Mr. Tozer, forgive me for disturbing your rest. But I have come to a decision about you and your daughter and her friends."

Tozer glanced curiously at the Buloffs. "Did the Colonel and his wife help you to that decision?"

"Not at all. You are my friend, Mr. Tozer—why should I listen to two such treacherous people as the Colonel and Madame Buloff when it involves you?"

"What's going to happen to them?" Tozer didn't really want to know, yet he had to ask the question.

"Oh, nothing serious. Not yet anyway, though one can never tell about the future, can one? I am a magnanimous man and I have made them an offer they cannot refuse. The Colonel will work much closer with me from now on. So closely, in fact, that I am putting him under the protection of my loyal guards, Tso and Kwang, who will take care of him as carefully as they do of me."

"And Madame Buloff?"

General Meng glanced at her as she stood side by side with her squat husband, holding his hand. "Madame and I have come to a business arrangement. I am taking over the Blue Delphinium tea rooms. Henceforth on my visits to Shanghai I shall be, as you Americans say, on the free list."

"And us? What about us?"

"You, Mr. Tozer, are about to take your departure."

"Now?" said Tozer, and looked out at the black night beyond the terrace. "Can't we wait till dawn?"

"What's the matter?" said O'Malley; and Tozer told him. "Good God, he's asking us to commit suicide! It'll be difficult enough taking off down that road in daylight—it'll be bloody impossible tonight!"

"Do you want to tell him?" said Tozer drily; he knew the futility of arguing with General Meng. "It's that or nothing. I've come to know him too well. But I'll try." He turned back to Meng, explained the danger of trying to take-off in the darkness. "At least let us wait till first light, General—"

"I'm afraid not, Mr. Tozer. Much as I enjoy your company, you and that machine have become an inconvenience to me. If I allow you to wait till daylight General T'an—those are his forces down on the other side of town, I have learned—will see that I am letting you take-off without any attempt to stop you. He wants that machine and if you are still here at daylight I shall be obliged to let him have it. You see, I think he is going to be the winner between him and the dog Chang. And you know what gamblers we Chinese are, Mr. Tozer—always try to back the winner. I have decided to come to an arrangement with him."

"What if we should be killed?"

"No one will regret your death more than I," said General Meng. "It will be a terrible weight on my conscience. For my sake, do your best to take-off safely."

"If we take-off now," said Eve, "how are you going to convince General T'an that you didn't let us get away?"

"It is dark down there on the road. They will only hear you start up your engine and then they will hear rifle shots. In the morning, if you are gone, I shall tell General T'an that you overpowered some of my guards and got away. If you crash, I shall tell him the same story."

"You are fiendishly clever, General," said Tozer. "I mean that, of course, as a compliment."

"How else could I take it?" said the Lord of the Sword.

Five minutes later the four foreigners, their belongings brought out for them, were down by the Bristol. O'Malley looked down the slope of the road, dim now in the shadow of the palace wall and the cliff on which it was built. He walked down the road with Kern, then the two of them came back to Eve and her father.

"The road's dried out, so there's no worry about the surface except for some cart tracks. Our problem is going to be getting the nose up in time to clear that house at the bottom of the hill. With two of us on the wings, that isn't going to be easy."

"I'll ride on one wing," said Eve. "I'm the lightest."

"You ride in the rear cockpit. No argument, Miss Tozer."

"Mr. O'Malley—"

"Shut up," said O'Malley politely. "Mr. Tozer, I'm afraid you are going to have to ride outside. It won't be comfortable and you'll be stiff and cold by the time we get to Hong Kong, but I think you can do it."

Tozer nodded. "Who will be the pilot?"

O'Malley looked at Kern. "We're equally good, Conrad. Do you want to toss?"

Kern produced a coin. "A pfennig, worth nothing now. Unless you would rather use an English coin?"

"No, the pfennig will do."

Watched by the Chinese, the two Russians and the two

Americans, Kern spun the coin in the air, caught it and held it on the back of his hand. "Tails," said O'Malley.

"You win, Bede. I have confidence in you."

They all shook hands with General Meng, Colonel and Madame Buloff. Bradley Tozer smiled at the General. "Don't forget, General—if there is anything you want, get in touch with Tozer Cathay in Shanghai. I think you owe us some business."

"That will depend on General T'an—he may already have contracts with Jardine Matheson. Good luck, Mr. Tozer."

Tozer shook hands with the Colonel but said nothing to him. Then he took Madame Buloff's hand and kissed it. "If ever you come to America, Madame, send me an invitation to the opening of your first tea room."

Madame Buloff, still holding her husband's hand, smiled. "You will be our Number One client."

Eve and O'Malley had already climbed into the cockpits. Kern, in his own flying suit, and Tozer, in O'Malley's, took their places on the wings, roping themselves to the inboard struts. Kern pulled down his goggles and Tozer adjusted the pair that had belonged to Sun Nan. They lay flat to reduce wind resistance at take-off, and grasped the forward edge of the wing. O'Malley glanced at them, then looked ahead down the road. They would be taking-off into a dark void and the house at the bottom of the hill would not be visible until the very last moment. When it might be the very last moment for them all.

Colonel Buloff had volunteered to swing the propeller. He grasped it and waited for the word from O'Malley. The latter could feel the sweat in his hands and his legs seemed suddenly to have gone weak; all at once he wished he had not won the toss, that the responsibility of getting them safely off the ground was Kern's. But it was too late now: he had claimed to be as good a pilot as the German and he had to prove it. He raised his hand and Colonel Buloff swung the propeller.

The engine coughed, then burst into roaring life. O'Malley warmed it up while General Meng's soldiers started shooting in every direction but the aeroplane. Then O'Malley raised his hand again and two soldiers jerked the chocks away. The Bristol began to roll down the hill.

It went down the narrow road, gathering speed quickly. The dark cliff loomed over it on the right, as if to fall on it; it seemed to force the plane out towards the edge of the road and O'Malley had to fight against the urge to over-correct. Eyes strained, he concentrated on the dim strip spinning up beneath the nose, conscious at the same time of the invisible house down at the corner rushing towards them at the same increasing speed. Flat on the wings, Kern and Tozer held tightly to the thin edge of the canvas, feeling it cutting into their hands with the fierceness of their grip; every bump of the wheels was magnified through their chests and bellies till they felt their insides would be forced out of their mouths; the wind tore at their faces, pushing their goggles against their eyes. In the rear cockpit Eve sat tense, leaning forward to peer past O'Malley's head into the darkness. The plane was gathering speed, but not fast enough: they were not going to get off the ground in time. Suddenly she saw the dim shape ahead, coming up at them so fast it was impossible to distinguish it properly: but she knew it was the house at the bottom of the hill. They were going to go straight into it. She sat right back in her seat, legs stretched out, stiff as the gun beside them, not ready to die but knowing it was now.

Then she felt the pressure on her stomach as O'Malley lifted the nose sharply. The Bristol creaked, seemed ready to break up; but it held together, went up in a steep climb. Kern and Tozer clung desperately to the wings as they were raised almost perpendicularly. The house flashed by beneath them, only a foot or two below the wheels. The plane kept climbing, slowly flattening out, and O'Malley gently banked it and set course for the south and Hong Kong.

Kern and Tozer cautiously raised themselves, rolled over and sat up. They turned their backs to the wind, wrapped themselves round the inboard struts. Kern looked back at Szeping, the palace and the domain of the Lord of the Sword fading into the night. He raised his eyes and looked further, to the west, to the darkness there in which he could see nothing: not China nor India nor Asia Minor nor the Balkans nor even home. He was staring into the long night of history: small worlds, once smug and safe, that had gone forever.

Then he looked at O'Malley and Eve, smiled and waved. There was three hours' flying ahead of them, but they, all four of them, were safe. All he and Tozer had to do was not fall off.

AUTHOR'S POSTSCRIPT

That adventure ended happily.

They landed in Hong Kong in a field where an ant-hill housing development now stands. O'Malley and Kern were paid their £500 and a bonus of another £500; for a moment they were rich beyond the dreams of adequacy. The Bristol Fighter was sold by Tozer Cathay to Jardine Matheson who sold it to General T'an Yen-kai, who sold it to another general named Chiang Kai-shek. It was still being flown in 1936 when it was used to bomb and strafe an army, on its Long March, led by an ex-schoolteacher named Mao Tse-Tung. There is no record of its eventual fate.

Eve Tozer and her father went back to America, where the Boston *Globe*'s social column reported that "Miss Tozer has just returned from an interesting vacation trip to China." No one bothered to interview Bradley Tozer. He arrived home on the day after a bomb exploded in Wall Street. All the capitalists in America were suddenly in jeopardy from either Anarchists or Bolshevists, take your pick. Any capitalist who had dealings only in China was safe and, therefore, dull copy.

O'Malley and Kern followed the Tozers to America in October. Because they were aces with 32 kills each, which made good advertising, they were invited to join Colonel Billy Zinnemann's Flying Circus. They were paid $75 a week—if the week was a good one. Frequently they earned no more than a locomotive engineer on the Union Pacific, Baltimore and Ohio or any of a dozen other railroads they flew over.

They visited the Tozers at the Tozer winter home in Palm Beach, Florida, in January 1921. Seeing Eve again, both men realized they were deeply in love with her; but, being friends and gentlemen, neither said anything to each other or to her. Nor to Wilbur Frankenhorn III, a New York banker, who was also a Tozer house guest and whom Eve married in Boston in June 1921.

O'Malley and Kern continued to barn-storm, flying for other air circuses and for themselves. In 1923 they went to California and became motion pictures stunt fliers and bit-part actors. Kern had romantic success with several leading ladies and O'Malley, a less ambitious lover, with several supporting actresses. His longest affair was with a girl who made a career of being in the background in all Ramon Novarro pictures.

Baron Conrad von Kern was killed during the filming of *Wings*, when he defied the director's instructions and attempted a stunt that the director had described as "suicidal". Kern had been drinking heavily over the past year, talking with bitterness of what was happening in Germany, and O'Malley, though deeply saddened, was not surprised at his friend's death nor the way he died.

O'Malley left Hollywood and took a job flying mail for Pan American World Airways to Cuba. In 1931, on a vacation visit to a national air meet in Cleveland, Ohio, he met Eve Tozer Frankenhorn again. Divorced from her banker husband, childless, restless, she was in Cleveland to compete in the Thompson Trophy air race. She finished tenth, two places behind O'Malley. A month later they were married. They went to England for their honeymoon, so that Eve could meet Martin and Marjorie O'Malley, who, Tanganyika and the Empire now safe for posterity, were living in retirement in Sussex. While in England O'Malley and Eve bought a Bristol Fighter and shipped it home, presenting it to a small aviation museum in Florida.

They had three children, all girls, and nine grandchildren. Bradley Tozer became an ill man, sold Tozer Cathay to Jardine Matheson in 1939 and died on 8 December 1941 in Boston. His fortune, not as large as expected, was left to his daughter, his son-in-law and his three granddaughters.

O'Malley became an American citizen and spent World War II ferrying aircraft across the Atlantic to Britain. He had a forced landing once in Greenland but was rescued by a US Navy patrol ship. He was attacked once by three Dornier Do-17's, but managed to bring his unarmed bomber safely down in England. From then on he refused to fly an unarmed aircraft, but to his chagrin was never attacked again. After the war he became an executive with Pan American and remained with that corporation till he retired in 1959.

The Tozer winter home in Palm Beach had been sold in 1936 and the O'Malleys built a smaller place in Fort Lauderdale. When that city became a magnet for the nation's roistering college kids on vacation, O'Malley, who had become increasingly conservative as his world shrank and changed, offered to get the ancient Bristol out of the museum, take it up and strafe the kids off the beaches. He was dissuaded from that course by his three daughters, whose own kids, unbeknown to their grandfather, were on the beaches.

Eve Tozer O'Malley, gracious in her old age, died in January 1974. William Bede followed her six months later. He was found one morning by the custodian of the aviation museum, sitting in the pilot's cockpit of the old Bristol Fighter. Death, the coroner said, was due to natural causes. Which can describe a broken heart or just the desire to live no longer.

The adventure was finally over.

Best Of Bestsellers
from WARNER BOOKS

___**THE CARDINAL SINS**
by Andrew Greeley   *(A90-913, $3.95)*
From the humblest parish to the inner councils of the Vatican, Father Greeley reveals the hierarchy of the Catholic Church as it really is, and its priests as the men they really are.

THE CARDINAL SINS follows the lives of two Irish boys who grow up on the West Side of Chicago and enter the priesthood. We share their triumphs as well as their tragedies and temptations.

___**THY BROTHER'S WIFE**   *(A30-556, $3.95)*
by Andrew Greeley   *(In Canada A30-650, $4.95)*
A gripping novel of political intrigue does with politics what THE CARDINAL SINS has done with the church.

This is the story of a complex, clever Irish politician whose occasional affairs cause him much guilt and worry. The story weaves together the strands of power and ambition in an informed and clear-eyed insider's novel of contemporary politics.

___**THE OFFICERS' WIVES**
by Thomas Fleming   *(A90-920, $3.95)*
This is a book you will never forget. It is about the U.S Army, the huge unwieldy organism on which much of the nation's survival depends. It is about Americans trying to live personal lives, to cling to touchstones of faith and hope in the grip of the blind, blunderous history of the last 25 years. It is about marriage, the illusions and hopes that people bring to it, the struggle to maintain and renew commitment.

Mystery...Intrigue...Suspense

—FLETCH AND THE WIDOW BRADLEY
by Gregory Mcdonald   (B90-922, $2.95)
Fletch has got *some* trouble! Body trouble: with an executive dead in Switzerland. His ashes shipped home prove it. Or do they? Job trouble: When Fletch's career is ruined for the mistake no reporter should make. Woman trouble: with a wily widow and her suspect sister-in-law. From Alaska to Mexico, Fletch the laid-back muckraker covers it all!

—FLETCH'S MOXIE
by Gregory Mcdonald   (B90-923, $2.95)
Fletch has got plenty of Moxie. And she's just beautiful. Moxie's a hot movie star. She's got a dad who's one of the roaring legends of Hollywood. She's dead center in a case that begins with a sensational on-camera murder and explodes in race riots and police raids. Most of all, she's got problems. Because she's the number one suspect!

—DUPE
by Liza Cody   (B30-367, $2.50)
Anna Lee is the private investigator called in to placate the parents of Dierdre Jackson. Dierdre could not have died as the result of an accident on an icy road. She had driven race cars; the stretch of road was too easy. In search of simple corroborating evidence, Anna finds motives and murder as she probes the unsavory world of the London film industry where Dierdre sought glamour and found duplicity...and death.